An Armada Three-in-One

*Three Great
Nancy Drew® Mysteries*

Nancy Drew® Mystery Stories in Armada

For contractual reasons, Armada has been obliged to publish from No. 51 onwards before publishing Nos. 37–50. These missing numbers will be published as soon as possible.

Nancy Drew® in

Carolyn Keene

This Armada *Nancy Drew®* *Three-in-One* was
first published in the U.K. in Armada in 1986
by Fontana Paperbacks,
8 Grafton Street, London W1X 3LA.

Armada is an imprint of Fontana Paperbacks,
part of the Collins Publishing Group.

Published pursuant to agreement with
Simon & Schuster Inc.

Printed in Great Britain by
William Collins Sons & Co. Ltd, Glasgow.

1
The Greek
Symbol Mystery

Nancy Drew® in
The Greek Symbol Mystery

Illustrated by Ruth Sanderson

The Greek Symbol Mystery was
first published in the U.K. in a single volume
in hardback in 1982 by Angus & Robertson (U.K.) Ltd,
and in Armada in 1982
by Fontana Paperbacks,
8 Grafton Street, London W1X 3LA.

Contents

1

Mystery Plus Mystery

"Nancy, do you think you could help solve a mystery for me while you're in Greece?" asked Mrs. Thompson, a friend and neighbor of the Drews. A tinge of sadness crept into the woman's hazel eyes.

"Oh, I'd love to," the titian-haired eighteen-year-old replied. "What's it about?"

Nancy's father, Carson Drew, a well-known River Heights attorney, had just given her an intriguing assignment to follow up in Athens. Now the young detective would have two mysteries to solve!

"I'll explain," said Jeannette Thompson, seeing the excitement in Nancy's face. "I've been sending money to the Papadapoulos family for about a year, but the last few payments disappeared."

"Disappeared?" Nancy repeated. "Were they stolen?"

"I don't know. I didn't send the money directly to Greece. There was an agency in New York—the Photini Agency—which transferred my donations. The main office is in Athens, and I assume that Mr. Georgiou, the New York manager, forwarded the money to Athens. Then it went to the family."

"You say that some of the money disappeared," Nancy went on. "Do you mean the family never received it?"

"That's right," Mrs. Thompson replied. "I used to get very sweet thank-you notes from the mother, but they stopped coming. Then, last week, I heard from her again. Mrs. Papadapoulos said she was writing because she had not heard from me in so long! Apparently, she contacted the Photini Agency in Athens about the missing payments. They told her that probably I had lost interest. Can you imagine such a thing?"

Nancy shook her head in bewilderment. "No, I can't," she said. "What about the New York office?"

"It closed suddenly."

Mrs. Thompson explained that she had tried to telephone Mr. Georgiou several times but there was never any answer. "I finally asked the police to investigate, and that's how I found out the office had closed. According to the post office, all mail was to be sent to Mr. Georgiou in care of the Athens address."

"What's his first name?" Nancy asked.

"Dimitri."

"Did he endorse your checks?"

"Yes, with the name of the Photini Agency stamped underneath," the woman said. "I can show you one."

Mrs. Thompson disappeared into her bedroom and soon returned with a small metal box. It contained numerous cancelled checks. She leafed through them quickly.

"Here you are," she said, handing one to the young detective.

Nancy stared at the signature on the back. It was bold and distinctive. Obviously it belonged to a person of confidence.

"Did you ever meet Mr. Georgiou?" Nancy asked.

"No. All the arrangements were made through the mail. I had seen an ad to sponsor needy children in Greece and that's how it all started. There are three children in the Papadapoulos family, but my donations were primarily intended to help send Maria to school."

Nancy's mind was racing. Had Dimitri Georgiou kept the money for himself? How many other poor

Greek families had he robbed? Or had someone else taken the money? But who?

Nancy squeezed Mrs. Thompson's hand. "We'll do all we can," the girl detective assured her.

"We?" the woman asked.

"My friends Bess and George are going with me," Nancy explained.

Bess Marvin and George Fayne were cousins and Nancy's closest friends. They often helped her solve mysteries, even those in distant countries.

"Well, my dear, is there anything else I ought to tell you?" Mrs. Thompson asked.

"I'd like to make a copy of Dimitri Georgiou's signature," Nancy said. She pulled a small notepad and a felt-tip pen from her handbag, then carefully imitated the handwriting. "Clue number one," she said, slipping the pad and pen back into her bag.

When Nancy reached home that afternoon, she immediately called Bess and George to report her visit with Mrs. Thompson. "So," she concluded, "between looking for Helen Nicholas's cousin, her missing inheritance, and Mrs. Thompson's money, we'll have plenty to do in Athens!"

"I'll say," George replied. "I can't wait!"

Hannah Gruen, the Drews' housekeeper who had helped rear Nancy since she was three years old, when her mother had passed away, overheard the conversation. "Your trip sounds like trouble to me," she said, frowning.

"Oh, Hannah," Nancy said, chucking the woman's chin affectionately. "You worry so."

When the young detective and her friends boarded the plane for New York the next day, she grinned. "Last night Hannah dreamed that we'd be greeted at Athens airport by gorgons—monsters with snakes for hair!"

Plump Bess Marvin ran a hand through her blond waves and shivered. "Thanks for telling me. I'm nervous about flying as it is."

George laughed. "Didn't you say Hannah was having a permanent today, Nancy? I bet that's what inspired the nightmare!"

As the three girls settled into their seats, George yawned. "How long do we have to wait in New York between flights?" she asked Nancy.

"Three hours."

"In that time," Bess said, "we could take a sightseeing tour of the whole city."

"That's just what I had in mind," Nancy said.

The cousins looked at her in surprise. "Are you serious?" George asked.

Nancy nodded. "Here's the address of the Photini Agency in Astoria. We might pick up a clue."

"Out there? We'll miss our plane!" Bess objected.

"No, we won't."

"Didn't you know that every New York taxi has wings?" George chuckled.

"Just so long as ours has four good tires," Bess replied.

The flight to New York took little more than an hour. Within twenty minutes after landing, the trio had flagged down a cab. It looped onto a service road that fed into a busy highway.

"That's the building over there," the taxi driver said, taking the exit for Astoria.

Bess gaped at a line of people holding signs and marching up and down the block.

"Who's on strike?" George asked.

"The tenants," their driver replied as they pulled close.

Nancy took some money from her wallet and handed it to the man. "We'll get out here. Thanks."

"Not me," Bess said. "I'm going back to the airport."

As George nudged her cousin out the door, Nancy caught sight of the storefront that bore the name PHOTINI. A peppery-haired man was sweeping out the empty store.

"Let's talk to him," Nancy suggested.

But as they started to slip through the picket line, brusque voices shouted at them. "Hey, where do you think you're going?" one cried out. "Yeah, that's what I want to know!" yelled the other.

George stared into a pair of angry eyes. "We're only trying to—" she began apologetically.

The man behind them snapped like a firecracker. "Say, who are you anyway?" he asked George. "You look like Mr. Sully's daughter!"

"That's her, all right," another man added in an accusing tone. "You tell your father we're going to see that all his buildings are condemned by the city!"

"She's not—" Nancy interrupted, but was cut off as the crowd pressed closer to the girls. She grabbed George by one arm while Bess hung onto the other.

"We're cousins," she murmured. "Her name is Fayne and mine is—"

Her words trailed off as the men barked back. "Go home, Miss Sully. We're the new landlords here!"

The men laughed harshly, forcing the girls to step off the curb into the street.

"Those men aren't going to let us within two feet of that agency," George declared.

"I knew we should've stayed at the airport," Bess put in as the cleaning man retreated into the store.

"Let's go," Nancy said in disappointment. She waved to an oncoming taxi. "I hope our batting average improves when we get to Athens."

The girls were still discussing the side trip when they boarded their plane, an Olympic Airways jet. While Bess went ahead to find their seats, Nancy

17

stopped to talk with the copilot. He was young and had dark hair that spun in waves across his forehead.

"I flew a small plane once," Nancy told him. "I can't imagine sitting behind controls like these."

"Well, as long as we aren't in motion yet," the copilot replied, ducking into the front compartment, "be my guest."

"Oh, are you sure it's all right?"

"Just don't touch anything. Okay?"

She nodded and slipped into the comfortable bucket seat next to him. "This is fantastic!" Nancy exclaimed, leaning toward the bank of knobs and gauges.

Suddenly a man's voice bellowed at the pair from behind them. "What is this? Some joke? You let a girl try to fly this plane? Are you crazy?"

The copilot tried to explain but could not get a word in as the angry passenger kept complaining. Finally, Nancy stood up and stared calmly at the burly man. His face was the shade of a pale tomato.

"If you're going to fly this plane," he yelled, "I'll see to it we never leave the ground!"

"You have nothing to worry about," Nancy replied. "I'm only a passenger like yourself."

"Then what are you doing in the pilot's seat?" the man demanded.

Nancy explained. She had just finished when

one of the flight attendants approached the group. "Please be seated, Mr. Isakos," she said to the man and handed him a Greek newspaper.

Instead of thanking her, he merely shrugged. "Girls should be kept in their place—certainly nowhere near the controls of an airplane!"

George, who had heard part of the conversation, was angry at the man's presumptuous tone. "In case you didn't know," she said as he walked down the aisle, "Amelia Earhart was an ace pilot and so is Nancy Drew!"

Isakos did not answer her. He slid into a seat not far from the girls.

Nancy frowned. "We'll probably have to listen to his complaints all the way to Athens!"

She purposely averted her eyes from his as she moved toward her seat. Halfway there she noticed a piece of paper on the floor. She glimpsed the name PHOTINI printed boldly in the upper left-hand corner, and picked it up.

"What's that?" Bess asked as Nancy slid into her seat next to George and fastened her seat belt.

"I don't know," Nancy said.

The three young detectives stared curiously at her discovery. It was the torn letterhead of the Greek agency that was under suspicion! Beneath the printed address was a most mysterious-looking doodle:

2

Stolen Note

Instantly Nancy pulled a small magnifying glass from her handbag and trained it over the unusual doodle. "It looks like the Greek letter phi," she said.

"But what are those curlicues at each end?" Bess whispered.

"Maybe that means the doodler is going in circles!" George replied, grinning.

"Or it could mean something important," Nancy said. She strained her neck to look out the window as the plane taxied into the lineup ready for take-off. The runway shimmered in the heat.

"Do you think it'll be this hot in Greece?" Bess asked.

"Hotter," George teased. "I've heard it gets to at least 120 degrees in the shade—"

"Of an olive tree," Nancy added absently.

Paying small attention to the light banter between her friends, she stared at the note again. Suddenly, she realized there was some faded, almost invisible handwriting on the Photini letterhead.

"Look at this!" she exclaimed, handing the piece of paper and her magnifying glass to George.

"Let me see it, too," Bess said.

"In a minute," her cousin replied. She held the glass over the words Nancy had indicated. "All I can make out is *Záppeion* and *Maïou*."

"*Záppeion*," Nancy repeated. "Isn't that the place in Athens that has a huge military exhibit?"

Her listeners shrugged. "I don't know about that," George said, "but I think *Maïou* means the month of May in Greek."

Bess was able to detect one or two more words in the message, and together they reconstructed the sentence: *rendezvous stó Záppeion tís íkosi pénde Maïou*. Nancy filled in the letters with her pen as the plane's engines began to roar and the flight attendants returned to their stations for take-off. Once the plane was in the air, Nancy summoned one of them.

"Will you please translate this for me?" she asked, indicating the message in Greek.

The young woman wrinkled her forehead for a second, then answered. "It says 'meeting at Záp-

22

peion on the 25th of May.' That was a month ago."

"Where exactly is Záppeion?" Nancy inquired.

"It's not far from my apartment—behind the King's Garden in the heart of Athens. If you haven't been there, you ought to go."

"I'm sure we will," Bess said. "What other sight-seeing do you recommend?"

"Oh, there is so much—the National Archeological Museum or the Benaki, for instance. And you must see Plaka, the old section of Athens. Also, monastiraki, the flea market."

"Isn't that the place Helen Nicholas told us about?" Bess whispered to Nancy.

"Yes, she said it's within walking distance of our hotel."

When the flight attendant excused herself, Nancy pulled out the notepad with Dimitri Georgiou's signature. She compared it with the message on the letterhead. The formation of the letters was the same!

"So I guess we can conclude Dimitri wrote this," George said, "and met someone at Záppeion on May 25th. But who and why, and was the meeting relevant to our case?"

"The point is," Nancy said, drawing two sets of crisscrossed lines on the back of the letterhead, "whoever he wrote this to is probably on this plane."

"But we don't want him to know we're looking

for Mr. Georgiou, do we?" Bess declared. She formed an X in a corner box of the tic-tac-toe pattern she had just drawn.

"If you mean we shouldn't ask someone to claim the letterhead," Nancy went on, "I agree."

She and Bess played a few games of tic-tac-toe. Then dinner was served. There was a generous portion of moussaka on each tray, along with fresh green salad garnished with feta cheese and small black olives.

"I love eggplant," Bess said, savoring her last forkful.

After the meal, the girls slipped on headphones to listen to music and later to the sound track of the in-flight movie. To their delight, it had been filmed in Athens. Nancy paid less attention to the story than to the twisting alleyways the girls would investigate tomorrow!

When it was over, the lights in the plane remained dim. Restless passengers got up to stretch while others, including the young detectives, asked for pillows and blankets.

"Good night," George yawned presently.

" 'Night," Bess said.

Nancy wedged her handbag next to her, then closed her eyes, sinking soon into a deep sleep. It was only an hour or so later that she awoke as she felt her handbag being shoved against her. Groggily she glanced into the aisle. She saw no one there.

It must've been my imagination, she concluded, and drifted off again.

Sunlight flooded the plane a few hours later as it droned across southern Europe. It was three A.M. in New York but nine o'clock there.

"We just lost six hours," Bess yawned.

"Cheer up," her cousin replied. "You'll gain them all back when we go home."

"Promise?" the other girl said.

She closed her eyes again while Nancy opened her handbag.

"It's gone!" she cried suddenly.

"What's gone?" George asked.

"The paper—the letterhead!"

"Are you sure?" Bess put in.

"Look for yourself," Nancy said.

She pulled out her wallet, a checkbook, various cosmetics, an airplane ticket, and passport, leaving only a set of small luggage keys in the bottom of the bag. The Photini letterhead was, indeed, missing.

"Maybe you threw it away with your dinner napkin," George suggested.

Nancy shook her head. "Don't you remember we played tic-tac-toe on the back of it, then I put it into my purse before we ate?" She sank back into her seat. "Someone took it," she added.

She told about being half-awakened the night before when she felt the bag being moved. "But I guess I was so tired I just dismissed it."

"Don't feel bad," Bess consoled her. "At least we know that one out of all the passengers on board has contact with Dimitri."

"So all we have to do is interrogate 300 people!" George quipped.

Nancy wrinkled her nose. "You and Bess take coach and I'll go through first class," she replied, chuckling.

The girls dismissed the incident temporarily from their minds as they debarked and collected their suitcases. Outside, the sun blanketed the area of Glyfada in thick layers of heat.

"It's sweltering," George declared, feeling the temperature seeping through her sandals.

"We'll get used to it," Nancy said and darted toward a taxi stand. Within moments, the girls were on their way to the Hotel Skyros, a charming place located near Omonia Square.

"Gor-geous!" Bess exclaimed as a porter led them to their room.

It was large, with sliding glass doors that opened onto a terrace view of the Acropolis. On the walls were embroidered tapestries and beside each bed was a small flokati rug.

"When we get up in the morning," said Bess, "we'll think we're floating on an Athenian cloud!"

Nancy and George laughed as they opened their suitcases.

Nancy removed a folding umbrella and remarked, "This could have stayed home!"

Before she could unpack anything else, there was a knock on the door. The porter had returned with a basket of delicious-looking yellow apples.

"For you," he said, setting it on the table in front of the glass doors.

"Thank you," Nancy replied.

"Maybe Ned sent them," Bess suggested after the porter left, referring to Nancy's special date. "Is there a card?"

"I don't see any," Nancy said. "Perhaps it's a welcome gift from the hotel."

She was tempted to sample it but decided to hang up her clothes first. George, on the other hand, scooped an apple off the top. As she bit into it, she glimpsed something green and scaly inside the basket. It was slithering upward between the fruit! George dropped the apple on the floor and stepped back.

"There's a snake in here! Nancy! Bess!" she cried.

Now the venomous head emerged. George held her breath and took another step away as Nancy reached for her umbrella.

"Don't move!" she told George, then slid the tip of the umbrella under the reptile.

It swooped forward abruptly, then swung back again.

"Oh!" Bess shrieked. "Be careful!"

"Sh!" her cousin chided her.

Seconds ticked by slowly as Nancy edged closer, hoping to bait the snake onto the umbrella. This time, to her relief, it curled across the folds of the material.

"Get the wastebasket and one of the flokati rugs," Nancy said to Bess. "We'll use it as a cover."

Trembling, Bess obeyed Nancy's instructions. She placed the basket near the table, dropped the rug in a heap next to it, then darted out of range. Nancy turned slowly and steadily on her heels, never letting her eyes leave the poisonous creature, and lowered the umbrella into the basket.

"Whew!" she sighed in relief as the snake slid off.

Instantly George stuffed the rug over it while Nancy dialed the hotel desk.

"Someone will come to dispose of it," she told the girls.

"When?" Bess asked, still shivering.

"Soon, very soon."

As promised, a young hotel worker appeared within minutes. He did not say anything, but when Nancy handed him the wastebasket and lifted the rug, he gasped. He turned quickly and ran down the hall with it.

"Give him the apples too!" Bess said. "Porter! Porter!" she called after him, but it was too late. He had disappeared through a stairway exit.

"It's just as well," Nancy said, removing the apples from the basket. "Maybe there's something else hidden inside."

"Like a scorpion?" Bess squirmed.

"If anything, there are probably dollar bills," Nancy announced mysteriously. "Remember the Greek myth about the Golden Apples? They were guarded by a snake that twisted itself around the pillars of Heracles, and that's how the dollar sign came into being."

"I always thought apples were a love gift from Aphrodite," Bess said dreamily.

Ignoring the comment, Nancy glanced inside the basket. "Nothing here," she said, refilling it.

"So now what?" Bess asked, flopping down on her bed. "I'm beat."

"You're just suffering from delusions," George giggled. "Come on. Get up. We have work to do."

"Right this minute?" Bess muttered.

Nancy glanced at her watch. "We may be able to catch Mr. Vatis before he leaves his office," she said, referring to the attorney who handled Helen Nicholas's inheritance from her uncle.

The girls took a taxi to the address Mr. Drew had given Nancy for the law firm Vatis & Vatis. To their astonishment, the attorneys had moved and another name was painted on the entrance.

Inside, Nancy introduced herself to the receptionist, who smiled politely when she heard Nancy's question concerning the law office. "All I know is that the father, Vatis Senior, died some time ago. I have no idea where his son is. No one else does, either."

"Thank you anyway," Nancy said in disappointment.

Turning to leave, she and the others almost bumped into a man who was standing behind them apparently waiting to talk to the young woman. The girls apologized and left, a little embarrassed.

"I wonder where Vatis went," Bess remarked.

"Who knows?" George sighed. "The question is, where do we go from here?"

3

Unwanted Mask

"We're not far from Plaka," Nancy replied to Bess's question.

"Then what are we waiting for?" her friend asked. "I hear it's mysterious and exciting!"

Within ten minutes, the girls found themselves in the quaint district of old Athens where the capital of modern Greece had formed in the early 1800s.

"The houses are charming," Nancy observed.

The buildings rose in craggy steps like layers of stone carved out of an ancient hill. Most were trellised with vines and had window boxes and clay pots filled with colorful flowers. Jasmine and honeysuckle permeated the air.

"Smells wonderful," Bess said. She breathed

deeply as they wandered down the narrow, winding street.

They had paused in front of a small Byzantine church when a bearded clergyman wearing a black robe darted ahead to enter. Nancy gazed up at the faded red dome.

"It must be several hundred years old," she said. "Shall we go in, too?"

"Sure," George replied.

The odor of incense filled the church as the service ended, and in the entrance thin, white candles burned dimly, creating a soft glow around the icon on the stand next to them. It was a small wood panel on which a saint's picture had been painted. The bearded priest placed a beautiful silver box in front of it.

"What's he doing?" Bess whispered as he hurried out.

"He's leaving a present for the saint," Nancy explained. She stepped closer.

To her surprise, there was a nautical crest engraved on the lid of the box. Was the young man related to a shipping family? If so, might he know Constantine Nicholas?

"Come on!" the girl detective exclaimed, leading the way out.

By now, the Orthodox priest was far ahead of them. To Nancy's dismay, he disappeared quickly into the crowd of pedestrians at the foot of the hill.

"Oh, dear," Nancy said with a sigh as they lost sight of him completely.

The smell of roasted corn now drew the girls farther into monastiraki, where a variety of wares hung across open shop doors.

"Look at those embroidered blouses," Bess remarked. "Aren't they pretty?"

"I'm going to buy one," George announced.

"Me too," her cousin replied.

Nancy had her eye on two lovely linen tablecloths across the way. She bought them, then stopped in front of another store window. The sign above it said CHRYSOTEQUE.

"That must mean 'gold store,' " Nancy said as Bess and George caught up to her. "Just look at all that fabulous jewelry!"

Even more intriguing was the gold mask displayed in the middle!

"It's beautiful," George remarked.

The girls leaned forward for a closer look when suddenly it was pulled out of the window.

"I guess somebody wants to buy it," Bess said, and entered the shop followed by Nancy and George.

To their amazement, though, there were no customers inside. Behind a curtain at the rear, angry voices shouted at each other.

"Maybe we should leave," Bess murmured as a young boy appeared from behind the curtain and raced out of the store in tears.

Then a woman stepped into view and smiled. "May I help you?" she asked.

"I was interested in the mask in your window—" Nancy said.

"That's been sold," the shopkeeper replied curtly. "We have no more like it."

"In that case," Bess put in, "I'd like to buy this pin." She pointed to one in the form of a mask. "What do you think, girls?"

"Don't forget you have to lug all this stuff through customs," her cousin reminded her. She gazed at her friends' shopping bags. They were filling up rapidly.

"But this won't weigh a thing," Bess insisted and asked the shopkeeper the price.

"Not much at all, less than a thousand drachmas," the woman said.

"How many American dollars is that?" George inquired.

"Three—four."

"It's more like thirty," Nancy whispered to Bess.

"Even so," the girl said, "I'll take it. Somehow, spending drachmas is more fun than spending dimes!"

George rolled her eyes to the ceiling. "I'm going

34

to save my traveler's checks for something I really want," she said as they stepped outside. "Like a cruise on the Aegean."

By now, the girls were beginning to feel tired from their long walk. Nancy laid her heavy shopping bag on the sidewalk whenever she could. She had done so twice, and the second time the bag was nearly trampled on by tourists who window-shopped beside her.

"Let's get out of here," Bess suggested at last. "I can't take all of these people."

The girls walked toward Syntagma Square, where a din of children's voices circled an old man who wore a flat hat made of natural sponge. He carried others over his arm. They were all different shapes and sizes.

"*Barba Yanni! Barba Yanni!*" a small boy cried, eagerly trading a few coins for a big sponge.

"He sure won't need an umbrella," George said. "That sponge could soak up an entire cloudburst!"

"I'd like to soak up something cool," Bess said as they passed an ice-cream vendor.

"How about sitting down, too?" George asked.

The three found a sidewalk table. After they gave their order, a young man pulled up a chair.

"You American?" he asked in halting English.

"Yes, we are," George replied.

"I show you Athens," he announced.

"Oh, we couldn't—" Bess said.

"No, thank you," Nancy interrupted coolly.

"*Entaxi*," he said, heaving a sigh. "Okay, girls. So long."

Giggling, Bess leaned toward her friends. "I think we broke his heart," she said, watching him leave.

Instantly George changed the subject. "May we see your tablecloths?" she asked Nancy, who promptly opened her shopping bag.

"Hey, what's this?" she said, discovering an extra package. It was wrapped like the others from the jewelry store. She pulled it out and removed the paper.

"It's the gold face mask we saw in the window!" Bess exclaimed.

"How did it get into my shopping bag?" Nancy wondered.

George shrugged. "It sure looks like a real ancient piece," she replied, "not a reproduction."

She took the mask from her friend and turned it over, examining it closely. "How about this?" she declared, pointing to a gold-colored sticker affixed to the metal behind the chin.

"It's that doodle!" Nancy said excitedly.

"Doodle?"

"Yes, like the one someone drew on the Photini letterhead. It's the letter phi, but instead of curli-

cues at each end, this one has the head of a snake."

"The whole symbol is actually the body of a snake," Bess observed. "What do you suppose it means?"

"I don't know, but I'm going to find out," Nancy said, announcing her plan to return to the jewelry shop immediately.

"Right this minute?" Bess asked. "Can't we relax a bit longer? I really feel dizzy."

"Maybe you ought to go back to the hotel," George said, as her cousin rose unsteadily from her chair.

"I think you're right," Bess replied. "It must be the heat or something."

Nancy insisted that George accompany her cousin, adding that she would not be long at Chrysoteque's. To her disappointment, she found the jewelry store closed.

Siesta time, Nancy thought, snapping her fingers. Maybe the archeological museum could give her some information about the mask!

She took a taxi there and found it also was ready to close for a few hours. The guard at the door rattled at her in Greek as she pleaded in English to be let in.

It's no use, Nancy thought anxiously.

Then she showed him the gold mask. To her astonishment, he grabbed it from her and said something in Greek. Nancy shook her head in puzzlement. He took her arm and pulled her toward an office at the end of the corridor.

I hope he's taking me to see the curator, she murmured to herself. And I hope he speaks English!

When they stepped into the room, the guard flew past a secretary to an inner office. Seated behind a desk was a brown-haired man with a trace of gray in his sideburns. The guard spoke in Greek and laid the gold mask in front of him.

"I am in charge of this museum," he said to Nancy in a thick accent. "Who are you and where did you get this?"

The girl detective introduced herself, explaining, "I found it in my shopping bag."

"In your what?" the curator replied.

"In—"

"Just a minute," he interrupted and dialed a number on his telephone.

Within seconds, another man appeared breathless in the doorway. The curator told Nancy he was a detective who had been recently assigned to the museum after a series of art thefts.

"The mask was stolen from this museum, Miss Drew," the curator announced. "Did you know that?"

"No. How could I?"

The detective's glaring eyes made Nancy suddenly feel like a criminal.

"As a matter of fact," the curator went on, "this mask should now be in the United States with a traveling exhibit."

"You mean to different museums?" Nancy answered.

"Then," the detective interrupted in sparse English, "you know something."

"No, I—no, I don't. I was shopping at the flea market and—"

"And you bought this mask?" the curator asked.

The guard, who understood no English, remained stone-faced while the detective laughed. "A joke—she bought mask monastiraki! Ha!"

The three men conferred quietly for several minutes. The curator turned the mask over. He seemed to be making comments about the symbol on the back, then pointed accusingly at Nancy.

This is ridiculous, she thought. They think I'm a thief!

"When the thieves realized they could not sell the mask, they got rid of it," the curator stated. "Does that make sense to you, Miss Drew?"

"I suppose so. Maybe they figured you were close to catching them and planted the mask on me."

"Perhaps you belong to gang," the detective put

in haltingly. "You American girlfriend or cousin to one of the members?"

"No," Nancy said indignantly. Trying to remain calm, she added, "Even if I were, which I'm not, I'd hardly have stepped into such a flimsy trap."

"Even so, we must keep you here until we know otherwise!" the curator exclaimed.

4

The Intruder

As the curator spoke, a flush of anger rose in Nancy's cheeks. "You are going to hold me?" she repeated.

"That is correct, Miss Drew," he replied. "We cannot let you go, now that you have given us the first clue to the thieves. Tell us about this symbol."

"I can't—I don't know how it got on the mask or who put it there." Nancy asked if she might make a phone call to her hotel.

"You may use this telephone."

To the girl's relief, George answered on the first ring. When she heard Nancy's predicament, she was astounded.

"We'll—I mean I'll—come to the museum right away," George said. "Bess still isn't feeling well, so she'd better stay here. Bye—"

"Wait, George. Don't hang up," Nancy said anxiously. "Please call my father. He'll know what to do." She put down the receiver, hoping Mr. Drew, though thousands of miles away, would somehow come to her rescue.

George immediately asked the hotel operator to place a call to the attorney's office. She was told it could take a couple of hours to go through.

George hung up and said to Bess, "Nancy can't wait that long. I'm going downstairs to the kiosk, the magazine stand, on the corner. There's a public telephone inside."

"Shall I go with you?" Bess asked, lifting her head off the pillow.

"You stay put." George drew the half-closed drapes fully shut, then left.

Bess snuggled under the blanket and curled herself into a comfortable knot. Sleep overtook her quickly and it was not until something shuffled in front of her bed that she awakened. Groggily, she turned her head toward the door, glimpsing the back of a man as he shut the door quietly. Bess gasped. It was only the ring of the telephone that kept her from running after him.

"Hello," she said shakily.

"Where's George?" Nancy asked before Bess could tell her about the intruder. "It's been almost an hour since I talked to her."

Suddenly Bess's eyes shifted to the table where

the basket of apples had been. It was gone!

"Oh, Nancy!" she cried out. "Something awful happened!"

"To George?"

"No, no. Someone broke into our room—"

"What!"

"A man. He took the apples. I didn't get much of a look at him, but I'm not staying here another minute. I'm coming right to the museum."

Bess said good-bye, splashed cold water on her face, then dressed and grabbed her purse.

At the museum, Nancy sank into a chair in the curator's office. She thought anxiously about George, the strange intrusion at the hotel, and how she could free herself from the detective who glowered at her. Then, to her great relief, she heard a familiar voice in the corridor.

"George!" she cried, racing to the door.

The girl's short dark hair was tousled from running and she was out of breath.

"I'm sorry I took so long," George panted. "The hotel phones were tied up and the one at the kiosk was out of order. So I went to the American Embassy. I spoke to one of the attachés who—"

"And who are you?" the curator interrupted George.

"George Fayne. I'm Nancy's friend and—"

Just then Bess walked into the room. "Oh,

George, I'm glad you're here," she said, then quickly introduced herself to the curator.

"Nancy is working on a case. You have to let her go!" Bess added.

"Oh, really?" the officer snapped.

"I can prove that Nancy is a detective!" she declared.

"You're making it worse," George murmured, causing Bess to stop talking.

The general silence lasted only a few seconds. Then the curator's secretary summoned him out of the room. The detective joined them, leaving the guard to watch the girls.

"What's going on?" Bess asked.

Nancy and George shrugged. "Maybe the wheels of justice have started to turn," her cousin said.

The prediction proved correct. Nancy was released shortly, but not without a warning.

"You may be helpful to American police," the detective said, "but you are not to us. So stay out of our case."

Despite the stinging remark, Nancy smiled politely and said good-bye. Leaving the mask behind them, Bess and George followed her out of the museum.

"You're not going to give up working on the mystery, are you?" Bess asked.

"You heard what the man said," Nancy replied, but the mischievous gleam in her eyes told the others she had no intention of quitting.

Again Bess mentioned the intruder, which troubled her listeners.

"That guy may have been in our room before we returned," George said, "and slipped out onto the terrace when he heard us coming. I thought it was odd the drapes were half-closed but figured the maid had drawn them."

"What's even stranger," Bess added, "is that he took the basket of apples he probably sent us in the first place."

"That's only an assumption. Maybe the apples were intended for somebody else," Nancy pointed out.

"More likely," George put in, "the poisonous snake was. After all, who, other than our friends, knew were were coming to Greece?"

Their next stop, the girls agreed, would be the Photini Agency. It was located on the upper floor of a bank building in the heart of the city. Staff members darted from files to desks, creating an air of busyness in contrast to the vacant office in New York.

"This place sure isn't going out of business," Nancy commented, then asked to see the manager.

He was a short, friendly man with dark eyes. "I

am Mr. Diakos," he said, greeting them warmly.

Nancy introduced herself and the others, adding that they had recently visited the agency in New York.

"Ah, then you know about our poor pitiful village families," Mr. Diakos said. "They need constant help."

Apparently, Nancy thought, he thinks we're interested in sponsoring somebody.

"Here, look at her," the man went on, pulling open a desk drawer and producing a photograph of a small, sad-faced child. "Such a pretty girl, but you see? No smile."

"I—" Nancy tried to interrupt.

"And look at this one." Mr. Diakos showed her another picture. "He is her brother. They live in Athikia." Next he removed a manila folder from a second drawer. "All these children come from Angelo Kastro, another town on the Peloponnesos. Their families are very poor and—"

"Mr. Diakos, I'm afraid we are only interested in one specific family at the moment," Nancy cut in at last.

"Oh, yes?" the manager fluttered his eyelids.

"Papadapoulos is the name. They live in Agionori."

Without waiting to hear more, Mr. Diakos asked a secretary to check their file. No one by that name was listed. Puzzled, Nancy revealed Mrs. Thompson's story about the missing payments and Dimitri Georgiou's disappearance.

"Have you seen or heard from him recently?" George asked.

"No, I haven't, but that did not seem strange to me. I'm new to this position and it's taken me a while to adjust."

"Did this office send Mr. Georgiou lists of names for sponsorship on a regular basis?" Bess spoke up.

"Yes, but only a few were picked by Americans."

"What happened to the rest?"

"They still need support."

"Is it possible," Nancy suggested, "that Mr. Georgiou signed up sponsors without reporting them to you?"

"Of course, but why—how could he do such a thing? It's terrible to steal from the poor!" The idea stirred Mr. Diakos into a rage. "Dimitri Georgiou will pay for this!" he blazed angrily.

"But we're not sure he took the money," Bess said, trying to calm the man.

"Well, someone did!" he declared.

Before leaving, Mr. Diakos took the girls' hotel address and phone number. "If I hear anything about Dimitri's whereabouts, I will let you know."

"Another dead end," Bess said in disappointment. "Now what?"

"Let's go to the Nikos Shipping Company," Nancy suggested. "But first we should visit Dad's friend, Mr. Mousiadis. He might be able to lend us a car." She pulled the man's business card out of her pocket. "It's not far from the Hotel Skyros."

When they reached his office, they were met by an efficient young assistant who introduced them to Mr. Mousiadis. He was a tall, sturdy man with a pleasant face. He ushered the girls to comfortable chairs. Before Nancy needed to ask, he offered her the use of his car.

"That is very generous of you," she said. "Thank you, I—"

He lifted his hand as if to stop her from saying more. "You father told me why you are here and I am happy to help you. Unfortunately, I must leave for Italy tomorrow, so I won't be able to show you around. Even so, maybe my four wheels can!" He smiled broadly. "But I have a suggestion for you."

"What is it?" Bess asked.

"If you have time, please buy a *máti*, an amulet to protect yourselves. *Ná mín avaskathí*. May no evil come to you." He handed Nancy a set of car keys, saying he would be back in a week.

The streets of Athens were congested with private cars and taxis which honked and weaved in front of one another, sometimes dangerously close. Nancy gripped the steering wheel tightly as she drove to the outskirts of the city. There the narrow roads opened onto a highway. She followed it to Piraeus, the busiest port in Greece.

"There it is!" George exclaimed, spying a gray building with the name NIKOS across the top.

Inside, Nancy asked for Helen's cousin, Constantine. She was not surprised to learn he no longer worked there.

"Do you know where he is?" Nancy asked, looking at the man squarely.

"No. Constantine is a wild boy with wild friends. He spent all the money his parents left him, then—poof!—like smoke—he disappeared!"

"What about the lawyer, Mr. Vatis?" Nancy probed.

"Out of business."

George muttered, "I have a feeling we River Heights detectives are out of business, too!"

"Not yet, I hope," Nancy said. She asked the man for permission to board one of the Nikos freighters. He gave her three passes and, to her bewilderment, a snapshot of a handsome young man.

"Constantine," he said with a nod. "You may keep it."

"He looks like Helen, don't you think?" Bess commented, observing the soft brown eyes and wavy hair.

"A little," Nancy agreed. She stowed the picture in her purse and noted the man's directions to a freighter berthed near the shipyard.

"Someone will let you on board," he said. "I hope you enjoy your visit and your vacation in our country." The girls thanked him and left.

"What do you figure we'll find?" George asked.

"Some cute sailors," Bess answered, dimpling.

"Or a few Greek rats!" George quipped.

Her cousin shivered as she eyed the large gray tanker in front of them.

"Well, let's go aboard," Nancy urged, and the girls walked up the gangplank.

They gave their passes to a crewman who spoke to them in Greek.

"Here we go again," George sighed. "Does anyone speak English here?" she asked him.

The man stared at her. He shrugged and walked away, leaving the visitors to explore the ship alone. They stepped below deck. Suddenly the freighter began to move.

"Where are they taking us?" Bess cried.

5

In the Ditch

The young detectives raced upstairs. Already the freighter had slipped a few feet out of its tight berth.

"Stop!" Nancy shouted to a crewman while George and Bess waved their arms frantically toward the dock.

"Let us off!" they exclaimed.

The crewman jabbered back in Greek, then yelled to another man who bolted through an iron door.

"What'll we do if the boat keeps going?" Bess said anxiously.

"Jump overboard and swim back," George teased.

"Won't be necessary," Nancy said. "We're going back!"

"Phew!" Bess exclaimed. "That was a close call. We could've been kidnapped—"

"And left to die on some sinking island!" her cousin said as the girls stepped onto the dock.

"Tomorrow we'll do something a little less eventful, okay?" Nancy said, and suggested a visit to Maria Papadapoulos's home.

"Does her family know we're coming?" George asked on the way there.

"Not unless Mrs. Thompson wrote to Mrs. Papadapoulos. Anyway, she gave me a letter of introduction to bring along."

The car rolled on smoothly for several miles, passing groves of olive trees along a highway that curved along the Canal of Corinth. When they reached the hillside village, Nancy shifted to low gear on a steep incline. For a moment she dropped her gaze, unaware that a small pickup truck was speeding down the narrow curve toward them.

"Oh, no!" George cried in alarm.

The truck was gaining speed. In a few moments the two vehicles would collide! There were no side roads or driveways to escape into, only a deep, muddy ditch!

"Hang on!" Nancy told the others, steering sharply to the right out of the truck's path.

The car bucked into the ditch like a bronco. Its rear wheels kicked high as the front ones spun forward in the dry mud, spewing it in all directions, before the vehicle finally came to a complete halt.

Nancy let go of the wheel and sank back against the seat. "That was a close one!" she exclaimed. "Are you all right?"

"Uh—okay," Bess said weakly.

George grinned. "I feel like a cowgirl, and glad this animal has stopped! How about you, Nancy?"

"I'm okay." Actually, her hands and arms ached from clenching the wheel so tightly. She took a deep breath and said, "Let's try to push the car out."

"We'll never be able to budge it," Bess predicted.

"Where's the old positive thinking?" George said brightly, and anchored herself behind the right rear bumper. "Ready?" She glanced at Nancy, who stood in a similar position on the left side.

"Ready!"

Bess lined herself between them. "One, two, three, push!" she said. But the car did not move. "Is the brake off?"

"Yes," Nancy puffed. "Let's try again. Two, three, push!"

This time the car slipped ahead, but not far.

"It's useless!" Bess declared, collapsing on the trunk.

George rested against it, too, while Nancy walked to the front. The wheels were choked with mud.

"What we need is a crane," she sighed.

In the distance, a stout woman in an old cotton dress emerged from a small farmhouse. With her were several children who hung close to her as she hurried toward the girls. She chattered at them in Greek, and looked piteously at the car.

"*Parakaló*, just a minute, please," Nancy said, reading the small Greek-English dictionary she took from her purse. Quickly she flipped through it, picking out *voíthia*, *autokínito*, and *mihanikó*, which meant "help," "car," and "mechanic."

The woman nodded with understanding and patted one of the children, saying, "Zoe! *Grígora! Grígora!*"

"That must mean 'Hurry,'" Bess whispered to Nancy.

"*Fére tón Babá!*" the woman continued.

Shortly, the little girl returned with her father, a man not much taller than his wife but as muscular as she was plump. He circled the car quickly, then got inside and started it, pressing the gas pedal to the floor. The others stood back as mud churned under the racing wheels. Suddenly, the car lurched forward.

"*Efharistó, efharistó*, thank you," Nancy said when the car stood on the road once again.

The couple smiled happily as the girls gave each child a shiny American coin. They grinned and waved good-bye to the travelers who set off for the Papadapoulos home, a small stone house down the road.

"Welcome," Mrs. Papadapoulos greeted them. She was a slender, dark-haired woman with a pale face. A little girl with huge dark eyes clung to her skirt.

Nancy handed her Jeannette Thompson's letter of introduction.

"Cannot read," the woman said. "Maria, you—"

Her daughter, who was nine or ten years old, spoke. "Mama knows only a few English words."

"But you speak very well," George remarked.

"That's because I went to school in Athens."

Maria glanced at the letter and seeing Mrs. Thompson's name at the end of it, she grinned. "She is a nice lady. She helped us a lot, but she stopped."

As she talked, her listeners looked past her at the rugs and afghans handwoven with red and brown wool. They were a striking contrast against the pure white cotton cloths trimmed in needlepoint that hung over the tables and chairs.

"Mrs. Thompson never stopped helping you," Nancy assured her. "Somebody stole the money!"

Maria gasped and sputtered in Greek to her mother, who looked equally shocked. Her eyes brimmed with tears which subsided only when

George asked to see some of her handiwork. Quickly Maria brought a cloth bag. Her mother opened it and pulled out a beautifully embroidered shawl.

"How lovely!" Bess murmured. "Is it for sale, Maria?"

The little girl repeated the question in Greek. Mrs. Papadapoulos shook her head. "A gift," she said, wiping her eyes.

"That is very kind of you," Bess said sweetly, "but I can't take it unless I pay for the shawl. It's not for me. I want to give it to someone else."

When Maria explained to her mother, she reluctantly accepted a small sum of money. Then, digging back into the bag, she produced a pretty white handkerchief with an unusual lace edging. She handed it to Bess. "For you," she said. Pulling out two more, she gave them to Nancy and George.

"*Efharistó*," the girls answered gratefully.

"I suppose," Maria said, "Mrs. Thompson will not want to—"

"When she got your mother's letter, she was very upset," Nancy interrupted.

"I wrote it for my mother—"

"Well, she realizes how much you all have depended on her."

Before the girl could continue, the door swung

open and two small children, younger than Maria, ran in.

"*Éla, éla.* Michali! Anna!" their mother exclaimed. "Come here, we have guests."

She sent them to fetch glasses of fresh goat's milk for the visitors. Bess swallowed hers quickly.

"It's delicious," she said. "You ought to make goat's milk candy."

"Think so?" Maria giggled. "How much milk would it take? We only have three goats!"

"In that case," Bess said, excusing herself, "I'll be right back." She returned with a large picnic basket filled with delectable food from Athens.

"Where did you hide that?" George asked in amazement.

"In the trunk," Bess replied smugly.

Her friends helped lay out the meal. Despite everyone's hearty appetite, there were plenty of leftovers for the Papadapoulos family.

When the girls were on their way back to Athens, Nancy and George praised Bess extravagantly. "It's the first time you didn't go for second helpings!" George teased. "Now that you've started the diet, how about sticking to it?"

Bess did not retort.

As they drove along an attractive bathing beach, Nancy gazed longingly at a strip of white sand dotted with sunbathers. "If only we had brought our swimsuits," she said with a sigh.

"That's my second surprise," Bess piped up, announcing she had packed everyone's gear. "I was hoping we'd have time for a dip!"

Eagerly Nancy parked the car and Bess removed the beach togs. The girls hurried to the ticket booth and bathhouse. They changed quickly and, after dropping their towels on the coarse sand, ran into the surf. Nancy and George dived under a wave, feeling the cool water tingle against their skin, while Bess began to sidestroke near shore.

"It's wonderful," she thought as the salt water licked her face. Then, changing direction, she let her toes touch bottom. Instantly, she let out a cry of pain!

6

Hunting a Suspect

Hearing Bess's cry, Nancy and George swam toward her from opposite directions. They sliced through the water quickly but were still several feet away when the lifeguard reached her.

"My foot hurts," Bess was saying to him as she limped onto the beach.

The young man knelt to look at the red mark on Bess's skin. "You were stung by a jellyfish," he said, then stood up again. "You'll be all right. I have some—"

"What happened?" George interrupted as she and Nancy caught up to the pair.

Nancy's gaze traveled to the bite. "Do you have any rubbing alcohol?" she asked.

"No," the lifeguard said, "but I have a solution of ammonia."

"Ammonia!" Bess gasped. "Ick!"

The young man ran to a canvas bag next to his chair and removed a bottle of clear fluid. Within seconds he was pouring some of it over the large welt.

"Ou-ouch!" Bess cried out. "That burns. It hurts more than the jellyfish!" She shook her foot vigorously and to her relief the sharpness of the sting abated quickly.

"You see, I told you you'd be all right," the lifeguard grinned. "Alexis is never wrong."

For a long moment Bess returned the smile, dimpling her cheeks as she blinked in the sunlight. "Alexis?" she paused for the rest of his name.

"Hios."

"The shipping family?" Nancy inquired.

"That's right. We're from the island of the same name."

"Then why are you here in Loutraki and not sailing on some gorgeous yacht?" Bess asked.

"I will be on one later this summer. Would you all like to go?" he said hastily.

The sunlight danced on his deeply tanned shoulders, making the visitors wish they had more time to spend on the beaches of Greece.

"I'd love to," Bess replied.

"But we don't plan to stay the whole summer," George put in quickly.

"We're really here on business," Nancy explained. "As a matter of fact, it involves the shipping family of Nicholas, who own the Nikos line."

"Oh, yes. I know them."

"You do?"

"Of course," Alexis said. "The shipping community is a very close-knit one."

"Then maybe you know Constantine Nicholas," George put in. "Do you?"

"Yes."

"Well, we're looking for him. I mean Nancy is."

Alexis seemed somewhat guarded as he went on. "I understand he disappeared with a lot of money, some of it his inheritance from his parents and the rest stolen. It's possible, though, the story is only gossip."

"What else have you heard?" Nancy prodded.

"First, can you tell me why three pretty American girls are so eager to know?"

Briefly, the girl detective mentioned that her father was Helen Nicholas's lawyer and that he had asked Nancy to search for Helen's missing cousin, Constantine. "The stolen money you referred to— was it stolen from Uncle Nicholas's estate?"

"Maybe. I know that the old man hoped Constantine would carry on the business after his death. But now he's gone, and no one knows where."

Alexis could shed no more light on the subject, and the young people began to chat about Greece.

"Have you ever been to Lycabettus Hill?" Alexis inquired.

"Where's that?" Bess asked.

"In Athens," he said. "It has a spectacular view of the city. There's a small church, too, and a restaurant. Maybe you would all like to go there with me this evening."

"Sounds great," George replied.

"Shall we meet about eight thirty?" Nancy said as the girls picked up their beach towels.

"Fine. Just tell me where you're staying," Alexis said.

"The Hotel Skyros," Bess replied, waving goodbye. "See you later."

The young detectives changed into dry clothes and as they were starting back for Athens, Nancy mentioned Mrs. Thompson. "I ought to phone her about our visit to Agionori."

"Forget using the hotel phone," George said. "It takes forever to get through."

Consequently, after Nancy returned the car to the garage, the trio headed for the kiosk near their hotel. Nancy dialed Mrs. Thompson's home telephone number, listening to it ring several times before hanging up, then tried Helen Nicholas. She did not answer.

"Maybe Dad's in," Nancy murmured, making the third call.

To her delight, he picked up the phone immediately, and Nancy related her current news.

Bess, meanwhile, pulled George aside. "Do you see that guy up the street?" she asked.

A tall man with black hair was pacing back and forth in front of an iron fence.

"What about him?" George replied.

"I think he's the one who took the basket of apples from our hotel room!" Bess said.

"Oh?" George said. "Let's watch him."

As soon as Nancy finished her conversation, Bess told her about the suspect. Suddenly she let out a stifled cry.

"And look who else is coming," Nancy remarked.

Approaching the stranger was Isakos, the unpleasant man they had met on their flight to Athens!

"Follow me!" Nancy urged her friends. She led them onto a side street that curved back to the one where the men were standing.

The girls walked briskly toward a profusion of bougainvillea vines entwined around an iron fence and parted the flowers enough to see Isakos's red face. He was moving his lips, but the words were barely audible. Then his voice rose.

"At two or three tomorrow morning no one will be around St. Mark's!" he insisted. "It will be perfect. We can take—"

"Don't speak so loudly!" the other man cautioned him.

"I can't hear everything they're saying," Bess whispered to Nancy.

"Sh!" her cousin warned.

They heard only a few more words, including a vague reference to mosaics, before the pair moved down the street. They crossed it, apparently aiming for the Hotel Skyros.

"Do you suppose the men are staying there?" Bess asked, following her cousin and Nancy through the square.

"If not both, then I bet one of them is," Nancy said upon entering the hotel. She stopped at the desk to inquire.

"Why, yes," the clerk answered, "there is a Mr. Isakos in Room 986."

"Thank you very much," Nancy said.

"Do you wish to leave a message?"

"N-no," Nancy replied. The number of the man's room was racing through her mind. Theirs was 968! Had the venomous snake in the basket of apples been meant for Isakos? If so, why?

The same questions occurred to George. "Our room isn't far from 986," she said as they took the elevator to the ninth floor.

When the girls reached it, no one was in the hallway.

"All clear," Bess said, tiptoeing with the others to Isakos's door.

They listened a bit, but heard nothing.

"Maybe the other guy left," George whispered.

"And maybe he's on his way back," Bess pointed out. "We'd better go."

The girls hurried to their room to rest awhile before they showered and changed. Less than an hour before Alexis was due to meet them, Nancy slipped into a pretty turquoise skirt and blouse. Bess put on a white eyelet dress, and George, a tan silk outfit.

When they strolled out of the elevator onto the first floor, they found Alexis seated in a comfortable chair under a palm tree. His deep tan was a striking contrast against his white shirt.

"Hi!" the girls greeted him, prompting the young man to rise.

"I have some news for you," he said mysteriously.

"You do?" Bess asked eagerly.

"I think I saw Constantine."

"Where?" Nancy asked in surprise.

"Near Plaka. I tried to catch up to him, but couldn't. There were too many people around."

"Maybe Constantine works at the flea market," Nancy said thoughtfully. "We ought to go there in the morning to find out what we can."

The other girls agreed, but as they approached Lycabettus Hill, the conversation quickly changed.

"How do we get up there?" Bess inquired.

"On the funicular," Alexis said, pointing to a cable car ready to ascend through a tunnel. "It will take us to St. George's Church."

"Speaking of St. George's," Nancy said as they boarded one of two compartments, "is there a St. Mark's Church nearby?"

Alexis pondered a minute. "Not that I know of," he said.

"Well, I'm thinking of some place called St. Mark's that may have some unusual icons or mosaics," Nancy went on.

"Oh, yes. The monastery."

"Is it in Athens?"

"No, no. It's on the northern outskirts." As Alexis spoke, the car began to slide through the dark tunnel, breaking slowly away from the buildings below.

"This is fantastic!" George exclaimed when they reached the top of the mountain.

The church was small and white, a stark contrast against the awesome view from the hill. Alexis swept his arm toward the Acropolis, where a rainbow of lights played over the temple ruins, then pointed out the King's Palace and, in another direction, the harbors of Piraeus.

"We'd never have come here if we hadn't met you," Bess said to Alexis. "Thank you."

"My pleasure," he answered. "I hope to convince your friends to stay all summer."

The evening wore away quickly and at the end of it, the girls promised to keep in touch with their new friend.

Next morning, the girls awakened early and directly after breakfast went to the jewelry shop in monastiraki.

Nancy's first question to the shopkeeper was, "Do you recall the name of the man who bought the gold mask?"

The woman glanced in bewilderment from Nancy to the other girls. "Gold mask? What gold mask?" she repeated.

"The one you had in your window," Nancy said.

"I don't know what you are taking about."

"Surely you remember all of us," the girl went on.

The shopkeeper remained silent. It was only when Bess decided to purchase a gold filigree bracelet that she smiled a little.

"A very pretty choice. Excuse me while I wrap it."

"Weird," George commented as the woman slipped behind the curtain, but hearing a low murmur of voices, she said no more.

Nancy tiptoed near the curtain. She caught a few Greek words, *símera, ti óra, stís októ, apópse,* and finally the name of the girls' hotel!

"Something's about to happen at the Hotel Skyros!" Nancy gasped.

7

Burglar Attempt

Before Nancy could tell her friends what she had overheard, the curtain was flung back. The shopkeeper appeared, holding Bess's purchase.

"Is there anything else you would like?" she asked the girls.

"No, thank you," George replied, signalling her cousin to leave.

Outside, Nancy opened her Greek-English dictionary, then said, "Something related to the three of us is going to happen at our hotel tonight about eight o'clock!"

"What!" Bess exclaimed.

"But where?" George asked. "We can't cover the entire hotel. There are fourteen floors—"

"And a lobby," Bess interrupted, adding, "Are

you positive the shopkeeper was talking about us?"

"No, I'm not," Nancy said, "but my hunch is yes. Anyway, we should stick around to see what happens."

That evening, the girls strolled through the hotel at the appointed hour. As a precaution, Nancy asked the hotel desk and telephone operator not to reveal the girls' room to anyone. Bess offered to post herself near the busy side entrance.

"Where are you two going to be?" she asked.

Before either could answer, a call came over the loudspeaker for Nancy Drew to answer the phone. "George, will you check that out for me?"

"Sure. Where are you going?"

"Upstairs to our room."

"Alone?" Bess asked fearfully.

"I'll be okay. You stake out the side entrance and don't worry. I have a feeling that phone call is meant to keep us away from our room."

The girl detective took the elevator to the ninth floor. Instinct told her to step out cautiously. As she approached her door, a man suddenly appeared from the stairway exit. In his hand was a key which he inserted in the lock of her room!

"Stop!" she shouted, racing toward him.

He whirled quickly and hurled something in her direction, then dashed to the stairway.

"Stop! Stop!" Nancy cried again, dodging the ob-

ject. She ran after the intruder, tracking him to the floor below. He dashed into an elevator with a couple who were just entering. The door closed just before Nancy got there.

He's probably going to the lobby! Nancy thought.

Instantly, the girl detective flew back to the stairs, bolting down each flight with amazing speed. Upon reaching the ground floor, she gazed about breathlessly, hoping the man would still be in the lobby. There was no sign either of him or of the couple who had ridden with him.

Nancy hurried to the desk. "*Parakaló*, excuse me," she said. "I'm looking for someone." She described the suspect and the couple and added, "Are they staying in this hotel?"

"I don't recognize the man but the couple sound familiar. They are staying here. Their name is Zimmer. I believe they are members of a charter tour from Massachusetts."

Just then, George spotted Nancy and ran toward her. "That phone call was from a newspaper reporter." she said. "He wants to write an article about you."

"About me?" Nancy said. "Why?"

"It seems he heard you were in Athens to solve a mystery and wishes to know what it's about."

"You didn't tell him, did you?"

"Are you kidding? I wouldn't tell anyone. I said, 'What kind of a detective would I be if I told you over the phone?' "

"And what did he say?"

"He didn't want all the details—just enough to make an interesting story. 'Even so,' I said, 'I really can't help you.' " She paused. "I believe he thought I was you until I slipped and told him I wasn't Nancy Drew."

"Then what happened?"

"He was furious and hung up."

"Did you find out his name?" Nancy inquired.

"Yes, it's Irwin."

"And which paper does he work for?"

"He's a free-lance writer. At least, that's what he said. He claims he's developing a column that focuses on Americans living or visiting in Greece."

"I think," Nancy told George, "that Irwin, if that's his real name, was only trying to keep me from going to our room, while his buddy went in." She told about her ride to the ninth floor and what had happened. "The man looked like the one who took the apples—"

"Where did he get the key?" George asked. "Do you think he works at this hotel?"

"Possibly. Or maybe he stole a master key and had a duplicate made before anyone discovered the original was missing."

"Terrific," George said, shaking her head in concern. "If you're right, then he could return at any time."

"We don't have much of value for him to steal," Nancy said. "What really bothers me is that he can harm us. Apparently, the apples were meant for us after all."

George nodded worriedly. "We'd better change rooms before—"

Just then Bess ran up to them. "Wait until you hear this!" she panted.

"What?" Nancy asked.

"A man ran out of the elevator and almost bumped into me. I heard him say 'Drew.'"

"Why didn't you follow him?" George pressed her cousin.

"I tried to, but he got away from me. He jumped into a car and they took off."

"They?" George asked.

"There was another man behind the wheel."

"Did you notice a couple with them?" Nancy continued.

"Come to think of it, there were two people in the elevator, but they didn't go with him. They looked as mystified as I was when he cut out in front of them. I'm positive the rude one was the man we saw with Isakos!"

Suddenly, Nancy recalled the object he had

hurled at her in the hallway near the girls' room.

"Let's go upstairs," she said. "On the way I'll tell you what happened to me."

When Bess heard about the intruder, she turned pale. "We'll have to move out of here!" she insisted. "What if the guy slips us another poisonous snake?"

"If you would feel safer in another room," Nancy said, "we can arrange it. I'm staying where we are."

"But why expose yourself to danger?"

"What's to prevent him and his pals from finding us in another room? If we leave the hotel, we might lose track of our enemies. I don't want to do that. I want to catch them!"

"Nancy's right," George agreed. "We're a team, and facing the danger is winning half the battle!"

The girls stopped near room 968.

"There it is!" Nancy cried, seeing something that lay on the hallway carpet. She hurried forward and picked it up. "It's a metal stamp," she said.

On the bottom was the strange serpentine symbol that appeared on the gold mask!

8

Valuable Outburst

Were the intruder and Isakos working together as art thieves? Nancy wondered. If so, had one of them planted the mask in her shopping bag, hoping the police would arrest her if she tried to return it?

"This is absolutely incredible," George said, staring at the stamp.

"It must be used to identify all the stuff stolen from the museum," Bess suggested.

But why was the stranger carrying the stamp with him? Why, too, had he thrown it away so carelessly? Was it done in a fit of frustration?

No immediate answers came to the three detectives as they went into their room.

"Maybe we ought to investigate St. Mark's monastery," George said, "It wouldn't surprise me if Isakos and his friend try to steal some of the icons."

"And stamp them with this," George added.

"Uh-huh. I have a feeling we're in for another long night," Bess moaned. "Didn't Isakos say something about two or three in the morning?"

"Why don't we take a nap for a few hours?" Nancy suggested. She removed Mr. Mousiadis's car keys from her purse and put them next to her digital alarm clock. "Seeing these when I wake up will spur me out of bed." She laughed.

None of the girls slept soundly. When they awoke, it was one o'clock.

"All set?" Nancy asked cheerily.

Bess lifted her head from the pillow, then mumbled something and turned over.

"Come on, sleepyhead!" her cousin prodded her.

"Go away," Bess murmured, but forced herself to get up.

Once she dampened her face, Bess was as eager as the others to begin their journey into the hills. But the monotonous drone of the car engine soon made her sleepy again.

"How much farther do we have to go?" Bess asked when they reached the edge of the city.

"Only a few more miles," Nancy replied, stifling a yawn.

Soon she turned the car onto a narrow roadway that twisted between darkened houses and rows of cypress trees that grew more dense as the iron gate of the monastery came into view. A lone candle was burning dimly in a window.

"How do we get in?" Bess whispered. "The gate looks locked."

Nancy pulled the car to a halt and shut off the headlights. "Where there's a will, there's a way," she declared.

Careful not to make any noise, the three sleuths crept out into the moonlight and moved toward the gate.

"We're in luck," Nancy whispered excitedly. "The bolt's broken."

"Maybe someone forced it!" Bess declared.

"Or maybe it's just rusty," her cousin said, helping Nancy swing back the heavy gate.

Quietly they stole across the paved courtyard, glancing at the candlelit window, and hid near a tree. Suddenly a loud wail drew monks from their cells.

"What's going on?" Bess whispered to the others.

She stuck her head out from behind the tree trunk to watch the men scurrying through the chapel doors at the far end of the courtyard.

"Do you want them to see us?" George asked, yanking her cousin back next to her.

"They won't. It's pitch-black," Bess retorted.

"Sh!" Nancy signalled them to stop talking.

She noticed a glow of light dance on and off across the pavement. Perhaps one of the monks had remained in his cell, turned on a lamp for a moment, then shut it off. But to her surprise the light flickered several times. Was it a signal?

The cousins had also noticed it, but kept quiet as a man in a long black robe darted in front of their hiding place. The wailing sound had stopped and the other priests quickly returned to the courtyard, immediately dispersing to their rooms.

"Let's go to the gardens," Nancy said in a low voice.

Bess grasped her friend's arm. "What if they all come out again?" she asked nervously.

"What if, what if," George grumbled. "What if the sky falls down, Chicken Little?"

With a deep frown, Bess stepped away from the old gnarled tree.

"Stand where you are!" a deep voice ordered.

"Oh!" Bess gasped, freezing in fear.

Nancy whirled and found herself facing the grizzly detective who had tried to arrest her at the museum! "Have you been following us?" she asked.

On the way to the monastery, Nancy had noticed a pair of headlights bearing down on her car, but it had whipped past when she parked.

"I—how you say—have had my eye on you all."

"But I didn't tell anyone where we were going," the girl sleuth said.

"Doesn't matter. Your hotel has been very helpful to the police."

"You mean that someone at the Skyros has been reporting our comings and goings to you?" George inquired in disbelief.

The detective ignored the question. "You have no right to be here," he charged. "This is private property."

"We're investigating something," George explained indignantly.

Afraid that Bess, out of fright, might reveal too much, Nancy said quickly, "We have reason to believe that someone is planning to steal things from this monastery. He may be doing it this very minute!"

"Ridiculous!" the detective sneered.

"If you don't believe us," George spoke up impulsively, "we'll show you!"

"We will?" Bess asked in surprise.

In the back of George's mind and Nancy's was the thought that the man in the black robe might have been Isakos or his partner! Nancy glanced at her watch. It was almost 2:30 A.M.

"He went down there," Nancy said, pointing to a stone passageway across the courtyard.

She led the way to a small room. The wooden door was open a crack and George pushed against it gently. Nancy noticed the walls were devoid of any decoration. There was only a simple altar where a monk knelt in prayer. He jerked up suddenly when the door hinge squeaked, but he did not turn around.

"Oh, excuse me," George apologized. She closed the door.

When the group stood once more in the moonlight, the detective chided them severely. "If I catch you doing something like this again, I will have you sent home!"

"But—" Bess muttered.

"Not another word," the man snapped. "Go back to your hotel at once!"

He strode through the iron gate, escorting the girls to their car to make certain they left before he did.

"What a pill!" Bess commented.

"You can say that again," George agreed.

Nancy, on the other hand, kept her thoughts to herself. Disappointed as well as weary, she drove back to Omonia Square, parked the car, then walked across the street into the empty lobby of their hotel. Even the desk clerk was snoring peacefully in a chair.

"First thing in the morning," Bess stated as they reached their room, "I'd like to go back to the jewelry shop in monastiraki—the one we went to before."

"How early?" George asked.

"Oh, seven or eight," Bess teased.

"You two go ahead," Nancy yawned. "I'm going to sleep."

"Not all day, are you?" Her friends giggled, knowing how unlike Nancy that would be.

The next morning, Nancy was the first one up. Despite the fact she had slept only six hours, she was remarkably refreshed. Bess and George also felt a new surge of energy.

"I can't wait to ask that lady the million-dollar question," Bess said mysteriously.

"Which lady and what question?" George asked.

"The lady in the jewelry shop—" her cousin replied, catching herself before saying more.

When the trio entered the shop, two women stood behind the counter. "You buy *more*?" the older one asked, recognizing the girls.

"No, not today, thank you," Bess said, quickly adding, "Is Constantine Nicholas here, by any chance?"

George glanced at Nancy for her reaction.

"He works here, doesn't he?" Nancy put in.

The younger woman flashed her brown eyes at the girl. "He's not—I don't know where he is. What do you want with him?"

"I merely—" Bess started to say.

"And if he should come back," she thundered excitedly, "he belongs to me. You cannot have him!"

Bess was shocked by the implication. "You don't under—"

"I understand—"

Cutting off the reply sharply, the older woman lashed out at her in Greek. Nancy knew it was useless to ask more questions.

"Bess? George?" she said quietly, nodding toward the door. They excused themselves as Constantine's friend stepped angrily behind the curtain.

As the girls turned the corner up the street, they broke into laughter. Bess said, "She thought I was trying to steal her man!"

"In a way," Nancy said, "I'm glad she did. We picked up a lead on Constantine. He will probably stop by that shop sometime."

"So we should go back again, too," George advised, "but without you, Bess."

Her cousin made a face as Nancy spoke. "Isn't it wonderful—we finally found someone who knows Helen Nicholas's cousin!"

9

The Strange Statue

As the three girls continued their stroll, they found themselves at a sidewalk cafe in the middle of Syntagma Square. A soft breeze rustled their hair while they studied a menu.

"*Parakaló*, I'll have a glass of *visináda*," Nancy told the waiter.

"That sounds interesting," Bess said. "*K'ego*, me too."

"*Triá*," George joined in. Then, turning to Nancy, she asked, "What is it?"

The girl shrugged, a mischievous smile on her face. "I don't know, but Helen Nicholas told me to try it sometime. It's supposed to be very popular here."

In a few minutes, the waiter brought a tray of tall glasses filled with sweet cherry soda.

"Ooh, my favorite!" Bess said happily after she finished a long sip.

George, in the meantime, took a notepad from her purse and tore off several pieces of paper.

"What are you doing?" her cousin asked as she watched the girl write a word or two on each sheet.

"I thought we ought to play tic-tac-toe again. It might help us solve our Greek symbol mystery."

So far George had written the words *inheritance*, *Helen*, *Constantine*, and *Dimitri*.

"Don't forget *Isakos*," Bess put in.

"Or *ship*, the *gold mask,* and *symbol*," Nancy added.

On the remaining pieces of paper, George wrote down *Papadapoulos* and *Mrs. Thompson*.

"That's a lot of clues," Bess remarked. She arranged the words in tic-tac-toe fashion, hoping to make sense out of all the connections. "It's no use," she said at last. "They don't fit together."

It was Nancy's turn next. She set her glass of soda near the edge of the table and picked up the piece of paper bearing the name *Constantine*.

"I'll put him here," she said, placing the paper in the right-hand corner of the imaginary block.

"What about *Helen*?" Bess asked, resting her head on her arm.

"In the bottom left corner," Nancy said, then

quickly arranged six other pieces so that the game board looked like this:

symbol	gold mask	Constantine
ship	inheritance	Dimitri
Helen		Isakos

"Where do the Papadapoulos family and Mrs. Thompson fit in?" George asked.

"Oh, they're just innocent bystanders," Nancy replied.

"And what about the blank space in the middle?" Bess pointed.

"Maybe it's an unknown clue," Nancy suggested.

"Or," Bess went on, "you could put your name in there."

She was about to tear off another piece of paper from George's pad when a large cat jumped up and charged across the table without warning.

"Oh!" George exclaimed.

The glasses teetered, then two of them fell over before the girls could prevent it. Soda spilled on some of the papers while the rest floated away in the gusting wind.

Nancy dived after them, instantly catching two. The others, however, fluttered in the path of a Greek girl, who retrieved them.

"Here you are," the young woman said pleasantly, handing the papers to her.

"You're Constantine's friend," Nancy said, recognizing her from the jewelry shop.

"That's right, I-I'm very sorry about what happened there," she replied contritely.

As the two walked toward Bess and George, a waiter was mopping up liquid from the table. The cousins gasped to see the young woman again.

"I am Stella Anagnost," she said, introducing herself.

"And I'm Bess Marvin," Bess replied, extending her hand. "This is my cousin, George Fayne."

"And you are?" Stella asked as she glanced at Nancy.

"Nancy Drew." The girl detective's thoughts were focused on Stella's change of attitude. Although Nancy was eager to ask questions, she waited for Stella to speak first.

"Do you know where Constantine is? I mean, have you any idea at all?" the pretty girl said.

"No, we don't," George answered.

"I know he must be in some sort of trouble," Stella said anxiously. "He hasn't been to the shop in a long time and he has stopped calling me. The last time I saw him he acted very strange—"

"Stella!" A man had stopped by their table and addressed the Greek girl angrily. "You have work to do. Come with me!"

Aghast, the young detectives stared at the stranger, who resembled the man they had seen with Isakos. What was Stella's connection with the men? they wondered. He grabbed her arm and dragged her out of the chair.

"Just a few more minutes," she pleaded. "They can help me find Constantine—"

"Stop it, stop such nonsense!" the man exclaimed, forcing her to go with him.

"But Mimi—" Stella spurted. She tried to break away from her captor, but was no match for him.

"Mimi?" Bess repeated, watching the pair disappear into a taxi.

Before the man stepped inside the car, a small silver money clip fell out of his pocket. He did not hear it hit the pavement as he shouted at Stella, jumped in, and was driven away. Nancy raced to retrieve the clip.

"Look at this!" she exclaimed and showed it to her friends. On the back of the money clip were the initials *D.V.* "Mimi is a Greek nickname for Dimitri," Nancy recalled from her study of the Greek dictionary.

"Too bad his initials aren't *D.G.*," George remarked. "Otherwise he might be the missing Mr. Georgiou."

Nancy pocketed the new clue. "When we see Stella again, we can return it to her and get some more information."

"You mean *if* we see her again," George replied. "It looks as if she's mixed up with the wrong kind of people. They may really hurt her if she steps out of line."

"I think her biggest trouble is Constantine," Bess declared. "She's crazy about him."

"Well, since the jewelry shop will be closing in a few minutes," George said, "we may as well hang on to the money clip and do some sightseeing before we miss Athens altogether."

"I agree," Bess said.

"How about going to the Acropolis?" Nancy suggested. She gathered the pieces of paper on which George had written the important clues. "These go into the purse, too."

The rays of the afternoon sun were tongues of fire as the girls began to look for a cab. Each car, it seemed, already had passengers.

"It's getting frightfully hot out here," Bess complained, feeling a trickle of perspiration drain across her neck.

Nancy finally managed to flag down a free cab, which they took. The windows were lowered, allowing hot air to circulate freely as they sped through the crowded streets.

When the cab reached the entrance to the Acropolis, the visitors stepped out to walk the rest of the way. They paid an entrance fee at the gate, then began the long, hard climb. Ahead of them was the Parthenon. Like a crown jewel, the temple stood majestically among the ancient ruins.

"It's fantastic, isn't it?" George said, admiring the tall Doric columns flanked by marble porticoes.

Nancy's gaze traveled to the north side where a magnificent colonnaded hall had once overlooked the old marketplace. "You know, a number of sculptures were taken from here in the early 1800s," she remarked.

"Were they stolen?" Bess asked instantly.

"No, no. Lord Elgin, who was the British ambassador in Turkey at the time, received permission from the government to remove the pieces. Athens was then part of the Turkish Empire."

Bess's expression remained quizzical. "What did Elgin do with the sculptures?" she inquired further.

"He sold them to Great Britain, which in turn placed them in the British Museum in London."

"What a story," George commented. "I understand that more recently other statues were also removed by the Greek government."

"That's right," Nancy said. "Because of pollution and the fact that tourists had started to chip off marble for mementos."

Bess shook her head in disgust as they all collapsed into silence and drew near another set of columns. They heard a low, indistinct murmur that seemed to shift from one column to another.

"I wonder where that's coming from," Bess remarked finally, turning around to catch the view below.

Red-tiled roofs on the houses of the Plaka below clustered like bright color on an artist's palette, hypnotizing her. Then, as Bess turned to join her companions, who had temporarily left her side, she realized the clasp on her purse was loose.

Oh, I hope I didn't lose any money, she thought, and pulled out her wallet to check.

To her surprise, a small boy dashed from behind a column and grabbed it.

"Come back here!" Bess cried out, alerting Nancy and George to the young thief. "He stole my wallet!"

They chased him down the stone steps, sprinting fast over the ragged marble!

10

Surprise Visitors

"Wait for me!" Bess shouted, running behind the other girls.

They were several feet ahead, trying to keep the young thief in sight, but lost him in a crowd of tourists now beginning their ascent. Nancy and George froze to a halt.

"Why did you stop?" Bess panted as she caught up to them.

"He disappeared," Nancy explained.

"Besides," George said, "I'm getting a blister under my heel." She stooped to loosen the strap of her sandal.

"But what about my wallet?" her cousin exclaimed. She broke into tears. "That was all my money!"

"No, it wasn't," George reminded her. "You still

have traveler's checks in your suitcase, don't you?"

"I suppose so," Bess said, "but I just cashed one for fifty dollars and that kid took every cent!"

Nancy slipped an arm around Bess's shoulder. "We'll report it to the police," she assured her.

"And if there's anything else you need to buy," George said, "I'll give you the money."

"You will?" Bess smiled appreciatively.

"We both will," Nancy replied.

The girl dried her eyes with a tissue and followed her friends to the bottom of the hill. Almost immediately, they caught a taxi and went to the nearest police station, where Bess explained what had happened.

"I don't know," the captain said, shaking his head. "Your wallet may be lost forever. But we try to find boy. Tell me, was there American money inside?"

"Yes, some," Bess replied. "Why do you ask?"

"Most likely, he will take it to a money exchange. They give better rates than the hotels— more drachmas for the dollar."

"Maybe we can do some investigating on our own," Nancy declared. "How many money exchanges are there in Athens?"

"Oh, quite a few," the captain replied. "But with hundreds, even thousands of tourists here—no one at an exchange would remember boy." The officer frowned slightly and added, "If we catch him, we tell you."

"*Efharistó*," Bess said as everyone turned to leave. "Now what?" she asked Nancy. "I suppose there's no sense trying to check out all the money exchanges."

"True," the girl detective replied, "but I have a hunch the boy probably stopped at one near the Acropolis."

"I think we passed one when we were in the taxi," George said. "It's that way." She pointed toward a narrow street bordered by apartments.

Quickly, Nancy darted to the traffic light. The cousins trailed after her, crossing the intersection and walking briskly to the other side past the buildings. Soon they reached another corner and their destination.

"Look at that line of customers," George remarked.

"Which line?" Bess asked. "There are about five of them."

"Come on," Nancy said, stepping inside.

The room was crammed with people. Several were seated on benches along the wall, but most of them were standing.

The young detectives separated. Bess looked for the small boy who had stolen her wallet while Nancy and George tried to speak to the clerks.

"Excuse me, excuse me," George said as she weaved in front of two people.

"Wait your turn," a woman in line replied.

"But I only want to ask the teller a question."

"Yeah, well, that's all *I* want to do." The woman squeezed close to the person ahead of her. "I've been standing here for almost an hour," she said, "and you'll have to do the same."

George took a deep breath and gazed in Nancy's direction. Somehow, she had managed to reach another teller. But when the girls met in the back of the room, Nancy looked disappointed.

"I guess the captain was right," she said. "They're all too busy counting money to pay attention to faces." Suddenly, she became aware of the fact that Bess was missing. "Hey, where's Bess?"

"She must have left," George said, rising on tiptoe.

Within a few seconds, however, Bess emerged from the crowd. She was holding a small boy by his shirt collar. "Here's the culprit!" she exclaimed with pride.

"Mommy!" the child cried.

"That's not him!" George said.

"Of course it is," her cousin insisted. "The boy who took my wallet has dark brown hair cut short like this, and he was wearing a blue and yellow T-shirt."

"Well, the one I saw had on blue jeans," Nancy

put in. She stared at the boy's blue slacks.

"How can you be so sure they were jeans?" Bess replied.

"I'm a witness," George chimed in. "And Nancy and I were a lot closer to him than you were."

"Where is your mother?" Nancy asked the boy.

"In line. We just came to Athens today."

The girl did not allow him to continue. Obviously, he was not the thief.

"I'm sorry," Bess said sheepishly. "Here." She handed him one of her tissues.

He buried his nose in it for a second, then slipped back into the crowd.

"Let's go," George declared, "before his mother decides to have you deported."

"It was an honest mistake," Bess defended herself.

Without making any further investigation, the trio returned to their hotel, where they found a message waiting for them. It was written on hotel stationery.

Nancy read it aloud. " 'Surprise! We checked in here today. Give us a call at 1110.' "

"Uh-oh," Bess said. "Don't fall for it."

"There's no signature," George commented as she looked over Nancy's shoulder.

Only a room number," Nancy said. "Maybe it's a ruse to trap us."

"Count me out," Bess said quickly. "There's

probably a bushel of apples and snakes waiting for us!"

"I hardly think so," her cousin said. "After all—"

"Even if I'm wrong, I vote to ignore the message completely."

"What if it's from Dave?" Nancy teased. Dave Evans was a special friend of Bess's.

"In that case—" Bess started to say. "But on second thought—"

"Look, why don't you stay in our room while we check out 1110?" Nancy interrupted. "If we don't come back within a reasonable amount of time, send a search party."

"Good idea," her friend agreed.

Bess stepped off the elevator on the ninth floor, leaving her friends to continue to the eleventh. It was still early evening. Several people passed Nancy and George in the hallway, but they recognized no one. Despite the knowledge they were not alone, the girl detectives cautiously approached the door marked 1110. The sound of bouzouki music from a radio floated toward them. Nancy glanced at George and pressed the buzzer.

Soon the door clicked open and two mocha-brown eyes stared at Nancy!

11

Clue on the Dock

"Helen Nicholas!" Nancy exclaimed in surprise and hugged her friend.

"And Mrs. Thompson!" George cried happily when she saw the other woman in the room. "We're so glad to see you! When did you arrive?"

"Just a little while ago," Helen replied with a smile. "I have missed Greece so much. Where's Bess?"

"In our room. I'll call her right away." Nancy dialed their number and invited her friend to join everyone.

When Bess saw Helen and Mrs. Thompson, she giggled. "And here I thought you were kidnappers!"

"Kidnappers!" the women chorused and Helen asked, "Has somebody threatened you girls?"

"Not exactly," George answered.

"We'll tell you everything that's happened so far," Nancy promised, "after you give us your news and tell us what's behind this surprise visit."

"Yes, what made you decide to come?" Bess asked.

"Mostly hearing Helen talk so fondly about the time she spent here as a child," Mrs. Thompson replied. "I just felt I had to see Greece myself. Of course, I dearly want to meet Mrs. Papadapoulos and her children, especially Maria."

"It also occurred to us we might arrange to import some of her handmade embroidery," Helen said.

"That's a fantastic idea!" Nancy exclaimed.

"Helen has agreed to be my interpreter," Mrs. Thompson explained. "Without her help, I'm sure all that beautiful embroidery would probably end up being shipped to penguins in Antarctica!"

"Of course, it would brighten up their tuxedos!" George quipped.

Everyone laughed, then Helen changed the subject. "Now tell us about your adventures in Athens."

Nancy explained what had happened to them, mentioning the mysterious clues they had found. Helen and Mrs. Thompson listened transfixed.

"You're in danger," the older woman said. "I'm not sure it's such a good idea for you to stay here."

"Oh, please don't worry," Nancy said gently. "We're used to this sort of adventure. Besides, now that you're here to help us, we'll round up those crooks in no time!"

This made Mrs. Thompson smile. George quickly asked, "Tell us what you two would like to do this evening."

"Ever since I stepped off the plane, I've wanted to go to Herodotus Atticus," Helen replied.

"The big amphitheater near the Acropolis?" Nancy asked.

"That's right. I saw so many wonderful plays there as a child. Euripides' work was always my favorite."

It was decided that everyone would meet in the lobby at 8:30 P.M.

"Does this mean we're going to skip dinner?" George asked, causing a smile to ripple across her cousin's face.

"Haven't you adjusted yet to the fact that everybody in Greece eats late?" Nancy replied. "We're bound to find a restaurant or tavern open near the theater."

As predicted, there was a festive-looking café within a block of their destination. Helen, however, begged her companions to visit the theater first.

"There is nothing playing tonight," she said, "so we won't stay long."

Bess's stomach growled in discontent. Nevertheless, she followed the others to the theater. Although it was closed to the public, Helen spoke to a guard who consented to admit the group.

"Isn't it marvelous?" Helen cried in delight.

She stepped lightly down a stone aisle and paused to gaze at rows of seats that fanned out from the big stage. She motioned the others to join her. George, Mrs. Thompson, and Bess went ahead of Nancy, who stopped to adjust the strap on her sandal. She became aware of two men talking below her in Greek but paid little attention to them until she heard the name Nicholas!

Excitedly, the girl detective hurried down the steps toward Helen. "Did you hear that?" she whispered.

Helen nodded and held up her hands for the others to be quiet. She was trying to overhear the rest of the conversation.

Suddenly, her eyes flashed. "Nancy!" she gasped. "My cousin is hiding in Pireaus!"

"And to think we were just there!" Nancy said.

"I guess it's time for a return trip," George put in.

"But in daylight, please," Bess commented, gazing up at the dark-blue sky.

The next morning, Nancy volunteered to drive everyone to Piraeus. The harbor was filled with ocean-going tankers and freighters that dwarfed the smaller boats.

"Where shall we go first?" Bess asked.

"I suggest," Helen said, "we park the car and just walk around a bit."

"That's fine with me," Nancy agreed.

All of the conversations they overheard were in Greek. Helen listened closely to one or two of them.

"Anything important?" Bess inquired afterward.

"Possibly," Helen replied. "The men over there said the police have been inspecting freight shipments for some stolen ancient vases. Then I heard the name Isakos."

"Isakos!" the girls chorused.

Nancy scooted to the workmen. "What do you know about Mr. Isakos or Constantine Nicholas?" she asked. Helen, who was behind her, translated the question. The men merely shrugged their shoulders.

"They claim they don't know anything," Helen told her.

"But you *heard* them," Nancy said.

Helen repeated the question. This time, however, she spoke at length. The men in turn gave a long answer.

"What did they say?" Nancy asked Helen eagerly when the exchange of words had ended.

"Not much, really. They didn't tell me any more than I overheard originally. Only that the police have been asking them if they knew a man by the name of Isakos. Apparently, no one does."

The group walked on until suddenly George stopped and pointed to something on the wall of the wharf.

"Look at this!" she exclaimed excitedly.

The initials *D.G.* were carved in the wall. Drawn around the letters was the figure of a serpent!

"What's so unusual about that?" Helen asked. "It's only graffiti."

"There are things scribbled all over the place around here," Mrs. Thompson said.

"But this could refer to Dimitri Georgiou," Nancy pointed out.

"Oh, my goodness! Do you really think so?" Helen responded.

"Definitely."

Ahead of the group was a shipwright who was repairing a hole in the hull of a freighter. Nancy hurried forward, mentioning Dimitri Georgiou's name. The man stopped working and nodded.

He knows him! Nancy thought.

He climbed down his ladder and disappeared for a moment, returning in a few moments with a tall, muscular man.

"Dimitrious Georgiakis," the shipwright smiled,

now revealing a prominent space between his upper front teeth.

Nancy and her companions, who stood near her, responded with disappointed faces. Helen told the men they were looking for someone else.

"Will you ask them, too, if this boat goes to the States?" Nancy requested.

"*Óhi*, no," was the answer.

"I wonder," Nancy said, "if the fake artifacts are shipped first to another country like Italy or France before they're sent on to the United States."

"For what purpose?" George asked.

"To protect the identities of the people involved here."

Interrupting their tour of the harbor, the young detectives decided to talk to the local police.

"*Astinomikós tmíma?* Police station?" Nancy asked a passerby.

The old man lifted his feeble arm and spoke in Greek.

"He's telling us how to get there," Helen explained. "It's not far."

"Can we walk?" George asked.

"Yes."

The group found their way easily. Nancy, again with Helen's assistance, spoke to the police officer in charge. She mentioned their search for Constantine Nicholas.

"I know nothing about him," the officer replied.

"Then what have you found out about the art thefts from the museum in Athens?"

"Nothing I am at liberty to reveal. May I ask why you are so interested to know?"

"Nancy is an amateur detective," Helen answered.

"Oh, I see. Well, this case is meant only for professionals to solve."

The remark nettled his listeners, who said little more than good-bye.

"We're not making a whole lot of progress, are we?" Bess remarked as she walked with the others to the car.

"Where could Constantine be?" Helen murmured. "There are so many factories here."

"And ships," Mrs. Thompson added.

"He could be anywhere," Nancy said, turning on the ignition.

The car sputtered as she pressed down on the gas pedal, then stalled. Nancy tried to start it again, but this time there was only a soft click as she turned the key back and forth. The engine was dead.

"There wasn't a thing wrong with this car before," George said.

Had someone tampered with it?

12

The Banded Freighter

Nancy released the hood and peered under it
while Helen and the others questioned those nearby. Was anyone seen near their car?

"Nancy, dear, come here a minute." Mrs.
Thompson called out.

The girl emerged from under the hood and
closed it. Her friends were gathered in front of a
small boy.

"Did you see someone?" Nancy asked, squatting
on her feet.

"*Óhi, óhi,*"

"Are you sure?"

The boy weakened. "Big man. Very red face.
Gray hair. Mean," he said haltingly.

Isakos! Nancy thought. "Where did he go?" she
asked.

"Gave me money," the boy went on. "Not tell anyone."

"But you must tell me where he went," Nancy persisted. "He did something very wrong."

Gently, she laid her hand on the boy's shoulder and stood up.

"Over there," he muttered under his breath. He pointed to the dock, adding something else in Greek.

"He thinks the man went aboard the freighter with the big white stripe around its middle," Helen translated.

"To that one?" Nancy asked. She indicated the ship berthed near the wall marked with the snake symbol.

"*Nai.*"

"No?" Mrs. Thompson sighed.

"On the contrary," Nancy smiled. "*Nai* means yes!"

"Shall we get the police?" Bess asked. "Isakos is three times bigger than all of us put together."

"They'll only tell us to stay out of their business," Nancy said. "Why don't we split up and see what we can find out ourselves?"

"Good idea," George said. "Who's going with whom?"

"Perhaps you and Mrs. Thompson could try finding a mechanic to fix the car, while Helen and I investigate the freighter."

"What about me?" Bess asked.

"You post yourself near the dock to watch for overinterested onlookers."

Bess caught sight of a young policewoman approaching. "See you later," she said to her group, hurrying toward the officer.

When Bess reached her, she was already talking with two young sailors, one of whom was Greek and the other a light-haired Scandinavian.

"Excuse me," Bess said, interrupting the conversation.

The fair-complexioned man winked at Bess. "American?" he asked with a lilting accent.

She nodded.

"Swedish, like me?"

"No," blond-haired Bess answered shyly, "at least, not that I know of."

The policewoman, who was not much older than the sailors, stepped forward. "Do you need some help?" she asked.

"Y-yes, I do," Bess said. Thankful the woman spoke English, she drew her away from the men. "I'm looking for three people, Constantine Nicholas, Dimitri Georgiou, and a Mr. Isakos."

"Just a moment," the policewoman replied. She spoke briefly to the sailors.

"Maybe I can help you," the Swedish man said to Bess. "Constantine Nicholas is connected with the Nikos Shipping Company. I work for them myself once in a while."

"Have you seen him recently?"

"The other day. He wanted to send cargo on the White Band freighter."

That's the one the little boy mentioned! Bess thought. "Does he do that frequently?" she asked aloud.

"Yes and no. Several weeks ago he was around here a lot. Then he disappeared. Of course, I move from job to job. One day I'm in Haifa and the next I'm here. Now he's back, too."

As the young man spoke, his dark-haired companion sidled closer to Bess, causing her to ease toward the policewoman. Bess glanced disdainfully at the Greek sailor.

"Where does Mr. Nicholas live? Here or in Athens?" the officer inquired.

"I'm not sure," the Swedish crewman replied. He ran his forefinger along the crest of his nose. "And I doubt that anybody in Piraeus could tell you."

His companion, meanwhile, leaned toward Bess. "What kind perfume you wear?" he asked in halting English.

"Tea rose," the girl said curtly. "I don't think you can buy it here." She looked straight past him to address his friend again. "I've seen a picture of

Mr. Nicholas, but I'm wondering if he has changed his appearance since it was taken."

"Well, he has a beard and mustache now," the Scandinavian replied.

"Oh, he does? I'm glad to know that."

Thinking the policewoman might glean something else useful, Bess gave her the name of the girls' hotel. "Please don't mention it to these men, though," she whispered.

"Don't worry." The young woman laughed. "That one loves to flirt—especially with pretty American girls."

Bess giggled as she ran toward the white-banded freighter. Nancy, Helen, and a policeman were standing on deck. They were talking to a couple of crewmen. Their voices were heard above the girls'.

Sounds like trouble, Bess thought, speeding up the gangplank to the deck.

"Where do you think you're going?" someone shouted at her.

Bess stopped short. "My friends are up there," she said, turning around to face a short, chubby man in work clothes.

His stern eyes traveled to the deck, then back to Bess. He mumbled, nodding her to move on.

"I found out something important," she whispered to George as soon as she was on board.

"Tell me later."

At the moment, the policeman was involved in a heated discussion with one of the ship's officers.

"They say we have no right to be here," Helen explained to the girls. "But the policeman has told them he will arrest every one of them if they don't obey him."

"I just heard him mention Constantine's name," George said.

"He's asking where my cousin is," Helen replied.

To the girls' surprise, the ship's captain now addressed the group in English. "My name is Fotis. Are you friends of Constantine Nicholas?"

Before Nancy could answer, she noticed steely eyes peering at them from the corner of the deckhouse. The man ducked back for a moment. Then, not realizing he was in Nancy's line of vision, he stuck his head into view again.

"Isakos!" she exclaimed, and quickly darted after him.

13

Boat Chase

Breaking away from the group, Nancy raced toward the man. "Mr. Isakos!" she shouted.

"Where are you going?" the ship's captain bellowed at Nancy. He ran after her with Bess, Helen, and the others following.

The girl detective halted at the end of the deck, where thick coils of rope lay between metal crates heaped in front of a lifeboat.

He's gone! she thought as Fotis grabbed her by the shoulder.

"You have no business upsetting my ship like this!" he hissed.

Ignoring the comment, Nancy suddenly caught sight of Isakos's shirt collar.

"There he is!" she exlaimed. "In the lifeboat!"

Before anyone could catch him, though, the burly man leaped out of it, crashing through piles of crates. He dashed to the other side of the deck and vaulted quickly over the railing. Bess and the policeman sped after him while Fotis gripped Nancy's arm.

"Let me go!" she insisted, pulling away abruptly to join her friends. "Can we chase him?" Nancy asked when she saw Isakos fleeing onto a small cabin cruiser.

Shouting to the crew in Greek, the policeman raced toward the gangplank. Helen and the girl detectives followed him, running every step of the way to a patrol boat moored nearby.

"We'll never catch him!" Helen cried as they watched Isakos disappear behind a jetty.

Nancy, too, became tense as their own boat chugged slowly into the harbor, picking up speed only after they passed an incoming barge. They skirted the jetty and found themselves in the open sea with only the shoreline in sight. Could Isakos's small boat have outdistanced theirs so quickly?

Impossible, Nancy thought.

Then she saw it. The boat lay abandoned on the beach.

"There's a trail of footprints," Nancy observed as they pulled close to shore.

"Bess and I will stay with the boat if you and the

officer wish to search for the man," Helen offered.

"We'll be back before you catch any fish!" Nancy called.

The footprints were still wet, making them easy to track. They led to an unmarked road which seemed to be in the middle of nowhere.

"Isakos must've been picked up by a passing car," the policeman concluded.

"Or a waiting one," Nancy said.

When they returned to the patrol boat, she saw the eager expressions on her friends' faces and shook her head.

"No clues? Nothing?" Bess asked, obviously disappointed.

"Zero."

As Nancy spoke, the officer took the cabin cruiser in tow and headed back to the harbor. Shortly, the white-banded freighter came into view. Fotis stood on deck, holding binoculars.

"He's watching us," Bess remarked. "Are we going to board the ship again?"

"I do have some questions for the crew," Nancy replied.

"And I intend to see their cargo," the policeman put in.

To everyone's amazement, Fotis was less irritable, almost compliant, when the group spoke to him the second time. He instructed a crewman to lead them below deck to storerooms that held a variety of crates. Many had olive oil labels, others cotton, and pelts of fur hung in large refrigerators.

Nancy whispered to Helen and Bess. "What better place to hide stolen artifacts—"

"Than in bales of cotton," Bess interrupted.

"Right." Helen grinned. "What companies import these?" Nancy asked the crewman.

He did not understand English, however, so Helen translated the question. "He doesn't know," she said.

"Has he seen your cousin? And what does he know about Constantine's shipment of cargo?"

Again Helen spoke to the man. "He says he has never heard of my cousin."

"I doubt that very strongly," Bess said. "The sailor on the dock told me Constantine shipped something on this freighter *recently*."

"Then either this man is lying or the person you spoke to was wrong," Nancy replied.

Now the policeman gave orders for two of the crates to be opened. The crewman balked, muttering in Greek. He threw up his arms as if to tell everyone he had just finished packing the boxes.

"I don't care," the policeman said brusquely, slipping from English back into Greek.

Watching every movement the man made, Nancy concentrated on the crates that contained bales of cotton. Was anything else inside? The crewman seemed to struggle unnecessarily with the staples that secured it. Nancy wondered if he was trying to stall.

Finally, though, the top loosened and the policeman wrenched it off. He opened the bale, then quickly dug into the contents, pulling out a cloud of fiber. It dropped gently to the floor.

Nancy sighed in disappointment. "I was almost positive—" she started to say, poking her hand into the cotton. "Is there anything else in the crate?" she asked the policeman.

"No."

"May we check the other crates?"

"He says they are all alike," the officer replied.

As the group returned to the main deck, they found Fotis waiting for them. "Satisfied?" he said with a smirk.

"Not really," Nancy said.

"I told you there was nothing of interest on my boat."

"That's not true," she declared abruptly. "We discovered Mr. Isakos."

"I never heard of the man," Fotis replied in a smooth tone. "But then, many people come on board when the ship is docked. We cannot check everyone."

He promised to keep in touch with the police and to hold Isakos should he appear on the freighter again.

"I'm sure he will," Bess said cynically.

"I think we would all learn more from the oracle at Delphi!" Helen added. "But don't look so sad. You are making good progress, girls."

"You're sweet to say that," Nancy replied as they left the ship. "Actually, I have a hunch that that freighter is deeply involved in a smuggling scheme. The problem is how to prove it."

14

The Vanished Lawyer

As Nancy, Helen, and Bess said good-bye to the policeman at the dock, they noticed Mrs. Thompson and George talking with a man in blue overalls. Next to him was a tow truck.

"Can't the car be fixed here?" Nancy asked anxiously when she reached the others.

"It already has been," Mrs. Thompson smiled. "We were just discussing the fact that someone deliberately tampered with the engine."

Nancy fixed her eyes on the mechanic. "Did you find any clues to the person's identity?" she asked.

"Clues?"

"Yes, a piece of torn clothing or a button, for instance," Nancy replied. The man shook his head and Nancy opened her purse. "How much do I owe you?"

"Already paid," he said.

"Put your money away, dear," Mrs. Thompson added.

"But I don't expect you—" Nancy began.

The woman shut her eyes, not wishing to hear further on the subject. When the mechanic drove off in his truck, she suggested that everyone have lunch.

"Mikrolímano," Nancy suggested. "It's one of the harbors in Piraeus."

"Are we going to fish for our meal?" Bess asked, grinning.

"Not unless you want lobster!"

The drive to Mikrolímano was short. When a string of restaurants next to the harbor came into view, Nancy pulled to a halt.

"That's the one I told you about," Helen said, pointing to a colorful store window displaying freshly caught fish.

Across the street and down a flight of stairs was a table-lined dock that overlooked the shimmering water with boats moored nearby. A number of customers were finishing their lunch when the visitors sat down. To their surprise, instead of menus, the waiter brought a message.

"It is for Miss Drew," he said.

Nancy opened it quickly, wondering how anybody knew she was there. "It's in Greek, Helen," she said, handing it over.

"The note says, 'I understand you are trying to find Mr. Vatis. I used to work in his office. Maybe I can help you,' " Helen translated.

"Amazing!" Bess remarked.

"That he worked for Vatis?" George asked.

"No, that he found Nancy."

The girls glanced down the row of tables, noticing one man seated alone. A napkin was tied around his neck and he was dipping a small chunk of lobster into melted butter.

"That must be the one who sent the note," Nancy concluded. "He looks familiar, but I can't place him exactly."

"Let's talk to him," Helen suggested. The two stood up and walked to the stranger's table.

"Mr. Vatis?" Nancy asked.

He laid down his fork and smiled. "I'm not Mr. Vatis, Miss Drew. I'm not related to him, and I'm glad of it." He gestured for them to sit down in the empty chairs at his table, introducing himself as Peter Scourles.

"Why are you glad you're not related?" Nancy asked.

"I did not approve of the way he handled estates for people. Your father is an attorney, is he not?"

Nancy nodded, perplexed that he knew so much about her.

"Well, then he would understand what I mean," the man replied. "As a matter of fact, the govern-

122

ment of Greece was about to investigate Vatis."

"For what reason?" Helen inquired.

"He disappeared with many important papers."

"Where did he go?" Nancy questioned.

"I don't know, but I think he may be hiding on Corfu. I recall he liked to vacation there and mentioned some hotel with a wonderful view of the sea. Unfortunately, I don't know its name."

Nancy glowed with excitement. Maybe she and her friends could fly to Corfu!

"Mr. Scourles," she said, "who told you about me and my father?"

"I heard of you when I lived in your country and more recently, while I worked for Vatis & Vatis. It was there I learned that Carson Drew represented a member of the Nicholas family in the United States. When Vatis left, I was hired by the law firm who took over his office. You came in the other day to ask for Mr. Vatis. I was standing by the reception desk and heard you introduce yourself."

"Why didn't you speak to me then?" Nancy asked.

Scourles shrugged. "I was in a rush and didn't think of Corfu. It occurred to me later."

Nancy and Helen thanked the man and went back to tell the others what they had found out. Bess and George were thrilled. "Let's go to Corfu tomorrow," George urged.

"I hope to," Nancy replied. "You'll go, too,

won't you?" She was looking at Helen and Mrs. Thompson.

"We'd love to," Helen said, "but we think we ought to see the Papadapoulos family."

They discussed plans for the next day, pausing only to order a sumptuous lunch of seafood and Greek salad. The salt air had increased everyone's appetite, so they added fruit for dessert. Soon the afternoon disappeared as quickly as the fleet of small boats anchored in the quay. The Americans returned to their hotel.

"There's a travel agency in the lobby," Nancy said as they stepped inside.

Yawning sleepily, Mrs. Thompson excused herself to go to her room. The others followed Nancy into a small office decorated with attractive posters of Greece.

"There's a wonderful hotel in Corfu. It's called the Cyclades," the agent told the foursome. "Reasonable, too."

"Does it have a great view of the ocean?" George asked.

"From the top floors, yes. From the lower floors, no. The hotel is in the heart of the business district."

"Hmm," Nancy murmured, then asked to see a brochure.

"If you are looking for a magnificent view," the

young woman continued, "these would be better." She pointed to several listings in the booklet.

"How about this one—the Hotel Kephalonia?" Bess suggested. "It looks gorgeous."

Nancy and George agreed wholeheartedly that it did.

Helen sighed. "If only I could go with you," she said, but she could not be dissuaded from making the trip with Mrs. Thompson to see the Papadapoulos family.

The next day, the girl detectives caught a late morning flight to Kérkyra. It took little more than an hour from Athens.

"I see a taxi," George said, after claiming her baggage. "Meet you out front."

"Okay," Nancy replied. When she and Bess collected their bags, they darted after her.

Aside from the parking lot that stretched against a clearing bordered by brush and trees, the landscape was uninteresting. But as the girls' driver weaved into the colorful shopping district, Bess oohed and aahed over the stores.

"No wonder Vatis loves to come here," she said.

Now the car climbed steadily past villas nestled in a hillside, taking the fork that led to a promontory.

"There it is!" Nancy exclaimed when a gleaming white building came into view.

The driver pulled to a halt at the entrance. Since he spoke fairly fluent English, Nancy asked if they might call him for further work.

"Of course," he said and gave his telephone number.

After the girls registered at the desk, Nancy inquired whether Vatis was staying there, too. The clerk merely shook his head.

"Guess we have to make a few phone calls," she told her companions when they were settled in their room. She pulled out the travel brochure and one by one began dialing local numbers. On her third try, Nancy was successful. "Vatis is staying at the Queens Palace!" she announced in delight.

"That would have been my second choice after this hotel," George said as Nancy hung up and placed a call to the taxi driver.

"I don't want to waste another minute," the young detective said eagerly.

"But the beach looks so inviting," Bess replied.

"We can take a dip later," Nancy pointed out. "Don't tell me you want to miss out on all the fun!"

"Me? Never!"

When they reached the Queens Palace, they learned that Vatis was staying in one of the cottages near the main building. They drove to it. Nancy requested their driver wait for them, then the girls walked to the lawyer's cottage.

"Doesn't look as if anyone's home," George remarked as Nancy knocked on the door.

They peered through half-drawn Venetian blinds. Seeing no one, they circled to the back entrance. A band of wet footprints led up from the beach.

"He must've gone swimming, changed, and left," Nancy concluded. "We'll have to come back later."

"I'd rather face him in daylight," Bess objected.

"He's not going to hurt you," George said assuringly. "Besides, there are three of us against one of him!"

Even so, when they returned that evening, Bess continued to feel uneasy. Before their driver finished asking if he should wait for them, she said yes.

"But please park the car up the road out of sight," Nancy added.

George offered to post herself near the road while Nancy and Bess looked through the window of Vatis's cottage. Inside, the light was on and a man moved about nervously. He was of medium height, dark-haired, and wore horn-rimmed glasses. Presently, he took something out of a suitcase, then lifted the telephone receiver. For an instant, the girls caught sight of an object in his hand.

"It looks like a gold cuff bracelet," Nancy whispered to Bess.

"Apparently he's trying to sell it," Bess replied,

overhearing a snatch of conversation which was spoken in English.

"That's right," the man said. "This bracelet was dug up in 1876."

In the pause that followed, Nancy whispered again to Bess. "1876! That's the year the famous archeologist Heinrich Schliemann discovered the gold death mask!"

"The bracelet was probably stolen from the same museum in Athens!" Bess gasped.

A muffled scream and the sound of dragging feet interrupted Nancy's reply. She and Bess swiveled around fast. George was gone!

15

Corfu Snafu

"Where's George?" Bess gasped.

"I don't know," Nancy whispered, completely mystified.

Several yards away, an engine purred, then roared off quickly. Leaving their post in front of Vatis's cottage, Nancy and Bess raced up the road toward their taxi and leaped in.

"Follow that car, please," Nancy implored the driver, and pointed to the pair of taillights that were fast disappearing down the hill. "Our friend has been kidnapped!"

Instantly, the man turned his cab around and lurched forward, rumbling over the rough road and trying hard to catch up to the other car.

"Faster! Faster!" Bess pleaded.

"I'm going to break the springs under my car," the driver yelled over the racing engine.

Ahead of them, the fleeing vehicle swerved onto another road and cut off two cars ready to make the same turn.

"Oh!" Bess gasped fearfully, as the taxi driver pressed hard on the gas pedal, speeding past the car in front of him. "We're going to get creamed!" She shut her eyes tight.

Nancy, on the other hand, kept calm. "He's heading toward that cliff," she said. "Can you overtake him?"

"This taxi is not a racing car, but I'll try," the man replied as the winding road dissolved in a sharp curve. The cab quickly lost momentum, and Nancy sank back against the seat in disappointment.

Bess, however, sat forward. "Where'd it go?" she asked, staring into the darkness.

"It got away," the driver replied. "Shall I turn back?"

"Let's go a little farther," Nancy urged.

The man grumbled but complied. Suddenly, the glow of his headlights fastened on a figure stumbling out of a ditch.

"It's George!" Bess cried, causing the driver to stop. She threw open the rear door of the cab and jumped out, along with Nancy.

"Are you all right?" Nancy asked the girl who staggered dizzily toward them.

"Fine. I'm fine," George said, but her eyes looked glazed. "I fell, that's all."

Bess and Nancy helped her into the taxi. They stared at the slight bruise along her cheekbone.

"Did he hit you?" her cousin questioned.

"No. He motioned for me to get out, but didn't stop fully. I stumbled and rolled into the ditch."

Nancy removed a tissue from her purse and blotted particles of dirt off George's face. "Who was he?" the girl detective asked.

"I have no idea. He was wearing a stocking mask. He said something in Greek, but I didn't understand it. The voice was a little familiar, but—"

"Do you want to go to the hospital?" the driver interrupted.

George shook her head and Nancy said no. "But are you sure?" she asked her friend.

"Positive. Let's go back to the cottage."

To the girls' dismay, Vatis had apparently left. Was George's abduction merely a ruse to lure Nancy and Bess away from the Queens Palace? They went to the main building and inquired if the man had checked out.

"Yes, he did, but he will be back in a few weeks," the clerk replied.

Instantly, Nancy telephoned the local airport. It

was probable, she thought, that Vatis planned to take a night flight back to Athens en route to some other exotic destination.

"What did you find out?" Bess asked when Nancy rejoined her and George.

"The last two planes just left. One for Athens and the other for Cairo."

"In other words, we're stuck in Corfu for the night," George said.

"It's probably just as well, for your sake," Nancy said. "You need to rest."

"We all do," Bess concurred, blinking her eyes sleepily.

Nancy had reserved seats on the first flight out of Corfu to Athens the next morning and, after breakfast, the trio took one last look at the tranquil sea.

"Too bad we have to leave so soon," George remarked.

"It'll be a long time before we come back, I'm sure," Bess sighed. She stepped out onto the velvet green lawn that swept toward the pool and gazed longingly at the beach below.

Nancy followed her, slipping an arm around her shoulders. Her eyes traced the short strip of sand along the water that lapped peacefully against it.

"Hey, look!" Nancy exclaimed suddenly.

Two men had come into view on the rocky precipice at the far end.

"They seem to be arguing," Bess remarked. "I'm pretty sure one of them is Vatis!"

"But who's the other man?" George asked. "My kidnapper?"

"Bess, you call the police," Nancy instructed.

She and George, meanwhile, hurried down to the beach and ran toward the precipice. The second man, whose back was to the girls, stormed away, disappearing quickly below the rocky ledge.

"Too bad we never saw his face," George said.

Nancy nodded. "But I want to talk to Vatis. Let's hurry before he leaves, too!"

Vatis seemed unaware of their presence. He stared, almost dazedly, into the gentle, deep water.

"Mr. Vatis?" Nancy addressed him.

"What do you want?" he barked, jerking around in fright.

"I've been looking for you," the girl detective said. "Or, rather, my father has been."

"Who are you?" the lawyer asked sharply.

"I'm Nancy Drew."

The sound of the name fell on him like a steel hammer. He gritted his teeth. "Leave me alone."

"I'm afraid I can't do that," Nancy said. "Why did you pretend to check out of the Queens Palace Hotel last night?"

"I don't know what you're talking about," Vatis blazed back.

He lunged at Nancy, grabbing her by the arms. She dug her fingers into his wrists to keep from crashing against the jagged stone.

"Let her go!" George demanded.

Vatis shoved Nancy back against her friend and leaped past them.

"Stop!" Nancy cried, ready to tear after him.

To her surprise, something glittery fell out of the man's pocket, tripping her off balance. It was the cuff bracelet he had tried to sell over the telephone. Quickly she snatched it up and looked inside. Stamped on the bracelet was the mysterious Greek symbol!

16

A Capture

Without wasting another moment, Nancy and George bolted over the craggy rocks to the beach on the far side.

"Vatis is getting away!" George exclaimed as Nancy sprinted ahead, clenching the cuff bracelet tightly in her fist.

"We'll catch you—you won't—" the young sleuth shouted haltingly as the man jumped into a small motorboat and sped away.

"What a shame!" George declared, emptying sand from one shoe.

"C'mon!" Nancy cried out and ran back toward the hotel.

By now, Bess was standing on the grassy overhang in full view of her friends. "The police are coming!" she called.

"Did you tell them to go to Vatis's cottage?" Nancy yelled up to her.

"No. Should I have?"

"Yes, and quick!" George replied.

As Bess hurried back into the hotel, Nancy and George leaped up the flight of stone steps that connected the beach with the pool area. Breathing heavily by now, they darted through the dining room and caught up with Bess at the lobby telephone.

"Let's go!" Nancy said, after Bess hung up. She took the girl's hand to hurry her along.

"Where are we going?"

"To the Queens Palace."

"But we don't have a car," Bess countered.

Parked outside, however, was their taxi driver. He greeted them pleasantly.

"All set to leave?" he asked, smiling.

"We can't go to the airport yet," George said. "We're after someone." She jumped into the back seat with her friends.

"Oh, no, not again!" The man groaned.

Nancy's lips parted into a smile. "I'm afraid so. Can you take us back to the cottage at the Queens Palace Hotel?"

The driver nodded reluctantly. He pulled onto the road, gaining speed at a moderate rate. "After that race last night, this car will never last through the summer," he sighed.

"We can't help it if there's a crook loose in Corfu," Bess said.

"You should leave him to the police to catch," the man replied.

After they passed the sign for the Queens Palace Hotel, a police car came into view. The taxi driver released his foot from the gas pedal, allowing the car to slow down.

"They're here already," Bess observed.

"Thank goodness," the driver mumbled in relief.

The girls stepped out quickly. Nancy skirted the police car to talk with one of the officers.

"What's happening?" she asked him.

"You keep back from the house," he ordered. "The man has locked himself inside. He may become violent."

Nancy produced the cuff bracelet and showed the strange marking inside. The young sleuth explained that she and her friends had overheard Vatis describe its value to someone apparently interested in buying it.

"And you say it was stolen from the archeological museum in Athens?" the policeman questioned.

"That's what I suspect."

A second officer, meanwhile, was shouting in Greek through the cottage door. He ordered Vatis to open it, but the man refused. Through the partially drawn blinds, the policeman watched Vatis frantically empty his pockets.

"It's gone! It's gone!" he grumbled to himself. "Those girls must have it!"

He lit a match, dropping it into a metal wastebasket filled with papers. Seeing smoke drift under the door, Nancy ran forward.

"He'll suffocate," she said as the police officer pulled her back. His colleague, meanwhile, smashed the window with a wooden club, tore down the blinds, and climbed inside.

Smoke billowed out and Vatis coughed as he gasped for air. While one policeman snapped handcuffs on him, the other one doused the fire. It had destroyed most of the papers. As the trio emerged from the cottage, Vatis glared at Nancy.

"Give me that bracelet," he growled. "It's mine. It was payment for legal services."

"From whom? Constantine Nicholas?" Nancy replied with equal confidence. "You were blackmailing him, weren't you?"

The man's eyes did not shift from hers as she went on. "You knew Constantine was mixed up with art smugglers and when he couldn't pay you for your work, you accepted this bracelet instead."

"Except," Bess added, "Constantine didn't know that Vatis was stealing the inheritance from him and Helen."

"Precisely," Nancy said.

Despite the accusations, the man did not seem bothered. He gave a self-satisfied grin.

"I will get the smartest lawyers in Greece to defend me. They will prove my innocence," he boasted.

The policemen, in the meantime, took custody of the stolen bracelet. "Someone else will be sent to investigate the cottage thoroughly," one officer said as they went off with their prisoner.

"We ought to check this place right now," Nancy said.

"But we won't be able to remove anything," George reminded her.

"No need to," Nancy put in. She took a small camera from her shoulder bag. "I was planning to take pictures before we left the hotel."

The young detectives went quickly to the wastebasket and examined the burnt papers. There were several readable fragments which Nancy photographed. Her camera automatically produced small color prints.

"We can have these enlarged later," she said, sticking them in her purse. "Right now, let's try to catch our flight to Athens."

The girls rode back to their hotel, asking their driver to wait for them. "We'll be out in a sec—" Bess said as they dashed inside.

The travelers reappeared with their luggage in less than fifteen minutes.

"Do you always rush everywhere you go?" the man asked, breaking into a laugh.

"Not always," Nancy said with a smile. "This really has been a most unusual two days."

In spite of the unexpected delays that morning, they reached the airport with time to spare.

"I don't believe it," Bess kept saying on the plane.

"What don't you believe?" George asked.

"That we solved part of the mystery."

Her remark prompted Nancy to pull out the photographs she had taken earlier. She studied them closely but could decipher only certain initials and parts of addresses.

"As soon as we get into Athens," she said, "I'm going to call Dad. He ought to be in his office now."

Even before she unpacked, Nancy placed the call from the hotel. To her delight, it went through with little trouble. She told her father about finding Vatis and the cuff bracelet stamped with the same intriguing symbol used by the art thieves.

"We'll take the first flight we can get reservations on," Mr. Drew said.

"We?" Nancy repeated.

"That's right. I—"

Suddenly the connection was broken.

"Dad? Are you there?" Nancy said. She pressed down on the receiver hook several times but the line was dead. "I wonder who's coming with him?" she thought, puzzled.

17

Nikos Deposits

"Maybe Hannah is coming with your father," Bess suggested.

"I doubt it," her cousin replied. "I think it's someone from his office."

"Don't you have any idea, Nancy?" Bess asked.

The girl shook her head and excused herself to take a shower. Secretly, she hoped the mystery traveler would be Ned.

"I ought to call Helen and Mrs. Thompson," Nancy said when she reappeared. "George, would you do me a big favor and take these photos to the camera shop on the corner?"

"At your service."

"Ask them to make enlargements as quickly as possible."

George left, and when she returned, her face was beaming. "They'll be ready tonight," she announced.

"Wonderful," Nancy said.

After dinner, the girls picked up the order and joined Helen and Mrs. Thompson in their room. Eagerly, they took turns telling about their visit with Mrs. Papadapoulos and her children.

"She has agreed to sew lots of beautiful things which we will sell in America!" Mrs. Thompson declared happily.

"That's great!" Bess said while Nancy produced one of the enlarged photographs for Helen to look at.

"Incredible!" the woman exclaimed, staring at it. "This is my uncle's will!"

"No wonder I couldn't read it." Nancy chuckled. "It's all in Greek!"

Helen Nicholas scanned the picture closely. "Apparently, he owned various companies, not just the shipping line," she said. "His interests were vast." She leaned back in her chair, fanning herself with the photograph. "And to think so much of this will now be mine."

"What do you suppose happened to the holdings other than those of the shipping company?" Bess asked.

"I have no idea."

"Perhaps Vatis acquired them somehow," Nancy suggested, "and sold them."

"But how?" Mrs. Thompson wanted to know.

"If the lawyer had access to Mr. Nicholas's papers, he could have forged Constantine's signature." Nancy paused, adding, "Tomorrow we'll try to find out where Lineos Nicholas kept his bank accounts. All right?"

Helen looked soberly at the girl. "All right," she said at last.

The next day, Nancy and Helen made a list of all the banks in Athens. They went from one to the other asking if Lineos Nicholas had maintained an account there.

"I'm getting so tired," Helen said as she pushed open the door of the fifth bank. "Can't we continue this tomorrow?" she begged.

"Tomorrow may be too late," Nancy replied.

"Too late for what?"

"For you. If Vatis was in cahoots with somebody here in Athens, they may know he's been arrested and try to steal the rest of your inheritance."

"Isn't it more likely the two of them would keep a low profile?" Helen retorted.

"Not if they want the money!"

"Well, there's no point debating about it," Helen said. "Where is the next bank located?"

"Not far from here," Nancy replied.

She indicated a brick building two blocks up the street. They walked to it quickly. Inside, a guard greeted them. Helen spoke to him in Greek, and to her delight, he said he remembered her uncle well. He had been sorry when he'd heard that Lineos Nicholas had died.

"Such a nice man," the guard added.

"Did he have a safe-deposit box here?" Helen inquired.

"As a matter of fact, yes. I've been wondering why no one has come to claim the contents."

"Have the bank charges been paid regularly?" Nancy asked, prompting Helen to translate the questions into Greek.

"*Nai*. Yes, at least, so far as I know."

"When is the next billing due?" Nancy asked.

"Tomorrow."

"Wonderful," Nancy said. She snapped her fingers as she and Helen left the building. "You and Mrs. Thompson must come here first thing in the morning."

"To pay for the use of the box?"

"No—to wait for the person who will."

"But how do you know the payment won't be mailed?"

"I don't, but it's worth being here to find out."

As the girl detective recommended, Helen and Mrs. Thompson left for the bank early the following day. The others remained at the hotel hoping for another message from Mr. Drew.

"There's a beautiful embroidered dress in one of the shops downstairs," Bess said, trying to gain the interest of her friends.

"Is there?" George said casually. She helped Nancy swing two chairs out onto the balcony of their room.

"I can see you're both absolutely thrilled about my discovery," Bess murmured as her friends sat down.

"We are," Nancy insisted. But she turned her face toward the shimmering rays of the sun and closed her eyes.

"Are you two going to sit up here all day?" Bess asked impatiently.

"Just until Dad calls," Nancy replied.

"In that case," Bess commented unhappily, "I might as well go shopping alone."

She took the elevator to the first floor and discovered almost immediately that the embroidered outfit was no longer in the window. When she inquired about it, the proprietor said it had been sold the day before.

"Thank you, anyway," Bess said in disappointment.

She took a few moments to look at a selection of pretty needlepoint pillows. Then, as she was about to leave, the dressing-room curtain parted open.

"Stella!" Bess exclaimed.

The other girl did not reply, however. She pretended not to recognize Bess and flew past her out the door of the shop.

"Don't you remember me, Stella?"

Bess trailed after her, but a group of arriving tourists quickly separated the young women.

I wonder why she was shopping in this hotel, of all places, the girl said to herself. Come to think of it, she didn't leave with any packages. Maybe she was in the store when I stepped in and she hid in the dressing room.

Then, suddenly, she saw Stella push open the revolving door of the hotel. The young woman dashed out into the square and hailed a taxi.

I'm just too suspicious for my own good, Bess chided herself. Even so, I'd love to talk to Stella again.

It seemed unlikely that Mr. Drew had telephoned Nancy yet, so Bess did not even bother to tell her friends where she was going.

"Monastiraki, here I come!" Bess decided.

She caught a cab and in a few minutes found herself at the jewelry shop. Strangely, the woman who had waited on her was not there. Instead, there was a completely new staff. Bess asked the man behind the counter for Stella.

"I do not know her," he said pleasantly.

"I'm also looking for Constantine Nicholas."

Again the man shrugged. "Perhaps Mrs. Koukoulis knew both of those people. But—uh—she sold the business to me rather quickly and I am not yet familiar with her customers."

"Or former employees?"

"They're all gone."

Very strange, Bess thought as she said good-bye.

By the time she reached the hotel and the girls' room, Helen and Mrs. Thompson had also returned.

"Where have you been?" George asked. She eyed her cousin's empty hands. "No dress?"

Bess shook her head and related her encounter with Stella Anagnost.

"I also have news," Helen remarked. "A boy brought an envelope to the guard at the bank. It contained the payment for Uncle Lineos's safe-deposit box—"

"Your hunch was right, Nancy," Mrs. Thompson interrupted.

"We asked the boy who he was," Helen said, "but he wouldn't give us his name."

"He did admit, however, that someone from the shipyards asked him to make the delivery," Mrs. Thompson explained. "The man told him to say it was from Constantine Nicholas, who couldn't come himself—"

148

"Because he is living in a monastery outside Athens," Helen concluded.

"Incredible!" George exclaimed.

"The question is, which monastery," Nancy said.

"It's Ayiou Markou," Helen put in.

"St. Mark's—the one we tried to investigate before!" Nancy exclaimed in excitement. "We'll go there tomorrow."

"Why not today?" Bess asked.

"Because Dad's going to be arriving with three big surprises!"

18

Barrel Trap

"*Three* surprises?" Bess repeated. "What are they?"

"If I told you, they wouldn't be surprises anymore." Nancy grinned, saying her father had phoned earlier.

That evening, when Mr. Drew knocked on the girls' hotel door, Nancy opened it with anticipation.

"Ned!" she cried happily.

"Hi!" he said, giving her a kiss.

"Hello, dear," Mr. Drew added from behind.

"Dad, I'm so glad you're here," Nancy said as Burt Eddleton and Dave Evans also poked their heads around the door.

"May we join the reunion?" Dave grinned.

150

"Can you!" Bess giggled gleefully.

"We had no idea you were coming to Greece!" George said to Burt.

"We didn't, either!" her Emerson College friend replied.

"What I want to find out," Ned said, "is why you went ahead and captured Mr. Vatis before we got here."

Nancy chuckled. "We'll make up for it."

"How?" Bess piped up.

"By giving us three crooks to catch—one per couple!" Nancy said.

"We could go into partnership," George declared. "I have the perfect name for our company—the Sleuth Snoops!"

Everyone laughed, then quickly became serious as Nancy related everything that had developed since Vatis's arrest.

"This photograph is wonderful," Mr. Drew complimented his daughter. He was gazing at the enlargement of Uncle Nicholas's will. "Perhaps Helen and I ought to pay a visit to Mr. Vatis."

"That's fine with me," Helen said.

She smiled at the attorney, who responded with equal warmth in his eyes. Nancy glanced from one to the other.

"Dad, should I go, too?" she asked, trying to suppress a feeling that she might be an intruder.

"No, dear, that won't be necessary," her father answered.

"In that case," George said, "the rest of us can tackle the monastery."

Mrs. Thompson cleared her throat to be heard. "If you don't mind, I'd like to take the time to do some shopping for Maria and the other Papadapoulos children."

"We don't mind a bit," Bess said, slipping her arm into Dave's. "The Sleuth Snoops can take care of the job!"

As planned, the six young people set off for St. Mark's monastery the next day. It was unusually hot and the fact that the air conditioner in Mr. Mousiadis's car was not working did not help. The moment they pulled into the courtyard of St. Mark's, Bess and Dave stepped out and headed for the cool stone bench under a large tree.

"Whew!" Bess remarked. "It's hotter 'n peppers."

"You can say that again," her friend said, and rested against the tree trunk, watching the others disappear through the iron gates.

"Aren't you coming?" George called to the couple.

"In a minute," Bess sighed. She was unaware that the foursome had also decided to split up in twos.

George and Burt headed for the gardens behind

the chapel while Nancy told Ned about the prayer room across the way.

"I'd like to see it," Ned said, suggesting that Nancy take the lead.

As they strode across the stone yard, a monk scurried out of his room. He brushed past the pair as if they did not exist.

"I guess they're not used to having visitors," Ned chuckled.

"Guess not," Nancy agreed, stepping into the shady corridor at the foot of the stairway.

To the right was the small prayer room. The door was half-open and no one was inside.

"Where does that go?" Ned questioned, glancing toward the end of the passageway where there was a large wooden door.

"I don't recall seeing that the last time I was here," Nancy commented.

"How could you miss it, Miss Detective?"

"It was easy," she said, frowning playfully. "It was two o'clock in the morning!"

She darted ahead and lifted the latch. The door swung open freely. Beyond was a medium-sized room with little in it. Against one wall was a plain wooden bench.

Suddenly, Ned spotted a huge wooden barrel on its side in one corner. "How do you figure that got through this door?" he asked. Both he and Nancy gaped at the enormous cylinder of wood.

"What interests me more," Nancy said, "are those panels of mosaic on that far wall."

From where she and Ned stood, they saw that the mosaics were precast in wooden frames. They looked like paintings whose colors were finely blended.

"It was clever to mount them that way," Nancy said. "They're attached to the wall on brackets so they can be removed easily and hung elsewhere."

"Just like other pictures," Ned agreed, grinning.

"These may be the mosaics I overheard Isakos talking about—"

Before Nancy could finish her sentence, a pair of black-hooded robes were hurled over her and Ned.

"Ned!" she cried out, but her voice was instantly muffled as rope was lashed around her waist, pulling the material down tightly over her head.

Her companion had been taken off guard as well and trussed up. Unseen hands pushed the helpless couple into the big barrel and the lid was fastened in place.

We've got to get out of here! Nancy thought with determination.

She kicked against the floor of the barrel, rolling into Ned, who struggled to free his arms from the rope that imprisoned him. His movements loosened his bonds slightly and he tried to speak.

"Are you all right?" he asked, gagging on a fold of the black material.

154

Nancy groaned in reply, if only to let him know she had not fainted from the heat and stuffiness.

If we don't get out of here soon, she thought weakly, I probably will pass out. Ned, too. Please, somebody, help us!"

As if she had been heard, Bess and Dave had begun to search for the couple. "Nancy? Ned?" Dave called several times.

"Maybe they're in the garden," Bess suggested.

At the same moment, the monk who had nearly bumped into Nancy and Ned emerged from the chapel at the end of the yard.

"May I help you?" he asked in English.

There was a gentleness in his voice that immediately calmed the young detectives.

"I hope so," Bess said respectfully. She described her missing friends.

"As a matter of fact, I do remember them," the man said. "I was in such a hurry I almost stumbled into them." He laughed lightly. "I shall have to do penance for that."

"Where did they go?" Dave questioned with growing impatience.

"I don't really know, but why not start by looking over there?" He pointed to the crumbling stairway.

"Good idea," Bess said, murmuring to herself. "Nancy probably would want to visit that little prayer room in daylight."

To her chagrin, it was completely empty.

"But there's another one," the kindly monk said, indicating the far door.

Bess and Dave ran ahead, pushing it open with gusto. The large barrel was rocking against the wall and voices groaned inside.

"Nancy! Ned!" Dave shouted, tearing off the wooden lid.

The couple was weak from the heat. They slid limply out onto the floor and lay still as their friends removed the stifling robes.

"Oh!" Nancy said, as she suddenly felt several degrees cooler. She swayed to her feet with Ned's help. He slipped his arm around her waist and led her to the bench.

"Thank goodness you found us," Ned told the others.

The monk, in the meantime, was staring at the wall ahead. "What happened to the mosaics?" he gasped.

Nancy and Ned turned to look. The panels were gone!

"What was up there?" Bess asked.

"Beautiful mosaics," Nancy said incredulously. "They must have been stolen—"

"By the people who forced us into that barrel!" Ned deduced.

"And I know who they are!" Nancy declared.

19

Mosaic Lead

"You know who stole the mosaics?" Ned asked Nancy in surprise.

"Let's say it's a hunch," she replied. Turning to the monk, she asked, "Do you happen to know a man named Constantine Nicholas?"

"Yes, but you don't think he's responsible for this?" he said, motioning toward the blank wall. "It doesn't seem likely. He has been here often, begging for help."

"Help?" Nancy repeated.

"He admitted he was in trouble. He tried to get out of it but couldn't. Whenever visitors appeared, he would put on one of our robes and pretend he was deaf."

Ned leaned close to Nancy. "Doesn't that sound

as if Constantine's the smuggler we're after?" he whispered.

The girl detective nodded, which prompted the monk to ask her, "How well do you know Constantine Nicholas?"

"I've never met him," Nancy said and briefly explained her mission.

A perplexed expression crept into the man's face. Finally he spoke. "I don't know whether the person who comes here is the one you are looking for. In any case, I will have to notify the police about the theft of our mosaics."

"I understand," Nancy said. "But we'll try to find them for you, anyway."

As the foursome emerged into the courtyard again, Burt and George waved to them excitedly. They were standing near the shrub-lined access to the gardens.

"What's up?" Dave asked Burt.

"Follow us," George said mysteriously.

Nancy walked briskly along the stone path that led to a landscaped terrace trimmed with zakinthos, white flowers that closely resembled snapdragons. Beyond them was a clump of olive trees. A man was walking slowly between them.

"Who is it?" Bess whispered.

Nancy trained her eyes on the man, who looked like the man in the snapshot in her purse. "It may be Constantine," she said. "Wait for me."

As Nancy stepped nearer to the man, she noticed the grass was thick and moist.

If he tries to escape, she thought, he won't get far.

She skirted the trees, calling out, "Constantine Nicholas!"

Her heart pounded as she waited for a response. None came, so she repeated the name.

He probably hopes I'll give up and go away, she thought.

To her surprise, the man halted. He stood quietly for several moments, then turned to face the girl.

"You *are* Constantine!" she said as a wave of recognition passed between the two.

"And you are Nancy Drew?"

"Yes, but how did you know?"

"I've seen your picture in the American newspapers."

"I have seen yours, too," Nancy admitted, pulling it out of her purse.

Constantine's sad expression changed only slightly. "It's no use anymore," he said. "I'm glad you found me."

The relief in his voice made Nancy feel that before her was not a hardened criminal but a mixed-up young man.

"I'll pay back everything with the money I'm going to inherit," Constantine said. "That is, if I can find the lawyer who took it and the bracelet I gave him."

Nancy gasped in surprise. She waited until the others had joined them and everyone was introduced before she asked, "You mean you never received your inheritance?"

Constantine shook his head. "I had no money to pay Mr. Vatis for the work he did on my uncle's will, so I gave him the bracelet. Shortly after that, I tried to contact him, but he had moved. I never heard from him again."

"He's in jail," George said. "I suppose we'll be able to find out from him whether your story and his match."

"Oh, I'm so glad someone caught him," the young man replied. "At least—" But his voice broke and he lowered his eyes unhappily.

"Were you involved in smuggling art treasures out of Greece?" Nancy questioned.

Constantine nodded.

"Is that how you got the bracelet?"

"Yes."

"And you planted the gold mask in my shopping bag. Why?"

"Yes, I did. The store was—what you call—a 'drop' for things stolen from the archeological museum before they were shipped abroad." He took a deep breath before continuing. "I wanted to return the mask. I couldn't do it myself but I figured that a smart American girl like you would find out where it belonged."

"But Nancy almost got arrested for doing so," Bess informed the young man.

He furrowed his eyebrows in bewilderment.

"They thought Nancy was part of your gang," George explained.

"How terrible!" he said. "That was not my intention at all."

"What was the purpose of stamping that symbol on the mask and the bracelet?" Nancy pressed on.

"It was a way to identify and separate the real artifacts from the fake ones which were being shipped to America as exhibits. I'm surprised you noticed the symbol."

"Was it your idea?" Nancy asked.

"No."

"Was it Isakos's?"

"No. I don't know who thought of it."

"Were the artifacts shipped on the white banded freighter?" George spoke up.

"Yes, but I don't know much about that part of the business."

"Your cousin Helen is here in Athens looking for you," Bess put in.

"And Mr. Drew is trying to settle the inheritance for her," George added. "He needs your help."

"I will do whatever I can," Constantine responded. "Where is Helen staying? Can you bring her here?"

"More likely we will be taking her to visit you in jail," Burt said.

Constantine nodded. "I know. But please let me stay here just a little longer. I'm safer here than I'd ever be in jail, and I need to speak with the monks."

Just then, the holy man who had helped rescue Nancy and Ned approached the group. "It is all right," he assured them all. "Constantine will not escape. We will watch him."

"Thank you." Nancy smiled at him.

The young people said good-bye and left the monastery. The drive back to Athens was filled with speculation about how the other smugglers could be caught.

"It seems to me," Ned said, "if we can round up the key people, the police ought to be able to catch the rest."

"I'm glad we found Constantine, at least," Bess commented as she gazed out the car window. "He's really cute."

"You think so?" Dave asked instantly.

"Yes, very. Dark hair, dark eyes—"

"Each to his own taste," Ned cut in as he swung the car toward a major intersection.

Suddenly, Nancy stuck her head out the open window on her side. "Stop the car, Ned! Let me out!" she cried, and unlocked the door.

He grabbed her arm before she dived into the moving traffic.

"What's going on?" Bess asked.

"I just saw Isakos again!" Nancy exclaimed.

Ned pulled the car to a halt and released his grip on Nancy. She flung open the door and raced after the burly man.

"Isakos!" she shouted, dashing across the street.

He turned, poised on the edge of the curb.

"This is the last time you will bother me!" he snarled. When she was within reach he lunged forward and shoved her back into the heavy, oncoming traffic. Car brakes squealed as Nancy tumbled into their midst!

20

Smugglers' Arrest

"Nancy!" a voice cried as she barely missed being struck by an oncoming car.

It was Ned. He ran in front of the vehicle, causing it to jolt to a stop.

"Ned, Ned—" Nancy murmured. With his help, she stumbled to her feet.

The driver of the car shouted angrily at the couple, then sped down the street.

"Are you okay?" Ned asked Nancy, resting his arm firmly against her back.

She nodded, unaware of deep bruises on her knees. "But I lost one of the smugglers!"

"No, you didn't."

"What?"

"You didn't." Seeing the bewilderment on Nancy's face, he squeezed her affectionately. "Look over there." He pointed to a crowd that had formed on the opposite block.

Nancy noticed George's head bob into view and spurred Ned to walk faster. When they reached the scene, she learned that two men who had seen Isakos push her into the street had tackled him and called the police. Isakos was sputtering in Greek.

"He threw me into the street on purpose!" Nancy told the policeman, but he did not understand her. Frustrated, she looked around quickly, calling out. "Can anyone translate for me?"

A university student stepped forward and in Greek repeated to the policeman what Nancy had said.

"Tell him this man is a thief and one of the art smugglers the authorities have been looking for. All they have to do is contact the archeological museum to confirm it."

"Nonsense," Isakos bellowed in her ear. "Pure rubbish."

"Like that basket of apples one of your pals sent you?" Nancy said, narrowing her eyes.

He laughed loudly, interrupting the student before he could translate her statement into Greek.

"Maybe you don't know about the snake in the basket," Nancy admitted. "After all, it wasn't delivered to your room, even though I'm positive it was meant for you!" She turned to the student again. "Tell the policeman I'm pressing charges against this man for trying to injure me! And this is not the first time, either. He tampered with my car, which could have resulted in a serious accident!"

Isakos glared at her. "You'll pay for this!" he blustered.

"On the contrary," Ned cut in, "you will."

When the six young people finally returned to the hotel, Mr. Drew and Helen were sharing their news with Mrs. Thompson.

"Vatis confessed," Helen said.

"He falsified records and forged Constantine's signature," Mr. Drew added.

"Even my uncle's, in order to get hold of the inheritance money," Helen concluded.

"Did he spend all of it?" Nancy asked.

"Fortunately, no. A valuable coin collection worth a great deal was kept in my uncle's safe-deposit box. Vatis never found the key to it, but kept paying for the rental. It was only a month ago that he told Constantine to take over the bills."

"I guess he figured he had enough money to live on for a while," Bess said. "What a greedy man!"

The next day, it was decided that she and Dave would take Helen and Mr. Drew to St. Mark's monastery.

"Constantine is waiting there for you both,"

Nancy told them. "Please don't be too rough on him, Dad."

"If I didn't know better," George said, "I'd suspect you were interested in the guy."

"Hardly," Nancy said. "Maybe I'm just a marshmallow at heart." She grinned.

"In that case," Ned remarked, "let's go out and have sundaes!"

"After we go to Piraeus," the girl detective replied.

She telephoned the harbor police requesting them to meet her group at the white-banded freighter.

"I thought the mystery was solved," Ned sighed as he drove up to the dock.

"Which one?" George laughed.

"There's always more than one, don't you know!" Burt added.

Ned turned off the ignition and the foursome got out.

"The freighter's leaving!" Nancy exclaimed.

"And there's Isakos's friend," George said.

"The same one who dragged Stella away from us," Nancy added as an Interpol agent arrived with the police. "We must stop that ship," Nancy said.

The men ran along the dock to a patrol boat and jumped in quickly. Nancy and Ned followed.

"We'll wait here for you!" George called.

The small craft churned through the water, catching up to the freighter in record time. The police ordered it to stop immediately.

"Hang on to me," Ned told Nancy as their boat pulled close to the ship. It rocked against the hull and the Interpol agent caught hold of a rope ladder. He climbed up first, followed by Nancy and Ned, then the police.

"What is the meaning of this?" Fotis questioned.

"You are under arrest," the Interpol agent said.

"On what grounds?"

"Shipping stolen goods."

"That man's involved, too," Nancy declared, pointing to Isakos's associate. "You're Dimitri Georgiou. Correct?"

"So what?" he snapped.

"You helped hide stolen artifacts from the museum in bales of cotton stored below deck," Nancy accused.

Although she and the police had checked a few random crates earlier and found nothing, her father had learned from museum authorities in the States that artifacts shipped from Greece were discovered in bales of cotton.

"I have nothing to say about that," Dimitri said.

"How does it feel to have taken money that was meant to help poor families?" Nancy asked him.

"I don't know what you're talking about!" Dimitri hissed, but the crimson color in his face assured Nancy that she was right.

"You're also the one who abducted George on Corfu, aren't you?" she went on.

Dimitri stared at her full of anger.

"How did he get to Corfu?" Ned asked. "Just a little while ago, he ran a fake charity in the United States. Then all of a sudden he was in Corfu with Vatis?"

"That's because his real name is Dimitri Vatis!" Nancy said. "He's Vatis's brother and former partner. The original law firm consisted of Vatis Senior and two sons, not just one."

"How did you ever figure that out?"

"His money clip provided the clue. Remember, it had the initials D.V. on it—V for Vatis."

"Did you wiretap my phone, too?" the man rasped furiously.

"No need to," Nancy replied. "Your reaction just now was enough proof. Either you had an argument with your brother and left the law firm for that reason or you believed that running the Photini Agency in New York would be more lucrative. Then, when you realized that the police might soon uncover your scheme, you returned to Athens."

"That's when you found out about your brother's connection with Constantine and the Nicholas inheritance," Ned added.

"See if any of this holds up in court," the man sneered.

"Oh, it will," Nancy siad, "because Constantine will testify to everything."

"I'm also positive that Isakos will have a few things to say," George remarked.

"Especially since you and he stole the mosaics from St. Mark's monastery," Nancy said.

"Too bad we got in your way," Ned remarked.

"That wasn't the first time," George pointed out. "The night the three of us went to investigate St. Mark's, you or Isakos set off that weird noise in the gardens to distract us."

"It went on by mistake," Dimitri declared.

"Sending that poisonous snake to Isakos didn't work, either," Nancy went on. Her listener grumbled, but did not deny her accusation.

"Why did he do that?" Ned inquired.

"He wanted to get rid of Isakos and take over his racket," Nancy explained, "which, by the way, took Isakos to the U.S. on occasion. We happened to meet him on one of his return flights on Olympic Airways."

"When did Dimitri become involved with Isakos?"

"He learned about him from his brother, who in turn was aware of the art smuggling scheme through Constantine. When Dimitri returned to

Athens, he needed a job. He contacted Isakos. It didn't take him long to decide to take over Isakos's organization."

"Do you think Isakos realized what Dimitri was up to?" Ned asked.

"No. They worked closely together. As a matter of fact, the snake symbol was Dimitri's idea. He threw the smugglers' stamp at me in the hotel corridor."

"But why would he throw evidence in your path?"

"To plant something conclusive on me. He figured he could have me arrested and out of the way, once and for all." She paused, digging into her purse. "I don't plan to keep anything that will indict the man. Here." She handed Dimitri's money clip and the stamp to the agent from Interpol.

The police ordered Fotis to return his ship to the dock, where it would be searched. When they arrived, Dimitri and Fotis were led off in handcuffs.

"Thanks to you girls," the Interpol agent said, "the main members of the gang are now in tow!"

That evening, when Nancy's group was all together again, the young detectives and their dates took turns telling about Isakos's and Dimitri's capture.

"And to think I missed it all," Mrs. Thompson

said. "But I have to admit I did buy some lovely presents for the Papadapoulos family."

"That's great," Nancy replied.

"What about Constantine?" Nancy asked Helen.

"Your father has arranged something wonderful for him."

Mr. Drew smiled. "Well, it turned out that his role in the gang was a minor one. He didn't actually steal anything. He was just a go-between and delivery boy. For that, the gang gave him a reward once—the cuff bracelet. Unfortunately, he had been living way beyond his means and lost his job. That's when Isakos enlisted him with the promise of a lot of money."

"Which he never got, of course," Helen added.

"Right. That's why he gave Vatis the bracelet as payment for legal fees. Vatis realized it was a valuable ancient piece and pressed Constantine to tell him how he got it."

"What about Stella?" Bess asked. "She acted so peculiar when I met her in the dress shop. Obviously she knew Dimitri—"

"As a result of being Constantine's girlfriend," Mr. Drew said. "Dimitri began making deliveries to Chrysoteque, the jewelry shop, when Constantine stopped. Apparently, Dimitri told Stella he would harm Constantine if she even spoke to you girls, much less ask for your help."

"No wonder she pretended not to know me while I was shopping," Bess said.

"Well," Mr. Drew spoke up, "I convinced Constantine to turn himself in. He'll be out shortly on light bail."

"You're terrific, Dad," Nancy said, hugging him.

"I say this calls for a celebration," Helen declared. "I'm going to plan one on my new yacht."

"Your new yacht?" Nancy asked, surprised.

Helen explained that shortly before his death her uncle had ordered one to be built. It was ready now.

"What a shame he never had a chance to sail on it," Bess remarked.

"But we will tomorrow!" Helen said gaily.

The following day, she led the group to a berth near the Nikos dock. The yacht, nearly two hundred feet long from bow to stern, glistened in the sunlight.

"She's gorgeous!" Nancy exclaimed.

Suddenly, she noticed the crest on the bow. It was identical to the one on the silver box the young priest had left at the church in Plaka!

"That's the Nikos crest!" Nancy exclaimed.

Bess and George stared in amazement. "You mean the priest we saw on our first afternoon in Greece was Constantine?" Bess asked.

"That's correct," Mr. Drew replied. "He told me

he gave the silver box that had been in his possession for a long time to his patron saint—to make up for his dishonest ways."

"Now, no more talk of such unpleasant things," Helen interrupted. "Someone must christen this boat for me. Will you, Carson?"

"I'd be happy to," the lawyer said. "What are you going to call it?"

"Well, since I wouldn't have had it without your daughter's help, I'm calling it the *Nancy Drew!*"

The girl sleuth was stunned into grateful silence. Now that her exciting adventure had come to an end, she found herself daydreaming about her next one. She did not yet know it would begin soon when she discovered *The Swami's Ring*.

Seeing the glow on Nancy's face, Helen continued. "Giving someone's name to a ship is the highest honor a shipping family in Greece can bestow on anyone. But then, you are the most wonderful young detective in the world!"

2
The Swami's Ring

Nancy Drew® in
The Swami's Ring

Illustrated by Paul Frame

The Swami's Ring was
first published in the U.K. in a single volume
in hardback in 1982 by Angus & Robertson (U.K.) Ltd,
and in Armada in 1983
by Fontana Paperbacks,
8 Grafton Street, London W1X 3LA.

Contents

1

Mysterious Patient

"Nancy, would you come over to Rosemont Hospital and help solve a mystery?"

Mystery! That was all the girl detective needed to hear from her former schoolmate, Lisa Scotti, who was now a nurse.

"Sounds exciting," Nancy said eagerly. "Tell me about it."

"A young man was just brought into emergency with bad bruises. He has amnesia—can't remember who he is, where he has been, where he was going, or what happened."

"Who found him?" Nancy asked.

"Some people from out of state. They had stopped along a wooded highway near the airport to stretch their legs and discovered him at the bottom of a cliff. Apparently, he fell or was pushed off. I'm surprised he doesn't have any broken bones."

"Me too," Nancy said, adding quickly, "I'll be right over. 'Bye—"

"Wait—don't hang up," Lisa interrupted. "Visiting hours don't begin until eleven."

Nancy glanced at her wristwatch. It was only ten o'clock.

"In that case, why don't I offer to do some volunteer work at Rosemont? Then I'll be able to see Cliff almost anytime."

Lisa giggled. "How did you know that's what all us nurses call him?"

"I didn't." Nancy laughed.

"Meet you on the fifth floor. Cliff's in Room 502."

As soon as Lisa clicked off, Nancy dialed the hospital phone number. Since she had attended an orientation program for Rosemont volunteers the previous summer, she was no stranger to the hospital. Surely she could start right away. At least, she hoped so.

"Nancy dear," Hannah called out when the girl dropped the receiver into its cradle, "would you rather have fish or fowl for dinner?"

"I'll take either so long as it's garnished with savory clues!" Nancy teased.

"Now be serious," Mrs. Gruen replied, poking her head out of the kitchen.

Over the years, a warm and wonderful cameraderie had grown between the young woman and the Drews' housekeeper. She had helped rear Nancy since the girl was three, when Mrs. Drew had passed away.

"I am being serious." Nancy smiled. Her blue eyes almost danced as sunlight captured her pretty face and reddish-blond hair.

"Don't tell me you're off on a mystery of your own before you finish the case you and your dad are working on," Hannah replied saucily. She was hoping the answer would be no. "What will your father say?"

Carson Drew was a prominent attorney in River Heights who had recently become embroiled in problems of the town's summer music festival. The evening before, he had told Nancy his fear that it might be forced to close because of a squabble among some performers. As he frequently did, Mr. Drew asked his gifted eighteen-year-old daughter for advice.

"If you mean that Dad's going to worry

185

whether I'll have time to work on two mysteries at the same time—" Nancy started to say.

"That's precisely what I mean."

Nancy did not agree, however. She knew how Hannah worried about her, but could not help teasing her once in a while.

"When Dad comes home, tell him I'm in the hospital."

"What?" the woman gulped.

"Not as a patient, though."

The housekeeper shook her head while Nancy pecked her cheek and said good-bye. Driving across town, she noticed the billboard announcement for the River Heights Music Festival, but kept her thoughts concentrated on Rosemont Hospital, where she shortly found herself.

After parking the car, she hurried into the building to register as a volunteer, then went directly to an elevator and pressed the button. The door slid open a moment later, but as she stepped forward, a large, burly man with a heavy, black beard shoved her aside.

"Hey—" she cried as the stranger hurried ahead and pushed an inside button, but the door closed before Nancy could enter. She glanced up at the bank of lights overhead. "He's stopping at the fifth floor!" she murmured. "I hope I don't bump into him again!"

It seemed to take forever for the elevator to return, but at last the young detective was on her way upstairs. Lisa was waiting for her.

"Some creep got off the elevator a minute ago," the nurse said, "and practically knocked me down."

"That makes two of us," Nancy replied as they walked toward Room 502.

When they were within a few feet of Cliff's room, they heard short, quick gasps and ran inside.

"Oh, no! Stop!" Lisa shrieked when she saw the hands of the bearded stranger clutching at Cliff's neck.

"Get away from him!" Nancy demanded. She and Lisa grabbed the man's arms.

Angrily, he wrenched himself away from the girls. "Where's the ring you stole?" he growled at Cliff.

"I'm going to call the police if you don't—" Lisa threatened.

Now the man stiffened. He loosened his fingers from Cliff's neck, allowing the patient to

slip back against the pillow. Cliff moaned softly and opened his eyes halfway, only to shut them again.

"Who are you?" Nancy asked the intruder.

He whirled on his heels and stormed out into the corridor.

"Come back here!" Nancy insisted. She hurried after him as fast as she could, but his long legs carried him swiftly away from her into the elevator which now descended.

Instantly, Nancy dashed through the stairwell door. She raced down the steps, taking two at a time, and upon reaching the main floor, burst across the lobby to the entrance.

"Oh!" she muttered in disappointment. The stranger had disappeared into a waiting tan-colored car with a blue racing stripe on the trunk. The vehicle sped down the street.

Puffs of exhaust from the tail pipe succeeded in covering up the license plate so that Nancy could not decipher it. Disgusted, she returned to Cliff's room, where Lisa was giving him a small cup of water.

"This is my friend, Nancy Drew," the young nurse said, introducing the two.

The patient, a rugged-faced man with light

brown hair, nodded weakly. "I wish I could tell you my name," he said with a hint of laughter in his voice.

"Cliff will do for the time being," Nancy replied. "You had a pretty rough experience just a few minutes ago. Do you know who that man was?"

"No, not at all."

"Nancy is an amateur detective," Lisa quickly inserted, "and she wants to help you."

Cliff smiled again. "Tell me about some of your cases."

The girl detective blushed modestly.

"As a matter of fact," Lisa put in, "Nancy has been out of the country for her two most recent mysteries. She found *The Secret in the Old Lace* in Belgium and went to Greece to decipher *The Greek Symbol Mystery*."

"You have an excellent memory," Nancy remarked, suddenly realizing what she had said. "Oh, I'm sorry, Cliff."

"This old head's not that sensitive." The patient chuckled. "I'm sure my memory was at least as good as yours, Nancy—once upon a time."

Before she could say more, he closed his eyes

sleepily and Lisa beckoned Nancy out into the corridor.

"I'd like to tell Bess and George about all of this," Nancy said.

Bess Marvin and George Fayne were cousins and Nancy's closest friends who often helped her solve mysteries.

"The more brains we get thinking about Cliff's identity," Lisa answered, "the quicker we'll find out who he is."

"Exactly."

Nancy excused herself to telephone the Marvin home. To her delight, Bess answered.

"Just a minute, Nancy. Let me put George on, too. She's here."

"Great, because I need to talk to *both* of you."

"Uh-oh," Bess said. "I have a feeling we're in for another adventure—n-nothing dangerous, I hope."

Nancy laughed lightly while her friend called George to an extension phone. Then, as briefly as possible, the girl told them about Cliff.

"I'd like you to meet him," Nancy said. "Can you come over to the hospital?"

"Sure," Bess and George chorused eagerly.

By the time they reached Rosemont Hospital, Cliff was awake again, and Nancy introduced her friends. Afterwards, George asked if any identification had been found on the patient.

"Apparently not," Nancy said.

"The only thing he was carrying was a knapsack," Lisa advised.

She pulled the heavy canvas bag out of the closet.

"Cliff, would you object if I went through it?" Nancy asked.

"No, of course not."

While everyone watched, she removed several articles of clothing and an envelope with money in it. Then her fingers felt the lining of the bag. An unexpected thickness in the material suggested a hidden pocket.

"Did you find something else?" Bess asked, breaking the silence.

"Could be."

She opened the pocket and rolled the contents into her palm.

"Don't keep us in suspense," George begged as Nancy took her hand out.

When she opened it, everyone gasped at the girl's discovery. It was a large, gold ring, extremely ornate and obviously meant for a very fat finger!

"That would swim on Cliff's hand," Lisa observed.

Nancy glanced at the young man, whose eyes were riveted on the unusual ring. Was this the one he had been accused of stealing?

2

Tommy's Accident

"Cliff," Nancy said, holding the ring out to him, "does this mean anything to you?"

He blinked his eyes as if struggling to remember. "I—I, no, it doesn't."

"I don't think it should be left unguarded in this closet," Nancy announced. "Can we put it in the hospital safe until I come back with my magnifying glass? I'd like to examine it further."

"Definitely," Lisa replied, "if that's all right with Cliff."

Lisa promised to take the ring downstairs as soon as she gave him his medication. Nancy, meanwhile, led Bess and George to the office of

Dr. Randolph, the director of Rosemont Hospital. He was a tall, heavyset man in his late fifties.

"It's nice to see Carson Drew's daughter on our volunteer staff," he said, greeting Nancy.

The lawyer was on the board of the hospital and a personal friend of Dr. Randolph.

"I suppose you've heard about your amnesia patient," Nancy said.

"Of course. He's the most exciting thing that's happened around here all week!" the man replied. "Not that it's so exciting for him, poor guy. We called Chief McGinnis to see if anyone on the police department's list of missing persons fits his description."

"What did you find out?" George asked.

"Absolutely nothing. The police wanted to know if Cliff had been physically assaulted," Dr. Randolph went on. "But there was no evidence of that, according to Dr. Anderson."

"In other words," Bess said, "there's no reason for the police to get involved—"

"Yet," Nancy added in a serious tone.

"Why, what do you mean?" Dr. Randolph replied.

The girl told him about the bearded stranger,

his accusation, and her discovery of the ring. "At the moment, it's our only clue to Cliff's identity," she said, "and I'd like to study it some more."

"Good idea, Nancy."

Promising to keep the man posted on all developments, she and her friends stepped out into the hallway.

"When I signed on as a volunteer, I was asked to help distribute flowers, so I'll do that now," the young detective told Bess and George. "Maybe we ought to put our heads together later."

"Call us when you get home," George said.

Nancy immediately headed for the main lobby, where several colorful floral arrangements were displayed on a counter.

"These are for the third floor, and this one's for the sixth," the clerk told Nancy.

She fastened her eyes on the latter in surprise. The card was marked TOMMY JOHNSON. Was it her neighborhood friend? Curious, she went to Pediatrics on the sixth floor first. The boy's mother was just emerging from his room.

"Mrs. Johnson!" Nancy cried.

Without questioning Nancy's presence at Rosemont, the woman blurted out her story.

"Tommy was riding his bicycle when a car cut in front of him. He and the bike toppled over. He hit his head on the curb and twisted his leg—broke it in two places."

Nancy winced at the thought. "Oh, how terrible! Has he been operated on yet?"

"No, but he will be this afternoon."

"These are for Tommy," Nancy said, indicating the small basket of flowers.

She stepped into the room, where the shade was pulled low to keep out the bright sun. Tommy, a small bandage over one eyebrow, was sleeping quietly. He did not move until Nancy placed the flowers next to him. Then his eyes opened slowly.

"Hi, Nancy," the boy said. "Did you come to visit me?"

"I sure did," the girl replied cheerfully.

She touched his cheek gently as an orderly appeared. "We must get him ready now," the young man said, signaling the girl to leave.

Mrs. Johnson had remained outside the door, waiting to speak to her.

"Did anyone see the car?" Nancy asked the woman.

Tommy's mother shook her head. "I don't think so, but I'm not sure," she said. "It happened on the corner of Hathaway Street and Elm Avenue."

Nancy squeezed Mrs. Johnson's arm as she promised to help find the hit-and-run driver. At her first opportunity, she would make a trip to police headquarters.

"Now I have two reasons to go," Nancy said without explaining further.

She said good-bye and headed for the fifth floor to speak with Lisa. To her surprise, the young woman had gone off duty.

That's strange, Nancy thought. I'm positive she was supposed to work until five o'clock. I hope she took care of Cliff's ring for him.

Instantly, the girl detective returned to the main floor and the admitting office, where she inquired about the valuable piece.

"One moment," the clerk said, and stepped into the inner office, shortly reappearing empty-handed. "I can find no notation about the deposit of a ring from Room 502, and it's not in the safe."

"Are you positive?" Nancy inquired.

"Quite," the woman bristled.

What had happened to Cliff's ring? Nancy wondered anxiously. And where was Lisa?

As quickly as she could, Nancy checked out of the hospital and headed for Lisa's home. It was near Hathaway Street, where Tommy's accident had occurred. When Nancy reached the busy intersection at Elm Avenue, she noticed a tall, thin man with a briefcase enter a jewelry store. He was wearing a business suit and a white silk turban that offset his brown face and fine Indian features. But of even more interest was the man running after him. It was the bearded stranger who had attacked Cliff!

I have to talk to him! Nancy said to herself.

She swung her car into a space halfway down the street, pushed a coin into the meter, and ran toward the shop. She paused before entering.

Lisa! she gulped when she saw the girl, who was talking with the businessman and the shopkeeper. Where was the other man? Had he seen Nancy coming and disappeared?

She was tempted to explore the alley next to the store, but the scene inside was more fascinating. Lisa was showing Cliff's ring to the shopkeeper. Suddenly, he left the counter, and the stranger pocketed the ring. He hurried to the door, which Nancy flung open with such force that he slipped off balance.

"You took that young woman's ring," Nancy accused, alerting both Lisa and the shopkeeper.

Instantly, the man shoved Nancy against the counter. He grabbed the door, ready to dart outside, but the shopkeeper and Lisa rushed forward, tackling him. Nancy dived into his coat pocket and quickly retrieved the ring.

"Let go of me!" the man shouted, unaware that the valuable trinket had been removed.

He tore away from the group and ran across the street to a bus that had stopped at the corner.

"We'll catch him!" Nancy exclaimed.

Without another word, Lisa hurried after her friend to Nancy's car. As quickly as she could, Nancy pulled around in the opposite direction. The bus was several stoplights away from her.

"Why didn't you put Cliff's ring into the hospital safe?" Nancy asked as they sped forward.

"I meant to, but Cliff suggested I take it to a local jeweler—to find out more about it. Next thing I knew, that man in the turban was standing there, asking all sorts of questions."

By now, Nancy's car had caught up to the bus at a bus stop, where several people debarked. She signaled to the driver to wait.

"What do you want?" the man shouted through his window. "I've got a lot of people to let off."

"One of them tried to rob us," Lisa called back.

Before Nancy could park, her friend had jumped out of the car and raced to the policeman on the corner, leading him quickly to the bus. When the last of several passengers had stepped off, Lisa and the officer jumped on board. There were only a few people left, and the man in the turban was not among them!

3

Mean Accusation

Through her rearview mirror, Nancy watched Lisa and the policeman step off the bus without the Indian. The girl detective immediately switched on her hazard lights, leaving the car double-parked, and leaped out.

"What happened?" she asked, hurrying toward them.

"I don't know. He must have sneaked off without our seeing him," Lisa replied.

The officer listened to the girls' story while Nancy displayed Cliff's ring. "Lucky you were on the scene, Nancy Drew," he complimented her.

Nancy's reputation as a keen detective was well-known to the police of River Heights.

"I was planning to see Chief McGinnis tomorrow," Nancy said. "But maybe Lisa and I ought to go to headquarters now."

"Good idea," the policeman grinned, "especially since I don't want to tow your car away."

The girls glanced in the direction of Nancy's flashing rear lights. She suddenly realized she had double-parked next to a patrol car!

"Sorry," she said sheepishly.

When the pair reached the station, Nancy explained that she had two important matters to discuss with the chief. One related to the identity of a local amnesia patient who had been assaulted in the hospital. The other had to do with the driver of a car that had nearly run down Tommy Johnson.

"I know about both cases," Chief McGinnis said, "but I have no lead on the first and only a very slim one on the second."

Nancy gave a description of the bearded man.

"I've seen him twice now," she said. "The first time he took off in a tan-colored car with a blue racing stripe on the trunk."

"What's the license number?"

Nancy shrugged. "I couldn't see it."

The chief hunched forward on his elbows and shook his head thoughtfully.

"Do you have any idea whom it belongs to?" Nancy asked.

"Yes, I think so. Of course, I can't be absolutely positive, but—"

"But what?"

"It sounds like the same car that caused the Johnson boy's accident."

Nancy was stunned into silence as her mind raced over the events of the afternoon. What was the connection between the Indian businessman and the bearded stranger?

"I have a hunch the bearded man may be the driver we're looking for!" Nancy exclaimed.

"You could be right," Chief McGinnis said. "I'll let you know if anything definite turns up on either of those men."

Nancy promised to reciprocate and said good-bye. As the girls headed for Lisa's house, the young nurse suggested that Nancy keep the ring.

"It'll be safer with you," Lisa insisted, adding an apology for what had occurred earlier. "I should have put it in the hospital safe."

"Just be glad we have it," Nancy smiled. "Besides, your visit to the jewelry shop turned up an interesting character."

"And some interesting information," Lisa

said. "This is the first chance I've had to tell you what Mr. Jhaveri, the jeweler, said about the ring. He's quite an expert on foreign jewelry, and he believes the design is Asiatic.

"The other man disagreed, however. He kept saying the ring was Middle Eastern. That's when Mr. Jhaveri said he would show me some pictures as proof."

"And that's when the Indian businessman tried to steal the ring," Nancy put in.

"Exactly."

"He didn't count on Nancy Drew," Lisa added, causing a blush of crimson to cross her friend's face.

They pulled up in front of the Scotti home and Lisa opened the car door instantly.

"I promised Mom I'd cook dinner tonight, so I'd better run," she said. "Thanks a lot. See you tomorrow."

Nancy said good-bye, all the while thinking about the scene in the jewelry shop. She was tempted to return there, but a glance at her watch told her she was more than an hour late for dinner.

Hannah is probably worried about me, Nancy thought. I can just imagine the phone calls she must have made to the hospital.

The girl pressed down on the accelerator, watching the speedometer needle waver just under the speed limit. Rush-hour traffic had eased up, and she found herself in the driveway of the Drew home within fifteen minutes. Mrs. Gruen opened the door with a mixture of disapproval and relief on her face.

"I'm sorry," Nancy said, hugging the woman. "I was on my way home when—"

"You caught two robbers, found three clues, and went to see Chief McGinnis," Hannah replied, unable to keep from smiling.

"How did you guess?"

"Because I know you. That's how." The housekeeper grinned.

Before Nancy said another word, she raced upstairs to freshen up. The aroma of home-baked peach pie trailed after her, speeding her back to the dining room table where her father was already seated.

"Do I have lots of news!" Nancy said excitedly.

Carson Drew, a distinguished-looking man in his forties, did not respond immediately. Nancy thought he seemed disturbed.

"Is something wrong, Dad?"

"Oh, no," he answered quickly.

"Sure?"

"Sure."

"I really am sorry about being late."

Her father merely nodded as he took a sip of water. "Bring me up to date on what happened today," he said at last.

Despite her eagerness to tell him, she could not help being distracted by Mr. Drew's sullen manner. Nonetheless, she revealed her encounters at the hospital, the discovery of the ring, and Tommy Johnson's accident.

"How terrible!" Hannah commented when the girl finished speaking.

For the first time since dinner began, Mr. Drew's expression was also animated. He asked several questions, then lapsed into silence until he rose from the table.

"Let's go into the living room, Nancy," he said.

What was on her father's mind? Nancy wondered in puzzlement. She sank into the deep, soft cushions of the chair by the fireplace and waited anxiously.

"I really don't know how to say this," Mr. Drew said slowly.

"Does it have to do with the music festival?"

"In a way, yes." Her father paused. "You'll have to stop doing your detective work for a while."

Nancy blinked in disbelief. "But why? What have I done?"

"Oh, *you* haven't done anything wrong. The townspeople of Castleton think *I* have."

"You've lost me, Dad."

"As I told you yesterday, I've been handling negotiations for the River Heights festival on behalf of River Heights."

"Negotiations between the city and the different performing groups who are appearing here this summer," Nancy put in.

"That's right," her father replied. "Well, I've been accused of theft."

"Theft?" Nancy repeated in utter astonishment. "That's absolutely crazy."

"Castleton claims that River Heights has deliberately stolen one of the theater companies it booked for its own outdoor pavilion."

"I still don't understand."

"It's very simple, dear. The Jansen Music Theater Company was scheduled to perform at the Castleton Theater, but Jansen canceled out on Castleton in favor of River Heights. The town council of Castleton thinks I'm responsible for the last-minute switch." Mr. Drew interrupted himself, laughing nervously. "It just isn't true, but I can't seem to convince anyone, including the mayor of River Heights!"

"But he's your friend, Dad."

"He is, but he's also in an awkward situation with Castleton, since both communities have been working together on some environmental issues."

Nancy took a deep breath. "I'll help you," she said.

"No, Nancy, I think it's better if you don't. A number of unexplained things have happened to the Jansen troupe, and I'm afraid something could happen to you."

"You know I can take care of myself," Nancy pleaded.

"I would feel better if you just contented yourself with the amnesia patient."

The firmness in his voice told Nancy she ought not to push him on the subject.

It's the first time Dad has ever told me to quit on something before I even started, Nancy said to herself.

Worse than that, her own father needed her help, but would not accept it!

4

Suspect?

"Nancy, I don't want you to worry about me or the festival," Mr. Drew said.

"But Dad—"

He raised his hand as if he didn't want to hear another word.

"I have two complimentary tickets to the festival tomorrow evening. Perhaps you'd like to take Ned."

Nancy's face lit up into a smile immediately.

"Promise me, though, you'll just enjoy the performance. No investigating, okay?"

"Whatever you say, Dad."

She leaped out of her chair to call her friend, Ned Nickerson, who was home on vacation from

Emerson College. At first Nancy was tempted to mention her father's predicament, but she refrained as Mr. Drew strode past her.

Instead, she conveyed the invitation, adding in a whisper, "I have a lot to tell you, too."

"In that case," Ned said, "how can I resist?"

It was decided that he would stop by for Nancy at seven-thirty the next evening. In the meantime, she had several things to discuss with Bess and George.

"Hello. Is George there?" Nancy said, after dialing the number of the Fayne household.

To her surprise, the girl was not home.

Maybe she went to see Bess, Nancy surmised. She was about to call the Marvin number when the doorbell rang.

"I'll get it," Nancy announced, dropping the receiver.

It was the two cousins.

"When we didn't hear from you, we figured something must've happened," Bess said.

"Right?" George asked.

"Right," Nancy said. "Come on in."

While she cut pieces of Hannah's peach pie for each girl, she told them everything that had occurred after they left Rosemont Hospital.

"Fortunately, I still have Cliff's ring," Nancy concluded, excusing herself to get it.

When she returned to the kitchen, she was also holding her magnifying glass. The trio took turns examining the ring. On close inspection, they saw that the intricate design consisted of finely intertwined water lilies. Inside the band was a well-worn initial, together with an indistinct figure standing on a flower. To the untrained eye, they could pass for mere scratches.

"I can't figure out what the letter is," Bess said. "Can you?"

"I'm not sure, but it looks like 'P,'" Nancy said. "Lisa said Mr. Jhaveri was about to show her a book when the businessman took the ring."

"Maybe we should go to the store tomorrow," George suggested.

"I was just thinking the same thing," Nancy said.

That night, Nancy slept uneasily as the ring tossed through her dreams. Someone on the stage of the River Heights Theater was throwing it toward her, but she couldn't catch it because of an imaginary rope that held her arms back.

"Nancy . . . Nancy," a voice was calling.

The girl mumbled back into her pillow as the shade on her window snapped open and sunlight poured across the room.

"Nancy, dear, it's after nine."

The young detective pulled the bedsheet over her head while Hannah tickled her foot.

"Time to rise and shine. Bess and George are waiting for you downstairs."

"Oh, my goodness," Nancy cried, bolting out of bed. "They're here already?"

After a quick shower, she slipped into a skirt and blouse, put Cliff's ring in her shoulder bag, and hurried to the dining room, where a glass of orange juice awaited her.

"Didn't we say nine o'clock?" George asked.

Nancy nodded. "I overslept," she said, gulping down the juice.

"Don't drink so fast, Nancy," Hannah scolded. "You'll get indigestion."

Despite the warning, Nancy hurried through breakfast, explaining that she had several things to do.

"I promised to be at the hospital for a couple of hours at least," she said. "Now that I'm running so late, maybe you ought to see Mr. Jhaveri without me."

"Are you sure?" Bess asked.

"Yes. Besides, I want to check on how Tommy is and make a few inquiries at the hospital."

"What about the ring?" George replied. "Shall we take it with us?"

"Definitely," Nancy said. "When you're done at the store, then please bring it to Rosemont."

While Nancy headed for the hospital, Bess and George went downtown. To their delight, Mr. Jhaveri remembered the unusual ring and was more than willing to discuss it.

"I didn't have a chance to show my book to your friend," he said, "but I will show it to you. Do you have time?"

"Oh yes," George replied eagerly.

"I will only be a moment," the proprietor said, disappearing into the anteroom behind the main counter.

For an instant, the cousins sensed that someone was watching them, but when they glanced toward the front window, no one was there.

"We're just being overly suspicious," Bess whispered.

Mr. Jhaveri returned holding a large book. "There are many wonderful stories in here about unusual pieces of jewelry and their owners." He leafed through the pages, stopping now and then to show photographs of fantastic jewels—rubies, diamonds, and emeralds cut in various shapes.

"Ah, here it is," he said at last. "The Maharajah Prithviraj of Lakshmipur."

Bess and George giggled as they looked at the roly-poly man whose face was as round as Hannah's peach pie. He wore a loose-fitting robe that concealed his rotund figure, and on every finger except one was an exquisite ring.

"It seems that the maharajah had a passion for water lilies," Mr. Jhaveri said. "They grew profusely in his garden pool—"

"And decorated his linen, silver, and jewelry," Bess said, reading the caption under the picture.

Was it possible that Cliff's ring had once belonged to the maharajah? the girls wondered. But, if so, how had it traveled from India to the United States?

The bell on the front door jingled suddenly, and the girls stared at the bearded man who entered. Was he the same person Nancy had chased out of Rosemont Hospital?

George quickly dropped the ring into her purse and shut the book.

"Are you finished with it?" Mr. Jhaveri asked politely.

"Yes, thank you," George said, trying to conceal her nervousness. She nudged Bess to leave. "We must be on our way, but I'm sure we'll be back."

"Don't hurry on my account," the bearded customer said. "I'm just browsing."

The girls did not bother to reply, but hurried to their car.

"Maybe we should've stayed around to check that guy out," Bess said.

"And risk having him hear something about the ring?" George replied. "No, ma'am."

She started the car, then noticed that the jeweler had emerged from his store. The bearded man was with him.

"Don't go yet, miss!" Mr. Jhaveri was shouting at the girls. "Please—come back!"

"What should we do?" Bess gasped. Her heart pounded nervously as the stranger raced toward them.

5

Untimely Ruse

"I'm positive that man is after Cliff's ring!" Bess exclaimed fearfully.

"Just keep cool," George said, turning off the ignition.

By now, the bearded man was standing next to the girl's car.

"I am Dr. DeNiro, the anthropologist," he introduced himself.

George recognized the name immediately. Dr. DeNiro was a professor at Oberon College, a local university and had recently returned from field work in Asia. An article about him had appeared in the last issue of the *River Heights Gazette*.

"I'm George Fayne, and this is my cousin, Bess Marvin," George said.

"How do you do?"

Bess smiled sweetly, lifting her eyes to the thin, almost invisible scar that traveled down the man's cheek and disappeared under the ragged beard.

"We're sort of in a hurry," George said.

"Well, I don't want to hold you up, but—uh," the man stumbled, "I am interested in the ring you showed Mr. Jhaveri."

The cousins remained silent, waiting for him to go on.

"May I see it?" Dr. DeNiro said.

George hesitated, then dug into her purse, as earlier suspicions were replaced by curiosity. Perhaps the professor could provide some clues to Cliff's identity!

"Here you are," the girl said, handing the ring to him.

He studied it intently, turning it over several times.

"I have been doing some research on the area of India where this was made," the man said. "With your permission, I would like to photograph the ring. May I?"

"It doesn't belong to us," Bess replied.

"Oh, I see. Well, in that case, could you put me in touch with the owner?"

The girls paused.

"Perhaps you could give me his name and telephone number," Dr. DeNiro continued.

"He's in the hospital," George said. Her mind was racing as it occurred to her that Nancy might wish to speak with the professor as well. "We're on our way to Rosemont Hospital now. Would you like to ride over there with us?"

The man checked his watch. "Oh," he gasped, "I'm twenty minutes late for my appointment. I'll have to call you."

With that, he sped across the street to a parking lot, leaving the girls in complete bafflement.

"The ring! He's got the ring!" George cried. She leaped out of her car and darted after the man, shouting his name at the top of her lungs. But he was already pulling out of the lot.

"What happened?" Bess asked when her cousin returned.

"He's gone."

"And so is Cliff's ring," Bess said. "We have to get it back before we see Nancy again."

George agreed and suggested that they go to Oberon College.

"Maybe we'll catch him on the way to class," Bess said hopefully.

The girls located his office in an old stone building near the student center. A note was tacked on the door: HOURS 1:30–3:00 P.M.

"He should be here in a few minutes," George observed with a sigh of relief.

The wait, however, seemed interminable, as a stream of students carrying notebooks filed through the corridor and stopped outside an instructor's door at the far end.

"Where is he?" Bess asked impatiently.

Then, as if in reply, the large, wooden, entrance door swung open and a young, brown-haired man, neatly dressed in a striped shirt and khaki pants, strode toward them.

"May I help you?" he asked, pulling out a key.

"We're looking for Dr. DeNiro," George said.

"You've found him." The beardless man grinned. "Are you registering for one of my courses?"

His listeners stared at him completely dumb-founded.

"Is something wrong?" the instructor asked.

"No . . . I mean, yes," Bess said. "Do you have a brother who teaches here?"

"No," he chuckled, "but I'm sure my department head would be pleased if I did. I've been away from campus for almost a month."

The realization that Cliff's ring was now in the possession of an unknown stranger made both girls shudder. They had been duped!

Instantly, George asked, "Are you missing any personal identification—driver's license, credit cards, anything like that?"

"No, not that I know of. Why?"

George explained about their encounter with the man at the jewelery shop.

"He said he was you!" Bess exclaimed.

"Me?"

By now, the young man had opened his office and invited the cousins to sit down.

"He said he was doing some research on India and wanted to photograph the ring we gave him," George explained.

"Well, it's true I am working on a government project related to India, but it hasn't been publicized." He paused for a long moment. "I do wonder, though, why someone would pretend to be me."

"All we know is that the ring may have belonged to a maharajah."

The young man slid back in his chair, staring at the girls, yet past them.

"It's possible," he said, "that the fellow expects to gain access to information I'm after."

"What kind of information?" Bess inquired.

"I'm afraid I can't tell you."

She and George concluded that the professor must be involved in a highly confidential mission. The question was, Did the ring figure into it, and if so, how?

Before they could discuss it further, a student appeared at the door. She was holding several notebooks.

"I may need to talk with you both again," Dr. DeNiro said, signaling the cousins to leave.

"And vice versa," George said. She jotted down her phone number. "Will you be here tomorrow?"

"Yes, I have a course in the morning and another one in the afternoon."

The cousins said good-bye and hurried to the car.

"This whole thing is getting pretty weird," Bess commented.

"I'm beginning to think Cliff lost his memory on purpose," George said.

"What? You think he's faking?" Bess replied. "I don't believe it."

"I don't either, really, but that doesn't mean it isn't possible. After all, he could be in serious trouble and need a place to hide out."

"I can think of nicer places than a hospital," Bess remarked.

"True, but maybe he was trying to escape when he fell. The next thing he knew he was in the hospital. Since he didn't want anyone to know who or where he was, he conveniently forgot his name."

"I still don't believe it."

"Well, it's just a thought," George replied.

The girls said little else until they reached Rosemont, where they went to Cliff's room promptly. A curtain had been pulled around his bed and Lisa was talking with a doctor.

"Where's Nancy?" Bess asked when Lisa had finished her conversation.

"She went to see Dr. Anderson," Lisa said with evident concern in her voice.

The cousins glanced at the curtain.

"Is Cliff all right?"

"Yes, he is now," the nurse replied. "But an hour ago he started screaming and choking."

Had the bearded stranger returned to attack Cliff again? the girls wondered.

6

Harpist's Predicament

"What happened?" Bess asked anxiously.

"Did that bearded guy—" George started to say when Nancy dashed toward them.

"Cliff had a terrible nightmare," she said, pulling the girls away from the young man's door.

"Oh, thank goodness it wasn't anything more serious than that," Bess said.

"Even so, Cliff needs to be in a different environment," Nancy remarked. "Dr. Anderson agrees."

"Is Cliff well enough to be moved?" George asked Lisa.

"That's up to the doctor."

"Even if he can leave," Bess said, "where would he go?"

"To my house," Nancy said. "Hannah will see that he eats three full meals every day—"

"If that doesn't bring back his memory, nothing will!" Bess laughed.

"And speaking of losing things," Nancy said, suddenly remembering the girls' mission downtown, "do you have Cliff's ring?"

The cousins gulped. That was the inevitable question they had been dreading.

"No, I'm afraid not," George said. She explained all that had happened, ending with their visit to Oberon College.

Nancy listened in shock. "That was our only clue to Cliff's identity," she said anxiously.

"I know it doesn't help to say we're sorry," Bess replied.

"But we are. We really are," George added.

Nancy slipped her arms around the girls' shoulders. "Don't worry about it. You're not easily fooled, so the impersonator must be a pretty slick character," she said, catching sight of Cliff's doctor down the hallway. "Excuse me a moment. I must talk to Dr. Anderson."

She hurried toward him, and after several minutes of conversation, rejoined her friends.

"He wants to keep Cliff here until after lunch tomorrow," she announced, "but after that,

Cliff will belong to the Drew family!"

"I wonder how Ned will feel about that," George mumbled.

"There isn't a jealous bone in Ned's body," Nancy replied confidently. "I'll tell him everything tonight."

But when she reached home later that afternoon, she admitted she wasn't only worried about the whereabouts of Cliff's ring. She was also reconsidering the wisdom of her new plan. After all, Cliff was only a few years older than Ned, and Ned had often complained that she spent less time with him than solving mysteries. The fact that this one happens to involve a young, handsome man could be the last straw, Nancy thought.

Her father, however, disagreed with her conclusion. "After all, our house probably is the safest place for Cliff," he said.

So when Ned arrived, Nancy announced her news cheerfully.

"Is something wrong?" she asked him, watching his buoyant smile shrink.

Ned shook his head. "We're running late," he said, "and I don't want to break any speed limits on the way to the theater."

"'Bye, everybody," Nancy said as they darted

to Ned's car. As she buckled her seat belt, she remarked, "Dad thinks Cliff will be much better off at our house than in the hospital."

"Guess so," Ned answered crisply.

He said little else, however, until they reached the theater, where several neighbors of the Drews greeted Nancy. Other townspeople, mostly members of the municipal board, stared coldly at her.

"Is it my imagination," Ned said, "or did the mayor and his wife just snub you?"

"Yes, they did," Nancy replied, feeling immediately uncomfortable. "But if you noticed, I smiled at them anyway. I'll explain later."

As the couple walked down to the front of the hall, they heard a rising murmur behind them. The mayor's wife was adjusting her summer shawl and leaning forward to talk to a councilman's wife. She, in turn, hissed back in a loud whisper. Nancy knew they were talking about her father.

"Can't you tell me what's going on now?" Ned said in a low voice.

"No—" was all the girl could say as musicians filed onstage.

When they were seated, a gray-haired man

with a baton went quickly to the podium, causing a round of applause that grew louder as a young, red-haired woman took her place at the gleaming harp downstage.

Ned glanced at the program. The first piece featuring Angela Pruett, the harp soloist, was "Introduction and Allegro" by Maurice Ravel.

"This is going to be even more interesting than I thought," Ned teased Nancy.

When the harpist began to play, however, the strings of the instrument squawked like a flock of birds, each one singing off-key!

"What's going on?" Ned whispered to Nancy.

"I don't know," she said, "and apparently no one on stage does either."

The orchestra stopped playing as the conductor and harpist exchanged puzzled frowns and a few words.

"We are terribly sorry, ladies and gentlemen," the conductor announced to the audience, "but Miss Pruett's harp seems to be badly out of tune. We will continue our program with the next selection and perform 'Introduction and Allegro' after intermission."

Nancy leaned toward Ned. "Strange, very

strange," she said. "That instrument should have been tuned and checked before the concert began."

"Maybe someone tampered with it," Ned replied mysteriously.

That's exactly what Nancy was thinking. But why would anyone want to ruin the performance?

She was tempted to go backstage during intermission, but decided to wait until the end of the performance. To her delight, the rest of it went beautifully and uneventfully.

"I really enjoyed it," Ned told Nancy as her eyes drifted to the musicians leaving the stage.

"That makes me very happy," she replied, suddenly grabbing Ned's hand.

"Gee, if I knew that's all I had to say—"

"C'mon, let's go," Nancy interrupted quickly. "I want to talk to Miss Pruett."

Ned shook his head disconsolately. "And I thought this was going to be a detective-less evening," he mumbled.

Nancy disregarded the comment as she asked an usher where the stage entrance was.

"Outside and to the left," was the answer.

Without another word, the couple hurried toward the exit. Nancy did not even pay attention to the stares from the mayor and his wife as she passed in front of them. A minute or two more, and she and Ned were climbing a flight of steps to the musicians' room.

"Miss Pruett!" Nancy called out to the young woman when she finally emerged.

The harpist glanced at Nancy with a fearful look in her eyes. "Yes?" she replied.

"I'm Nancy Drew, and this is my friend, Ned Nickerson—"

Noticing the programs in their hands, she asked, "Did you wish an autograph?"

"No—I mean, yes," Ned replied, broadening his smile. He handed her a pen.

The young woman quickly scrawled her name. "You have lovely handwriting," Nancy said.

Nonetheless, she observed a certain stiffness in the curve of the letters. Perhaps the performance had exhausted her, or, Nancy wondered, was she suffering from the strain of what had occurred earlier?

"Miss Pruett, I would like to ask you a few questions, if I may—about—" Nancy began.

"About the humiliating thing that happened to me?" the young woman replied, tears forming in her eyes. "There was no excuse—none!"

Nancy explained that she was an amateur detective who had a particular interest in the music festival because of her father's association with it.

"It seems to us that someone must've deliberately turned all the pegs on your harp," Ned declared.

Miss Pruett blinked her eyes as if trying to push the whole episode out of her mind.

"I appreciate your concern," she said abruptly, "but I'd rather not talk about it now, if you don't mind."

"Will you be here tomorrow?" Nancy inquired.

"Yes, but I can't stay after the performance," the harpist said, adding nervously, "I have some errands to do. Now please excuse me. I must go."

"But—" Nancy said, hoping to persuade her into granting an appointment.

The young woman walked away, however, and disappeared through a door at the end of the hall.

"She obviously doesn't want our help," Ned remarked.

"I have a hunch, though, that she really needs it," Nancy replied.

7

The Sister's Story

"Speaking of help," Ned said, "I could use some myself."

"You could?" Nancy replied, suddenly shifting her eyes to his.

He sighed, allowing the bewildered expression on Nancy's face to grow into curiosity.

"Don't keep me in suspense, Ned," the girl detective said as they headed for the car.

But the boy was savoring the attention. "I'd rather you tell me all your news." Ned chuckled.

"That's not a fair answer," Nancy said, somewhat hurt. "After all, we're supposed to be friends, and you're practically saying you don't want my help."

"I didn't say that at all," Ned retorted, suddenly wishing he had never started the conversation.

Nancy, in turn, settled into silence until they reached the newly opened diner.

"You might as well have said it," she murmured finally.

"And you're making a mountain out of a molehill," Ned said, turning off the ignition.

The girl suddenly buried her face in her hands. "I'm sorry," she said. "I guess I just overreacted because of Dad."

"I don't understand," Ned said. "What do I have to do with your father?"

"You don't. It's just that he doesn't want me to help him either."

"Let's go inside and order something," Ned suggested. "Then you can tell me everything."

"Okay," Nancy replied in a soft voice, and for a few moments she forgot her troubles as they entered the diner.

Counters and booths glistened against panels of beveled mirrors, and a string of colorful Tiffany lamps hung from the ceiling, transporting the couple to a bygone era.

"Some place," Ned remarked as they slid into a booth.

"You can say that again," Nancy said, opening the tall menu that had been handed to her.

Her eyes traveled down the length of unusual fare. "How about a Tango Fandango?" She giggled. "That's only five scoops of ice cream with melba sauce, coconut, chopped nuts, raisins, and whipped cream!"

When the waitress came to take their orders, however, both settled for simple hot fudge sundaes and tea.

Nancy then related the conversation she had had with her father earlier in the evening.

"But your dad would never do anything underhanded," Ned said, when Nancy finished talking.

"He mentioned that things had been happening to the Jansen troupe. He didn't say what, though."

"He also told you not to get involved."

Nancy lowered her eyes away from Ned as he continued to look at her. He had never seen the girl so obviously distraught.

"I just can't let people say such terrible things about Dad," she said. "I know he wants me to stay out of it, but I can't."

As she spoke, the waitress brought the sundaes. Nancy spooned a bit of the mountainous whipped cream into her cup, stirring it more than necessary.

"Listen, Nancy, if you want me to help you in any way," Ned said, "I will. But I'd also like to say I don't think you ought to go against your father's wishes."

"Well, Dad said he didn't want anything to happen to me. That was his main concern," Nancy pointed out. "But if you're with me, I'm bound to be all right."

The young collegian blushed and dug his spoon deeper into the ice cream, catching some of the fudge sauce that floated in the bowl.

When they were almost finished, Nancy grinned mysteriously. "You said you needed help on something," she began to say.

"Oh, yeah—well, it's nothing really," Ned stumbled in embarrassment. "I was just trying to send a little of your attention my way."

"Oh, I see," Nancy said as her companion went on.

"Now that we have this big investigation ahead of us, I'll be too busy to feel sorry for myself."

"Have I been that neglectful?" Nancy asked sheepishly.

The young man smiled in response, but

chose not to pursue the subject. It was after eleven o'clock, and he suggested they leave. When they reached the Drew home, however, they were surprised to see a visitor in the light of the living room window.

"It's Angela Pruett, and she's talking to Dad!" Nancy exclaimed.

She and Ned darted toward the front door that had been left unlocked. They stepped inside, aware of a sudden hush in the conversation.

"Is that you, Nancy?" Mr. Drew called out.

"And Ned," she replied, walking into the room. She smiled pleasantly at the harpist.

"I gather you all met at the performance this evening," the attorney commented.

"I was hoping we would see you again," Nancy told the harpist.

The musician leaned back in her chair and closed her eyes momentarily.

"Miss Pruett has been trying to find her sister for several days," Mr. Drew revealed. "It seems she went on some sort of spiritual retreat last weekend, but never returned."

"Where was the retreat being held?" Nancy inquired.

"Somewhere in the hills outside of River

Heights," the harpist replied. "I don't know exactly. Phyllis is very interested in Transcendental Meditation."

"We didn't realize you were from River Heights, Miss Pruett," Ned commented.

"I'm not. And please call me Angela," the harpist said. "As I told your father, Nancy, I took the festival job because I wanted to see my sister again. She ran away from home last year, and it was only a month ago that she wrote to me. She begged me, though, not to tell anyone where she was.

"The minute I had her address, I scouted around for some way to spend the summer here. Of course, I was hoping to convince her to come home before I left River Heights. She's not quite seventeen yet."

"Has she been living at the retreat?" Nancy asked.

"No. According to her letter, she took a room in someone's house. I believe it belonged to their son, but he's away at school now. I called Mrs. Flannery the minute I arrived. She said that Phyllis hadn't been home all weekend.

"I contacted the police, but they don't have any leads," Angela Pruett went on. "When I met you tonight, I realized that maybe I needed to hire a private detective, and I was wondering—"

Nancy's face broke into a soft smile. "I'm afraid you can't hire me, Angela," she said.

"Then you won't help me?"

"On the contrary. I will help you, but I won't if you insist upon paying me."

"We'll find your sister," Ned said confidently.

"That's right," Nancy joined in, slipping her arm into his. "We'll start tomorrow."

But as she made the commitment, she thought of Cliff, the missing ring, her hospital work, and Tommy Johnson. Somehow, she would have to make time for everything!

Ned called her early in the morning. "What's our schedule today?" he asked cheerfully. "I mean, are you ready for a hike in the hills of River Heights?"

Nancy laughed. "Maybe after I hike the halls of Rosemont Hospital!" she said. "I'm supposed to bring Cliff home—to our house, that is."

There was dead silence at the other end of the line, then Ned cleared his throat. "Well, when would that be?" he asked.

"Oh, probably around one o'clock."

In the back of Nancy's mind was a visit to Dr. DeNiro's office at Oberon College. But she refrained from mentioning it, since she would have to find out the professor's schedule before making an appointment to see him.

"Ned, would you like to come by about two?" Nancy said.

"Okay," he said with renewed enthusiasm. "For a minute there, I thought you were going to back out on our plans for today."

"Me? Never!" she said. "See you later." She then called Bess and George to fill them in on the events of the night before.

Their mothers, they said, were going shopping and had invited the girls to accompany them.

"I didn't want to disappoint Mom," Bess said. "Neither did George. But if you need us—"

"Don't give it a second thought," Nancy insisted. She told them of her plans for the day, adding that by the end of it she would be in touch again. "That is, unless Ned and I get lost!"

The morning at the hospital seemed to fly. Tommy Johnson had made considerable progress, and in between small errands, Nancy would stop in to see him. On her last visit, she brought him a big picture book filled with riddles.

"These are funny, Nancy," the young patient said, giggling at the pictures.

"Hickory dickory dock," Nancy said, pointing to the first one, "the mouse ran up the clock. The clock struck one and down he came. Hickory dickory dock."

"What time is it now?" Tommy asked.

"It's not quite twelve-thirty."

"Then the mouse has thirty minutes to go," he laughed.

"And so do I," Nancy said, ruffling the boy's hair. "I'll see you tomorrow."

She darted down the corridor and took the elevator to Cliff's floor. He had recovered from the episode of the day before and was fully dressed, waiting for someone to bring a wheelchair in which to take him downstairs.

"I'm so grateful to you," he said, "but I hope this won't be an imposition on you and your father."

"Nonsense," Nancy remarked. "You need to be in a different environment."

"I need some fresh air, too," he said, as the

pungent odor of antiseptics floated down the hall.

The girl detective had deliberately not said anything about the Drews' concern for the young man's safety. Why compound his anxiety? she thought.

When they finally arrived at the Drew house, Cliff seemed almost happy. Although he still felt somewhat weak, he greeted Hannah enthusiastically. She and Nancy showed him to his room, where he sank into a chair.

"You rest now until dinner," the housekeeper suggested, closing the door quietly.

Nancy briefly explained that she would be gone most of the afternoon but would make certain to be back before six.

"Where have I heard that before?" Hannah said.

"From me, of course." Nancy grinned.

She changed into her oldest jeans and a long-sleeved shirt, then answered a call from Angela Pruett, who was just leaving for a performance.

"Ned's coming over soon and we're going to try to find that retreat," Nancy told her.

"Then I'm glad I caught you. One thing I did

today was to reread Phyllis's letter. She described the retreat a little bit. Apparently it's near a large la—"

Suddenly the line went dead. They had been cut off! Nancy clicked the receiver several times, but nothing happened. She redialed, but got only a busy signal.

"I'll call the operator, she said to herself, and dialed zero.

"I will place the call for you and credit your previous call," the operator said in a matter-of-fact tone. "We regret the inconvenience."

Nancy hung on the phone, anxiously waiting to hear Angela's voice again.

"I am sorry." It was the operator again. "That number is out of order."

Now what? Nancy wondered. She had just missed hearing possible clues to the location of the retreat!

8

Tangled Trail

As Nancy stood by the telephone in the Drew hallway, her eyes darted to the figure hurrying up the driveway. She pulled open the door and let the warm breeze sweep inside.

"Hi, Ned!" Nancy cried. The glaze of disappointment disappeared from her face temporarily.

"All set?" he replied with a quick glance at her loafers. "If I were you, I'd put on sneakers for this trip."

"You're right—I guess," Nancy said with a faraway look.

"Is something bothering you?" Ned asked.

That was enough to make the girl detective

give a detailed account of what had just occurred. "I'm positive Angela was about to mention the name of some lake when we were cut off," Nancy said. "If only she weren't tied up at the theater now—"

"All we have to do is look at a large map of River Heights," Ned interrupted, following the girl into the house.

"I wish," Nancy said in an unhappy tone. "Do you have any idea how many lakes there are in this area?"

Ned shrugged. "A hundred?"

"No, not a hundred, but there are at least three or four big ones. It'll take days to scout each one."

"So?"

"So—we don't have that much time," Nancy went on. "Every day we spend searching for Phyllis Pruett will be one less spent helping Cliff find out who he is."

The girl's voice rippled a little, causing Ned to set his hands on her shoulders. "The important thing is that Cliff has a home now," he said gently.

Nancy lifted her face in a smile and sighed. "Guess I'm just a bit edgy these days."

Ned did not comment, but he sensed that Mr. Drew's trouble with the townspeople of River Heights was the source of Nancy's continuing distress. She hurried upstairs to change her shoes, pausing on the landing long enough to call down to Ned.

"How many lakes do you think we can cover by midnight?" She grinned.

"At least a dozen." Ned chuckled.

When Nancy returned, she was carrying a road map of River Heights.

"This has *everything* on it—even major landmarks like our new shopping mall on Oak Boulevard," Nancy said brightly.

"Does it also show Phyllis's retreat?" Ned teased, watching the map unfurl on the dining room table.

"That would be nice, wouldn't it?" Nancy remarked. She cast a glance at the two bodies of water indicated on either side of a mountain ridge near the River Heights Airport. A third one lay farther south near Castleton.

"They always say to try and kill two birds with one stone," Ned quipped.

"So we'll start with these two first," Nancy said, pointing to Swain Lake and Green Pond.

In less than an hour, the couple was following a steep road that led to the latter. At the top of the hill they found a lookout point where they stopped the car.

"There it is—Green Pond!" Nancy exclaimed as she gazed at a shimmer of greenish-blue water below that spread out fish-like behind an outcrop.

"See anything that looks like a retreat?" Ned asked.

"No, but there's a little bunch of stores at the bottom of this road," Nancy observed, "and people who visit the retreat do need supplies once in a while."

"Right on," Ned said as they leaped back into the car.

First stop was a delicatessen that offered an array of salads, cold cuts, and household items. The twosome were of only moderate interest to the few people standing in line at the counter. As soon as the customers left the store, Nancy spoke to the clerk, asking if he knew of any retreat in the area.

"Can't say that I do," he replied immediately, then pursed his lips. "But I have heard of something like that over on Swain Lake."

A surge of excitement pulsed through the girl. "Do you know where it is exactly?" Nancy asked.

"No, I don't, but you might take a ride over there. Someone's bound to be able to tell you."

"Thanks a lot!" the couple exclaimed, dashing outside.

"See, I told you we'd find it just like that," Ned said, snapping his fingers.

"It almost seems too easy," Nancy replied.

As they rode through the countryside, Nancy kept her eyes on the landscape, thinking that by chance she might glimpse a house or perhaps a hotel that had been converted into a retreat. All she saw, however, was an elderly man working in a garden carved out of the woodsy hillside.

"According to the map, Swain Lake should be no more than a few miles on the other side of the ridge," Ned remarked. Almost immediately, he spotted a road sign in the distance. "Maybe that's it."

He pressed down on the accelerator and within a few seconds reached the entrance to a motel lodge. Several cars were parked outside, and a young couple with two small children, an assortment of suitcases, and fishing gear emerged from one.

"Which way to the lake?" Nancy called out to the visitors.

"Down there," the man said, pointing to a trail behind the lodge.

Ned was eager to investigate, but Nancy suggested they inquire further.

"Who knows, maybe someone in the lodge can tell us exactly where the retreat is," Nancy said, "and save us a long walk."

"Not to mention a romantic hike through weeds," Ned concurred as he noticed a tangle of overgrowth along the trail.

The lodge was as rustic inside as it was outside. Gingham curtains hung on the windows, and there were straw rugs on the old floor that creaked under the visitors' feet as they approached the hotel desk. The young couple whom they had spoken to earlier had just finished registering, and the clerk glanced briefly at Nancy and Ned.

"May I help you?" he asked pleasantly, causing Nancy to explain the reason they were in the area.

When she finished speaking, her listener said, "I moved here only a little while ago. But let me ask one of the fellows in the back office. He may know about the retreat."

As he excused himself, the couple took advantage of the time to look at the handful of people seated around the lobby. All were dressed casually, with the exception of one man who was in a business suit. But as the desk clerk returned with a co-worker, the man disappeared upstairs.

"This is Mr. Keshav Lal," the clerk said by way of introduction. The man's mocha complexion, large, brown eyes, and name suggested to Nancy that he was probably from India.

"You are looking for Ramaswami?" Lal inquired.

"I don't know, am I?" Nancy said in surprise. Her heart was thumping fast as she realized that she was on the brink of an important discovery!

"Yes, we are," Ned said, seizing the information instantly. "Where can we find Mr. Ramaswami?"

"We call him Swami," Lal corrected. He laughed quietly. "But I'm afraid that is all I can tell you."

"I don't understand," Nancy said, adding, "If you attend his retreat, you must—"

Before Nancy could finish the sentence,

however, the man in the business suit suddenly reappeared. He leaned over the counter, tapping his fingers in irritation.

"My calls have been disconnected at least twice," he complained to the desk clerk.

"I'm sorry, Mr. Flannery."

Flannery! That was the name of the woman whom Phyllis Pruett had been staying with. Were the two related?

For an instant, Nancy glanced at him. There was a familiarity about his face, but she couldn't place it.

"Excuse me," she said, addressing the man. "I'm looking for a girl by the name of Phyllis Pruett. I believe she's been living with people named Flannery—"

"Don't know her," he said abruptly, letting Mr. Lal resume his conversation with the girl.

"Give me your name first, please," he said.

"I'm Nancy Drew, and this is my friend, Ned Nickerson."

As Nancy spoke, Lal flashed his eyes away from her at someone else—Flannery, perhaps.

"Now will you tell us where the swami is?" she asked, pretending not to have noticed Lal's reaction to her.

"By all means. You will find a large cabin at the foot of these woods near the lake," the man said. "There is a trail—"

"I think we saw it," Ned interrupted.

"Well, it is a fairly long walk—almost a mile."

"In that case, we ought to get going," she told Ned, adding as they left, "Don't look back, but that guy Flannery is watching us."

"And don't look ahead either," Ned remarked, "'cause the sky's about to burst wide open."

"It's not going to rain!" Nancy said. "Come on, I'll race you to the lake!"

The couple darted toward the trail that had buried itself in an overgrowth of vines and almost disappeared entirely. Now and then they paused to glance down the slope of trees, waiting for a glimpse of the cabin retreat.

"I hope we're on the right track," Ned said as he felt a drizzle of water on his neck. "Because if we're not, we're in for a flood."

"Oh, Ned, it's only a light sprinkle," Nancy insisted, but, as the boy had predicted, in less than a minute rain began to pour.

It tore leaves and small branches off the trees, obscuring the trail and the hikers' vision. How much farther did they have to go?

"Let's turn back!" Ned shouted through the torrential rain.

Nancy, who was ahead of him, said something in reply, but Ned did not hear it. He hung back, ready to head for the lodge again and hoping Nancy would follow. She plunged deeper into the woods, however, glancing around only for a second.

The rainwater had seeped through Ned's clothes. "Where are you going?" Nancy cried out.

"Back to the motel," Ned said. "Come on!"

But the girl detective was determined to stay on the path to the lake. What difference did it make if she got wetter? She was already soaked to the skin.

Reluctantly, Ned yielded and trekked after her. The rain let up in spurts, and finally the couple reached a small clearing at the edge of the woods.

"That must be the place!" Nancy exclaimed when a cabin came into view.

She raced forward, feeling a chill in her bones, while Ned observed a woman peering through the window in the door. The light behind her suddenly went out and she pulled the shade down.

9

Cabin Captive

As Nancy and Ned leaped up the steps, Nancy dived for the cabin door, pounding on it with her fists.

"Hello-o," she cried, ignoring the drawn shade.

"If this is supposed to be a popular retreat," Ned said, "there sure doesn't seem to be much activity around here."

"Maybe everybody's meditating," Nancy suggested.

But as she spoke, the doorknob turned and opened, revealing the woman again.

"I don't want no more people staying here," she snapped.

Nancy told her that they were looking for Ramaswami.

"Who?" the woman asked.

"The swami," Ned repeated. "Do you know of him?"

"Not personally. But a bunch of people got turned away from his place because it was full up, so they came here."

"When was this?" Nancy inquired.

"Last weekend," the woman said. "They stayed here one night. Paid me, of course, but what a mess they left—dirty dishes everywhere."

"Where exactly is the swami's retreat?" Ned questioned.

"Stay on that trail," the woman replied, pointing to an opening in the woods behind the cabin. "You can't miss it, and when you see Mr. Swami, tell him I don't want any more visitors!"

She closed the door on Nancy and Ned. The rain had ended, leaving puddles of water in the softened earth which the couple now treaded across. The warming rays of the sun that began to emerge penetrated their wet clothes, making their clothing more tolerable as they walked in the woods.

"Are you with me?" Nancy said to Ned in a half-teasing voice.

"What do you think?" came the reply.

"Well, for a minute there I thought—" But Nancy did not have a chance to finish talking.

There was a scuffle of feet and the sound of branches breaking, which caused her to halt quickly.

In that split second before she could see what had happened to Ned, hands grabbed her waist and a scarf saturated with a strange honey-sweet fluid was stuffed in her mouth. She yanked her body forward, struggling to free herself, but the pungent odor soon overwhelmed her and Nancy fell limp against her attackers.

Meanwhile, Bess and George had finished their shopping excursion a bit earlier than they had anticipated.

"Why don't we pay a visit to Cliff?" Bess suggested to her cousin. "I'm sure he'd like to have some company."

George agreed, and after the girls dropped off their mothers at home, they headed for the Drew house. When they rang the doorbell, however, Hannah did not answer it.

"That's odd," George commented.

"Maybe Hannah went shopping, too," Bess replied.

"Even so, I'm surprised Cliff doesn't hear the bell," George said. "Of course, he could be sleeping."

As the girls headed for the driveway again, they saw Hannah Gruen coming up the walk with a shopping cart filled with groceries.

"I told you so." Bess giggled and called out to the housekeeper. "We just stopped by to see Cliff."

"Oh, and having done so, you're leaving now, before I've even had a chance to give you a piece of cake," Hannah said, halting the cart.

"On the contrary," Bess replied. "We haven't seen Cliff at all. We rang the bell, but he didn't answer it."

The housekeeper appeared perplexed. "He must still be sleeping."

Everyone stepped inside the hallway. Hannah set her packages down in the kitchen, then went upstairs. Cliff's room was empty!

"Cliff?" she called out.

There was no response.

"Will you girls check downstairs for him,

while I look around up here?" Hannah asked Bess and George.

They darted from room to room, glancing through windows to see if perhaps he had gone outside. They panicked as they realized that the young amnesia victim had disappeared!

"This is terrible, terrible!" Hannah cried. "I wasn't out of this house more than an hour. Oh, what if something has happened to him? It's all my fault!"

The girls tried to comfort the woman, wishing that Nancy were there and wondering what to do next.

"Let's call the police," Bess declared nervously.

"Good idea," George said, dashing to the hall telephone. But she picked it up and put it down instantly. "We shouldn't jump to conclusions," she said. "After all, there's no sign of a break-in anywhere, and Hannah, you locked all the doors before you left, didn't you?"

"Yes—oh, certainly."

"Well, then, it seems to me that Cliff may have simply decided to go for a walk."

Somehow, though, that did not seem likely to Bess.

"I suggest we wait a little while before calling the police," George went on.

"But what if you're wrong?" Bess replied anxiously.

"If I'm wrong, then I'm wrong."

"That's the craziest logic I ever heard," Bess said, racing to the telephone.

"Okay, suit yourself," George said, stepping away from her cousin. "But you're going to feel really foolish when Cliff walks in the door."

Hannah, in the meantime, had paid little attention to the banter between the girls. She sat frozen in her chair, hearing Nancy's earlier request repeat itself in her mind.

"No matter what," the girl detective had told the housekeeper, "please don't leave Cliff alone while I'm gone today."

But the refrigerator needed replenishment and Hannah had attended to the errand as quickly as she could, when she was unable to persuade the local store to make a delivery.

"The police are coming over right away," Bess said now, drawing Hannah out of her stupor.

"Thank goodness," she answered vaguely. "Someone must find Cliff before Nancy comes home."

The young detective, however, lay bound on the damp floor of a cabin, near an old iron stove. The odor of mildew that cloyed the air had replaced that of the insidious drug, and Nancy's eyes flickered open.

She was at once aware of the sweet, antiseptic taste in her mouth and the fact that the scarf had been removed. She lifted her head, then let it sink back as a dull ache thudded through her skull.

Where am I? And where's Ned? she wondered dizzily.

The log ceiling dripped water now, sprinkling Nancy's face unevenly and causing her to slide out from under the leak. As she moved, she noticed something dark and slippery crawling over a crack in the floor. It was moving slowly, steadily toward her. A water snake!

Completely helpless, she shrieked in horror, but the sound caught in her throat and she continued to drag herself away from the creature.

"Oh!" Nancy cried as the viper raised its head, poised for a venomous strike.

Instantly, the girl swung her knees up, catching the rubber soles of her sneakers in a loose floorboard. To her amazement, it popped up and made the crack split wider. The snake plunged forward, tumbling into the pit of earth below.

Despite her relief, Nancy shivered, gazing through a rain-spattered window overhead. The sky was dark now, and even if she could loosen the rope around her wrists and ankles, she wondered if she could escape.

Her log prison was surrounded by tall trees, and without the benefit of the sun, she had no idea where she was nor how she could find her way to Swain Lake Lodge.

The other, more troubling thought was, What had happened to her friend, Ned Nickerson? Where had their abductors taken him?

I have to find Ned! I must! Nancy thought with determination.

10

Ned's Rescue

At the same time, Bess and George were talking with a young policeman in the Drew living room. Although the River Heights Police Department had a description of Cliff on file, the officer requested additional information.

"Since the young man has been staying here," the officer said, "has he undergone any physical changes?"

"Hardly," Hannah remarked from a corner chair. "He came here only today."

"Oh, I see," the policeman said, clearing his throat. "Well, did he say anything at all that might give a clue to where he went? Judging merely from the looks of things, I'd say he might have left voluntarily."

George flashed an I-told-you-so glance at her cousin.

"Do you suppose he could have gone back to the hospital for some reason?" Bess suggested.

"Now why would he do that?" George muttered.

As she spoke, the policeman was examining a spot on the carpet which the others had overlooked near the entranceway.

"Chloroform," he said crisply.

His listeners gasped. "Then Cliff was kidnapped!" Bess exclaimed.

"But the front door was locked when we got here," George pointed out.

"Maybe Cliff recognized the person and let him in," Hannah put in.

"Or maybe—" the policeman said, heading for the back door. Bess and the others trailed after him. "Just as I thought," the young officer concluded. He pointed to a hole in the kitchen screen door.

The cousins now stepped outside, pinning their eyes to the ground for footprints.

"There! Look there!" George cried as prints loomed from the driveway. They traveled across the dampened grass to the back steps.

"He must've been very tall," Bess said, observing the long stride and large footprints.

While the mystery of Cliff's disappearance had not been resolved, Nancy, too, was seeking an answer to freedom. She twisted her arms, causing the rope to cut into her wrists, but steeled herself against the pain, looking for something, anything with which to sever the rope.

There! she gasped, spotting a thick nail that protruded from the base of the wall. It wasn't much, but it might work!

The young captive pulled close, hooking the rope over the iron head. Back and forth she rubbed the twine, hoping to wear down the strong threads, but they held firm.

I'll never get out of here! Nancy moaned.

Her arms ached now, and she lay back against the wall, intending to relax only for a minute, but instead falling fast asleep. When she awoke, two birds were chirping on the window ledge above and the sky had begun to lighten.

Morning had come, and Nancy had lost precious time in her search for Ned. Although the hours of rest had given her renewed energy, her body felt stiff and she longed for freedom even more.

Again she worked on the rope, stopping only when she heard the sound of footsteps outside the cabin.

Was it her captor? the girl wondered.

Panic-stricken, she froze and quietly lifted the rope off the nail.

Who is it? she thought anxiously as the door creaked open, revealing muddy sneakers and blue jeans.

"Ned!" she cried happily.

"Nancy, are you all right?" he asked immediately.

As Nancy spouted several questions, Ned began cutting the rope at her feet with a penknife. The rope binding Nancy's wrists did not sever so easily, but after several minutes of steady pressure, it, too, came free.

"Your wrists—" Ned murmured when he saw the deep red bruises.

"I'm fine," Nancy insisted, even though she felt a twinge of pain. "Really I am, Ned."

But the boy suspected otherwise.

"Forget me. Tell me what happened to you," the girl went on. She got to her feet slowly, with Ned's help.

"They dumped me in another shelter a few yards from here," he said, adding, "I still have a throbbing headache from the chloroform."

"They must've given you an extra dose," Nancy commented. "I didn't see who the men were. Did you?"

"Nope, and so far as I know they never came to check on me."

Nancy paused momentarily as they stepped outside into the sunlight. "I just don't get it—why us?" she said.

"Maybe someone doesn't want us to find the retreat," Ned suggested, a thought that had occurred to Nancy as well.

"But why?" she repeated. "Retreats are places for quiet and meditation, not for trouble."

Nancy linked her arm into Ned's, leaning on him until the stiffness in her legs had passed. Although she would have liked to continue the hunt for the swami's retreat, she knew that she must get home quickly. The Drew household would have realized Nancy had not come home and they would be frantic.

"How far do you think we are from the lodge?" the girl asked Ned.

"I have no idea, but my guess is that we're at least a mile away."

The thought of the long trudge back through

the same tangled woods made Nancy groan. But as the sun's warmth enveloped her again, she smiled.

"At least we don't have to swim through another flood," she remarked, letting Ned lead the way when the trail narrowed to a thin footpath.

By the time they reached the lodge, they realized that they had returned along a different route. But where it lay in relation to the one they had taken the day before remained a mystery.

"I wonder if there's a road to the retreat," the young detective said as they headed for the car. "Maybe I ought to ask Mr. Lal." And without giving Ned a chance to reply, she raced into the building.

There were different clerks on duty, however, and when she asked for the Indian man, she was informed that he was not in and wouldn't be back for a few days.

Nancy returned to the car, reporting the little she had learned.

"Don't worry," Ned said. "We'll track that retreat down eventually."

"I hope so," Nancy replied. She lapsed into

silence, saying no more on the subject until they were inside the Drew home. Then, before Hannah or Mr. Drew could reveal their news, the couple spilled out their story in detail.

"By the way, where's Cliff?" Nancy inquired when she finished speaking.

"Oh, Nancy, please don't blame me," Hannah pleaded, causing the girl's face to close in fear.

"Has something happened to him?" she asked.

"We don't know," Mr. Drew replied.

"He's been kidnapped!" Hannah blurted out. "Someone came in while I went food shopping and took him!"

The woman fixed her eyes steadily on the girl. "Bess and George were here, too, when we found out he was missing. We called the police right away."

As the reality of what had occurred sank in, Nancy sat down next to her father. "This is awful," she said. "I should never have left the house."

"Nothing else was taken," Hannah remarked.

"Only Cliff," Nancy murmured dejectedly.

The housekeeper bit her lips as a rim of tears

developed in her eyes. "Excuse me, every-body," she said, and left the room.

"Maybe I should go too," Ned said. "I'll call you later, Nancy."

The girl stared at her father for some offer of advice. "I don't know what to suggest, dear," he said. "I'm sure the police will find Cliff."

"But he was our responsibility, Dad," Nancy answered.

She telephoned Bess and George, and after they agreed to meet her for lunch at a down-town restaurant, Nancy decided to talk with the Drews' neighbors.

To her delight, she learned that the son of one couple had noticed a car speeding away from the Drew home the previous afternoon.

"Cool car," the boy said. "Stripes and every-thing."

"Did you notice the license plate?" Nancy asked excitedly.

"I noticed *everything*," he said, repeating the number. "197-MAP."

By now, Nancy's heart was pounding as she wondered if the vehicle was the one she had seen at Rosemont Hospital and the one that might have caused Tommy Johnson's accident!

She raced back to her house and telephoned the information to the police, who promptly fed it into a computer. It was only a matter of minutes before the girl had an answer.

"We have traced the owner of the car," the officer reported. "His name is Dev Singh. He lives near the river."

Nancy quickly jotted down the address, eager to reveal the discovery to her friends.

What intrigued her most, however, was the man's name. Was he from India? If so, might he be the man who had accompanied the bearded stranger to Mr. Jhaveri's shop?

11

Cancellation!

While Nancy stared at the unusual name she had written on a notepad, she also noticed a bright yellow flier poking through the morning mail on the hall table. It was an announcement from the River Heights Music Festival, which she opened quickly.

"Canceled?" she said, mystified, as her eyes fell on the large stamp mark that obliterated the names of several artist groups, including the Jansen Theater Troupe, which was scheduled to perform that evening.

I wonder if Dad knows about this, the girl detective thought.

Carson Drew, however, had already left for a business appointment, and the only way she could get some answers was to go to the River

Heights Theater herself. Taking a quick glance at her watch, she pocketed the flier and dashed to her car.

It was no surprise to Nancy when she arrived that at least thirty ticket holders to the festival had begun to descend on the box office. Many of them were carrying the cancellation notice and complaining angrily.

"Excuse me," the girl found herself saying over and over as she weaved through the crowd now queuing up into long lines.

"Hey, kid," one man snarled at Nancy when she stepped in front of him. "Where do you think you're going? I was here first."

"I only want to find out where the manager is," Nancy insisted.

"Don't we all," he replied, as a tall, angular man strode into view.

"Ladies and gentlemen, I am Mr. Hillyer, the manager," he said, "and I want you to know that none of the performances have been canceled. The notice is a mistake—"

"I'll say it was!" one irritated woman cut in loudly, causing the people around her to echo the complaint.

"Please—please. Let me explain," the manager replied. He raised his hand, signaling the crowd to be quiet. "Your tickets will be honored at every performance. Nothing has been canceled. Believe me."

Somebody must've gotten hold of the festival's mailing list and sent that announcement just to stir up trouble, Nancy concluded.

She waited for the crowd to disperse, then approached the manager.

"I'm Carson Drew's daughter," she said brightly, watching the man's relaxed demeanor fade.

Had the ill will of some of the townspeople toward the attorney filtered down to the festival management?

"What can I do for you?" the manager answered coolly.

"Well, I was wondering if you had any idea about the person who sent that cancellation notice."

"Why don't you ask your father?" the man snapped, and before Nancy could come to her father's defense, he excused himself.

Now, more than ever, she was determined to vindicate the Drew name.

All the way to the restaurant where she was to meet George and Bess, the girl constructed her next move. When they were all finally seated at a vacant table, Bess's eyes sparkled.

"You're awfully happy today," Nancy commented.

Bess shook her head excitedly, while George smiled pleasantly. Had the cousins made some important discovery? Nancy wondered.

"Don't keep me in suspense," she told them. "Did you find Cliff, or do you know where—"

"No, nothing that spectacular," George mumbled.

"But I think we've figured out an ingenious way to find his ring," Bess put in. "Since it's so unusual—"

"And valuable," George added.

"All we have to do is put an ad in the newspaper," her cousin finished.

"But if the guy who ran off with it is a thief, why would he even consider selling it back? I'm sure he's not stupid."

"True, but I bet he's greedy," Bess replied, "and if the reward is tempting enough, he might just fall into the trap."

Nancy half agreed, but was far from convinced and changed the subject momentarily. She brought the girls up to date on everything that had happened so far, ending with the information about Dev Singh.

"Do you have time now to check out his address?" Nancy asked her friends.

"Sure," George said. "Let's go."

The threesome ate their lunch quickly, then headed for Nancy's car, as another idea occurred to Bess.

"Mr. Jhaveri's store isn't far from here," she noted. "I'd like to find out what he thinks Cliff's ring is worth."

So the girls changed direction and walked a few blocks up the street. There were only four customers inside the store, and when they dwindled to one lone woman admiring the contents of a display case in the corner, Nancy and the girls spoke to the jeweler.

"How much would you estimate the ring we showed you is worth?" Nancy asked.

"Oh, that's hard to say. The gold itself could bring a handsome price."

"Can't you be more specific?" Bess pressed him.

"Offhand, I'm afraid not. But if you give me a little time to think, I may be able to give you an answer."

As he talked, Nancy thought she detected someone in the office behind the man. But then she realized it was only an unframed photograph that reflected in a wall mirror. She had not paid attention to it on previous visits. This time, however, she found herself transfixed. It was a picture of someone who bore an uncanny resemblance to Keshav Lal!

"Is something wrong?" George whispered to the girl.

"N-no," Nancy said, blinking her eyes in another direction. Then, on impulse, she asked Mr. Jhaveri if he knew Lal.

"He's my cousin," the man remarked with a touch of surprise in his voice. "You know him?"

"I met him at the Swain Lake Lodge," Nancy said, stringing out her thoughts slowly. "It just hit me that you might have some information about the swami's retreat."

Mr. Jhaveri shook his head vigorously. "I've never been there," he said.

"But you are aware of it," Nancy said.

"Yes, of course. Many of us Indians are, but I personally am not a follower of Ramaswami."

Nancy was even tempted to inquire if he knew someone by the name of Dev Singh, but decided not to until she had investigated him further. Instead, she continued her current line of questioning.

"Mr. Lal directed me to a trail," Nancy said, "but I'd bet there's another, easier route."

The man simply shrugged his shoulders, and as the lady customer came forward, he took advantage of the opportunity to escape from the girls.

They left, puzzling over their latest discovery.

"He seemed awfully nervous when you mentioned Lal's name," George told Nancy.

"I know, but why?"

No answer occurred to any of them as they drove to the address which the police said belonged to Dev Singh. When the young detectives reached it, however, they were completely stumped, because standing on the site was not a house or an apartment building, but a place called Hamburger Haven!

"Too bad we already ate lunch," George said, as their car hummed in the driveway.

"And too bad we're not getting anywhere," Bess added with a sigh.

Nancy, too, had secretly begun to feel defeated, but she flashed an optimistic smile at her friends. "I have a hunch there's an answer to this mystery just around the corner!" she exclaimed.

12

Escape Lane

"What makes you so optimistic?" Bess asked Nancy as she backed the car out of the driveway.

"Because I just realized we're on the wrong street." The girl laughed. "Singh's place is on River Lane, not River Drive."

She pointed to the bold green sign that hung a quarter of a mile down the road. There was an exit off the drive for River Lane.

The ride along the water's edge was exhilarating as the girls rolled down the car windows and let the breeze carry in the fresh, sweet smell of grass and wildflowers.

"Wouldn't it be nice to have a picnic down here?" George suggested.

"Why, I can't believe you said that, George Fayne," her cousin teased. "You, a girl who never thinks about food."

"It's a great idea," Nancy interposed, believing they'd all be ready for a celebration when the latest mysteries were solved.

The question was, Would they ever be?

She turned off the drive, jogging onto one street, then another, until she was on River Lane. It curved into the countryside, no houses immediately visible behind fences of hedge and poplar trees. Then, with no forewarning, the road stopped.

"Now what?" Bess said, as Nancy halted the car.

"This is getting to be ridiculous," she remarked unhappily and swung the car around. "I didn't see one house number, did you?"

"Uh-uh," George said.

"Me neither," Bess added, but on the return ride Nancy slowed the car down considerably, pausing at a trail of gravel off the road. "Driveway?" Bess said.

"We'll soon find out," Nancy said, making the sharp turn.

The car dipped into several potholes, which caused Nancy to keep her eyes trained for others and not on the house at the top of the hillock. When they pulled in front of it at last, they all sighed, feeling the ride itself had been an accomplishment.

"It doesn't look like anyone's around," Nancy commented shortly.

"There's no house number, either," Bess said, suddenly feeling queasy. "I don't know if this is such a hot idea, Nancy. I mean, what if Singh does live here and he tries to kidnap us too."

"For one thing, there are three of us and only one of him," George declared.

"How do you know?" her cousin replied.

Undaunted, however, Nancy went boldly up the front steps to ring the doorbell. No one came immediately, and she stood on her toes to glance through the small windowpane at the top of the door.

"This must be Singh's place," she told the others as she stared at a pair of batik wall hangings with Indian motifs.

"Oh, let's get out of here," Bess pleaded, but her listeners did not pay attention.

Nancy cupped her ear against the door, sensing for a moment that she had heard noises from within. Had Singh brought Cliff there?

Had the young man heard the car approaching, and was he struggling to let the visitors know of his imprisonment?

The girl detective was determined to find out!

"We can't just break in," Bess warned, while Nancy skirted the house to a side window, trying to open it.

"But what if Cliff is tied up in there?" Nancy countered.

"Even so, I vote we bring the police back with a search warrant," Bess said.

But as she spoke, they could hear the purr of a car engine at the bottom of the driveway.

"Oh, somebody's coming!" Bess exclaimed nervously. "What'll we do?"

"They'll see us for sure," George said, glancing at Nancy's car.

"C'mon!" Nancy declared, leaping toward it. "Those potholes will slow them down a little bit."

She turned the ignition and pressed the accelerator gently, letting the car roll forward onto a crescent of grass that curved around the far side of the house.

"It's the best I can do for now," the young detective said. She switched off the engine and listened to the sound of the other one growing louder. "You wait here," she told her friends. "I want to see who it is."

"But Nan—" Bess cried fearfully.

Her friend nonetheless stepped out of her car, leaving the door open in case she wanted to dive back in fast, and ran to the high bushes that hugged the front wall. She peered through the thick cover of leaves, listening to two men. They sat talking and, to her relief, did not seem to notice the wheel marks of the car that lay ahead. Their car, she observed quickly, did not match the description of the one her neighbor's son had seen at the Drew home.

Who are they? Nancy wondered as the driver finally appeared. Then, almost instantaneously, his companion slid out into view.

It's the man in the business suit I saw at Swain Lake Lodge! Nancy gasped, suddenly realizing that he and the bearded stranger who had attacked Cliff in the hospital were one and the same! With him was the tall Indian man who had been with him in Mr. Jhaveri's store!

We have to get the police! the girl said to herself.

She darted to the car, telling her friends everything as the men went inside the house.

"But we're stuck!" Bess cried. "And as soon as they realize we're here, we'll be done for, too!"

Nancy, however, had studied the slope of lawn that sprawled alongside the driveway that now held an obstacle—the men's car!

"Hang on!" she said, starting the ignition again, and spun the vehicle across the gravel and down the grassy incline, bypassing the potholes and lurching onto the road.

Bess had closed her eyes in a shiver of fear as Nancy urged the gas pedal.

"There's a public phone on River Drive," George remarked, seeing the glass booth come into view.

Without saying a word, Nancy screeched the car to a halt and leaped out, dialing River Heights police. She told them where she was and where she suspected Cliff was being held captive, then returned to her friends.

"They're on their way," Nancy said, "and they advised me to stay here."

"Thank goodness," Bess replied, still trembling as a patrol car with two officers inside whizzed toward them.

In the driver's seat was the young officer who had gone to the Drews' home when Cliff was reported missing. He signaled Nancy to follow.

When they turned onto River Lane, Nancy flashed her headlights, indicating the gravel driveway several yards ahead. The patrol car slowed down, pitching over the potholes with caution and coming to a halt when they reached the car parked in front of the house. Nancy and the girls pulled in behind them, hurrying after the officers.

"Open up!" the young policeman yelled, knocking hard on the door.

To Nancy's amazement, someone responded immediately. It was the Indian man whom she had seen arrive only moments before.

"Are you Dev Singh?" she asked at once.

"Why no, and I never heard of him." His high cheekbones resolved into deep-set eyes that gaped at Nancy in puzzlement.

"Let me see your identification," the policeman said, prompting the man to pull out an immigration card that bore the name Prem Nath.

"I've been in this country only a short time, so I don't have any credit cards." He chuckled softly.

The other policeman, meantime, flashed a search warrant, saying, "We're looking for a young man who was kidnapped recently."

"And you think I am responsible?" the Indian replied, laughing.

"Where is the man you came with?" George asked.

"What man?"

"His name is Flannery," Nancy said crisply, even though she suspected that it was an alias.

"I don't know what you are talking about. Now please—"

But the officers moved past him, the girls also, and they spread out to look in every room. Flannery was not there, and neither was Cliff! Had Flannery ducked out of the house to hide among the trees? Nancy was tempted to search the grounds, until the police spoke apologetically to the man.

"We're sorry to have troubled you, Mr. Nath," one of the men said, satisfied that he had committed no wrongdoing.

Nancy, however, remained unconvinced. She knew Flannery, or whoever the man was, had taken Cliff's ring. Unfortunately, though, he had escaped capture this time. It was useless to pursue the subject with the police until she had more definite evidence.

"I just don't get it," George said. "The car was registered in Singh's name at this address, but there's a guy named Nath living here."

"Doesn't matter," Bess said. "According to Nancy's neighbor, he saw Singh's car leave the Drew home, but he didn't say Cliff was in it. We assume so, but there's nothing conclusive to prove it."

"Maybe Singh did live at the house at one time, but moved out before his car registration came due for renewal," Nancy added. "Anyway, as you say, Bess, none of this matters a whole lot. We just want to find Cliff."

As she drove toward home, she began to think about Swain Lake Lodge again. What was Flannery doing up there?

13

Technical Attack

By the time the girls reached the parking lot where Bess and George had left their car, they asked Nancy about her plans for the rest of the day.

"As a matter of fact," she said, "I haven't any—"

"I don't believe it," Bess said.

"Other than visiting Tommy, calling Angela Pruett, hunting for Phyllis, and—"

"St-o-p!" George teased, putting her hands over her ears. "Don't you ever take a break?"

"Oh, sure." Nancy laughed. "I was just going to ask if you'd like to see *Oklahoma* tonight? The Jansen Theater Troupe is putting it on."

"I'd love to," Bess said happily, "and maybe Dave would."

"How about the six of us going together?" George put in.

Nancy nodded in agreement, asking the cousins to check with their friends Dave Evans and Burt Eddleton while she called Ned.

"Can you make reservations, too?" she asked the girls.

"No problem," Bess said. "Talk to you later."

"'Bye," Nancy replied, heading her car for Rosemont Hospital and a quick visit with Tommy Johnson.

To her amazement and delight, she found him walking in a leg cast with the aid of crutches.

"You'll be out of here in no time," she said to the little boy.

"I hope so," he declared, smiling. "There's nobody to play with around here."

He lay the crutches against his bed, allowing Nancy to help him up.

"Well, what about me?" she asked, pretending to pout.

"You're different, Nancy," he said. "Everybody else just wants to take my temperature."

The girl laughed, opening a small shopping

bag and peering inside with great relish.

"What's in there?" Tommy said eagerly.

Nancy strung out the surprise until she thought the boy would jump out of bed. "Here you are," the girl said, producing a toy racing car.

"Zowie!" Tommy cried happily. He ran the tiny wheels up and down his cast, then over the mattress, onto the night table, and back again.

Nancy giggled. "I'm sure your doctor never dreamed that cast would turn into a racetrack!"

When she left the boy's room, he was still playing with the car, rumbling like an engine, and laughing in between.

"I'll be back," the girl told him, though she wasn't sure when her next visit would be.

She stopped by the nurses' station to leave a message for Lisa Scotti, and was pleased to find her friend there in person.

"The strangest thing happened this morning," Lisa whispered to Nancy. "We got a phone call from someone who said his name was Cliff."

"You're kidding!" Nancy replied.

"Of course, I was positive it was some crackpot," Lisa went on.

"Why do you say that?"

"Because I knew Cliff was staying at your house."

"Not anymore," Nancy said, revealing the full story.

Lisa was completely shocked, saying she wouldn't have bothered to tell Nancy about the call except that she had stopped by the hospital.

"Oh, Lisa, you must tell me everything that happens if it's pertinent to Cliff's case."

"Now that I think about it," Lisa said, "the voice did sound like Cliff's, but I can't be certain. There was a lot of static in the background."

"What did he say?" Nancy questioned.

"Not much, really, but it had something to do with singing."

"Singing or the name Singh?"

Lisa shrugged. "As I said, the voice wasn't too clear."

If only the young nurse had known about the disappearance, Nancy thought, she might have tried to trace the phone call.

Thinking of missed opportunities, Nancy decided to try contacting Angela Pruett again. The telephone seemed to be working, but the harpist was not home—all the more reason, Nancy mused, why she should attend the performance at the River Heights Theater that night.

Nancy spoke briefly to Ned, who had already heard from the other Emerson boys, and despite a minor problem that had to do with the availability of a car for the evening, everyone had decided to meet at the Drew home.

The sky had thickened with clouds and there was the promise of another rainstorm.

"Don't forget your umbrella, dear," Hannah advised Nancy as the group left, but Ned waved his, a large, black one that could amply cover two people.

When they arrived at the theater, Nancy was struck by the small, scattered audience.

"Where is everybody?" Burt asked.

"Maybe they were afraid to come out in a storm," George said.

"But it isn't even raining yet," her cousin stated.

Nancy, however, surmised that a number of ticket holders had received the cancellation notice and for whatever reasons had not yet called the theater for a refund. If they had, they would have been told the announcement was a hoax!

She thought no more about it, though, as the orchestra filed into the pit. She looked for

Angela, but someone else—another woman—was seated at the harp.

"Where is she?" Ned whispered to Nancy.

"I don't know."

But as the overture swelled, the young detective temporarily pushed her concern to the back of her mind. The medley of tunes was a welcome respite from earlier events of the day, soaring to a climax and dissolving when the curtain opened.

The stage, however, remained pitch-black for several minutes as the first actors entered. Then harsh red lights came on.

"What's going on?" Bess said.

That was what everyone wanted to know. The actors moved mechanically through the scene, saying their lines and singing with as much ease as they could muster. But the red lights turned blue, then amber, and the din of the audience competed against the sound on stage, causing the lead singer to stop in the middle of his number.

"Ladies and gentlemen," he said, as the overhead lights went out abruptly. "House lights, please," he instructed someone offstage.

Nancy slid out of her seat and hurried to the

back of the theater, without waiting to hear the announcement.

"I'm coming with you," Ned whispered.

"No, stay here," Nancy said. "I'll be back in a second."

She darted through the lobby doors, spying another one marked EMPLOYEES ONLY. Did it lead to the sound booth where the technician controlled the sound and lighting systems?

Nancy turned the knob, ready to climb the inside stairway, when a young man bolted out the door. He was no more than twenty and had shoulder-length brown hair that blew off his neck as he ran down the front steps.

"Stop!" Nancy cried. She dashed after him, but her high dress heels slowed her down.

The boy had jumped in a car and roared away in the darkness before she could catch him. Instantly, she hurried back into the theater, racing to the employees' door and up the steps.

"Oh!" she gasped upon seeing a man slumped forward over a board of dials.

Next to him lay a wooden rod that had obviously been used to knock him out!

"What's going on here?" a voice barked behind her. It was the festival manager. Nancy turned sharply, giving him full view of the injured man. "Are you responsible for this, Miss Drew?"

"Me?" Nancy said, aghast. She felt her former irritation, but kept her temper in check and quickly explained what had happened. "He needs a doctor. Excuse me while I find one."

The stream of people prevented Nancy from getting an usher's attention, but as her friends appeared, she made her way toward them.

"Someone attacked the man in the sound and lighting booth," Nancy advised them. "We have to get a doctor for him."

"Is he bleeding?" George asked.

"No, but he's out cold."

Ned raced away from the group, negotiating through the slow-moving crowd to a man in a theater uniform at the far end of the lobby. Briefly, Ned reported the situation and the two of them hurried to a telephone in a rear office.

By the time they emerged again, Nancy had gone back to the booth, leaving the others to wait for Ned and the emergency squad.

The technician moaned quietly. His fingers curled over a switch, then spread out as he tried to lift his head.

"He'll be all right," the festival manager said.

He glared at Nancy. "Trouble seems to abound when you and your father are in our midst," he said sarcastically.

The young detective gulped, ignoring the comment. Instead, she leaned close to the technician.

"Please try not to move too much," she said gently. "You could have a concussion."

The man blinked his eyes slowly, murmuring, "I'm okay. That kid only tapped me."

But the eyes closed again, and the fingers stopped moving.

Ned, in the meantime, appeared in the doorway. "Rosemont is sending an ambulance right away," he said.

"That's good," Nancy said, noting the lump that had swelled through the victim's thinning hairline.

"There is no need for you to stick around," the manager told the couple. "I will take care of Vince from here on."

Nancy, however, did not wish to leave the theater until the ambulance arrived, so she and Ned returned to the lobby. The two large, glass doors were open now, and an approaching siren soon stopped as the hospital vehicle pulled in front.

"What was the announcement I missed?" Nancy asked her friends as two men in white uniforms wheeled in a stretcher.

"The star apologized for the interruption," Bess said, "but said they couldn't go on under such circumstances."

Burt revealed a handful of money. "Everybody got a refund on their tickets," he said.

"I wonder why they didn't offer to honor them for another evening," Nancy said.

"Well," George replied, "I did overhear one woman say to another that she doubted that she would want to come to such a poorly run operation again."

"What's on tomorrow night?" Dave inquired.

"Nancy has the schedule," Bess said.

"Whatever it is," Nancy put in, "I have a strong hunch that unless they strengthen security around here, the program could fall apart like this one did."

Now the group watched the ambulance team carry Vince through the employees' door. His head did not move as he lay on the stretcher.

How long would it be, Nancy wondered, before he could tell her about the incident? Had Vince expected the visitor, or was it a surprise attack?

14

Flannery Foolery

While the group followed the stretcher out, the festival manager hurried briskly toward his office.

"Boy, he's unfriendly," Bess said as they stepped out under the dark sky.

He was more than unfriendly, Nancy thought. He was downright antagonistic.

Since the performance had been cut short, the young people decided to stop somewhere for a light snack, giving them a chance to discuss a plan of action.

"Come to think of it," Nancy said, "I've yet to meet Dr. DeNiro."

"Young or old?" Ned asked.

"Young," Bess smirked, causing a mock frown to form on her listener's face.

"And rather nice-looking," George said.

"I thought you said you wanted to go to the Flannery house," Ned said to Nancy.

"Oh, that too."

"Well, I'm free tomorrow, if you want company," the young man offered.

"I could use an extra pair of eyes," Nancy teased.

"How about my sunglasses, then?" George said in a laughing voice.

"I'd rather take Ned, thank you," Nancy grinned.

As the conversation faded into light banter, the group temporarily forgot about the latest developments in the mysteries. When Nancy's telephone rang early the next morning, however, she was surprised and happy to hear Angela Pruett's voice.

"I've been so concerned about you!" Nancy told the harpist.

"I'm sorry. I should have called you sooner," Angela said, wavering as she went on. "But I received a short message from Phyllis."

"Yesterday?" Nancy interrupted.

"Yes, and she said she wanted to meet me at

Swain Lake Lodge in the afternoon."

Nancy listened intently as Angela explained how she had waited almost two hours for her sister to arrive, but she never did.

"I finally inquired at the desk," Angela said. "That's when I discovered a second message from Phyllis. All she said was that she couldn't come after all."

"Were both messages handwritten?" Nancy questioned.

"No. The first one was, but it was scribbled. The second one was phoned in by a woman, the clerk said."

"But not necessarily by Phyllis," Nancy remarked in a suspicious tone.

She immediately revealed her own experience at the same lodge, which now more than ever seemed integral to the mysteries she sought to solve. She described Lal and asked if Angela had seen him.

"No, I haven't," the harpist replied, pausing. "Now I'm wondering if I should go back to the lodge today. Phyllis said she might be able to come."

Somehow, the idea did not sit well with Nancy.

"The whole business seems very odd to me,

and I have a feeling you'll just find a third message," she sighed. "Anyway, don't you have a performance tonight?"

"I'm not sure," Angela said. "There's been some talk of canceling the rest of the week."

She had not yet heard about the catastrophe the night before, so Nancy gave her the details.

"Then I'm sure everything will be postponed," Angela said. "The festival has really turned into a fiasco, and what worries me most is that I may be out of a job sooner than I anticipated. I'd have to go home, and I can't. I just can't."

"We'll find Phyllis before that happens," Nancy assured her. "As a matter of fact, I'd like to see Mrs. Flannery. Do you have the address handy?"

Nancy refrained from telling the woman about the man identified as Flannery, whom she had seen at the lodge and later realized was the person who had attacked Cliff. There was no point in further upsetting Angela, Nancy decided.

So when the harpist gave her the information, the young detective merely thanked her and said she would be in touch. Ned was to arrive within the hour, so Nancy hurried to get ready.

When the doorbell rang, she greeted the young man in a new summer skirt and puff-sleeved blouse that complemented her lightly tanned complexion.

"Hi!" Ned smiled. "I gather we're not going on a hike in the woods today."

"Not in these I'm not," Nancy chuckled, taking a glance at the bare, white sandals she wore. "I'd probably wind up with a terrific case of poison ivy!"

"And who wants itchy feet when you're chasing down kidnappers!" Ned said, leading the way to the car.

They found the Flannery house without too much difficulty, and to their delight, Mrs. Flannery was there. She was at least twelve or fifteen years older than her visitors, a judgment they drew based on the line of her face. Her figure, on the other hand, was taut like an athlete's, and she exuded energy as she spoke.

"Yes?" she said crisply when she opened the door.

Nancy and Ned introduced themselves and said they were looking for Phyllis Pruett.

"She hasn't been here for a week," the woman said. "I haven't the vaguest idea where she went, and—"

"Did you call the police about her disappearance?"

"Who said anything about a disappearance?" Mrs. Flannery charged back. "She's only been gone a few days. I don't keep tabs on her, anyway. She pays me rent, and she comes and goes as she likes."

She started to close the door, but Nancy moved forward.

"May we come in for a minute?" she asked sweetly.

"Look, I have a lot of errands to do."

"It will only take a moment," Ned added, knowing that Nancy was hoping to pick up some clue to the whereabouts of the missing girl.

"I'd like to see her room, if you don't mind," Nancy said.

The woman rolled her tongue over her lips, then drew in air, hesitating to reply.

"You have no objection, do you?" the girl detective continued.

"No, why should I? Except maybe I don't know if Phyllis would appreciate letting strangers into her room."

"We're not really strangers," Nancy said quickly. "I'm a personal friend of Phyllis's sister, Angela, and she knows I'm here."

"Oh, uh-huh."

Still, the woman hung on the door, allowing less than foot space for anyone to enter. It was true that someone else might have reacted similarly to the girl's request, but Mrs. Flannery seemed unusually reluctant. Nancy would have inquired about the man whose name was the same as hers, except that she thought it unwise to reveal too much now.

Mrs. Flannery pulled the door back at last.

"Okay, come in," she said, "but you can't stay long."

She led the couple up a stairway and into a corridor that connected to a room at the end. The door was open, and the woman explained the layout.

"She had her own hot plate, as you can see, a small bathroom, bed, stereo, TV—everything she wanted."

But Nancy was less interested in the furnishings than in the disarray of clothing left on a chair.

"It looks like she left in a hurry," the girl remarked.

"You think so?" Mrs. Flannery said. "To me, it's just a typical teenager's mess."

Nancy and Ned looked at each other, reserving their answer.

On the desk was a brochure with a photograph of someone attached. Nancy stepped toward it, but Mrs. Flannery sidled in front of it.

"Are you done?" she asked, slipping her hands along the edge of the blotter.

"I'd like to see that pamphlet." Nancy said.

"Pamphlet? What pamphlet?"

"The one you're trying to hide, Mrs. Flannery," Ned replied.

"I'm not doing any such thing," she sputtered, permitting Nancy to pick up the pamphlet. "I just don't think it's right for you to come snooping in here."

Nancy, in the meantime, was studying the cover, which was entitled, *The Most Important Discovery Of Your Life!*

Clipped to it was the picture of an aging man in a long, printed tunic. His stringy, gray hair hung sparsely around his wrinkled face. He was painfully thin, perhaps from frequent fasting, and as she read a few short passages inside the booklet, she realized her assumption was correct.

The man was the ascetic whom Phyllis had chosen to follow. He was Ramaswami!

15

Surprise Return

As Nancy gazed at the small photograph, she spoke to Mrs. Flannery. "This must be the retreat that Phyllis went to," she said, catching the woman's eyes on hers.

"I suppose so."

"Do you know how to get there?" Ned asked, hoping she might reveal an easier access than the one they had taken.

"No. I have no interest in the place whatsoever. Never did and never will."

Nancy, meanwhile, had noticed that there was no specific address given, only a telephone number which she memorized promptly. Aside from that information, there was little else to glean from the pamphlet, so she put it back on the desk.

"Hmm. What's this?" Nancy murmured, spying the edge of a letter that Phyllis had begun to write.

"Now that's really prying," Mrs. Flannery said accusingly, as the girl's fingers slid the paper out from under another one.

To the girl's surprise, there was only the greeting to Angela and a half-finished sentence that read, *I have learned something terr—*.

Terrible or terrific? Nancy wondered. And why had Phyllis left the letter unwritten? Had something urgent interrupted her?

She did not voice her thoughts openly until she and Ned were in the car again. Then, the couple discovered they had reached the same conclusion.

"It's my turn for hunches," Ned said, "and I think Mrs. Flannery knows more than she's telling."

"You get an A-plus." Nancy grinned. "And I'd like to find out what it is."

"Well, maybe if we come back in the dead of night and stalk her every move, we'll be able to—just like that!" Ned snapped his fingers with confidence.

"Not a bad idea," Nancy said. "Not bad at all."

"I was only kidding," her friend replied.

"I know, but I'm not. Maybe we'll bump into Mr. Flannery again!"

"In that case, maybe we ought to bring a policeman along," Ned said.

"With me to protect you?" Nancy teased, raising the boy's eyebrows.

He swung the car onto the street, heading for their next destination, Oberon College. They passed through the busy shopping district into a residential area filled with stately houses. Beyond them was a brown brick wall that surrounded the campus.

"It's pretty, isn't it," Nancy said.

"Not as pretty as Emerson," Ned replied.

Nancy ignored the touch of sour grapes she detected in her friend's voice. "I wonder where the professors' offices are," she went on, still admiring the roll of green lawn that framed the assortment of buildings.

"Over there," Ned said. He indicated a small sign with an arrow that was posted near the parking lot.

They left the car and immediately crossed to

the building that looked more like a small, Tudor mansion than an office.

"Did you call ahead for an appointment?" Ned asked, suddenly realizing that Nancy had not mentioned any specific time they were to see Dr. DeNiro.

"No, I didn't have a chance to, but I'm hoping we'll catch him between classes."

As it was, there seemed to be a steady flow of students on the connecting pathways, and Nancy and Ned gathered momentum. They quickly discovered the professor's door and knocked.

"Come in," a voice replied.

There was a shuffle of papers as the young couple stepped inside.

"Dr. DeNiro, I'm Nancy Drew."

"And I'm Ned Nickerson," Ned said. He stuck out his hand to shake the professor's, but his was hurriedly stuffing a folder into a briefcase.

"I have a class now," the man said briskly.

"Well, we're friends of Bess Marvin and George Fayne. I believe you met them the other day," Nancy said.

"Oh yes, of course."

Suddenly, he let the briefcase tumble on the desk and sat down, gesturing to Nancy and Ned to do the same.

"As a matter of fact, I was planning to call them today," he said.

"You were?" Nancy replied in surprise.

"A most peculiar thing happened yesterday. Here, I'll show you."

He pulled out a lower drawer in his desk and dug to the back for a small packing box. Remaining shreds of brown paper were still wrapped around it. He removed it completely now and opened the lid. Inside was a thick wad of cotton which he drew out quickly.

"Oh!" Nancy exclaimed as a piece of gold jewelry rolled across his palm. "That's Cliff's ring!"

"Are you sure?" Ned asked, taking it from the man and handing it to Nancy.

"It's unmistakably the same one," she replied. "The lily design and the scratches inside. Can you tell me how and where you got this, Dr. DeNiro?"

"It came in the mail," he said. "It was addressed to me here at the college."

"May I see the wrapping paper?" Nancy requested. But to her chagrin, there was no return address on it.

Now she wondered why the ring had been sent to the professor. It seemed to her that his impostor was too clever to have let it slip through his fingers so easily. Might he have given it to someone who forwarded it to Oberon College by mistake?

"Has anything else unusual happened to you recently?" Nancy inquired.

"No, not really. I am busily trying to finish a project—"

"A government project?" Nancy put in, remembering what Bess and George had told her.

"Yes, and I've had my nose buried in books for days."

"I don't mean to pry, Dr. DeNiro," Nancy went on, "but I wonder if the man who was posing as you could be related to your current work."

"Let's say it's not impossible, but unlikely. The same thought occurred to me when I spoke with your friends, but after digesting it a bit, I concluded that my statistical studies would be of little interest to anyone other than someone in my field.

"On the other hand," the instructor continued, "the person could have read my name in the *Gazette* article and conveniently remembered it."

Nancy agreed. "In any case," she said, "I am greatly relieved to have the ring back. Now if we can only find its owner."

Dr. DeNiro's bewildered reaction prompted the girl to explain further. "Sounds like Cliff's in a lot of trouble," the man said, "and if anything relevant should turn up, I will contact you immediately."

"Or, if you can't reach Nancy," Ned inserted, "you can always call me."

They gave him their telephone numbers, which he pocketed, then said he was running late for class. The couple thanked him for his time and followed him up the walkway, separating at the juncture to the parking lot.

"Weird, weird, weird," Ned muttered as he drove the car along the winding pavement.

"And lucky," Nancy said, flashing the ring in her hand.

Suddenly, her eyes settled on a young man carrying a canvas bag toward a campus laundry room. He had brown hair that trailed across his shoulder, and his build was slight like that of

314

the boy she had chased out of the River Heights Theater!

"Slow down, Ned," Nancy said.

The window was down on her side and she stuck her head through it, trying to see the boy's profile as he strode toward a door.

"Who is it?" Ned questioned.

"It looks like the kid I found with Vince in the sound booth," Nancy said.

She opened the car door and stepped out quickly, leaving Ned to idle the engine in a no-parking zone. She raced to the door she had seen the young man go into, but when she looked behind it, he was nowhere in sight.

"Where did he—" Nancy said, in the same instant realizing that he had disappeared around the corner of the building and was running toward a car near a dormitory.

Nancy raced back to Ned's and leaped in.

"We have to follow him," she said. "I'm pretty sure it's the same guy."

The other vehicle now swerved onto the pavement, screeching its wheels as it flew past the couple.

"Did he see you?" Ned said, bearing down on the accelerator.

"I hope not," Nancy said. "I don't think so."

The boy ahead of them cruised down the road in the direction of the business district. He whipped through an amber light just before it turned red, which forced Nancy and Ned to a frustrating halt.

They didn't speak as they watched the silver hatchback dart between cars and pitch through a second light as their own turned green again.

"We can't lose him," Nancy finally said, causing Ned to press down on the pedal.

"Don't worry. We'll catch him," Ned assured her.

The hatchback was still in view, but when a sign for the River Heights Music Festival appeared overhead, the car spun quickly off its track. Ned had been concentrating on it so intently that he did not see another one barreling toward the approaching intersection.

"Watch it, Ned!" Nancy screamed as her eyes caught sight of the sports wagon. But Ned had already sailed into the path of collision!

16

Hazy Report

Instead of jamming on the brakes, which would have been Nancy's instinct, Ned lurched the car forward. The sports wagon careened past the rear bumper, barely missing it before coming to an abrupt halt.

"Why don't you watch where you're going?" the driver yelled back at Ned, then sped around the corner.

Nancy, meanwhile, had sunk against the car seat, feeling the tension in her muscles spin out in a shiver.

"Oh, Ned," she gasped, as he urged the pedal again. "I thought we were going to get crumpled for sure."

"Oh, ye of little faith," Ned said, squeezing her hand lightly. "Now, don't tell me you think I'd foul up a chase by getting us into a car accident."

Nancy shook her head, smiling. "Where did that hatchback go, anyway?" she asked.

"He was heading for the River Heights Theater, and I figure we ought to as well."

"But definitely," Nancy said, straightening up in the seat.

It was amazing how the incident at the intersection, despite the fact that their own car had never stopped moving, had given the hatchback enough time to vanish completely.

"Maybe he turned off onto one of these side streets," Nancy declared. She gazed down the ones they passed, looking for some evidence of the silver car. "I don't see it anywhere," she said at last.

But when they reached the theater, they noticed a trail of engine oil in the driveway and followed it.

"There!" Nancy exclaimed, spotting the elusive hatchback.

It was sitting in a parking space near the manager's office. Ned pulled in next to it and as he shut off the ignition, Nancy stepped out. Ned walked close behind her as she dashed to the door, opening it quickly and announcing herself to an officious-looking secretary.

"Mr. Hillyer is in conference at the moment," was her reply.

Was he talking with the boy whom Nancy suspected had attacked Vince? She and Ned waited a few minutes before interrupting the woman again.

"It's really urgent," Nancy said, half surmising that the manager had given instructions not to admit Nancy.

"As I told you, Mr. Hillyer is tied up. I have no idea how long he will be, and I suggest you call for an appointment."

Nancy strode quickly past the woman, knocking on the office door. She heard two voices clouded by the partition and stepped back, somewhat embarrassed.

The receptionist was on her feet by now and glaring at Nancy. "I suggest you leave," she snapped.

"We can't," Ned returned with equal brisk-ness.

The woman gritted her teeth and pressed the

intercom, advising the manager, "Miss Drew is here and she refuses to go."

"I'll be right out."

As the man emerged in the doorway, Nancy observed someone in the visitor's chair. His hair peeked out from the high back.

"Shall I have you thrown out of here by our security guards?" Mr. Hillyer rasped.

Nancy overlooked the comment. "I have reason to believe that the young man in your office clubbed Vince over the head last night."

"That is absolutely preposterous," the manager said.

"But I told you before how a boy almost knocked me down as he came out of the sound booth only minutes before I found Vince."

Hillyer had intentionally closed his ears. "He happens to be the son of a fine family from Castleton. He called me this morning about a job. He's had some experience in summer theater and we may hire him, especially since he just completed course work at Oberon with honors.

"Frankly, Miss Drew, knowing that we don't have your wholehearted support on the subject, I probably *will* hire him."

"But—" Nancy said, still trying to capture the man's attention.

"Good-bye, Miss Drew, and please don't bother me again."

Nancy knew it was useless to inquire about the boy's name, because neither Hillyer nor his receptionist would volunteer it. Nonetheless, she had picked up some interesting tidbits which she stored for future reference.

"Come on, Ned," she said, pausing to look at the performance schedule on an outside bulletin board.

The word POSTPONED had been stamped across two programs, including a spectacular trio of violinists and what had been advertised as the rare appearance of a famous jazz pianist. The Jansen production, however, seemed to be continuing.

"I'm game for another round of *Oklahoma*," Ned smiled. "Maybe we can at least see two scenes worth—"

"Before the stage collapses?" Nancy laughed. "Well, I had something else in mind for this evening—like a trip to the old Flannery homestead!"

"I knew you wouldn't give up on that one,"

Ned sighed. "In that case, I'd better do a little weight lifting this afternoon to build up these tired muscles."

"And I'm going to put in a call to the swami's retreat," Nancy said.

They returned to the Drew home, where they agreed on a time to meet later.

"See you at nine," Ned said, and drove away.

Nancy hurried into the house, where to her amazement she found Hannah in a complete dither. She had personally called Chief McGinnis to inquire about the ongoing search for Cliff.

"The police think they've found him!"she exclaimed.

"What?" Nancy replied.

Could it be possible that the young man and his intriguing ring had been discovered the same day?

Hannah bobbed her head excitedly. "Yes, it's true. It's true. The chief says someone saw him hitchhiking. The description fits, according to what he told me."

"Where is he now?" Nancy pressed.

"We don't know, exactly," Hannah said, losing some of the animation in her face. "All they have is a report, and they're scouring the area where he was seen."

Nancy now dialed headquarters, asking to be put through to the chief at once. Within seconds, she was told a similar version of the story.

Chief McGinnis chuckled, however. "We get reports like these all the time, you know," he said, "and I'm afraid Hannah has been so worried about Cliff's kidnapping that she didn't hear my final comment before she hung up."

"What was it, Chief?" Nancy inquired.

"Just that eight out of ten reports on missing persons don't usually lead anywhere."

The disappointment Nancy felt was no less than Hannah's when she related her conversation.

"No matter what the chief says," Nancy remarked, "I intend to remain optimistic."

"Good girl," Hannah said, hugging her. "And when that young man comes back, I'm going to bake him the biggest coconut layer cake he ever laid eyes on!"

"Mm, sounds delicious," Nancy said, sniffing the faint odor of something else in the oven.

"Oh! The tarts!" Hannah cried. "They'll burn for sure!"

She dashed into the kitchen, leaving the young detective alone to mull over the numerous details in the mysteries that beset her. Suddenly, she realized that only she and Ned knew about the unexpected return of Cliff's ring, and she raced upstairs to her room. She sprawled out on the bed, resting the telephone alongside her.

She called Bess and George first, then her father. All of them were ecstatic about the discovery.

As it entrenched itself in her mind, Nancy finished her conversation with Mr. Drew and closed her eyes. She saw the gold ring swirl vigorously around the figure of a man whose face was indistinct. But as she ran toward him, a beard grew along the chin, then floated away, leaving a smooth complexion and large eyes several shades darker than his skin.

"Jhaveri," Nancy murmured before slipping into a deeper sleep.

When she awoke, she discovered the phone partly off the hook and a twilight haze creeping between the trees outside her window. She jolted out of bed, resetting the receiver, and changed into slacks and a light sweater.

The dinner hour faded quickly as the young detective let a large noodle slide off her fork.

"Why didn't I think of it before!" she exclaimed.

"What, dear?" Carson Drew inquired.

"The ring!" Nancy said excitedly.

In the course of her nap, two elements of the mystery had joined themselves—Cliff's jewelry and Mr. Jhaveri's jewelry store. Flannery, alias DeNiro, had been there on one occasion, at least. Had he tried to sell the ring to Mr. Jhaveri after stealing it from Bess and George?

"I have an idea that Mr. Jhaveri wanted to ship it back for some reason," Nancy said. "Since the man had introduced himself as Dr. DeNiro from Oberon College, Mr. Jhaveri sent the ring there!"

17

Moonlight Intruder

Nancy's declaration about Cliff's ring caused Mr. Drew to smile. "I assume, then, you are planning a trip back to Mr. Jhaveri's shop," he said.

His daughter grinned. "First, however, I'm going to do a little investigating around the Flannery house. Ned said he'd go with me."

"When is that scheduled for?"

"In about two hours," Nancy said.

"Tonight?" the attorney questioned in surprise.

Nancy related her visit with Mrs. Flannery and her determination to find out whether the man who called himself by the same name was her husband.

"He wasn't there this morning," Nancy said, "but I figure he ought to show up eventually."

Although the young detective would have liked to reveal everything that had occurred during the day, she chose not to. She knew, for instance, that Mr. Hillyer's reaction to her would upset her father unnecessarily, so she avoided the subject.

"I think I'm on the way to convincing the mayor of my innocence," Mr. Drew said unexpectedly.

"That's terrific, Dad," Nancy replied.

It was the first time he had even made reference to the situation in a while. Yet, despite the note of optimism, Nancy did not see an observable change in her father's face. He still seemed distressed.

"So I don't want you to worry anymore," he continued.

Had he only told her half the truth in order to allay her fears? Nancy wondered. But she didn't ask any questions, allowing the rest of the meal to pass quietly.

Before long it was nine o'clock, and Nancy slipped into a jacket, thinking Ned would arrive punctually. To her surprise, though, half an hour had elapsed when the bell finally rang.

"I tried calling you this afternoon, but all I got was a busy signal," Ned said. He explained that his parents had asked him to do a number of errands and he knew he'd be late.

Nancy promptly recalled how the phone receiver had slipped off the hook as she slept next to it.

"I wonder if I missed any other important calls," she said, waving good-bye to her father.

"Well, if you did, I'm sure they'll call back," Ned declared.

The couple strolled across the driveway to Ned's car, unaware for the moment of the silver hatchback that was parked a short distance up the street. In spite of the moonlight that glinted on the hood, it remained concealed under a low-hanging tree. The driver, however, kept his gaze steady on the Drew house.

When Ned finally backed the car out onto the street, the hatchback's headlights turned on and the engine started to purr. The driver waited several seconds before pulling away from the curb, then followed the young detectives.

They headed for the Flannery house. Ned had paid only scant attention to the car in the rearview mirror. It had maintained a fair distance, but when Ned's car halted at the end of a block, the hatchback suspended the chase, waiting for the pair to emerge.

"The downstairs lights are still on," Nancy said to Ned as she gazed at the Flannery house.

"If we see the guy you're looking for," Ned said, "do you want to talk to him?"

"I'm not sure. Let's play it by ear."

"Okay. You're the boss on this one."

"Gee, thanks," Nancy smiled.

Together, they stole up the driveway, hiding behind a tree trunk when Mrs. Flannery moved in front of the living room window.

"Did she see us?" Ned asked.

"I don't think so."

But the girl knew their shadows could be seen on the pavement. She shrunk back, leaning against the bark. From where they stood, they were able to see a back window as well, and as one light in the front turned off, others switched on in the kitchen.

"Somebody's eating," Ned commented. He had craned his neck to peer between the lower branches and caught sight of black hair. "Come on. Let's get closer," the boy said.

They ducked out from their secret place and edged forward, stopping only when they heard the kitchen window being cranked open. Instantly, the two young people dodged discovery, pulling next to the house and accidentally stepping into a garden of petunias.

"Yuck," Ned said as he shook dirt off his sneakers.

Nancy, however, was more concerned about the footprints that might be noticed, and sprang to the ground to cover them up quickly. As she did so, voices drifted outside. One was low, yet recognizable.

"That is the man we saw at Swain Lake Lodge!" she told Ned.

After all the mysteries she had solved, she had learned to use all her senses with amazing accuracy.

"How can you be so positive?" Ned whispered.

"Trust me," the girl said, raising a finger to her lips.

Then, even Ned heard Nancy's name! But what precisely was being said about her?

Nancy closed her eyes to concentrate, but the whistle of a boiling teakettle interfered. She was also oblivious to the figure crouched behind the front hedge. It was the driver of the hatchback. He had crept up the sidewalk when the couple moved up the Flannery's driveway and darted behind bushes before coming to a standstill.

Ned, in the meantime, had let Nancy slip forward under the kitchen window.

"If she comes snooping around here again," the man was saying, "you know what to do."

"Sure, and I'll dump her at the lake."

Nancy winced, imagining another horrifying night in the forest shelter. Or worse, she thought.

"Well, she won't be back," Mrs. Flannery continued. "Good thing you waited until now to come home."

"When she trailed us out to the house on River Lane," her husband said, "I figured she'd turn up here sooner or later."

There was a clatter of cups and saucers and the sound of running water which interrupted the conversation temporarily. Then the lights went out, plunging the driveway into total darkness.

Instantly, the figure behind the hedge bolted toward Ned and seized him from behind, chopping a well-placed blow to the neck. The boy sank to the ground without a cry.

Nancy let out a shriek, quelling it as the boy dived for her too!

Now the lights went on in the kitchen again, and the back door opened and closed.

"Who's out there?" came Flannery's deep voice.

Nancy turned as the boy's fist shoved her down on the pavement, causing her to roll within inches of the man's feet. He grabbed her quickly, and dragged her into the backyard, and up the porch steps, letting her attacker escape.

"Let go of—" she cried, but he covered her mouth with his hand.

"What about her friend in the driveway?" Flannery's wife said.

"Just leave him. We'll be gone from here long before he comes to."

Nancy struggled as the pair secured her to a chair, binding her arms and legs so tightly she felt almost nauseated.

"You can't get away with this," the girl said, causing Mrs. Flannery to stick a soft roll in her mouth.

Nancy bit into it angrily, gulping down part of it. The rest broke off, dribbling crumbs on the floor.

"Was that good?" the woman sneered. "Here, have another piece."

She took a larger chunk of bread this time and stuffed it in Nancy's mouth.

"Where's Singh's car?" the woman now asked her husband.

"Up at the retreat."

As the young detective listened, questions whirled through her brain. What was the men's connection with the retreat? Was Ramaswami involved with them and the retreat merely a cover-up? Or was the swami being used in some evil way?

If only the Flannerys would reveal more information! Nancy thought.

But they disappeared upstairs, leaving her alone for almost twenty minutes. The sound of hurried footsteps creaking across the floor above convinced her they were packing.

Maybe Ned would come to sooner than they expected, Nancy hoped, but that did not prove to be the case.

It was almost two hours later before the young man regained consciousness. A dull ache drove across his spine as he realized he was lying along the edge of the Flannery's drive-way. A stray petunia wrapped around the toe of his sneaker reminded him of the sequence of events.

"Nancy?" he muttered weakly, but there was no answer.

He lifted his head slowly, the pain doubling rapidly and forcing him to drop it again.

"Nancy, where are you?" he cried out louder than before.

But the only response was the pad of a cat across the driveway into the yard of an empty house, causing the young man to roll on his side. He looked toward the kitchen window that was closed now. Nancy, who had stood under it, was gone! Surely she would not have left Ned as she had unless someone had over-taken her, too! Who was it—the same stranger who had attacked Ned?

18

Scorpion Scare

Soon after the incident had occurred, the driver of the hatchback had leaped out of sight. He had raced the car down to the corner and swerved onto a main road that led to the River Heights Theater.

The Jansen troupe's performance was under way, and the boy determined there was only an hour left before it finished. He turned into the parking area, which was less full than the night before, and stopped his car near the exit. He jumped out, holding a metal canister with punctures in the lid.

Smirking, he darted into the empty lobby, where he waited a moment as the buoyant melody emanating from the orchestra began to end. He then opened the door a crack, removed the lid of the canister, and freed from its prison a large, black scorpion. Urged forward, the insect crawled out, revealing its monstrous claws and poisonous sting!

The boy pulled back, shutting the door without being seen and listening for the first shriek of discovery.

The venomous animal, however, followed an even trail down the middle of the aisle until it was past the halfway mark. Then the glow of stage lights captured it and several couples in end seats screamed frantically.

"Help!" a woman cried as the jointed legs of the scorpion scurried off the carpet.

The man seated next to her shouted over the growing din in the audience. "It's a scorpion!" he exclaimed.

"Take the side exits!" another voice yelled.

Now the pandemonium struck the performers. The conductor ordered the musicians to leave the pit and the actors on stage fell into disarray as the house lights came up, sending the scorpion under a row of now-vacant seats.

"This is the last straw," one woman snapped in disgust as she charged out of the theater. "I

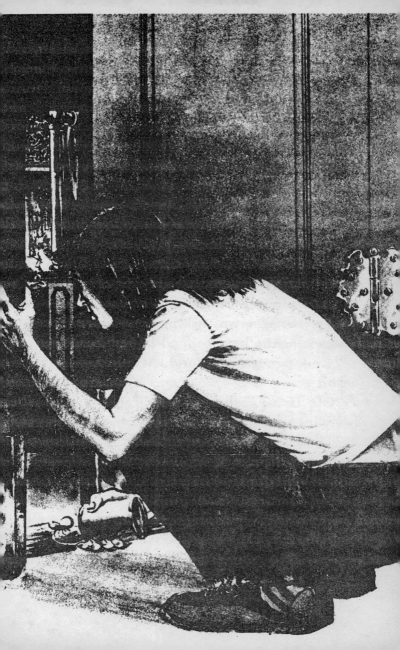

wouldn't come here again if you paid me!"

Her complaints were echoed by practically everyone who fled through the lobby in fear of the venomous creature.

"Please—please," the festival manager muttered helplessly. "We'll take care of everything."

But his weak promises went unheard, as he watched the departing crowd head for the parking lot. There the boy who had deposited the scorpion in the theater laughed. He waited, however, until the last car left, then went back inside where the festival manager had called the police to report the incident.

The manager was asking for emergency assistance as the boy stepped forward.

"Gee, what happened, Mr. Hillyer?" he asked.

"Oh, Brady," the manager replied. "Somebody let a scorpion loose in the theater."

"That's terrible," the boy said, trying not to appear overly concerned as he went on. "Do you suppose you'll have to shut down the festival after all?"

"I guess your real concern is whether we'll be able to give you the job we talked about."

"Yes, sir," Brady said.

Mr. Hillyer heaved a long, steady sigh. "Frankly, my boy, I doubt that the festival can last much longer. The Jansen troupe has already informed me they are canceling their contract with us."

His listener was almost gleeful to hear the news, but he remained solemn.

"So maybe if the Castleton Theater still wants them," Brady said, "the Jansen company will go back there."

"We've had problems ever since Jansen made the last-minute switch," the manager said.

"As you know, Pa works the sound booth for the Castleton Theater," the boy replied, "and he told me all about it."

Hillyer was too distraught to pursue the conversation further. He let the young man leave when the police arrived. Brady hopped into his car, turned the radio up, and drove away.

Ned, in the meantime, had managed to pull himself off the Flannerys' driveway. He dragged his feet toward the backyard, noting darkness throughout the house. He told himself that he would risk an unpleasant encounter with the couple when he inquired about Nancy.

339

But as he climbed the porch steps, he noticed a trail of bread crumbs.

That's odd, he thought. Why would anyone throw out food for birds at night?

He didn't think about it further as he knocked on the door. No one came, however. Maybe they couldn't hear him, he surmised, and he darted to the front, still trying to ignore the throb under his skull.

He rang the bell a long time. There was still no answer. Had the Flannerys left the house?

As Ned returned to his car, he did not observe the flat tire against the curb. He started the ignition and began to steer, rolling the vehicle forward. Suddenly, he was aware that one wheel was spinning on its rim. He cut off the engine and jumped out to examine it. The small valve cap on the tire had been removed and air had been allowed to escape!

Had his attacker done this? Ned wondered. Yet, somehow, that idea was hard to comprehend. How, for instance, could the stranger have abducted Nancy and pulled off the nozzle without her slipping away? Perhaps there were two people involved in the abduction.

Before he could mull over the question, Ned dived into his trunk and took out an air pump which he quickly hooked up. He gazed along the curb for the missing cap and discovered it had been thrown up on someone's lawn.

Several minutes later he was on his way to the Drew house, where a downstairs light had been left on for Nancy. It was approaching midnight as the boy pressed the bell.

It was a surprise that Hannah, rather than Mr. Drew, came to the door.

"Is Mr. Drew asleep?" Ned asked as the housekeeper's eyes traveled beyond the boy.

"Where's Nancy?" she said, disregarding his question.

"She's gone."

From the somber tone of the boy's voice, Hannah knew that trouble lurked in his explanation.

"Mr. Drew received an urgent call from the police," she said. "He's been down at the River Heights Theater for almost forty-five minutes."

Ned quickly revealed what had happened to him, adding, "Nancy just vanished into thin air."

"Oh, dear," the woman frowned. "Well, don't waste your time here. You'd better find Mr. Drew right away."

The young man pulled out of the driveway,

still feeling sluggish, but he propelled himself as fast as he could to the theater. When he arrived, he was astonished to find the lawyer defending himself against Hillyer's rash accusations.

"*That* is all *your* fault!" the manager grumbled. He was pointing to an empty metal canister and another container alongside it that now held the dead scorpion.

"You are being ridiculous," Mr. Drew said in an even voice. "How could I have any connection with what happened here tonight?"

"Ever since you forced the Jansen troupe out of their arrangement in Castleton—"

"I didn't force them, Mr. Hillyer. The town of River Heights made an offer which received the approval of every board member. I, for one, did not even know that Jansen had a pre-existing deal with Castleton. The mayor of River Heights informed me he had seen them perform elsewhere and suggested we line them up here. When I called their business manager, he made only a glib reference to a pending contract. But the impression he gave me was that it wasn't very satisfactory. It isn't my fault they accepted our proposal instead. Obviously, it was a better one than Castleton's!"

Mr. Drew had spoken with a clarity that rivaled the temper of his listener.

"All I know," Hillyer went on, "is that we will lose a tremendous amount of money if we have to close down the festival."

"Mr. Hillyer, rather than sputtering about that, wouldn't it behoove us all to try and figure out who is causing all the trouble?"

Although Mr. Drew had seen Ned, the intensity of his conversation and the police officers who flanked the two men prevented him from addressing the boy. Ned, also, did not wish to interrupt. But as the discussion wore on, he listened with greater interest.

"Tell me, Mr. Hillyer, did you not see anyone strange enter the premises?" one officer questioned.

The manager had steered his vision away from Mr. Drew. "No, I told you that before."

"But who was that kid with the long hair?"

"He must've been passing by when he saw the mass exodus. He knew the show couldn't have finished yet, so he decided to find out what had happened."

"What's the boy's name?" Mr. Drew inquired, but Hillyer continued to direct his statements to the policeman.

"We'd like that information, if you don't mind," the officer countered.

"Brady Tilson."

"And what's your connection with him?"

"I don't have a connection, officer. I merely offered him a job this morning."

Now Ned stepped closer, wondering: Was this the boy whom he and Nancy had followed from Oberon College? If so, he was the one whom Nancy suspected of having attacked Vince, the sound and lighting technician! Had he returned again to plant the poisonous scorpion?

As the men's conversation diverted to the exact moment when the disruption had occurred, Mr. Drew spoke. "From what I overheard Mr. Hillyer say earlier, Brady arrived only minutes after the trouble started—around ten o'clock or so."

"Ten-thirty would be more exact," an officer put in.

Ten-thirty, Ned repeated to himself. That was only a short time after his attack. Might there be a connection between the two events?

19

Prisoners' Retreat

Ned let the men finish speaking before he took Mr. Drew aside. The festival manager glanced gruffly at the boy as the officers made a few final statements.

"What's up, Ned?" Mr. Drew said, adding, "I assume that you dropped Nancy off at the house."

"No, sir. I-I don't know where she is."

The lawyer could see a visible tremble in the boy's body. "Tell me everything that happened, and don't leave anything out," he said.

But before the young collegian could complete his story, the festival manager and the police began to leave the building.

"Everybody out, Mr. Drew," Mr. Hillyer said

sharply, leading the way to an exit.

"We'll talk again tomorrow," the attorney informed the man.

"Not if I can help it," he said.

"Well, I'm afraid you may not have a choice in the matter," one of the officers said from behind.

When they were all outside, Mr. Drew requested the policeman join him and Ned.

"I couldn't help overhearing the discussion about Brady Tilson," Ned told the young officer.

"Do you know him?"

"No."

"But my daughter Nancy apparently had an encounter with him last night," Mr. Drew put in.

"That's right," Ned continued. He explained the sequence of events in the sound booth just as Nancy had related them to him. "But when we came to see Mr. Hillyer this morning, he ignored us."

"As you can see, officer," the attorney went on, "Mr. Hillyer refuses to listen to anything from the lips of anyone named Drew."

The policeman nodded. He would have called Hillyer back from the parking lot, but following Mr. Drew's remark, realized he would just be inviting another unproductive scene.

"When can we talk to your daughter?" the officer inquired.

"That's another problem," Ned answered for Mr. Drew. He displayed the welt across his neck and told how he had been struck from behind.

"Nancy's been hard at work on the kidnapping of that young amnesia patient," Mr. Drew said, assuming the disappearance was well-known in the River Heights police department. "Tonight she and Ned went on a small excursion to the home of Mr. and Mrs. Flannery."

The officer seemed puzzled. "What's their connection?" he asked.

"Well, I think Nancy suspected Mr. Flannery of being the person who attacked Cliff in the hospital," Mr. Drew said. "She wasn't absolutely positive, however. Did you run into the man?" he asked Ned.

"Yes and no. We overheard him mention Nancy's name, but we didn't see the face, so I'm not a hundred percent sure he's the one we saw at the lodge."

"Any idea who gave you the welt?" the policeman questioned.

."That's what I've been leading up to. I have a hunch it could be Brady Tilson," Ned answered.

"And not Flannery," Mr. Drew interposed.

"No, definitely not. He and his wife were still inside when I was hit."

The young man blinked his eyes wearily, and he swayed off one foot as the adventures of the evening swirled through his head.

"We'll search the Flannery place now," the officer assured Mr. Drew. "Maybe your daughter's still there."

Although Ned was positive Nancy had been taken away by someone, he knew he had no evidence to prove it. No one had come to the door when he knocked and rang, but that didn't mean the young detective wasn't trapped inside.

"Can I go with you?" the boy asked the officer. He shook his head.

"Do me a favor, son. Go home and get a good night's rest—unless you want to have that bruise checked first. You could have a slight concussion, you know."

Ned insisted he felt fine, but Mr. Drew studied his weary face. "You'll stay in the guest room tonight," he said. "I'll call your family and explain. I'm sure it'll be all right."

The young man nodded gratefully.

"What about Nancy, though?" he asked.

"I'm afraid we'll have to leave everything up to the police now," Mr. Drew sighed.

He himself was deeply worried about his daughter's safety, but he managed to retain his composure after the police said they would contact him shortly.

By next morning, however, the telephone had not rung and the attorney dialed headquarters. He learned that the Flannery house was vacant. Teacups and saucers that had been left in the sink overnight indicated that the occupants had departed recently. Officers, nevertheless, intended to search the grounds in daylight.

When Ned finally awoke, Mr. Drew relayed the information, asking if any other clues to Nancy's whereabouts had occurred to the boy.

"Just that I'm positive she's with the Flannerys," he said. "At first, I thought the guy who hit me had probably kidnapped Nancy. But if Brady was my attacker, then he obviously didn't take Nancy with him to the theater."

"Well, I think the police must've come to the same conclusions by now," Mr. Drew said. "So where do you suppose Flannery is?"

"Maybe at Swain Lake Lodge."

Mr. Drew considered the idea. "I doubt it. He wouldn't want to be seen in a public place with his prisoner."

"Then, maybe—" Ned let the sentence hang, thinking momentarily about Phyllis Pruett.

He shot out of his chair to the telephone. He didn't know Angela's number, but he quickly obtained it from the River Heights Theater office and dialed again.

"Angela Pruett?" the young man said, "This is Ned Nickerson."

From there on in, plans were made for him to pick her up at her hotel. He gave only a brief explanation before turning to Mr. Drew again.

"I'm going to find the swami's retreat if it's the last thing I do," he announced, "because that's where I think Nancy is!"

"Perhaps you ought to take along some extra muscle," the attorney said, "like Bess and George and the boys."

"Excellent idea," Ned declared. "Would you like to come too, sir?"

"Seems to me you have a full car already," Mr. Drew said, "but I wouldn't miss this trip for anything. I'll follow in my car."

It took almost an hour before Ned was able to round up everyone. Bess and George were completely shocked by the news of Nancy's abduction. Angela was equally astounded by the connection unraveling between the Flannerys and her own sister's disappearance.

"And what about Cliff?" Bess said.

The detectives wondered if they were on the right track. Had the retreat really become a hideaway for prisoners?

Mr. Drew followed the group in his own car, having left a strict message with Hannah not to reveal their destination to anyone. He did, however, pass the word along to Chief McGinnis.

The most pressing concern at the moment, though, was how to reach the retreat. Since their harrowing experience on the trail, Nancy and Ned had not returned to hunt for a road.

"Even so," Ned told his friends, "somebody near the lake must know if one exists. If not, we'll have to traipse through the woods."

"Uh-oh," Bess said, glancing at her bare ankles. "Hope we don't get bitten along the way."

"You should've thought of that sooner," her cousin said.

"Well, I can't think of everything, George Fayne."

Dave interrupted unexpectedly. "It seems to me that you two enjoy picking on each other," he said.

"We're not picking on each other," Bess said defensively. "George is merely looking out for my best interest."

Her friend pursed his lips, swallowing his words, as George giggled. Burt, meanwhile, had asked to look at the road map Ned kept in the glove compartment.

"Swain Lake isn't far from the airport," Ned told him, which helped the Emerson boy locate it more quickly.

"As I recall," Burt remarked, "there's a road that runs up into the hill around that area."

"You're probably thinking of the one Nancy and I were on the other day," Ned said. "It leads to the lodge, but not to the retreat, which I assume is somewhere at the foot of the lake."

"Come to think of it," George said to Bess, "don't you remember Nancy saying that Cliff was found near the airport?"

"Yes, that's right," Bess said excitedly. "It's possible that he was on his way back from the retreat!"

"Or on the way to it," George said. "At the moment, it really doesn't matter which direction he was heading—just that he was in the vicinity."

"I vote we go to the airport," Bess told Ned.

"I agree," Angela said.

"Maybe we will find an access to the retreat, after all," Dave encouraged their driver.

"You could be right," Ned replied, and when signs for the airport came within view, he followed them.

The airport itself had been modernized during the past year. New terminals had sprung up, and according to all reports, another one would be under construction shortly. Mr. Drew was temporarily bewildered as he kept his car in line with Ned's, wondering why they had veered off in this direction. Nonetheless, when the young man waved in the rearview mirror, the lawyer knew there was a reason.

It did not reveal itself, though, until the travelers climbed a steep road that curved away from the airport and into a densely wooded area. The road sloped toward a gully, weaving a thread of narrow pavement around it that unraveled along a large fork of water.

"Look! This has to be Swain Lake!"

George exclaimed to her companions.

She let her eyes trail out over the deep blue pocket, catching sight of a tan car parked by a large cabin. If it hadn't been for the car, she might have missed the building because of its dark log frame that blended against the trees. As Ned drove closer, the girl detective thought she spied a blue racing stripe on the trunk!

"Isn't that Dev Singh's car?" George asked her cousin.

Although neither of them had ever seen it before, it fitted Nancy's description.

"I'm beginning to get jealous," Ned said in a joking tone.

"Of what?" George inquired.

"Well, you both seem more tuned in to every little detail about this case than I am."

"Not every detail," Bess said. "After all, who got to investigate the lodge?"

"And visit Mrs. Flannery," her cousin added.

Ned grinned. "I have a headache to prove it, too!"

He slowed the car, motioning Mr. Drew to look in the direction of the lakeside cabin.

"We're sure that's the swami's retreat!" Ned exclaimed. "Stick close, okay?"

20

Intriguing Discovery

Mr. Drew followed the line of Ned's pointing finger and settled his eyes on the cabin. It stood at the foot of a small, sandy incline several feet from the water, and the attorney concluded that theirs was a back view of the building.

As Ned drove farther, he, too, realized that the cabin was nestled beneath an embankment, carefully concealed by a thickness of trees. Ned almost passed it, but the sound of a sputtering car engine below made him stop.

Was it the tan car George had spotted? the young detectives wondered.

Their driver pulled ahead instantly, burying the car behind a roadside shelter. Mr. Drew followed suit and waited with the young people as the distant engine continued to churn and then stop abruptly.

Ned took the lead now with Nancy's father and crossed the road. They walked behind the trees, keeping the uncovered cabin windows in view at all times. They did not notice any movement until they heard a crackle of twigs and leaves under the steep embankment. Then the group froze.

Had the person who tried to start the tan car seen them?

Bravely, Ned went forward, and the crackling noise stopped. He gulped nervously, wondering if someone would suddenly spring at him, but the silence lasted, and he waved the rest of his friends forward.

"I can't slide down that," Bess whispered to George. She gaped fearfully at the deep spur of slippery gravel beneath them.

"Well, we'll just leave you here, then."

Bess gazed at the forsaken wilderness around her. "I'll go. I'll go," she said, and took Dave's hand.

One by one the group, including Angela, who had remained quiet, strung out along the slope, ducking low as large, almond eyes peered out of the cabin window. The face pulled back quickly and the door opened, causing the visitors to drop behind a thick overturned log that lay near the base of the building.

George's blood pounded through her veins as she raised her eyes, catching sight of the stranger as he turned in their direction. It was Mr. Jhaveri!

Had the River Heights jeweler suddenly become a devotee of the swami? George wondered.

She lowered her head quickly, and they waited, breathless, for the man to go inside again. When he finally did, though, he didn't shut the door fully.

Ned scurried to the back of the building, taking Burt with him, while the others remained out of sight. The boys discovered a basement window partially covered by tall weeds. Tearing them aside, they stared in at several unmade cots that sagged over the cold, damp floor.

"Doesn't appeal to me a bit," Burt remarked. He followed Ned to the far corner, where another small window revealed the top of someone's head resting against the wall!

Ned pressed his face against the glass, hoping

to see who it was, but the hair color eluded him in the glare of sunlight. Burt tugged on his arm for some sort of answer, but Ned merely shook his head.

"Nancy? Phyllis?" he called through the crack in the frame. There was no response.

The others, including Mr. Drew, were about to circle in the direction of the parked car when a voice stopped them in their tracks.

"Now, ladies and gentlemen," the man said, flashing a mouthful of gleaming teeth, as the group swung to face him.

"Prem Nath!" Bess exclaimed.

"Ah, so we meet again," he said pleasantly.

He moved out from his hiding place under the embankment and shook the dry earth off his sweater.

"We heard you coming." He grinned.

"We're looking for our friend, Nancy Drew," George said. "This is her father."

"Oh, I'm honored to meet you, sir."

Mr. Drew nodded stiffly. "Where are you keeping her?" he asked.

"Obviously, there is some misunderstanding, Mr. Drew. Your daughter is not here." He paused. "We are peaceful people," he said, but a shout from above broke the calmness in his voice.

"The police are coming!" someone cried. "I just picked it up on the shortwave radio!"

"Let's get out of here!" another voice yelled, pulling Nath out of his tranquil posture.

He dived toward the visitors, pushing his way to the front stairs, but Mr. Drew tackled him.

"Where's my daughter?" he repeated again. His face flushed in anger.

"Let go of me!" the Indian rasped.

Mr. Drew shoved the man back against Bess and George, while Burt and Ned raced to the front, charging into the men who sought to flee the cabin.

"Oh!" Bess shrieked as Dave tripped one of them, causing him to flip over on his back.

Ned recognized him instantly as Keshav Lal, the fellow who had steered him and Nancy down the tortuous trail!

"You creep!" Ned yelled, now aiming for Flannery, who ran down the steps.

Flannery pushed a fist at the boy's jaw, but missed as Ned ducked, grabbing his arm and twisting him to the ground!

Mrs. Flannery, in the meantime, was screaming inside the cabin as Nancy suddenly caught her by surprise. She flung a tablecloth around the woman's waist and dragged her back, throwing her onto the couch.

"Nancy!" George and Bess exclaimed when they saw the titian hair.

They dived past the scuffle on the ground and raced up the steps toward the girl's prisoner, wrapping the cloth in knots around the arm of the sofa.

"Phyllis Pruett and Cliff are here, too!" Nancy told her friends.

"Speaking of Phyllis, where's Angela?" George said suddenly.

"Angela came with you?"

By now, sirens were approaching the cabin, and within seconds, patrol cars had pulled into view. Officers with handguns poised slid down the embankment, capturing the men who had already been subdued by the Emerson boys and Mr. Drew.

"Hands up," a policeman shouted, as the trio slowly got to their feet.

Having heard Nancy's voice, Mr. Drew hurried into the cabin

"Nancy—you're all right!" he said.

"Oh, Dad, I told you I could take care of myself." Nancy smiled, feeling her eyes grow moist.

Now Ned and the others surrounded her.

"You were all so brave," Nancy told them.

"It was Ned's idea," Bess said, causing the young man to blush.

He slipped his arm around Nancy's shoulder, saying, "I thought you had vanished forever."

"Me? Never," she replied, pecking his cheek and gulping as she remembered the other two captives.

They were already coming up the basement stairs with Mr. Jhaveri behind them. "I freed them, too, Nancy," he said, as Phyllis and Cliff stood in the room.

"Cliff!" Bess exclaimed.

"Correction, please." He grinned. "It's Randy."

"You mean you've got your memory back?" George said gleefully.

"One hundred percent. The minute I saw this place I remembered everything," he said.

Mr. Drew urged everyone to join the police, who had snapped handcuffs on the three men;

and before the former amnesia patient could tell his story, the lawyer hurried toward the underhang where Angela Pruett had secreted herself during the capture.

"We found Phyllis," Mr. Drew said in a quiet voice.

Upon seeing her sister, Angela ran forward and slipped her arms around the girl. "You should never have run away," Angela told her.

"I know, Angie. I'm sorry."

They whispered to each other as Nancy informed the police that Mr. Jhaveri had released her and the other two prisoners.

"Apparently," Nancy said, "he was an innocent victim of his cousin's greed. Keshav Lal had been a disciple of the swami. He was his assistant, as a matter of fact, until recently, when Ramaswami departed for another section of the country. He discovered that Lal had been intercepting valuable gifts to him and selling them through his relative, Mr. Jhaveri.

"Mr. Flannery here even tried to sell a beautiful gold ring which belonged to Randy. That was Flannery's big mistake."

Nancy's friends stepped closer.

"You see," Nancy went on, "we had told Mr.

Jhaveri about the ring on different occasions. He had seen Bess and George hand it over to Flannery, who at the time called himself Dr. DeNiro, and when he was asked to sell it, Mr. Jhaveri panicked."

"I know I should have immediately returned it to the girls," the jeweler said, "but I was frightened, really scared. If I told them how it had come into my possession, I would have had to tell them about Keshav. He had often given me trinkets to sell for him. I never questioned him about them, and he never discussed where they came from. But when he brought in the ring, I realized his friend had stolen it from the girls. So far as I knew, he was Dr. DeNiro from Oberon College, and I shipped it back to him, hoping he wouldn't bother me again."

Now Randy spoke. "I had come to the retreat frequently. It was almost like home to me, I suppose, because of my childhood days in India. My parents are still serving as missionaries there, and before I left for the states to study, they gave me a maharajah's ring. He presented it to them in exchange for all they had done for his people. I, in turn, had been thinking of giving it to Ramaswami to help him with his work.

"But the last weekend I spent here, I remember feeling very uneasy. I had spoken to Lal about the ring, and I would have given it to him for the swami, except that I overheard Lal's conversation with Dev Singh."

Randy now glanced at Prem Nath. "This man here," he said. "Believe me, Mr. Singh, I will make sure that Ramaswami gets *his* ring!"

So Randy's kidnapper had cleverly falsified an immigration card to cover up his real identity! How shrewd he had been to have it ready when the young detectives and the police challenged him on River Lane!

"Anyway," Randy went on, "I realized Lal had started a little business for himself at the swami's expense. So I waited for a chance to see Ramaswami alone, and when I did, I told him everything, not realizing that Lal was listening. I left quickly then. I didn't have a car, so I hitchhiked some distance and cut through the woods toward the airport. Next thing I knew, Lal and Singh had jumped me. They apparently didn't have time to hunt for the ring in my knapsack."

"They left it up to Flannery to retrieve it," Nancy remarked.

As she spoke, the captives fixed their jaws angrily and Phyllis offered her story. She said she had run away from home. "I was just mixed up at the time," she stated. "Angie, you have to believe me. I wasn't trying to hurt anyone."

"I believe you, Phyllis," Angela Pruett answered gently, urging her sister to continue.

"I was so upset," Phyllis said, "that when I heard about the swami's retreat, I thought to myself, that's for me—peace and quiet. It was great, too, until I overheard the Flannerys talking about Ramaswami. They said Keshav was worried he would find out what they were all up to.

"So I assume Mr. Lal wrote those messages that were supposedly from you just to make me think you were all right," Angela interjected. She looked at the prisoner whose face had settled into a rigid stare.

"I was determined to warn the swami. Of course, I didn't know that Randy had already done so," Phyllis went on. "But before I could pack or write you a note, Angie, the Flannerys pulled me out of my room and forced me into their car. Mr. Flannery drove me up here and threw me into the cellar, where he tied me up."

The conversation now shifted to the attack on Ned. "I saw the boy who did it," Nancy admitted. "He's the one who knocked out Vince."

"Well, if you can make a positive identification," her father replied, "then that little case will be solved too."

"One question still," George interrupted. "Who called the police today?"

"Your housekeeper, Mr. Drew," one of the officers said. "Chief McGinnis said you had told him where you were headed, but it was Mrs. Gruen who pressed us into action."

"Thank goodness for Hannah," grinned Nancy, as the prisoners were led away.

While the disappearances of Randy and Phyllis had been solved, it was only during the next couple of days that the problems surrounding the River Heights Theater began to straighten out.

Brady Tilson was brought in for questioning and he reluctantly admitted his guilt. He had created all the disruption at the theater because he wanted to force a shutdown. He said his father had lost his job at Castleton's outdoor pavilion because Castleton had been unable to replace the Jansen troupe on such short notice.

River Heights, Brady claimed, had actually stolen Castleton's production and audience, and he was determined to get it back! The first thing he did was to steal the festival's mailing list and pick up handfuls of fliers left on a table in the River Heights Theater lobby. He then stamped CANCELLED on them, and sent them out to as many people as possible.

When Mr. Hillyer heard the story, he sent a personal apology to Mr. Drew and Nancy, noting that Vince, the sound technician, had verified everything. At the same time, telephone calls from the mayor and various board members besieged the Drew household, causing Nancy to wonder if the flood of apologies and compliments would ever end.

Despite the excitement, however, she could not help thinking of where her next adventure would lead. To her amazement, she would soon find herself on the trail of *The Kachina Doll Mystery!*

In the meantime, she would enjoy the feast which Hannah had been preparing for days. When Randy arrived with Phyllis and Angela, they peeked into the kitchen, but the housekeeper had scooted them out quickly.

She reappeared only when Bess, George, and the Emerson boys arrived. Nancy had counted the plates and discovered two extras. But before she could say anything, Hannah told everyone to close their eyes.

"We have two surprise guests this evening!"

"Hi, Nancy!" a small voice giggled, causing all eyes to open. It was Tommy Johnson, and with him was Lisa Scotti!

The little boy was still wearing a leg cast, but with Lisa's help, he hobbled quickly toward the young detective and hugged her.

"Oh, Tommy, you look wonderful!" Nancy cried happily.

Knowing that the men responsible for Tommy's injuries would now face a stiff penalty was enough to satisfy the onlookers—Nancy, in particular.

She grinned at Hannah. "I'd like to give special thanks to the person who really saved the day for all of us!" Nancy exclaimed.

Everyone applauded enthusiastically, but following Hannah's signal of modesty, turned their applause toward Nancy.

"You really deserve it," Ned whispered to the young detective.

3
The Kachina
Doll Mystery

Nancy Drew® in

The Kachina Doll Mystery

Illustrated by Paul Frame

The Kachina Doll Mystery was
first published in the U.K. in a single volume
in hardback in 1982 by Angus & Robertson (U.K.) Ltd,
and in Armada in 1983
by Fontana Paperbacks,
8 Grafton Street, London W1X 3LA.

Contents

1

A Friend's Plea

"Nancy, you have a letter from Arizona," Hannah Gruen called. "Do you know someone out there?"

Nancy Drew, her titian hair tousled by the early spring breeze, came into the kitchen through the back door. She smiled at the housekeeper, who had cared for her since her mother's death many years ago, then took the offered envelope.

"Maybe it's an advertisement," Nancy said, studying the strange figure printed in the corner of the buff-colored envelope. However, it was a handwritten letter, not a pamphlet, that she took out of the envelope.

"Why, it's from Heather McGuire," she murmured as she unfolded it to check the signature. "Remember her, Hannah?"

"The pretty girl with red hair and freckles?" Hannah asked.

Nancy nodded. "She and her older brother moved away two years ago after their parents were killed in a plane crash. We planned to keep in touch, but I got involved in solving my mysteries and I suppose she was so busy making new friends she didn't have time to write either."

"Well, is she all right?" Hannah asked.

Nancy scanned the letter and a frown marred her usually smooth forehead. "I don't know," she admitted. "Let me read this to you."

"I'll make some hot chocolate while you do," Hannah suggested. "It's rather nippy outside. You must be half-frozen after your walk."

Nancy smiled indulgently at the housekeeper. "That sounds wonderful." She began to read the letter.

> *Dear Nancy,*
> *I know you'll be surprised to hear from me after so long, but I don't know where else to turn. I remember how wonderful you have always been at solving mysteries, and now Chuck and I have one that we can't seem to do anything about.*

Nancy paused. "Chuck is her older brother," she explained.

"The one Bess used to think was so handsome," Hannah agreed.

Nancy laughed. "That's right, she was heartbroken when they told her they were going to Arizona to live with their grandfather. I'll have to call Bess and tell her about this letter."

"Does Heather say what the mystery is?" Hannah asked.

"That's the next part." Nancy went on reading.

A few years ago, Grandfather bought an old ranch near the Superstition Mountains east of Phoenix. We decided last year to make it into a fitness-health resort, and we've been working on it ever since. We planned to open by next fall when the tourist season starts here. Now, however, I'm not sure we will ever open.

"The main attraction of the ranch is a wonderful, old building that we have modernized for our hotel. Everyone calls it the Kachina House, because the old man who built it painted a number of pictures of colorful, Indian Kachina dolls on the walls

of the central hall that are beautiful.

"We finally completed work on the in-side of the building and moved in just after Christmas. That's when we learned about the Kachina's curse. Absolutely nothing has gone right since, Nancy, and even Chuck is beginning to believe that there is something haunting this house. If you can't help us, I'm afraid the Kachina Health Resort will never be more than a dream.

"We have plenty of room here, so if you and possibly George and Bess could come out for a spring vacation in the desert, you would be very welcome. Once you get here, maybe you will be able to find a way to end the curse.

Nancy put the letter down with a sigh and accepted a cup of hot chocolate from Hannah.

"She sounds desperate," Hannah observed, picking up the envelope. "Is this a Kachina?" she asked, indicating the drawing in the corner.

Nancy nodded. "If I remember correctly, they are wooden statues carved by members of the southwestern Indian tribes. The dolls represent various Indian spirits. I've seen pictures of them. They are very beautiful and can be quite valuable, too."

"This one doesn't look very friendly," Hannah commented, handing back the envelope. "What are you going to do?"

"Do you think I could turn down such a plea?" Nancy asked, her blue eyes sparkling. "This sounds like a real problem, and Heather *is* an old friend." She finished her drink and got to her feet. "I think I'd better call Dad and find out if he will agree. Then I have to talk to George and Bess and see if they'd be interested in going."

Hannah watched her go with a smile, sure that Mr. Drew would not object to the trip. It had been a long winter for all of them, and the prospect of a mystery to be solved was all the young sleuth ever needed to keep her happy.

Nancy was still on the telephone talking to her father when the doorbell rang. Hannah went to admit George Fayne and her cousin Bess Marvin, Nancy's best friends. She directed them to the study, sure that Nancy would wish to talk to them at once.

"Just the two people I wanted to see," Nancy greeted them as soon as she put down the telephone receiver. "I have something to show you—a letter from Heather McGuire." She handed them the note, then waited patiently while the two girls read it.

George, a slim brunette who had long ago learned to like her masculine first name, looked up first. "You are going, aren't you?" she asked.

Nancy nodded. "I just talked to Dad and he gave his permission. Now what about you two, do you want to go?"

"Do I?" George could hardly contain herself. "I'd love it. Imagine, a vacation on an Arizona ranch."

"What about the curse?" Bess asked, anxiety detracting from her pretty features.

"What about Chuck?" George teased. "You used to think he was quite something. Isn't he worth facing the curse?"

Bess giggled, showing her dimples. "Well, I guess as long as Nancy is going to be there, it will be safe enough. And I do want to help."

"Good," Nancy said. "Now why don't you call your families, then we can make some real plans."

"It's a shame the boys are all so busy at Emerson College," George commented. "They'd probably love to go to Arizona with us, Nancy."

Nancy sighed. "And I'm sure we could use their help," she admitted, thinking of her handsome friend Ned. "But we'll just have to make it on our own, I'm afraid."

Things moved quickly once George and Bess obtained permission from their families. Plane reservations were made for early Friday morning, leaving them just one day to pack the summer clothes they would need once they reached Arizona.

Nancy called Heather that evening and, though their conversation was brief, her friend's gratitude was obvious. That proved to Nancy just how worried Heather was about the rumored curse and what it could mean to her future.

Thursday, Nancy took a little time to go to the library and study the single book it had on Kachinas. The book was filled with photographs of the strange and beautiful wooden dolls, and did give her some information.

The Kachinas had originated as a part of the religion of the Hopi Indians and several other tribes. The dolls themselves represented the spirits of all the visible things in the Indian world. There were Cloud Kachinas, various animal Kachinas, plant and bird Kachinas, and even Kachinas representing abstract ideas like death or the power of the sun.

There wasn't time to read all the details that filled

the book, but as she replaced it on the shelf, Nancy realized that none of what she'd read had even hinted at the Kachinas' being involved in any curses. Could there be some other explanation for what was happening? she asked herself.

Hannah was waiting for her when she returned to the house, and she looked concerned when she handed Nancy a letter. "This came while you were out," she explained.

"It's from Arizona," Nancy observed, not recognizing the handwriting as she opened the envelope. The single sheet of paper she took out showed a crudely drawn Kachina lying on its back, an arrow protruding from it. Pasted-on letters cut from a newspaper made the message very clear.

STAY OUT OF ARIZONA, NANCY DREW.

Hannah gasped as she took the sheet from Nancy. "You can't go, Nancy," she murmured.

Nancy took a deep breath. "But I must," she said. "Don't you see, Hannah, this just proves how desperately Heather and Chuck need my help. It's obvious that no ghost sent this."

"But you could be putting yourself in danger," Hannah protested. "And your father should be told."

Nancy looked at her watch. "He's already on his way to Canada," she reminded Hannah.

"But, Nancy . . ."

"We don't want to worry him, and I'll be very, very careful, I promise," Nancy reassured her. "Now, why don't you help me with my packing? I'm never sure exactly what I should take."

Hannah's gaze told her that she wasn't fully reassured, but she followed the young detective upstairs without further protests. Nancy's heartbeat quickened as she realized that she would soon be on her way to face whoever had sent the threatening letter!

2

The Kachina's Curse

"I can't believe it," Bess said as they walked out of the terminal building into the glow of the late afternoon sun. "It was winter when we left River Heights and now it's spring."

"You'll be able to smell the citrus orchards once we leave here," seventeen-year-old Heather told them as she led the way to where her older brother Chuck was already loading their luggage into a station wagon.

"Is something wrong, Heather?" Nancy asked the slim redhead. Though their reception had been warm, she'd quickly detected a worried glint in her friend's green eyes. "Something you haven't told us?"

Chuck turned his dark head their way, his blue

387

eyes grave. "It's Grandfather," he said. "He's in the hospital. We took him in last night."

"My goodness," Nancy gasped. "What happened?"

"It was the Kachina's curse," Heather answered bitterly. "I didn't really want to believe in it before, but after this, I can't deny it."

"There are no ghosts," Chuck snapped, helping George, Bess, and Nancy into the back seat of the station wagon. "It was a fire in the mountains, nothing else."

Nancy frowned, sensing how troubled her friends were. "Suppose you tell me what happened," she suggested. "Maybe we can figure things out together."

Chuck got in and started the station wagon, while Heather settled herself and half-turned toward the trio in the back seat.

"It happened after we went to bed last night," Heather began, her dappling of freckles much less obvious now that her face had been tanned by the Arizona sun. "We were sleeping, but Grandfather woke up. He said he looked out the window and saw a glow of light off toward the mountains."

"A fire, you mean," Chuck corrected. "Another signal fire, no doubt."

Heather sighed. "The moon was almost full last

night, so Grandfather didn't bother to turn on any lights. He went out in the hall, and that's when he says he saw the Kachina figure."

Chuck grunted, but seemed to concentrate on the traffic as they left the airport area and moved into the city. Heather glared at him, then went on.

"Grandfather started after whatever he saw, and in the poor light, he caught his foot on a rug and fell. We found him in the hall."

Chuck nodded. "He has a broken wrist and a badly wrenched knee. The doctor says he'll have to stay in the hospital for at least a week, till his knee is healed and they're sure there isn't any other damage from the fall."

George and Bess expressed sympathy, but Nancy said very little, though her bright eyes sparkled at this new evidence of a mystery. "Has this Kachina figure been seen before?" she asked after a moment.

"Frequently, if you believe the general gossip," Heather answered. "Not that we did. I mean, we've lived there since the end of December and neither of us has seen anything."

"What about your grandfather?" George asked.

"He didn't believe the stories either," Chuck answered.

"Is there anyone else in the house who has seen

the figure?" Nancy asked. "Anyone I could talk to, I mean?"

To her surprise, Chuck and Heather exchanged glances before Heather answered. "You might ask Ngyun. He's always roaming around the place, so he might have seen something."

"Ngyun?" Nancy asked.

"He's the nephew of Maria Tomiche. She's our housekeeper now and will be the resort dietician when we open," Chuck said. "Her husband Ward teaches at the local school. He's been tutoring Ngyun so he can enter an American school in the fall."

"The boy's just been here about two months," Heather went on. "Maria's brother, Kyle Little Feather, was in Vietnam. He met and married Su Lin, Ngyun's mother, there. He'd planned to bring her and Ngyun to Phoenix as soon as he could, but things got very bad for them when the war ended. Su Lin was able to get out with Ngyun, but Kyle was killed."

"How sad," Bess murmured.

Heather nodded. "Maria didn't hear from Su Lin, didn't even know if they'd escaped till about a year ago. She was very happy when she finally got word and she's been wanting to meet Su Lin ever since, but Su Lin has been ill and finally wrote and asked if she could send Ngyun to his father's family till she was well again."

"How old is Ngyun?" George asked.

"Twelve," Chuck answered, a note of anger in his voice.

Heather giggled. "Don't mind him," she said. "He's unhappy with Ngyun at the moment."

"We just didn't need any more problems," Chuck contributed, sounding far older than twenty. "He's the real cause of Grandfather's accident, not some mysterious Kachina figure."

"What do you mean?" Nancy asked, thinking of the threatening letter she'd received.

"Grandfather was out in the hall because he thought he saw something on the mountain, and that something was probably another of Ngyun's signal fires. That kid has burned two big cactuses and one palo verde tree."

"You don't know that for sure," Heather corrected.

"Well, do you know anyone else who'd ride around the ranch starting small fires?" Chuck asked.

Heather's face was suddenly sad. "No, of course not, but he says he didn't set them, Chuck, and Maria believes him. I mean, he didn't deny starting the first fire." She turned back to Nancy. "He's never had a chance to learn much about his father's people before, and I'm afraid a lot of his ideas come from the old movies on television. He was trying to make smoke signals when he started a fire on the ridge. He was told not to do it again, but several things have been burned since."

"What about the fire your grandfather saw?" Nancy asked, pursuing the question.

"We don't really know," Chuck admitted. "By the time we got back from the hospital, there wasn't any sign of it. I suppose it could have been a trick of the moonlight." His tone made it clear, however, that he didn't believe this explanation. "Most likely though, it just burned out. Desert fires do that, if there isn't any wind."

"Nancy, do you suppose you could handle another case while you're here?" Heather asked, taking Nancy by surprise.

"What do you have in mind?" Nancy asked immediately.

"Well, it's Ngyun. The fires and some of the other things that have happened since he came to the ranch have caused a stir among the neighboring ranchers, and I was hoping that you might be able to clear his name."

"Clear his name?" Nancy frowned. "I don't understand. If he's been doing all these things, how can I help?"

Heather turned her eyes back to the roadside, with its palm and citrus trees. "I guess what I'm asking is that you investigate what has happened," she said, now gazing at Nancy. "You see, Ngyun claims that he only lit the one signal fire, and he denies leaving gates open and all the other little things he's supposed to have done. Maria believes him and, well, we really need to know. If he isn't telling her the truth, Ward says she will simply have to send Ngyun back to his mother's people."

"I'll do my best," Nancy promised, thinking that her vacation on the ranch was already promising to be a very busy one.

"How soon will we get to the ranch?" George asked, changing the subject.

"Oh, we still have quite a drive," Chuck answered. "Kachina Resort is near the Superstition Mountains." He pointed toward the east, where rugged cliffs rose out of the desert landscape.

"The Superstitions," Bess murmured. "Isn't there supposed to be some kind of lost mine in those mountains?"

"The Lost Dutchman Mine," Chuck confirmed, smiling at her. "You'll find people in Apache Junction selling maps to it."

"What is Apache Junction?" George asked.

"That's the little town closest to the ranch," Heather answered.

"Oh." Bess's round face lost a little of its usually happy expression. "I didn't realize we were going to be so far out in the country," she said.

"Don't worry, we won't let the Kachina get you," Chuck teased.

"I wasn't afraid," Bess protested. "It just seems sort of wild out here."

"We felt that way at first, too," Heather said. "But we've come to love the area now." She opened the car window. "This is my favorite time of year, too. Smell the orange blossoms."

The heavy odor drifted in on the light, spring breeze. "Orange blossoms," Bess whispered. "How romantic."

"It really is a business," Chuck corrected. "Those groves ahead are all citrus trees. A month ago, they were still loaded with oranges and grapefruit, but most of it has been picked and sold by now. We have quite a few trees on the ranch, too, so you girls can pick your own grapefruit for breakfast if you like."

"I can hardly wait," Bess said, then blushed as George and Nancy laughed.

"I'm sure Maria will have something much more

substantial prepared for us," Heather assured her. "I told her we'd wait and have dinner at the resort."

George and Bess greeted the news enthusiastically, but Nancy's mind was already on what lay ahead. Investigating a ghostly Indian figure had seemed an interesting challenge, even after the threatening letter arrived, but now that it had actually harmed someone, the whole mystery was much more serious. And, of course, there was the boy Ngyun to be considered, too. Determining his guilt or innocence in the accidents around the area could have very grave consequences for him.

"Nancy," Heather broke into her thoughts. "I'm sorry to meet you with so much bad news. It's just that having the resort means everything to all of us, and this talk of a curse could ruin us before we even start."

"Then we'll just have to stop it, won't we?" Nancy told her, hoping she sounded more confident than she felt at the moment.

Suddenly, when they were rounding a curve, a speeding car from the opposite direction swerved from its lane and came at them head on!

3

Horse Thief

Chuck had no choice but to wrench the wheel to the right and drive off the road. The girls screamed in fright as the car teetered precariously on two wheels for an instant as they moved off the hard surface. The road at this point dropped down a stony incline for a few feet until it evened out in a field overgrown with scrubby weeds.

Finally, the station wagon stalled and came to a halt in the field. Chuck's hands were still tightly clamped around the steering wheel, and he let out a deep sigh.

"That driver must have been out of his mind, coming straight at us like that!" he complained.

Bess, who had been holding on to her cousin's

arm, let go and shook her head in despair. Is that how people drive around here? she wondered.

"I think that man forced us off the road deliberately," Nancy declared. "He wanted us to have an accident!"

"I agree," Heather said. "But why would anyone do such a thing?"

"Maybe it has something to do with the Kachina doll mystery," Nancy said, thinking of the threatening note she had received before leaving River Heights.

"I don't know," Chuck said. "It doesn't make sense. Did anyone get the license number?"

No one had, it all had happened too fast.

"Well, let's see if we can get this car started again," Chuck said. After a few attempts, the engine turned over, and he drove along the field to a spot almost level with the road, and eased the car back onto it. Once they were again on their way, his shaken passengers calmed down.

Though the signs of habitation grew more sparse after they left Mesa, Arizona, the desert never really became desolate, for there were homes scattered throughout the area. Nancy was fascinated by the tall saguaro cactus, with their branching arms so often lifted toward the cloudless, blue sky. Since it was spring, many of them wore crowns of creamy flowers.

The road narrowed and Chuck turned off onto a gravel lane. "Homestretch," he announced. "The ranch starts as we cross the cattleguard. You can see the house just over there."

Nancy followed his pointing finger, and her gasp was echoed by Bess and George. "It looks like a castle!" she exclaimed.

Heather laughed. "That's what I said the first time I saw it."

"It's really more of a fortress," Chuck said. "Those walls are several feet thick, and most of the windows weren't put in till just the last fifty or sixty years. When it was originally built, this was still Indian country and Mr. Harris meant to be safe inside."

"It looks like a part of the mountains," George observed.

"Much of the rock used in the building did come from the Superstitions," Heather acknowledged. "We decided not to change anything about the outside. I think it's more impressive just the way it is, don't you?"

"It's fantastic," Bess breathed. "I had no idea it would be anything like this."

"What are the other buildings?" Nancy asked,

forcing her gaze away from the weathered, golden-beige walls of the huge, old house.

"The low one on the right with the corrals is the stable," Heather began. "The smaller ones on the other side are extra guest cottages. There is a pool house behind the main building, and a pool, of course. There will be tennis courts and a racquet-ball court, but we don't have them done yet." She sighed. "We haven't even finished the interiors of the cottages."

"It's quite a big undertaking," Nancy acknowledged. "Do you have much help?"

"Just Maria in the house. Ward, Maria's husband, helps when he can, and Mr. Henry has let his sons Sam and Joe work for us part-time." She smiled. "Mr. Henry is our nearest neighbor. His ranch is the Circle H over that way." She pointed away from the mountains. "He's been very helpful."

"We'll be able to have ten to fifteen guests in the house itself," Chuck explained, "and when we get through, we should have room for as many as twenty in the cottages."

"What exactly will you do here?" George asked as they rode along the drive between lacy, pale green trees that were full of tiny, yellow flowers. "I mean, this isn't a dude ranch, is it?"

Chuck shook his head. "We're calling it a health

resort. What we plan to do is offer a place for people to come who want healthy outdoor exercise and a proper diet."

"Diet?" Bess's voice wasn't exactly filled with joy. Everyone laughed and she quickly joined in.

"It's not going to be just for losing weight," Heather explained, "although Maria is a dietician and will set up menus for people who do want to shed some pounds. I've studied at a studio in Mesa so I can teach aerobic dancing and rhythm fitness classes, and, if things go well, someday we may be able to put in a golf course. To start, we'll have hiking in the Superstitions, horseback riding, of course, and swimming. We hope to have a sauna ready by fall, and there will be racquetball and tennis. When people come, we'll treat them individually, setting up whatever kind of diet and exercise program they want."

"It sounds wonderful," Nancy said. "Just different enough from the ordinary resort to attract attention, but offering what more and more people are interested in—a healthy vacation."

Heather smiled at the compliment, then her happiness faded. "Healthy if we can get rid of the curse," she amended. "We can't take in a single guest if there really is some ancient apparition stalking our halls."

Chuck snorted derisively as he followed the rough driveway along the side of the old building, which was shadowed now by the thick growth of mesquite bushes and cactus. As they rounded the end of the dun-colored building, Nancy gasped in surprise. The scene ahead was totally unexpected.

A low hedge marked the line between the arid grandeur of the cactus and the dusty desert and a lush, green lawn, flowering bushes, and citrus trees, which scented the warm air. A large pool gleamed aqua in the center of the spreading gardens. A lovely, white building rose behind it, which Nancy assumed was the pool house and home of the future sauna.

"It's lovely!" she exclaimed.

"Water in the desert," Chuck explained. "We thought the contrast would be interesting for our guests."

"Shocking is more like it," George told him.

"It's like a sudden oasis," Bess agreed.

Chuck stopped the station wagon and everyone climbed out.

"Oh, I'm so glad we brought our bathing suits," Bess said. "We can lie by the pool and go home with lovely tans."

"You give them the tour, Sis," Chuck said. "I'll take the luggage in and tell Maria we're home."

"We hope to build three more cottages over there," Heather began. "They can accommodate as many as six people each, so we'll have families. It's tentative now. I mean, we can adapt our plans as we go along. Find out what our guests like best and try to supply it."

"Nothing could be lovelier than this," Nancy told her honestly. "I mean, driving up and seeing everything so completely desert and cactus, then coming around the corner to this garden. I love both aspects and I'm sure your guests will, too."

"We'll have pool parties and cookouts and maybe overnight rides into the desert or mountains, too," Heather went on. "Grandfather knows the area very well and he's been showing Chuck and me all the old trails into the mountains."

Bess sighed. "I'd love to come back when you have a lot of handsome guests to ride with."

Heather's green eyes gleamed as she winked at Nancy. "Won't you enjoy riding with Chuck?" she asked innocently. "I thought you liked him."

Bess blushed, then dimpled as she realized that she was being teased. "You're all terrible," she told them. "None of you has an ounce of romance."

"Well, right at the moment . . ." Heather began, then stopped as a door opened in the rear of the massive, stone building.

"Heather, oh, Heather, I'm so glad you're home." An Indian woman of about thirty came out into the dying sunlight. She was neatly clad in a bright, cotton print dress, and her black hair was fastened back on her neck. She would have been pretty had her expression been less troubled.

"Maria, what is it?" Heather asked, then quickly made introductions as they met on the white stone path that led from the concrete apron of the pool to the rear door of the main building.

"It's Ngyun," Maria began. "Mr. Henry just came by to ask if by any chance Ngyun had come home with an Appaloosa filly."

"What?" Heather asked.

Maria looked uncomfortable. "It seems that one is missing from the J Bar T Ranch, and someone called Mr. Henry and told him they'd seen a boy leading the horse in this direction." She paused, then added, "A boy on a black and white pinto."

"Well, has he come home with the filly?" Heather asked.

Maria sighed. "He hasn't come home at all. You know how upset he was about your grandfather's fall last night. Well, this morning he made himself a lunch and rode out. I haven't seen him since."

"Did Mr. Henry say where he was seen?" Heather asked.

Maria shook her head.

"It's not quite dinner time yet, so suppose I show my guests to their rooms. Then maybe Chuck and I can drive around and see if we can locate him," Heather said soothingly. "But don't worry so, Maria, Cochise isn't the only pinto horse around and Ngyun isn't the only boy in the area, either."

Maria smiled, but there was no happiness in her face.

"We could help you search," Nancy offered quickly. "We don't know the area, but the more pairs of eyes looking . . ." She stopped as the sound of hoofbeats came from the front of the looming building.

In a moment, a boy on a black and white pinto trotted into view. Trailing behind, held firmly by a lead rope, was a dark bay filly, whose haunches displayed the distinctive white blanket with brown spots of an Appaloosa. The boy guided the pinto right up to the hedge before stopping him.

"Hi," he called. "Look what I find running in desert. She pretty."

"Oh, Ngyun," Maria wailed. "Why . . ."

Nancy stopped the woman with a light hand on her arm. "You found the filly in the desert?" she asked, stepping forward, then introducing herself.

Ngyun smiled at her shyly, then nodded. "I know

she belong someone, but I afraid she get in road if I not catch her. Bring her here safe."

Heather looked at Nancy, then nodded slightly. "Why don't you take the filly and Cochise down to the stable," she suggested to the boy. "I'll go inside and call the J Bar T and tell them you found their missing horse."

The boy, who was small for twelve, nodded and turned the pinto around easily. As he rode away, Maria shook her head. "They'll call him a horse thief, won't they?" she asked no one in particular.

Heather offered no argument as Nancy and her friends followed her and Maria toward the imposing, old house. As they stepped into the shadow of the building, Nancy shivered though the day was still warm. There was, she sensed, trouble ahead!

4

Dangerous Warning

The inside of the huge building was surprising. One door led from the rear entry to a large yet cozy-looking room filled with sofas and chairs grouped for conversation or, in one corner, around a television set. A second door, the one they entered through, led into a very modern kitchen, which was filled with delicious scents.

Bess stopped and sniffed appreciatively. "This is even better than the orange blossoms," she observed.

"Dinner will be ready in about an hour," Maria said with a grateful smile. "I was working on it when Mr. Henry arrived."

"You just go ahead with what you were doing,

Maria," Heather told her. "I'll talk to Mr. Henry after I call the people at the J Bar T."

Maria nodded. "Thank you, Heather," she murmured.

Nancy, Bess, and George followed Heather out of the kitchen into an airy dining room. There were several tables scattered around the big room that would accommodate four or six people each, but Nancy could see that there was space for twice as many. The walls were decorated with small, Indian rugs and blankets plus a number of paintings of western and desert scenes. Indian baskets holding dried flower arrangements decorated the side tables, giving the entire room a friendly, western atmosphere.

"I'll show you to your rooms before I take care of things for Maria," Heather began. "I'm just sorry that all this has come up right now. I was hoping we could have a nice, quiet evening, but . . ."

"You don't really think the boy took the filly, do you?" George asked.

Heather sighed. "I don't want to," she replied, "but there have been so many incidents. Everything seemed fine at first, but after he started riding so much . . ."

"He's a cute boy," Bess said. "And he certainly

speaks English well for having been here such a short time."

"His mother speaks some English and she insisted that he learn it, too. Also, he's trying hard to be like his father, though he can't remember him too well. He was barely three when Kyle was killed." Heather led them into a large hall and Nancy gasped with delight.

"Are these the Kachinas?" Bess asked breathlessly.

"Our private gallery," Heather confirmed, her tone a mixture of pride and resignation as she pointed to the beautifully decorated walls of the hall. "And home of our resident ghost, I guess."

"Now, Heather, you don't really believe all those stories, do you?" The man who stepped into the long hall of Kachinas from the other side was tall, well-muscled, and weathered.

"Mr. Henry!" Heather said. "I was just coming to talk to you." She told quickly about Ngyun's appearance with the filly and his explanation of how it had come into his care.

"I'll take the filly to the J Bar T Ranch," Mr. Henry said, "and I'll report everything to them."

Only when that was settled did Heather remember her guests. She quickly introduced Nancy, George, and Bess to the rancher.

"So you're the sleuth that Chuck and Heather are counting on to capture their ghost," Mr. Henry said, shaking Nancy's hand firmly. "I had no idea you'd be so young, Miss Drew, or so pretty."

Nancy blushed, unsure what to say.

"She'll do it, too," George said firmly. "No ghost is safe around Nancy."

"I'm certainly going to do my best to solve the mystery here," Nancy agreed. "I want to help Heather and Chuck make this resort a success."

"We all do," Mr. Henry assured her. "That's why I'm concerned about the boy. He's causing a lot of trouble in the area, and Heather, you're going to need the good will of your neighbors if you want this resort to work."

"I don't see how a few childish pranks could cause so much trouble," Nancy said, her mind on the shy smile and almond eyes of the boy who'd ridden in on the pinto. He'd seemed younger than twelve and quite defenseless.

"That filly is worth a great deal of money," Mr. Henry told her. "And there have been a number of other things. We've been lucky with the fires so far, but he could light up a barn or a house next, and that wouldn't be so easy for us to ignore."

Heather gasped and Nancy could see her paling at the man's accusing tone, but before she could say anything, Chuck came into the hall. A moment later, the rancher excused himself to talk to Chuck about some ranch business.

Heather turned back to the wall paintings with a sigh. "They really are beautiful, aren't they?" she said. "Someone suggested that we might be able to get rid of the ghost by painting over them, but I couldn't do that."

"Of course not," Bess agreed. "They are real art treasures."

"Which Kachinas are they?" Nancy asked. "I mean, what do they represent?"

Heather smiled and pointed out the feather-headdressed, red, white, and yellow Cloud Kachina; the feather-winged Eagle Kachina; the white-furred Bear Kachina; and finally a blue-masked, white-bodied creature known as the Prickly Pear Cactus Kachina. "The other three we haven't identified yet," she finished. "Maria says she thinks the one on the end is a Mud-head, but the other two even she doesn't recognize."

"They certainly are exotic," Nancy observed, standing in front of one of the unidentified figures, which sported a feathery topknot and a very carefully patterned body. "Your guests are going to love them."

"I hope so," Heather said with a smile. "Especially you three, since your rooms are right along this hall." She paused, then added, "I hope you and George don't mind sharing a room, Bess. We don't have all our furniture yet."

"Just being here is wonderful," Bess and George assured Heather as she pointed to the two doors that opened just beyond the bend in the hall.

"The front of the house is devoted to the lobby area and the resort office," Heather explained, "so all the bedrooms open off this hall. Grandfather, Chuck, and I have rooms at the other end at the moment, though we hope eventually to move upstairs and convert all the rooms down here for our guests."

"What about the Tomiches?" Nancy asked. "Do they live at the resort?"

"Yes, on the second floor, as a matter of fact. Ward and Chuck have been working on the modernization up there in the evenings. They have one end fixed, but that's all."

"Where did your grandfather see the Kachina spirit?" Nancy inquired, her mind returning to the reason for her visit.

Heather frowned. "Well, he said he came out of his room and started along the hall, but he'd only taken a few steps when he saw this thing in the moonlight. He thought it was an intruder, so he went down the hall in a hurry, then he caught his foot and . . . well, he said that the figure just seemed to fade into the wall about there." She indicated the Kachina that had attracted Nancy's eye.

Nancy stared at the painting for a moment, wishing that the masked face could give her some kind of clue. But the old paint was uninformative, and, after another moment, she shrugged and allowed herself to be directed to her room.

"I suppose if we're going to unpack before dinner, we'd better get started," she murmured as she stepped through the door which bore a freshly painted number on it.

"Don't feel rushed," Heather told them all. "We're just family, so Maria can hold dinner if you want to nap or something."

"Oh, no," Bess said quickly, "don't have her do that, not the way everything smelled in the kitchen. It must be nearly ready."

Nancy laughed as she closed her door and turned her attention to her suitcases, which Chuck had placed on the bench at the foot of her double bed. She got her keys out and started to open the large one first, anxious to hang her clothes in the closet so the wrinkles would come out. However, when she tried to unlock the bag, she found that it was already unlocked.

Could she have forgotten to lock it? Nancy asked herself as she opened the case. They had been rushed, but still. . . . Frowning, she began taking things out, trying hard to remember everything she'd packed and the exact order it had been put in.

Everything seemed all right, but when she reached for her new, blue knit shirt, the wrinkle in it moved and she jerked her hand back quickly. Nothing happened, so she carefully picked up one of the clothes hangers from the bed and lightly touched the "wrinkle." It moved suddenly, and to her horror, a brownish scorpion nearly two-and-a-half inches long scuttled out of her shirt, its deadly tail moving angrily!

5

A Scary Apparition

Nancy shrieked when she saw the ugly scorpion, but managed to control her nerves enough to use one of her unpacked riding boots to kill the creature before it could find a new hiding place. Only then did she catch her breath and really look at it.

"How did you get in that suitcase?" she asked the dead scorpion. "You didn't come with me from River Heights, that's for sure."

She picked up the vicious creature, with its poisonous stinger, and disposed of it in the corner wastebasket. Nancy looked around, sighing. It was possible that her unlocked case could have come open in the luggage area of the airport, or even here, but somehow she didn't think so. She had a disturbing feeling that someone had used the scorpion in another attempt to get rid of her. Was it the driver of the car that had forced them off the road when they arrived? The person who sent her the threatening note in River Heights?

In any case, her enemy obviously knew she had been invited by Heather and Chuck before she left home, and was desperately trying to keep her from solving the mystery. But who could it be? And what was his or her motive?

Nancy sighed. "This is getting stranger every minute," she said to herself. "And certainly more dangerous!"

Chuck and Heather seemed unsurprised when she casually mentioned the scorpion as they sat in the rear parlor after dinner.

"We don't see as many of them now as we did when we first moved in," Heather said, "but they are still around. It's wise to empty your shoes before you put them on in the morning, just to be sure."

"Ugh," Bess said with a shudder. "How could you do anything but scream, Nancy? I'd be scared to death if I found one."

"Then it's a good thing that we're sharing a room," George told Bess. "While you are screaming, the scorpion would just find a new place to hide."

"I don't think you'll need to worry, Bess," Chuck

said with a smile. "We had the exterminator out last week, so that little devil probably came from outside the house."

"I'm not so sure," Nancy said, then showed them the letter she'd received the day before.

Chuck looked grave after he finished reading it. "Now I'm beginning to think that scorpion was planted," he said. "And you probably are convinced that the car accident yesterday was deliberate, too."

Nancy shrugged. "I honestly don't know what to think," she admitted.

After a few moments of silence, the talk turned to other subjects, and soon the long day's excitement began to catch up with the three girls. Nancy was glad when Heather suggested that they make it an early evening. "I've invited some of our friends over for a barbecue tomorrow night," she explained. "I thought you might enjoy having a campfire in the desert."

"That sounds like fun," George and Nancy chorused.

"Without scorpions," Chuck told Bess, and they all laughed as the pretty blonde added her voice enthusiastically to theirs.

In spite of her weariness, Nancy found sleep difficult as she watched the moonlight tracing the delicate limbs of a palo verde tree which grew just beyond the single window of her room. She'd seen no more of Ngyun Little Feather, since he and the Tomiches ate in the kitchen rather than the dining room, but she found it hard to believe that the boy was a troublemaker. However, she could see no reason for anyone to falsely accuse Ngyun of starting fires or stealing the Appaloosa filly.

The Kachina paintings troubled her, too. They were beautiful and strangely fascinating, with their alien colors and forms. They were perfect for the resort, and as she'd stood in front of them, she'd felt no sensation of haunting or menace, only a kind of sadness.

Though she wasn't aware of drifting into sleep, Nancy knew as soon as she opened her eyes that a great deal of time had passed, for the moonlight no longer played brightly through her deep window. For a moment, she just lay still, then the sound came again and she sat up. Someone was out in the hall!

She slipped her feet into her shoes, trying not to think of scorpions, then pulled on her robe as she moved to the door, opening it as quietly as she could. The hall, which stretched in both directions, was dimly lit by the moonlight that came in the windows at each end, but shadows lay heavy along the inner walls and in the doorways that opened off it.

Suddenly, something moved out of the shadows at the near end of the hall and seemed to be coming toward Nancy. Sure that it was an intruder, Nancy stepped back into her room, closing the door to a crack, then peeping out. Only when the apparition reached her did she realize that it was no human form.

The Kachina drifted by, moving in and out of the shadows, seeming unaware of Nancy's eyes. Fearfully, she eased her door open and stepped out into the hall, determined to follow the creature and perhaps learn if it was real or part of a nightmare. Just then, the apparition reached the turn in the hall, and Nancy had to hurry to keep it in sight.

Her feet made soft sounds on the bare floor, but she wasn't really conscious of anything except following the Kachina. Then, suddenly, someone was coming down the stairs and a switch clicked, flooding the hall with light. The Kachina whirled for a moment, then disappeared into the wall.

"Miss Drew?" Maria Tomiche came up to her. "I thought I heard someone down here. I hope I didn't frighten you."

"Call me Nancy, please," Nancy told her, forcing

a smile though her heart was still pounding with excitement from following the Kachina.

"Were you looking for something?" the Indian woman asked.

Nancy peered around, suddenly aware that there were people sleeping behind the doors along the hall. "Could we go to the kitchen and talk?" she whispered. "I don't want to wake the others."

"Of course. Would you like some tea? I mix my own herbal blend and came down to have a cup myself. I often do when I can't sleep."

"I definitely could use a cup of tea," Nancy assured her, shivering now in reaction to her spooky vision. "I think I've just seen the Kachina ghost."

Maria nodded, seeming unsurprised as she stepped through the door that led into the kitchen. She busied herself making two cups of steaming, fragrant tea, added a small plate of pecan-rich cookies, then settled herself at the kitchen table with Nancy.

"You've seen the Kachina yourself, haven't you?" Nancy asked.

Maria nodded. "Its spirit has lived here for years, but it mostly appears when the moon is full, as it was last night and is tonight."

"You're not afraid of it?"

420

Maria shook her head. "The Kachinas are sacred to my people, so why should I be afraid? Besides, it has done no harm here. Mr. McGuire fell because he caught his foot in one of the small rugs, that's all."

"Do you know why the Kachinas haunt this house?" Nancy asked, suddenly sure that this quiet woman could offer her some valuable clues to the mystery she'd come to unravel.

Maria sipped her tea for a moment, then sighed. "I think it has to do with the man who built this house and the way he died," she replied.

"Do you know the story?"

"I know all the stories that were told," Maria answered evasively.

"But you don't believe them?"

Maria shrugged. "Big Jake Harris built this house and painted all the Kachinas. He was a friend of the Indians and he honored our ways. There was no reason for his death to be blamed on the old tribal chiefs. They wouldn't have scared him to death."

"What do you mean?" Nancy asked, intrigued by the woman's words. "Who said that's what happened?"

Maria looked at her suspiciously, then seemed to decide that Nancy was honestly interested. "The story is that Big Jake took something valuable from the Hopi, a treasure of some sort, and hid it in this house. When they came to reclaim it, he refused to give it up, so they threatened to burn him out or maybe they attacked the house or something. Anyway, he was a frail, old man and the fear was too much for him. He was found dead in the hall near that strange middle Kachina."

Nancy nodded, realizing that Maria must mean the spot where her apparition had disappeared. "But you don't believe that's what happened, do you?" she asked.

"My great-grandfather was among the chiefs blamed for Jake Harris's death. They were driven out of the area and died in exile in Mexico. My great-grandmother mourned him for years. She always swore that he and Jake Harris were old friends, that Jake would never have taken their treasure, so there was no reason for them to have frightened him to death."

"Do you think that's why the Kachina spirit still haunts this house?"

Maria nodded. "My great-grandfather and several of the other chiefs died shamed and alone for something they didn't do."

"Why do other people say the spirit appears?" Nancy asked, wanting to get the whole story.

"They say that the chiefs put a curse on this house because Jake Harris had hidden their treasure and they couldn't find it even after he was dead," Maria explained emotionlessly.

Nancy stared at Maria in surprise. "You mean that the treasure is still here?"

6

First Clue

Maria shrugged. "That's the story most people believe."

"But you don't?"

"People used to search this house and the surrounding area. I've heard stories about it ever since I was a little girl. No one ever found any treasure." Maria got to her feet briskly. "Would you like more tea?"

Nancy drained her cup, then shook her head. "It's delicious, but I think I should be getting back to bed. Thank you for telling me about the house and the Kachina spirit. You have given me plenty to think about."

"I just hope it helps you solve the mystery here so the McGuires can go on with the resort." Maria's expression softened. "And thank you for saying that you'd try to help Ngyun. He's really a very good boy, Miss Drew—Nancy. I just can't believe he'd do anything that would get him sent away from here. He wants so much to be like his father."

"I'll do my best on both," Nancy assured her, then made her way back through the now empty and quiet hall to her own peaceful room.

After her disturbing night, Nancy slept later than was her habit. When she'd washed and dressed in jeans and a bright, plaid Western shirt, she went outside to find Bess, George, and Heather still sitting around a table in the back garden. All three were sipping some of Maria's herb tea, their breakfast dishes empty on the table before them.

"We got too hungry to wait," Bess told her. "Anyway, we wanted you to sleep late. Maria told us that you had some excitement last night, so you would be tired."

"Did she tell you what happened?" Nancy asked, feeling rather strange about confessing to what she'd seen in the shadowy hall. It had been believable in the light of the full moon, but now that the bright Arizona sun was shining and the bees were buzzing around the citrus blossoms, it seemed more like a dream.

"She just said you'd seen something in the hall

and had tea with her before going back to bed," George answered, her eyes full of curiosity.

"Was it the Kachina ghost?" Heather asked as Maria came out with an omelet and a large glass of fresh-squeezed orange juice for Nancy.

Nancy recounted her night's adventures carefully, starting with the sound she'd heard in the hall. "At the time, I thought it must be an intruder," she said, "but now I realize that it was more like distant voices singing or chanting."

"An Indian chant?" George asked.

"It could have been," Nancy admitted.

"I wouldn't have followed it out into the hall," Bess murmured, shivering. "That's so spooky."

"What do you think it means?" Heather asked.

Nancy repeated the two stories that Maria had told her about the haunting of Kachina House.

Heather nodded. "I've heard both theories," she admitted. "But what does it help? Either way, we still have a ghost and we can't open our doors to guests till we get rid of it." Her voice was filled with despair. "I guess we should have sold the place to Mr. Henry when he offered to buy it last fall."

"Someone wanted it?" George asked. "You didn't tell us that."

"Oh, he wasn't interested in the old house, just the land. He has cattle, and he was going to expand his herd. We'd already done quite a bit of work on the house, though, so we didn't want to give up the resort idea."

"You sound as though you might change your mind now," Nancy observed, feeling sorry for the girl.

Heather's green eyes filled with tears. "I love it here, ghost and all, but if we can't open the resort, we'll have to sell. Grandfather invested everything we have in it. But we won't be able to maintain it, unless we make money, and we'll have to sell at a loss."

"Nancy won't let that happen," George assured her. "She'll find a way to stop the ghost."

The young detective ate her delicately spiced omelet without speaking, hoping fervently that she could justify her old friend's confidence. If the ghost had been simply someone's trickery, she would have felt surer of her next move. But last night's apparition was something she'd never encountered before, and she wasn't exactly sure what to do next.

"What would you three like to do this morning?" Heather asked, recovering her composure. "Our dinner guests won't be arriving till early afternoon, when we'll ride into the Superstitions. There's a pretty trail that leads to the place where Ward and Maria will have our dinner waiting."

"I'd like to get to know Ngyun a little better," Nancy suggested, remembering her other mystery. "Maybe he could tell us more about finding the filly."

Heather sighed. "I'm afraid he's already gone," she said. "I went to invite him to join us this afternoon, but Maria said he'd left just after dawn."

Nancy frowned. "Where does he go?" she asked.

"I don't really know," Heather admitted. "He gets on that pinto and rides out into the desert. He used to talk about learning to trail animals and watching coyotes and jackrabbits, things like that. But since the fires . . ." Her voice trailed off. "I don't think he trusts us anymore."

"Could we check the places where the fires have been set?" Nancy asked, determined to do what she could to help the unhappy boy.

"Sure," Heather replied. "You can see the blackened area up there on the ridge." She indicated a rocky ledge about a mile from the stable. "That's where he set the first one. He said he was learning to make smoke signals."

"And the others?" Nancy asked.

"Well, besides the one Grandfather thought he saw, there have been three, and the only other close one is about half a mile beyond that ridge. You can't see it from here, but when you get up on the ridge, the burned saguaro is off toward the mountains."

"So those two are within walking distance," Nancy mused.

Heather nodded. "I'd take you to see all of them today, but Chuck's already off with the jeep to run errands, and the roads are too rough for the station wagon."

"After this breakfast, I need the exercise," Nancy assured their hostess, then turned to Bess and George. "Are you ready for a nice walk in the desert?"

"You're sure you wouldn't rather lie by the pool and start a suntan?" Bess asked hopefully.

George and Nancy shook their heads, laughing.

As the three girls set off past the stable and corrals, they quickly discovered that the desert was far from desolate. The spring rains had brought green to the tufts of grass that grew everywhere, and there were delicate wild flowers on the gently rising and falling slopes of the hills that rolled toward the Superstitions. Yellow, blue, red, and white blossoms danced in the light breeze, and even the cactus exhibited flowers of varying hues.

"Why, it is really beautiful," Bess commented as

she stopped to watch a large jackrabbit bounding between two fat-bodied barrel cactuses, with their crowns of pale flowers.

"Look, there's a roadrunner," Nancy called, pointing to where the big bird was racing from one clump of grass to another. He paused, lifting his black-crested head to stare at them. Then, with a jerking of his long black tail, he was on his way again, disappearing behind a strange cactus that looked as though it was composed of monkey tails topped with scarlet flowers.

"Don't they fly?" Bess asked as the bird appeared on a small ridge ahead of them, still on his feet.

"They can," Nancy replied. "They just prefer to run."

Ahead, more desert wildlife left cover as several quail took flight. Nancy stopped, and in a moment the gray and brown birds with their dainty, black head plumes returned to the ground. Almost at once, a dozen little, yellow and brown–streaked balls of fluff emerged from the grass to join their parents. They disappeared into their thicket again as the girls detoured away from them on their walk to the ridge.

Once they reached the top, Nancy saw the charred remains of the fire. There were several stubs of scrap wood and the ends of some wooden kitchen matches. Bending closer, she could see that there were more bits of wood under the sand.

"It looks like someone tried to put this out," she observed. "Maybe Ngyun kicked sand over it and thought it was out, then it smouldered back to life."

"At least he didn't just go off and leave it to burn," Bess agreed.

"It wouldn't really matter," George contributed. "There's nothing around close enough to catch fire anyway."

"What about that cactus down below?" Bess asked, pointing toward the blackened skeleton of what had been a large and handsome saguaro cactus at the bottom of the hill.

Nancy picked up the ends of the kitchen matches and dropped them into her pocket, sure that they were a clue Ngyun had left, since she'd seen a box of kitchen matches on the big range in the resort kitchen.

The ground was rougher after they left the ridge. Small stones twisted treacherously under their feet, and the long spines of a big, prickly pear cactus reached out toward them as they slipped and slid down the incline toward the burned saguaro.

Once they reached it, Nancy looked around. "This doesn't seem like a very good place to light a signal fire," she said. "No one could see it."

"Maybe that was the idea," George suggested. "After being scolded for lighting the one on the ridge, he wouldn't have wanted anyone at the resort to see this next fire."

Nancy nodded, realizing that her friend could be correct. However, as she looked around the area of the blackened cactus, she quickly saw the difference. There was no neat pile of charred wood and, though she scraped the sandy soil all around the burned area, no sign of wooden match stubs.

"What do you think?" Nancy asked after she explained what she'd been looking for.

"I'd say this was deliberately set on fire," George said, frowning, "and not as a signal fire, either."

"But why?" Bess asked. "Why would anyone set fire to a cactus?"

Nancy could only shrug her shoulders. She was silent and thoughtful as they turned away from the blackened corpse of the saguaro. There was something wrong, and it had little to do with the burned cactus. She felt a prickling of fear and looked back just in time to see the massive saguaro sway and start to fall!

7

A Bolting Mare

There was no time to warn her friends. Nancy grabbed Bess and George by their arms and threw them and herself out of the path of the falling cactus. They all three stumbled and fell sprawling on the ground as the saguaro crashed to earth where they had been standing.

"What happened?" George gasped. "How . . .?"

"I saw it falling," Nancy explained. "I guess I must have loosened the soil at the bottom while I was searching for clues." She stopped, not sure that she believed her own words.

Bess shivered. "This place really is haunted," she observed. "Let's get back to the resort."

Nancy nodded, realizing that there was nothing else to be done here. Only the promise of the afternoon ride and the evening barbecue under the stars lifted her spirits from the unfamiliar feeling of confusion that both cases had brought her so far.

When the girls returned to the ranch and reported their experience to Chuck and Heather, he apologized for having neglected to warn them about the danger of the burned cactus.

"I've been wanting to pull it down," Chuck said. "But I just forgot about it after Grandfather was hurt. I'm glad you acted so quickly, Nancy."

"No one blames you," Nancy assured him. "And I don't think it just happened to fall down all by itself, although I was digging in the ashes around it."

"You mean—?" Bess stared at her friend in shock. The thought that someone might have toppled the cactus to hurt the girls had not occurred to her earlier.

Nancy nodded. "Could be another attempt of our unknown enemy to get rid of us. Unfortunately, I have no way to prove it."

Heather's face was worried, but she tried to cheer up her friends. "Well, whatever the reason was that the cactus fell, I think you should all relax by the pool now," she said. "Save your energy for tonight."

"That sounds like a wonderful idea," Bess agreed.

When time for the barbecue ride came, Nancy, Bess, and George were delighted to discover that the other guests were four young, male friends of Chuck's and a pert brunette that Heather introduced as Diana. Chuck had the horses saddled and waiting, and as soon as they finished the introductions, everyone went to the stable to mount up for the ride.

Chuck, with Bess riding beside him, took the lead, and Nancy quickly found herself alongside a dark-haired young man called Floyd Jerrett. He proved to be a pleasant companion as he pointed out the various formations among the weathered and somewhat overwhelming rock cliffs of the ever-closer Superstition Mountains.

"Did you ever go up there to look for the Lost Dutchman Mine?" Nancy asked.

Floyd laughed. "Everyone around here does," he answered. "I've ridden or hiked over most of the mountains since I was seven or eight. That's when I used to go out weekends with my father. We have even come across gold up there."

"From the mine?" Nancy was impressed.

"Oh, no, nothing that exciting. There are some small pockets of gold or short veins of it that wash out or are uncovered by the winter rains and floods. We've found nuggets and gold dust in the washes."

"If you girls are going to be here long enough, perhaps we can go prospecting," Tim, one of the other young men, suggested, smiling shyly at George. "We might find something, you never know."

"With Nancy's talent as a detective, we could even find the Dutchman's mine," Heather suggested from the rear of the group where she was riding with Diana's brother Paul.

"I can supply the maps," Diana offered with a giggle. "I must have twenty-five and they're all different."

"And all genuine," her date, Jerry Blake, added.

"Thanks, but I think I have quite enough mysteries at the moment," Nancy said, laughing easily.

"Nancy has seen our resident ghost," Heather told everyone.

Discussion of the Kachina spirit and the various stories about the old house kept them all busy as they rode up into the rugged mountains, following narrow trails that were flanked by sheer cliffs on one side and rather frightening, rocky slides on the other. Though Nancy loved to ride and found her bright chestnut mare Dancer a pleasure to handle, she was glad when the trail finally dropped down into a small canyon rich with trees and flowers. They reined in near the small stream that was fed by a spring.

The ranch jeep was parked at the mouth of the

canyon, and the sweet scents of food already filled the air as the young people dismounted and walked over to where Maria and her strong, dark-eyed husband were working at a small campfire. Nancy looked around and was disappointed not to find Ngyun in sight, but just as she opened her mouth to inquire about the boy, a flash of black and white appeared between the trees and he rode up to them.

Maria and Ward Tomiche greeted Ngyun with what looked like relief. When he rode to where the horses were tied, Nancy joined him. Talking to the boy was difficult at first, for he was very shy, but when she asked him about his horse, his attitude changed.

"He mine," Ngyun said. "Really mine. My grandfather say I have any horse in big herd. I take Cochise. He beautiful."

"You ride very well, too," Nancy told him. "Did your grandfather teach you?"

"Some," Ngyun answered. "We not see him much now. Uncle Ward and Aunt Maria help and Chuck. They say I like real Indian."

Nancy let the boy talk on, asking him questions about where he went and what he did. There was no hesitation in his answers, she noted. If he was lying or covering up, he was far better at it than any adult she'd ever questioned. His almond eyes fairly

437

glowed as he talked about the deer and the wild, piglike creatures called javelina that he'd seen in the washes leading from the mountains into the desert.

"When I learn to use bow and arrows good, I hunt them," he said. "Grandfather say he bring home dinner with bow and arrows."

"Don't get too close to the javelina," Ward cautioned from the fire, where he was helping Maria set out the various dishes of food. "They may look like long-haired pigs, but they have very sharp tusks and nasty dispositions. They can be dangerous."

"Dinner is ready," Heather announced before either Ngyun or Nancy could say another word.

Never had food tasted so good. There were mounds of barbecued ribs dripping with a delicious sauce. Beans, both the traditional, baked kind and the Mexican, refried variety, were offered. There were taco chips and a green mound of guacamole dip made from avocados and onions and cottage cheese. Fresh fruits and vegetables were set out in cold water, and there was plenty of icy soda to drink.

"Don't you love our fancy china?" Heather teased, passing out battered, tin pie plates and sturdy eating utensils as well as bandana-sized napkins.

"Everything is just perfect," George assured her

as she began heaping food on her plate. "The high sides on the pie plates keep the food where it is supposed to be."

Bess sampled the refried beans, which were delicately spiced with bits of hot peppers and onions. "Oh, this is heavenly," she told Maria. "But if you're going to feed your guests like this, I don't think they'll be losing any weight."

Chuck looked up with innocent eyes. "Oh, didn't Heather tell you, we have a new method of dieting. We feed you like this, but then you have to hike back to the ranch."

Mock groans were followed by loud protest, and everyone relaxed on the grass to eat, talking contentedly of past and future rides, picnics, and barbecues. Only when the plates had been scraped clean did Bess sigh and say, "I know I shouldn't ask after all that food, but is there dessert?"

There was general laughter, but when Maria nodded, everyone turned toward her. "Indian Fry Bread," she announced. "I've brought the dough out and I'll fry it here, then you put either powdered sugar or honey inside. It makes a perfect dessert."

"Fried bread?" Bess looked dubious, but when she received the first piece and dutifully poured on the honey, her expression changed. "Why, it's wonderful!" she exclaimed. "I must find out how to make it. Everyone at home will be fascinated."

Once the food was gone, Chuck and the other young men gathered more of the nearby dead wood—fallen limbs, trees, and bushes that hadn't come back to life with spring's magic. The campfire blazed as the sun suddenly slipped beneath the horizon, plunging them quickly into night.

Ward produced a guitar from the jeep and Chuck began to play while Bess looked at him dreamily. The familiar melody soon had everyone singing along. Nancy leaned her head back, staring up at the stars, thinking how lovely and peaceful everything seemed.

"Once the moon is up, we'll have to start back," Chuck told them between songs.

"Not the way we came, I hope," Bess murmured. "I'd be afraid of missing that trail in the dark."

"No, we'll take an easier route," Heather promised. "We don't want any trouble."

While they sang, Nancy noticed that Ward and Maria had packed up all the supplies, and once the jeep was loaded, they left the canyon. Ngyun vanished, too, not waiting to ride back with them through the cooling, night air.

"I'm glad you told us to tie our jackets behind our

saddles, Heather," Nancy said, pulling hers on before she mounted Dancer. "It feels good now."

"The desert can be quite cold at night," Heather agreed. "Even in the summer, it cools off once the sun goes down."

They were quiet as they rode back, following the edge of a wash that led through the rough hills. Nancy was so deep in thought, trying to decide what to do about the Kachina spirit, that she didn't notice when the mare slowed a little. Dancer dropped behind the other horses to nibble at a tuft of grass growing on the rough hillside the trail was skirting.

Suddenly, the silence of the desert night was broken by a rattling, and Dancer whinnied, nearly unseating the young sleuth. Though she'd lost a stirrup, Nancy clenched her knees to the mare's sides, trying to keep her moving forward on the trail. But the horse was too terrified. In a moment, they were slipping and sliding down the rocky slope toward the bottom of the wash.

Frightened, Nancy grabbed the saddle horn and did her best to stay still in the saddle so as not to throw the mare off-balance as she skidded toward the hard-baked earth below. Rocks and other debris fell with them, and she could hear the shouts of the others, but at the moment everything depended on the mare's surefootedness.

Dancer's plunging ended as she stumbled to her knees, nearly throwing Nancy over her head. Still the terrified mare didn't stop. She scrambled back to her feet and leaped forward, with Nancy hanging on for dear life!

8

The Rattler

The mare stumbled again in the roughness of the wash.

Nancy regained her balance and immediately tightened her hold on the reins, trying to steady the mare. She talked to the animal as calmly as she could while her own heart was still racing from the terror of their wild descent. "Steady, girl. It's all right, Dancer," she soothed, finally succeeding in stopping the trembling creature.

"Nancy, Nancy, are you all right?" Heather called.

"I'm fine," Nancy answered, getting off the horse. "But I think we should check Dancer. She went down on her knees when we hit bottom and may have injured her legs."

In a moment, Heather, Bess, George, and the others rode back along the wash, having come down a more gradual slope further along the trail. "I have a flashlight," Heather said, taking it out of her saddlebag and dismounting to join Nancy on the ground. "What happened?" she asked as they examined the mare's slim front legs.

"It was a rattlesnake," Nancy explained. "I was riding along and all of a sudden it seemed to come down the cliff after us. I tried to keep Dancer on the trail, but she was terrified, of course. It must have been right under her hooves. Do you think she could have been bitten?"

Heather ran a hand over the mare's legs, examining them a second time. "I don't see anything," she answered. "Her knees are skinned and she's probably pretty badly bruised, but she'll make it back to the ranch all right. We'll just have to go slow. If she starts to limp, you can always ride double with someone."

"You say a rattlesnake came down the cliff after you?" Chuck asked, breaking into their examination.

Nancy nodded. "I could hear it rattling as it came."

"That doesn't make sense," Chuck said. "Rattle-

444

snakes are shy of people. Are you sure it wasn't alongside the trail?"

"You'd already ridden by," Nancy reminded him. "If it had been along the trail, it would have been disturbed and rattling long before I got there, wouldn't it?"

"Let me have the flashlight," Chuck ordered. "And somebody hold my horse. I'll go up and see if I can find the snake."

"You be careful, Chuck," Heather warned, surrendering the flashlight to her brother.

"Are you sure you're all right, Nancy?" George asked, moving to Nancy's side now that Heather had finished examining the horse. "You weren't hurt at all?"

"Just frightened half to death," Nancy assured her. "It all happened so fast."

The others gathered around making suggestions about the snake and telling tales of their own brushes with rattlers. It was several minutes before Chuck slid back down the side of the wash.

"What did you find?" Nancy asked.

"Your rattlesnake," Chuck answered, holding out his hand so that she could see the odd-looking thing that lay in his palm. It rattled slightly from the movement, and Dancer snorted and pulled back against Nancy's steady hold on her reins.

"What is it?" Bess squeaked, stepping back just as the horse had.

"It's the rattle from a big snake," Chuck explained. "Some people cut them off dead rattlers and make them into tourist souvenirs. I found it lying on the trail."

"But how . . .?" Heather began, then turned to face Nancy, her eyes wide with fright. "Did you say it came down the cliff after you?" she asked.

Nancy nodded.

"Then someone must have thrown it from up there." Chuck uttered the words that had already begun to fill Nancy's mind with pictures of the possible consequences.

Heather gasped. "Nancy could have been injured!" she cried out. "If Dancer had lost her footing in that rock slide coming down, she could have been seriously hurt!"

"Well, nothing like that happened," Nancy said soothingly. "I'm fine and Dancer's all right, so I think we should just put this behind us and get back to the ranch." She did not want to mention their unknown enemy to Heather's friends, but she asked herself the same question Bess, George, and the McGuires did. Was this another deliberate attempt to get her off the Kachina Doll case?

The young people remounted and rode their horses along the wash. Once they reached the resort, Nancy, Bess, and George escorted the guests to their cars, but their good nights were subdued and everyone left rather quickly. Not knowing what else to do, the girls settled in the lobby, waiting for Chuck and Heather to come up from the stable.

"You think it was deliberate, don't you, Nancy?" George asked breaking the silence.

Nancy sighed. "Someone had to drop that rattlesnake down the cliff, and I was the only one riding by at the time."

"I agree," George said. "And it wasn't the Kachina spirit, either."

Nancy chuckled, "I'm sure it wasn't. As a matter of fact, the spirit seemed almost friendly last night. Whoever threw that rattler wasn't friendly at all."

"That's for sure," Heather agreed from the archway that led to the hall of the Kachina paintings. "We were just talking about that."

"And what did you decide?" Nancy asked as Chuck joined his sister in the doorway.

"That you'd better stop your investigation," Chuck replied.

"What?" Nancy looked from one to the other. "But I've just begun."

"That awful letter you showed us was bad

enough," Heather said. "And the accident and finding the scorpion in your suitcase and the toppled cactus. But this. . . . If it means things like this are going to happen, we can't let you go on, Nancy. When I wrote to you and asked you to come here, I had no idea that you would be in any kind of danger."

Chuck nodded. "The letter and the scorpion, maybe, were warnings. But you could have been killed tonight! That's more than a warning."

"I'll just have to be more careful in the future," Nancy replied firmly. "If someone is trying this hard to frighten me away, that must mean I'm making real progress, don't you think?"

Heather and Chuck seemed unconvinced, but after cups of thick, sweet, hot chocolate and cream prepared by Maria, they all went to their rooms without further discussion. A long, relaxing bath gave Nancy plenty of time to think, but she still hadn't a clue about the person who'd thrown the rattler down on her. She slipped between the cool sheets and pulled the bright quilt over her shoulders with a sigh.

She'd been asleep for several hours when the strange sounds woke her again. This time, she lay still and listened, identifying them as chanting, though she couldn't distinguish any words. After several minutes, she got up and padded to the door, quite sure what she'd find on the other side.

The Kachina she saw was much closer this time, and the moment she opened the door, it seemed to beckon to her, then moved on along the hall. Nancy followed without hesitation. As before, it floated along the hall till it reached the same painting. Then, with what appeared to be a signal of some sort, it disappeared into the painted wall, leaving Nancy alone in the hall.

Nancy stared at the painting for a long time, studying each individual section. It wasn't till her eyes reached the left hand that she realized something. The Kachina was holding what looked very much like a pencil or pen—something no Indian Kachina could possibly be concerned with!

Frowning, she went back to her room to get the powerful flashlight and the magnifying glass she kept there. Since Jake Harris had been a friend and admirer of the Indians and their Kachinas, she was sure that he wouldn't have put the writing instrument into the picture by mistake—which had to mean that it was a clue. But to what?

Using the flashlight and magnifying glass, she began to make an even closer inspection of the painting. She studied each individual brick, tracing it carefully, trying not to let her eye be confused by the complex design that Jake Harris had painted so long ago.

Eventually, she found what she was looking for. The pencil or pen was pointing to a brick that wasn't mortared into place like the others. Nancy slipped a fingernail into the tiny seam, trying to work the brick loose. It didn't move. She went back to her room for a metal nail file and used it to pry at the seam. The brick squealed and grated in protest as she dragged it out of the patterned design of the Kachina.

"Nancy?" George's head appeared around the door of the room she shared with Bess. "What in the world is going on?"

"I saw the Kachina again and it seemed to want me to investigate this painting, so . . ." Nancy lowered the brick to the floor. "Now we'll see what it wanted me to find!"

9

A Wonderful Discovery

Bess and George quickly joined Nancy as she directed the beam of the flashlight into the hole left by the brick she'd removed. The light reflected dully off what appeared to be an old, tin box.

"Have you found the Kachina's treasure?" Bess asked breathlessly. "Do you suppose the box could be full of gold?"

"I don't think so," Nancy said as she pulled the tin box out. "It isn't heavy enough."

"Maybe it has the treasure map in it," George suggested.

Nancy blew the dust off the box and lifted the lid with trembling fingers, then jumped nervously as another door opened down the hall and Heather emerged. "What's going on?" their hostess inquired as she approached the three girls.

"Nancy has found something," George explained. "The Kachina led her to it."

"What is it?" Heather asked, joining them in front of the painting.

"It looks like a diary or journal," Nancy answered, lifting an old, leather-bound book out of the tin box. She opened it with care.

"That's all that was in it?" Bess asked, taking the box and peering into it.

"It's Jake Harris's journal!" Nancy announced after she'd scanned the first page.

"Maybe he wrote something in it that will tell us where the treasure is hidden," Bess said hopefully.

"If there really is a treasure," Heather reminded her. "No one has ever been sure about that, you know."

"Look and see if there's a map," George urged.

Nancy leafed through the pages carefully. There were not a great many entries, and once the spidery script ended, there was nothing else. "No map," she told them. "Guess I'll have to read it and see if he's put a clue in his entries."

Bess, George and Heather peered over her shoulders at the open book. "I hope you *can* read it," Heather said. "His writing is so shaky and faded."

"I'll do my best," Nancy assured them. "Now, let's repair the painting and see if we can all get some sleep."

Heather shook her head. "To think that's been hidden there all these years. I wonder why no one else has ever found it."

"No one else is as good a detective," George stated firmly.

"I just followed the Kachina's guidance," Nancy told them. "It gave me the clue."

"And you investigated it and found the journal," Heather finished.

Chuck, awakened by their voices in the hall, came out to join them. He inspected the journal and listened as Nancy recounted how it had been found, then helped by replacing the brick she had pried out of the wall. That done, they all returned to their rooms. Nancy took the journal with her.

Though she was tired, she opened it at once. Even with the good light from her bedside lamp, she had difficulty reading the script. Yet she was immediately intrigued.

Deer Slayer was here today. He brought me a haunch of venison to trade for some canned goods, and we talked long about Winslow and his offer for the Ka-

chinas. Deer Slayer doesn't want to sell them, but the year has been a bad one and a few of his tribe are beginning to talk of all the food Winslow's money would buy.

Deer Slayer and some of the other tribe elders have asked me to speak for them in the bargaining with Winslow and I've agreed, though I don't think they should sell the figures. The ones they've let me use to copy for my wall paintings are so beautiful, it would be a tragedy to let them go.

Nancy turned the page as that entry ended. The next day's writing dealt with ranch matters, a missing heifer, the possibility of sending a few calves to the reservation for Deer Slayer's people. Later, there was another entry about Jake's meeting with Mr. Winslow and their discussions about the Kachinas.

The man is offering far too little for the Indians' treasure. He would cheat them of the very food for their children. I've advised the chiefs and elders not to even consider selling the Kachinas to him. If they must part with them, I'm sure I can con-

*tact a reputable trader who will at least
make it worth their while.*

Nancy yawned. Her eyes were burning from the
strain of deciphering the writing. The next entry
was more about his painting and the fact that Winslow had seen the pictures on the wall of the hall and
acted very strangely.

> *It seems that Mr. Winslow believes that
> the Kachinas are here. He has taken to
> riding out here at odd times and even
> asked to be allowed to spend the night. I
> think he hopes to become my friend to use
> me against the Hopi chiefs in his trading
> schemes.*

Nancy stopped for a moment and stared out at the
shadows of the palo verde tree. Had something
moved there? she asked herself. The hair on the
back of her neck prickled as though someone was
watching her, yet she could see nothing.

Fully awakened by the feeling, she continued her
reading. Jake seemed to be growing more and more
concerned about his Indian friends and about his
own safety. He described the way he'd pried the

brick loose and cleared the box-sized space behind it.

> *I'll paint a Kachina to guard my hiding place, and to guide my friends to this book, should something happen to me. Perhaps it is just the fancy of an old man too long alone, but I see things in the night—fearsome torches on the distant hills and shadowy figures nearer to my house. I sleep on the second floor now, with the stairs barricaded. I'll be glad when Deer Slayer comes to visit again and I can tell him what I've learned about this man Winslow. Once he tells Winslow that the Kachinas are not for sale, perhaps my ordeal will end.*

Nancy turned the page and stopped, startled to find that there was nothing written on the next page or the one after it. In fact, a quick flipping through of the remaining pages told her that there were no more entries at all. A closer inspection of the book, however, revealed the rough edges of three or four pages that had been torn from the journal.

Frowning, she closed the old book and carefully placed it in the drawer of the nightstand, then turned off the lamp. Moonlight glowed beyond her window, and she lay watching the feathery shadows of the palo verde as it stirred in the night wind.

The entries in the journal certainly seemed to prove that Maria's theory of the old man's death was the correct one. Jake Harris had been a friend of the Hopi, not an enemy, and there appeared to be no reason for them to have hounded or frightened him to death.

And what about the stories of hidden treasure? she asked herself. Could it be the Kachinas?

That seemed more likely, though Jake hadn't mentioned seeing any except the ones he'd used as models for his wall paintings. Nancy drifted off to sleep, still not sure what clues she'd gained from her late-night discovery.

Her dreams were haunted by frail, old men and floating, teasing, beckoning Kachinas. The chanting seemed to surround her, and the Kachinas circled and reached out to her in pleading ways. It was almost a relief when a great pounding on her bedroom door brought her back to reality.

"Fire!" Chuck shouted. "We've got a fire in one of the cottages!"

10

A Raging Fire

Nancy pulled on her jeans and a sweater right over her pajamas, slipped her feet into her shoes, and raced out to the hall. George and Bess emerged right behind her.

"Wh-what happened?" Bess asked in a shaky voice.

"Let's find out," Nancy replied, and the three of them quickly followed the cold draft of night air to the open rear door.

Once outside, the situation became obvious to them instantly. "It's the cottage farthest from the house!" George cried.

The little building was blazing like a torch in the darkness. Chuck and Ward were already spraying

water from the two garden hoses on the inferno, but seemed to be making no progress at all.

Nancy looked around quickly. "Did anyone call the fire department?" she shouted above the roaring of the flames.

"I did," Heather called as she and Maria came racing from the direction of the stable. They were carrying what looked like burlap feed sacks. "They'll be along as soon as they can, but in the meantime, we'd better wet these sacks and try to keep the fire from spreading."

Nancy nodded and they all helped Heather dip the feed sacks in the swimming pool. Once they were soaked, each took a couple and began chasing the sparks that were already floating away from the blaze.

The men, having given up on the cottage, were now using the hoses to wet the walls and roofs of the nearby buildings to keep the fire from spreading. This left it up to the girls and Maria to put out the small blazes that seemed to start everywhere in the grass, the hedge, even in the clumps of desert wild flowers and bushes nearby.

It was like a nightmare. While one spark was being extinguished, three more were igniting close-by areas. The smoke rolled over them and, as it reached the stable, set the horses to whinnying in terror. When the crashing of hooves became too loud, Heather left the others and went to open the stall doors, allowing the terrified animals to get out into the corrals if they wanted to.

By the time the small, rural fire truck arrived, Nancy and the others were smoke-stained and weary. They were all glad to stand back and watch as the firemen tamed and finally put out the roaring blaze. Only then did they have a chance to relax and sit down on the damp chairs near the pool.

"How did it get started, Chuck?" one of the firemen asked, and for the first time, Nancy recognized him as Floyd, the young man she'd ridden to the barbecue with earlier that evening.

Chuck shook his head. "Your guess is as good as mine," he answered. "I was sound asleep when it started. Heather woke me up."

All eyes turned toward the redhead. "I guess it was the smell of smoke that woke me," she said. "My room faces this way and when I opened my eyes, I could see the flames. It scared me half to death. I thought the whole resort was on fire."

Floyd looked around. In the pearly beginning of daylight, the charred places on the lawn and bushes were very clear. "You're just lucky that it wasn't," he said. "If you hadn't come out in time, the place could have gone."

"Anybody out here ready for sandwiches and coffee?" Maria called from the doorway. When there was a chorus of assent, she and Ngyun emerged with two big trays.

"When in the world did you do this?" Heather asked in amazement.

"As soon as the firemen arrived," Maria answered. "I knew you wouldn't need me any more and I already had Ngyun at work making sandwiches in the kitchen."

Everyone began to eat with enthusiasm, and Ngyun's shy smile soon appeared as everyone commented on his handiwork. The ham, cheese, and beef sandwiches did taste delicious and helped to lift their spirits in the cold aftermath of the battle with the fire.

Ngyun's smile faded, however, when one of the firemen frowned at the charred and smouldering building and commented, "I just don't see how it could have started accidentally, Chuck. There wasn't anyone staying in that cottage, and you weren't working on it yesterday, were you?"

Chuck shook his head. "We finished the rough work before Grandfather's accident, and I haven't had the time to do anything else since. I've been waiting for Grandfather. He makes all the final decisions about the wiring and finishing, you know."

"Are you saying that the cottage could have been deliberately set on fire?" Nancy asked, her attention caught by the idea.

"I not do it!" Ngyun protested, getting to his feet so quickly that he spilled the remainder of his milk in the grass. "I not set any fires!"

For a moment, no one spoke. Maria cleared her throat, but before she could say anything, the boy was gone, fleeing not toward the house, but toward the stable. In a moment, the black and white pinto appeared, Ngyun clinging to his bare back as they raced away from the house into the desert.

"I didn't mean to make him think I was accusing him," Nancy protested quickly, getting up. "Should I ride after him?"

"You'd never catch him," Maria told her sorrowfully.

"Why should he think you were accusing him?" George asked. "You were just asking a logical question."

"Perhaps he should be questioned," Ward observed, looking uncomfortable. "There have been so many fires since that first signal fire on the ridge. I don't think that Ngyun could have anything to do with them, but . . ." He let his voice trail off, shaking his head, then continued, "Burned saguaro cactus and fenceposts are one thing, but the cottage is something else."

"No!" Maria was on her feet, her face full of pain. "It can't be Ngyun," she cried. "Honestly, Chuck, he was in his bed when you pounded on our door. There's no way he could have done it. He wouldn't, I just know that he wouldn't."

"I think we're all jumping to conclusions," Floyd said. "The fire is too hot to check now, but I'll come back late this afternoon and look around. I'll see if I can find any clues to how it happened. Maybe that will give us some answers."

His words seemed to signal the end of the brief rest period. The firemen finished their sandwiches and coffee and began to gather up their equipment and put it back on the truck.

The rest of the group, including Nancy, Bess, and George, all set about cleaning up what they could of the debris that had been left behind. By the time the truck drove away, the sun was over the horizon and the new day had begun.

Once things had been set to right, Nancy wandered slowly toward the house. "What's wrong?" Bess asked as they started down the hall to their rooms, anxious to clean up.

"I'm worried about Ngyun," Nancy admitted. "I

promised to try to clear his name and now he thinks I've accused him of setting the cottage on fire."

"Do you believe there's a possibility that he did?" George asked.

Nancy considered, then shook her head. "I don't think he's guilty of anything except being alone too much and pretending to be the kind of boy he thinks his father was."

"Poor kid," Bess murmured compassionately. "But why would someone else set fires and let him be blamed? I mean, someone has to be doing all these things."

Nancy sighed. "I wish I knew who it was," she admitted, then brightened. "Maybe we'll find a clue after the fire cools."

"If there's a clue, you'll find it," Bess told her loyally.

After they parted, Nancy showered to remove the stains of her fire fighting, then dressed in a bright blue-and-yellow print, cotton dress. Ready to start the day, she went out to see if she could help Maria or Heather.

She found Heather alone in the lobby and asked her where Chuck was, hoping that he'd gone after Ngyun. Her hope was short-lived.

"Chuck has gone into town to talk to Grandfather. He wants to tell him about the fire and about the journal you found. Then, too, he feels he should tell him about that rattler someone threw at you last night." She frowned. "Chuck and I are still worried about you getting hurt, Nancy."

"And I'm worried about Ngyun," Nancy said, changing the subject.

Heather nodded. "So am I," she admitted, "but I don't know what to do about him. There are people who can't help setting fires, you know, Nancy. Do you think Ngyun could be like that?"

"Oh, I hope not," Nancy said, not liking the idea at all.

"Did you find out anything from the journal?" Heather asked, changing the subject.

"Not about any treasure," Nancy told her. "But it does make it clear that Jake Harris and the Indians were friends, so I very much doubt that they were the ones who caused his death."

"I'm glad of that for Maria's sake," Heather said.

"Do you think she'd like to read the journal?" Nancy asked. "Jake mentions several of the Hopi chiefs and elders by name. One of them might be her great-grandfather."

"Oh, she'd love to read it," Heather assured her. "She's always been so sure that the Indians were wrongly accused. It will make her happy to see some proof of their innocence. And after what happened this morning, I'm sure she could use some cheering up."

Nancy nodded, remembering only too well her part in Ngyun's hasty exit from their early morning gathering by the pool. "She must be very worried about Ngyun," she agreed. "I'll go and get the journal."

She hurried back to her room and opened the drawer in the bedside table. Her nails scraped the wooden bottom as she reached inside, then she stared unbelievingly into the empty drawer. The journal was gone!

11

A Flying Arrow

Nancy checked with George and Bess just to make sure that neither of them had taken the journal to read, but she wasn't surprised by their denials. "I had the feeling someone was watching me last night," she told them. "But who would take Big Jake's journal?"

"Someone who thought it might lead them to the treasure?" Bess suggested.

"Well, the thief will certainly be disappointed then," Nancy said. "There's no mention of any treasure in the journal."

Since everyone was tired from fighting the fire and from Nancy's earlier excursion in the hall following the Kachina, Maria served an early lunch so they could all settle down for naps. Afterward they planned to spend the warmest part of the afternoon in the swimming pool.

Even while she splashed in the water, however, Nancy kept watching the surrounding hills, hoping for a glimpse of the boy and the pinto horse. Later, after she'd changed out of her bathing suit, she made a search of the now smokeless ruin of the cottage. But there were no clues to be found in the charred wreckage of the building.

Floyd did no better when he came by later. "There's really not much I can tell you," he said after he finished inspecting the ruined cottage. "With so much raw wood around, it would be easy to set a small fire, and once the building was fully engulfed. . . . Unless someone saw something, I guess we'll never know for sure."

"It's just that there is no way it could have been an accident," Chuck stated as he joined them. "That's what Grandfather said when I told him. No careless cigarettes left burning, no lightning, no mice in the wiring, nothing like that. It just must have been deliberately set."

Nancy thought of the missing journal and quickly told the two young men about it. "Perhaps someone saw me reading it and set the fire to get us all out of the house," she suggested. "I mean, it *is* gone, so someone must have taken it."

"I guess if the thief thought the journal would lead him to the treasure that is supposed to be hidden here, he might do something so violent," Floyd mused. "But who could it have been?"

They all looked at Nancy, but she had no answers for them.

She continued to watch for Ngyun, and when she saw the pinto in the distance, she excused herself and walked to the stable. She stopped first at Dancer's stall, petting the mare and examining her scratched and swollen legs.

When the boy brought his horse in, Nancy went over to him and leaned on the top of the stall. "Have a nice ride?" she asked.

The boy nodded, but didn't look up at her.

"Did you happen to see any strange tracks, or anyone in a car or on horseback riding away from here?" Nancy went on.

This time the almond eyes turned her way. "Why?" Ngyun asked suspiciously.

"Someone set that cottage on fire and stole a book from my room," Nancy told him. "I thought you might have seen him."

"I go to mountains," Ngyun answered after several moments of considering the question. "No one live that way."

"But you do like to follow tracks?"

470

The boy nodded, his shy smile returning. "Grandfather start to teach me, but I not good yet. If he here, he trail whoever do it."

"You must know a lot about the Superstition Mountains by now," Nancy said, changing the subject as they started back toward the great, stone fortress of the resort.

"They different all the time," Ngyun answered. "Sometimes people ride or hike or dig gold. I see coyotes teach cubs to hunt and . . ."

He was interrupted by a shout from the house and excused himself politely to run to his aunt. Nancy followed more slowly, certain now that Ngyun hadn't set the fire in the cottage or taken the journal. If only she could prove it, she thought wearily. The poor boy must feel terrible, having people suspect him all the time.

Chuck came to meet Nancy, his face grim. "What did he have to say for himself?" he asked.

"About what?" Nancy was surprised by her friend's tone.

"The way he spent his day."

"He said he was riding in the mountains," Nancy answered. "Why?"

"I just got a call from Mr. Henry. One of his men rode in a little while ago to tell him that their catch pen and shed were burned, probably sometime early this afternoon. The men spotted the smoke, but by the time they got there, nothing was left but charred wood."

"And you think Ngyun had something to do with it?"

Chuck's attractive features softened a little. "I don't want to think that," he admitted, "but why would anyone want to burn an old shed and corral that no one is using?"

"Why would Ngyun burn it?" Nancy countered.

"He could have been angry because Mr. Henry was the one who came over and told us about the missing filly, and Ngyun thought he was accusing him of stealing her," Chuck reminded her. "Or maybe he was just playing Indians and settlers and thought no one would notice. It is in a remote area of the Circle H."

Nancy considered for a moment, then shook her head. "I'm sure he didn't burn your cottage, and I don't think we have two firebugs in the area, do you, Chuck?"

Chuck sighed. "I have a feeling it isn't going to matter what I think," he replied bitterly. "Mr. Henry's been a good friend to us and he's been very patient about open gates and straying cattle. This time he sounded really angry. I don't know how much longer we can keep Ngyun here."

"But where would he go?"

"His mother is now staying with relatives in the Los Angeles area. Living in the city would be rough on him, but if these fires keep up. . . ." He shook his head, not bothering to finish the sentence.

Nancy started to protest, then closed her lips firmly over the words. If Ngyun was to stay, it was obvious that she must clear his name and there was no time to waste.

She and George spent the next hour walking around the desert beyond the walls of the old house, but found nothing significant.

"The ground's been so marked up by the fire truck that it's impossible to see anything," George complained.

Nancy nodded. "And we have all the hoof marks from the horses yesterday going to the barbecue site. They obscure any other tracks that might have been made."

"Let's look under your bedroom window," George finally suggested. "Perhaps we can determine whether the thief came in that way."

This idea proved more productive. Though the ground was too hard to show footprints, Nancy soon discovered something when she examined the window itself.

"Look, George!" she called out. "See all those

smudges on the frame of the screen? That proves someone lifted it down, then replaced it."

"Did you leave the window open last night?" George inquired.

Nancy nodded. "The thief had no trouble getting in this way." She stepped back, then shivered, though the late-afternoon sun was warm beyond the shadow of the house. She had the eerie feeling that they were being watched. She turned slowly, scanning the ridges and washes that formed the landscape between the ranch and the nearby mountains.

George had wandered away from the window, still trying to find a telltale set of footprints. Nancy looked after her, then shifted her attention to a clump of cactus. A roadrunner darted from it to some bushes. Quail chirped sleepily from a closer stand of grass. And a shadowy figure was moving on the crest of one ridge.

There was something so threatening about the vague movement that Nancy dodged behind a sheltering palo verde without seeing clearly what had caused the motion.

The next moment there was a whistling sound, then a "thunk" made the tree's green trunk shiver. Startled, Nancy looked up to see an arrow quivering in the wood!

12

Trapped!

"Nancy, where are you?" George called suddenly from just around the corner of the house.

Nancy looked toward the ridge. "Stay where you are," she ordered, aware that the arrow had struck the tree and not her only because she'd no longer been standing in front of the green trunk. Never looking away from the ridge, and ready to dodge into the bushes at any sign of movement, Nancy made her way around the corner to where a thoroughly unhappy-looking George waited for her.

"What in the world is going on?" George demanded.

"Someone just shot this at me," Nancy told her, extending the arrow for George's inspection. "Luckily, I saw someone moving and dodged behind the tree, or—" she shuddered, unable to finish the sentence.

"Let's go inside," George said, a frown marring her attractive features. "This is just terrible! Someone's making an attempt on your life every day!"

"But why?" Nancy asked. "Why would anyone try to harm me, George? I haven't even come close to solving either of the mysteries here. I don't know why the Kachinas are haunting the house, and I haven't been able to clear Ngyun's name." The young sleuth clenched her fist in frustration. "So far all I've done is to get Dancer injured and lose Jake Harris's journal."

"You found it first," George reminded her as they walked into the cool kitchen, where Bess was sitting at the table sipping some lemonade and sampling the cookies that Maria was taking from the oven. "You must know something dangerous to someone."

"But what?" Nancy asked, putting the arrow on the table and sinking wearily into a chair. "And whom could I be a danger to?"

"What are you talking about?" Bess inquired.

"Nancy almost got shot with this arrow," George said and explained what happened.

Bess's face turned white. "Oh, Nancy!" she cried. "What are we going to do?"

Maria had been busy taking more cookies out of the oven, and had not paid attention to the girls' conversation. Now she came over to the table and stared at the arrow.

"Where did you find this?" she asked.

"Do you know whose it is?" Nancy countered, reviving as her detective instincts returned.

"It's Ngyun's," Maria answered without hesitation. "My cousin makes arrows and he does special fletching—the feathered part—for the family. See the pattern of red feathers worked into the black and gray."

Nancy nodded. "I knew the arrow was homemade," she admitted.

"Where did you find it?" Maria asked a second time. "Don't tell me he's been shooting the cactus again."

"Someone shot it at Nancy," George spoke up. "She moved out of the way just in time, so it hit a tree."

"Nancy!" Maria paled. "You don't think . . . Ngyun wouldn't . . ." The woman sank down in the empty chair, dropping the arrow as though it had burned her fingers.

"I'm positive it wasn't Ngyun," Nancy assured her, "but how would someone else get one of his arrows?"

Maria sighed. "He's lost some by shooting them into brush or cactus," she answered, looking only slightly relieved. "My cousin gave him a dozen when Ngyun's grandfather showed him how to use the bow, and I think he has eight or nine left. Would you like me to go up and see?"

Nancy shook her head. "I don't want him to think that I suspect him of shooting the arrow at me. In fact, I think it might be a good idea not to say anything about this to anyone else." She looked at Bess and George.

"But if you're in danger, Nancy, we should tell someone," Bess protested.

"I'll just have to be more careful till I find out who wants to get rid of me," Nancy replied. "Meantime, I don't want Chuck and Heather worrying any more. And I don't want them telling their grandfather. Mr. McGuire was very disturbed when he heard about the fire. Chuck says he might have to stay in the hospital several more days because of it."

"He'd be terribly upset if he knew," Maria agreed. "But if there really is someone out there who means you harm, Nancy, you must not take any more chances. I'd rather send Ngyun back to his mother and her people than have you risk your life trying to clear his name. And you know that Chuck and Heather would feel the same way about you trying to solve their mystery."

Nancy nodded. "They've already told me that," she admitted. "But don't you see, if someone wants to hurt me, there has to be a reason. I must be close to finding out the truth, and once I do, I'll be safe."

"You just be careful," Maria warned. "Very, very careful."

The next two days passed rather quietly. The girls made trips into the town of Apache Junction, shopping in quaint, little stores for the lovely Indian jewelry that seemed to be everywhere. With Heather's expert advice, they bought beautiful, silver and turquoise belt buckles to take back to the boys, and selected more jewelry as gifts for the members of their families.

Nancy found an exquisite Kachina doll in one of the shops and was unable to resist it. "It looks just like the one painted at the far end of the hall," she told George. "Won't it make a great souvenir to show everyone when we get home?"

"When is that going to be, Nancy?" Bess asked softly, not wanting Heather to overhear them.

"How much longer are we going to stay?"

Nancy frowned. "I can't leave without solving the mysteries," she protested.

"But nothing is happening," Bess reminded her. "And you did find out what the Kachina in the hall wanted, didn't you?"

Nancy nodded. "But I still hear the chanting every night," she confessed. "I look out in the hall whenever it wakes me, but the Kachina isn't there. I have a feeling it wants me to do something else, but I don't know what."

Bess appeared unconvinced, when Heather came over with a handsome, fetish necklace to show them. There was no chance to go on with the conversation while they admired the tiny, hand-carved birds that were strung on the silver wire.

Still, memories of the words haunted Nancy through the afternoon, and after dinner she found it hard to concentrate on the card games that Chuck and Heather had suggested to fill the evening hours. A spring rainstorm seemed to be brewing, which added to the feeling of tension in the air.

After several games, Nancy excused herself and wandered into the hall to stare once more at the Kachina paintings. They were so lovely, yet eerie and, in the shadows of evening, almost frightening.

Did they conceal further secrets? she asked herself. Were there other little differences like the writing instrument that had guided her to the loose brick?

Thinking that it might give her a clue, Nancy went to her room to get her Kachina to compare it with the larger painting. However, when she reached her room, she hesitated, then went to the window to stare out at the distant flickerings of lightning that seemed to be licking into the Superstitions.

The scent of rain was in the air and on the breeze that stirred the white curtains. When she listened closely, she could hear the far-off rumbling of thunder. Then, suddenly, she heard something else— the sound of hoofbeats. In the dim light, she saw a black and white pinto headed toward one of the washes.

Nancy hesitated only a moment before racing through the house and down the path to the stable. If Ngyun was riding out in the night, she had to follow him! There wasn't even time to tell the others where she was going. If she waited, she would surely lose him in the stormy night.

Fumbling in the dark stable, Nancy saddled the bay gelding Pepper Pot and rode out as fast as she dared in the poor light. As they entered the wash, she slowed the horse a little and looked around, suddenly not sure where to go. Almost at once, she saw movement ahead, and once again there was a flash of black and white as the rider moved along the wash.

"Ngyun?" she called. "Ngyun, wait, please!"

Hoofbeats were her only answer, but since they seemed to be coming from directly ahead, Nancy urged the gelding to follow them. The wind was rising, spinning dust and small bits of sand off the top of the wash and driving them down on Nancy as she rode through the rough, ditchlike formation.

The thunder grew louder and the lightning flared more often, illuminating the scene like midday and making it easier for Nancy to guide Pepper Pot along the wash. It also gave her an occasional glimpse of the pinto's splashy haunches, but no clue to why his rider didn't slow when she called to him.

The rain came suddenly. There was a teeth-jarring crash of thunder and the skies seemed to break apart, spilling the water in sheets rather than drops. Pepper Pot slowed immediately, snorting and tossing his head, obviously wanting to turn back and run for the dry sanctuary of the stable.

Nancy allowed him to slow to a walk, then stood in her stirrups, peering ahead into the rush of water, seeking the pinto's familiar shape. However, there seemed to be nothing ahead. Nervously, Nancy urged Pepper Pot forward, following the narrowing wash as it led deeper and deeper into the hills.

"Just a little further, Pepper Pot," she told the bay. "We have to be close and Ngyun must be afraid in this storm."

The horse stumbled a little, slipping and sliding as the water gushed down the sides of the wash and turned the once hard-baked earth to mud. Lightning flashed and gave Nancy a glimpse of the scene ahead.

The wash seemed to end or at least narrow so abruptly that it was hard to imagine where a horse and rider could have gone. Yet Ngyun and Cochise were nowhere to be seen! Nancy drew her rein and waited for the next flash, berating herself for having been in too big a hurry to remember to bring her flashlight.

When the bolt came, the stark light showed only the steep walls at the end of the wash and the wet slopes of the hills above them. Then the rain increased again, pouring so hard that she could not see ten feet ahead of her. Defeated, Nancy allowed the bay to turn, weariness and despair making her slump in the saddle.

Where could Ngyun have taken Cochise? How could the boy and the pinto simply vanish out of the deep wash? Or had they even been here? For a moment, she doubted her own senses, then her courage returned and she shook her head.

"They were here, Pepper Pot," she told the gelding. "I know we were following them. I saw the pinto several times in the lightning flashes."

The gelding snorted, then suddenly plunged ahead, almost unseating her. Nancy struggled wildly to regain her balance, then tried to rein in the horse. Pepper Pot, however, had the bit in his teeth, and, fearing that she might make him fall in the rough terrain, Nancy was forced to loosen her hold again, giving him free rein.

Almost at once, she heard a strange rumbling. When she realized that it was coming from behind her, she looked back.

A wall of water cascaded through the narrow ravine, carrying with it limbs and branches torn from bushes and trees!

13

A Stormy Night

Nancy gasped as Pepper Pot headed for the steep wall of the wash. Wildly, he scrambled up the slope, barely managing to reach the top before he stopped, his sides heaving violently.

Had the horse hesitated a moment longer, Nancy knew, they both would have been carried along in the flood!

Trembling, she leaned her cheek against the horse's hot, wet neck and hugged him. He turned back to sniff at her knee, then began picking his way slowly along the ridge above the wash. Since she had no idea which way would take them back to the resort buildings, Nancy simply left the reins loose on his neck, trusting him to take them home through the stormy night.

She rode for what seemed an age before the rain ended as abruptly as it had begun. Once the pounding drops stopped, she straightened up and looked around. The wind, chilling since she was soaked to the skin, was already herding the clouds across the sky, leaving behind them black velvet sparkling with stars.

Almost at once, Nancy saw car lights ahead. They were coming in her direction and proved to be those of the battered resort jeep. It slithered to a stop beside her.

"Nancy!" George shouted, leaping out. "Thank heavens we've found you. We've been frantic. Where have you been? What happened?"

Nancy found herself lifted down from the saddle by Chuck. Once she was steady on her feet, he knotted the reins high on Pepper Pot's neck, then turned the horse loose with a slap on the haunch. "Go home, old boy," he said to him. "We'll be there to put you into your stall."

The gelding trotted off as Nancy began telling everyone exactly what had happened. "I don't know where Ngyun and Cochise could have gone," she finished. "They just weren't in the wash when I got to the end of it."

Heather frowned. "Ngyun is back at the house, Nancy," she said. "He's been there all evening. And

Cochise is in the stable. Pepper Pot was the only horse missing when we went down there looking for you."

"But I saw a rider on a pinto trotting away from the stable," Nancy protested. "And they were ahead of me in that wash. I'd never have gone so far from the house in the rain if I hadn't been following them."

"Did you really see Ngyun?" Chuck asked.

"Well, no, but . . ." Nancy stopped, then swallowed hard. "It was a trap, wasn't it?" she asked. "But how could the intruder have known that I'd follow him?"

"Maybe it didn't matter," George suggested. "I mean, maybe he just wanted you to see the pinto leaving the stable and believe that Ngyun was riding him."

Nancy nodded, her mind working feverishly. "When I followed, whoever it was must have decided it was a perfect opportunity to get rid of me. If it hadn't been for Pepper Pot, I'd have been trapped in the flood."

"You definitely picked the right horse to ride tonight," Chuck told her as he helped her into the crowded jeep. "He's saved me a couple of times."

No one said much as they bounced over the wet ground on the way back to the well-lit, stone house.

However, by the time Chuck stopped by the rear garden to let the girls out before going down to the stable to take care of Pepper Pot, Nancy had already come to a conclusion.

"Do you suppose the rider on the pinto was going to start a fire or cause some other kind of trouble?" she asked. "I mean, since I saw the horse leaving the stable, I had to believe that it was Cochise, and that would mean Ngyun could be blamed again."

"That would explain all the times someone has seen a rider on a pinto near trouble, wouldn't it?" George commented. "It's too bad you didn't get a closer look at your mystery rider."

"I will next time," Nancy promised with a sturdy smile. "Now, if you'll excuse me, I think I'll go take a nice, hot bath and get into some dry clothes."

"You come out and join us for some hot chocolate afterwards," Heather ordered gently. "I think we have some talking to do."

Nancy nodded, aware from the girl's tone that she would be asked once more to discontinue her investigation. But she couldn't stop now, the young detective realized, not when she was so close to clearing Ngyun of all the ugly accusations!

Later, however, as they sipped their hot chocolate, it took all her powers of persuasion to convince both Chuck and Heather that she had to go on with her sleuthing.

The morning dawned beautifully clear and sunny as though there'd been no storm at all. Nancy awoke, more than ready to go to work on the mystery of Ngyun's persecution. Heather offered to help by volunteering to call the nearby ranches and ask them about black-and-white pintos. By the time breakfast was over, she had a list of six possibilities to contact.

"While you do that, Heather, I think I'd like to ride out to the wash and see if I can figure out how my mysterious rider escaped," Nancy said. "Maybe I'll find a clue to his identity there."

"It seems to me we should come with you," George spoke up. "Right, Bess?"

"Just as long as we stay away from rattlesnakes and flooded washes," Bess answered.

"There's not a cloud in the sky," Nancy assured her. "I don't think we have to worry about floods."

"How about arrows and rattlers?" Bess asked.

"The only sure way to be safe is for me to find out who is pretending to be Ngyun—and why. Once we know that, we'll all be safe."

Riding along the wash in the bright sunlight was far different from the previous night, and Nancy found herself enjoying the fresh, morning air and the glimpses of all the desert creatures that seemed to be busy making their own repairs after the flood. The wash showed the marks of the racing waters, with gouges in the damp earth and the clutter of debris that had been dropped when the rain ended and the runoff slowed to a trickle.

As they rounded the bend near the end of the wash, Nancy stopped Pepper Pot and stared to her left. "I guess that's the answer to my ghostly rider's disappearance," she said, pointing to the rough trail that led from the floor of the wash to the rim. "In all the rain and confusion, I didn't even see that last night."

"Want to follow it?" George asked.

"Might as well." Nancy guided the obedient bay toward the narrow trail, then clung to the saddle as he made a rather bounding climb up it. George and Bess followed, sending a small hail of loose earth into the wash.

"It must have been someone who knows this area well," Nancy observed, looking around the open hills. "Whoever it was led me into that ravine on purpose, then got out of it just before the runoff from the surrounding hills turned it into a flood channel."

"Now we know why they call them washes," Bess murmured, looking back.

"So where do we go from here?" George asked.

Nancy considered, then pointed to a distant clump of trees. "If I'd just come out of that wash in the middle of a storm, I think I'd be looking for shelter," she said, "and those trees are the closest."

George nodded. "Heather says those spring thunderstorms never last long, so whoever it was would know that, too."

The shady ground beneath the trees was soft and still wet, since the strong Arizona sun couldn't reach it to dry it out as it had the rest of the area. Nancy dismounted at once, handing her reins to Bess. It took her only a moment to locate a set of hoofprints.

"Looks as if you were right," George said, joining her on the ground.

"It's too bad the area beyond here is so rocky," Nancy complained. "Otherwise, we could try some of Ngyun's tracking."

"The tracks lead that way," George said, following them to the edge of the trees and a few yards beyond. "Right into that loose shale."

"Now what?" Bess asked.

Nancy returned to the shade of the trees, walking under the low-hanging boughs till her eyes were

caught by a flash of bright red color on the thorny tip of a mesquite bush. She went to pick up the piece of cloth, then smiled. "Now we have two things to look for," she said triumphantly. "Someone with a pinto horse, and a red shirt or jacket with a big tear in it."

"Wonderful," George congratulated her. "Once everyone hears about this, Ngyun's name will be cleared and Maria won't have to worry about sending him to his mother."

Nancy sobered. "He'll be cleared when we *find* the person with the pinto horse and the torn clothes," she corrected, then added, "and maybe then we'll also find out why he did all these things and arranged it so they'd be blamed on Ngyun."

"It does seem strange," Bess and George agreed as the girls mounted again, and they all turned the horses toward the resort.

"Maybe Heather will have some answers for us when we get back," George suggested as they loped along.

They were feeling very pleased with their discoveries when they turned the horses loose in the corral after unsaddling them. "I hope you can get this settled so you can concentrate on the Kachina ghost," Bess told Nancy as they walked toward the rear garden.

To their surprise, no one came out to greet them, and when they entered the kitchen, neither Heather nor Maria even looked up. "Hey, Nancy found some clues," George called. "She can prove that it wasn't Ngyun in the wash last night!"

Maria turned to look at them, but there was no joy in her brown face, and Nancy could see the marks of tears on her cheeks. "What's happened?" she asked.

"It's too late," Maria sobbed, then fled from the kitchen!

14

Ngyun's Trouble

"What's happened, Heather?" Nancy asked.

"The sheriff was here," Heather replied, her own eyes filling with tears. "It was about an hour ago. He came for Ngyun. He said that some jewelry was stolen yesterday and a boy on a pinto was seen riding away from the area."

"Well, don't you listen," Nancy began. "I saw someone on a pinto last night, too, but it wasn't Ngyun, so I'm sure we can prove that the thief was the same person who tricked me into that wash."

Heather shook her head sadly. "I'm afraid no one will believe you now."

"What do you mean?" George asked. "We have a clue to the real culprit."

"It's too late," Heather sobbed.

"Why?"

"They found a stolen belt buckle in the stable. It was hidden in the saddlebags that Ngyun uses when he goes on an all-day ride and carries a lunch."

"Was that all that was taken?" Nancy asked after a moment of stunned silence. "Just a belt buckle?"

Heather stopped crying. "Well, no, but that was all they found out there. The sheriff said they would get the rest when Ngyun tells them where he's hidden it."

"How much jewelry was stolen?" Nancy continued her questioning.

"Quite a lot. The most expensive pieces were two matched squash-blossom necklaces. They were specially designed—a smaller, lighter one for the woman and a massive one for her husband. I guess they were done by a master designer, with lots of the best turquoise and the finest of silver work. There were also two or three bracelets and a couple of rings."

"Whom were they stolen from?" Nancy asked.

"From some winter visitors who have a mobile home in the desert a few miles from here. Their collection is worth a great deal of money."

"To Ngyun?" Nancy inquired gently. "What would a twelve-year-old boy want with a lot of jewelry? He's not some little thug who could pawn it."

Heather opened her mouth, but no words came out, and Nancy could see the dawning of understanding in her bright, green eyes. "That's what Maria kept saying," she murmured. "She said it had to be a mistake, that Ngyun would never take a lot of jewelry—he's not a thief."

"Perhaps we should go and talk to the sheriff, Heather," Nancy suggested. "Maybe if we explain about what happened to me last night . . ."

"We can't go anywhere till Chuck gets back with the station wagon," Heather said. "He'd already left for town before the sheriff came."

"What about the jeep?" Nancy asked.

"Ward and Maria were out with it getting supplies, so they weren't here when the sheriff came, either. Ward took the jeep and went after the sheriff and Ngyun as soon as I told him what had happened."

"Could we call the sheriff's office?" Nancy suggested.

"They weren't going there, I don't think," Heather said. "The sheriff wanted to take Ngyun to see the people who were robbed. So they could identify him and the belt buckle, I suppose."

"They'll have to say it wasn't him," Maria said from the doorway. "They'll tell the sheriff he's mistaken. It wasn't Ngyun."

"We know that, Maria," Nancy assured the woman.

Maria began to cry again. "I should have gone with Ward," she wailed. "I should be with Ngyun. He gets so frightened sometimes when he doesn't understand things. People think that just because he speaks English he understands everything, but he doesn't, and . . ."

"You were too upset," Heather reminded her. "You said yourself that you'd just frighten him more."

Maria collapsed into a chair again and Bess went to the stove to heat a kettle of water to brew the poor woman some of her own soothing tea. "What am I going to do?" Maria sobbed.

"We're going to clear him, Maria," Nancy told her firmly. "Just as soon as the sheriff comes back, I'll talk to him and perhaps we can get everything straightened out."

The words calmed Maria enough that she was soon up and bustling around making preparations for lunch. While she worked, Nancy questioned Heather about the neighbors' horses. "Several have pintos," was Heather's answer, "and no one admits to riding one last night."

Nancy sighed. "Well, I really didn't expect a confession," she admitted. "Still, it would be easier if there weren't so many."

Heather shook her head. "I just don't understand any of it," she said. "Why would anyone go to such lengths just to get a harmless boy sent away?"

"When we have the answer to that question, we'll know who is doing it," Nancy assured her.

Maria set the table with places for Chuck, Ward, and Ngyun, but when the food was ready, the men hadn't returned, so they ate without them. Though the food was excellent, no one had much of an appetite, and they were all relieved when they could busy themselves with clearing the dishes and tidying the kitchen. It helped the minutes drag by.

It was mid-afternoon before Ward drove up in the jeep. A moment later, he came in alone. Maria ran to meet him. "Where is he?" she demanded. "Where is Ngyun? Why didn't you bring him home?"

Ward's face was grim and stony, the pain showing only in his dark eyes. "The sheriff is coming with him," he replied. "He told me to go on ahead and talk to you."

"What happened?" Maria asked, the relief she'd showed before draining away. "He didn't do it, Ward, you have to believe that."

"It's not up to me to believe or disbelieve," Ward replied. "They identified him, Maria. The people said he was the one they saw riding near their trailer just before they missed their jewelry."

"But he admitted that he was in the area," Maria protested. "Heather told us that. He was on his way into the hills. Just because he rode by their mobile home doesn't mean that he did anything else."

"He had the belt buckle!"

Maria pulled away from him. "Do you believe it?" she demanded. "Do you believe that he took the jewelry?"

For a moment, Ward glared at her, then his dark eyes dropped. "I don't want to," he said, "but, Maria, what else can we believe?"

Before anything else could be said, the sheriff drove up, and in a moment Ngyun was clinging to his aunt while he tried hard not to cry.

The sheriff looked sad but stern. "Ngyun refused to tell us where the rest of the stuff is hidden," he began. "The Bascombs won't press charges if they get all their jewelry back. They had planned to leave tomorrow, so they don't want to make a big thing out of it."

"I not tell, Aunt Maria," Ngyun protested. "I not know!"

"Of course you don't, Ngyun," Maria said, hugging him for a moment. Then she held him at arm's length and said, "You must be hungry. Did you have lunch?"

The boy shook his head, and in a moment he and Maria disappeared through the archway toward the kitchen. Once they were gone, Nancy stepped forward and introduced herself to the sheriff.

With the help of George and Bess, she described her recent discoveries to him, including a full account of all that had happened to her since her arrival at the resort. She even showed him the letter she'd received before she left River Heights.

The sheriff was dubious at first, but with both George and Bess speaking up and listing some of Nancy's past accomplishments, and Heather explaining that she and her brother had invited Nancy to solve their strange case, he had to take her seriously. Maria joined them and the hope returned to her face as she listened.

"You seriously believe that someone has done all this just to frame the boy?" the sheriff asked when the young detective had finished.

Nancy nodded. "The person who rode away from the stable last night could have been there planting the belt buckle, Sheriff. Maybe my seeing him and following him was just a lucky coincidence."

"But why would anyone frame Ngyun?" The sheriff repeated his question.

Nancy swallowed a sigh. "I can't answer that question till I discover who is responsible for all the things that have happened," she admitted.

The sheriff shook his head. "Well, your theory seems sound enough, Miss Drew, but until you can offer some proof, I'm afraid I can't change my mind about the boy. If he doesn't produce the jewelry by tomorrow morning, charges will be instituted."

The young sleuth longed to plead further, but without proof she knew that she couldn't convince the sheriff of Ngyun's innocence. He talked for a few minutes with Ward and Maria, then the Tomiches and Heather saw him out the front door.

Nancy, sure that Ngyun must be feeling miserable, excused herself and went to the kitchen to tell him what she'd learned last night and this morning. However, when she reached the kitchen, she found it empty, the sandwich and glass of milk untouched on the table. Curious, Nancy walked to the back window and looked out across the garden just in time to see Ngyun heading toward the stable.

It took her only a moment to make a decision. She scribbled a quick note on the pad Maria kept beside the telephone, then ran out into the warm, sunny afternoon. By the time she reached the stable, Ngyun was already leading Cochise out the other side. Nancy didn't try to stop him, preferring instead to follow him.

If the sheriff wanted proof, the answer had to lie with Ngyun, she reasoned. Since he didn't seem able to explain what was happening to him, it was up to her to find the clues. Following him on one of his excursions seemed the best place to start. Nancy saddled Pepper Pot once again and set off in pursuit of the rapidly disappearing pinto.

The young detective rode for nearly an hour, catching only occasional glimpses of Ngyun and his hurrying mount. The boy never seemed to look back as he guided the pinto further and further into the low hills that marked the area of the resort closest to the Superstition Mountains.

They were practically in the shadows of the mountains when the boy finally stopped and slipped off Cochise. Leaving the pinto to graze in a small hollow, his trailing reins "ground-hitching" him so he wouldn't run away, Ngyun began to climb up a nearby, rocky outcropping.

Nancy stopped Pepper Pot at the edge of the same small patch of grass, trying to decide what to do. She meant to talk to the boy, but she didn't want him to think she was chasing him. With that in mind, she dismounted and let Pepper Pot join the pinto while she strolled across the grass and halted at the base of the rocky rise.

Ngyun turned to look at her when the horses snorted their greetings to each other, and Nancy could see the quick flash of fear in his dark, almond eyes. Then, to her surprise, he lifted a finger to his lips, cautioning her not to make any noise. When she nodded her understanding, he signalled her to climb up beside him. Curious, Nancy made her way up the steep incline, being careful not to create a landslide.

As they neared the top of the rugged hill, Ngyun again signalled caution, but this time Nancy had already heard the sounds coming from below. There were people somewhere beyond the rim above them, and it sounded very much as though they were pounding or digging!

15

Caught!

For a moment, Nancy stood stock-still. Then she moved the last few feet and peered over the rim.

In this spot, the cliffs of the Superstitions had formed the walls of what appeared to be a small canyon, well concealed by brush and rocky outcroppings.

Two men, one tall and blond, the other short, wiry, and dark, appeared to be digging in the cliff at the end of the canyon! A small, rough cabin had been erected in the center clear area, and there was a corral next to it.

What brought a gasp from Nancy, however, was one of the horses that stood in the corral. It was a pinto and looked almost exactly like Cochise!

Nancy looked at Ngyun, who had silently crept

up next to her. Together, they watched the men for several minutes, then Nancy let herself slip and slide back down the rocky rise to the grass. The boy followed at once.

"Who are those men, Ngyun?" she asked, keeping her voice low so the sound wouldn't carry.

Ngyun shrugged. "Prospectors, I think."

"On the resort land?" Nancy frowned. "Chuck and Heather never mentioned it."

"This belong to resort?" Ngyun seemed surprised.

Nancy looked around, trying to recognize the landmarks that Chuck and Heather had pointed out to her during their first days with the McGuires. Finally, she was sure. "The boundary of their land is supposed to be along that purple cliff there," she said, pointing off to the right. "The men must be on the resort land."

"Maybe they find gold," Ngyun suggested with a timid smile that was quickly gone. "Make everybody happy."

"Have you seen those men around here before?" Nancy asked.

The boy moved nervously, not meeting her gaze. "I watch here sometimes."

"Have they seen you?" Nancy asked, sensing that

506

there was more to the story, something that he wasn't telling her.

For a moment, he didn't answer. Then he sighed. "One time. Not here. They out in wash that go from canyon. I ride up. See what they do. They get angry. Big one shoot at me. I not come this way a while."

"They shot at you?" Nancy gasped, unable to believe her ears.

Ngyun nodded. "I not do anything. I just ride up to look, honest."

"I believe you," Nancy assured him. "Do you think they were prospecting for gold in that wash?"

Ngyun nodded. "They do same thing prospectors do in mountains. I watch a lot. I see plenty."

Nancy considered his words for a moment, then changed the subject. "Where were you going today?" she asked. "Why did you leave the resort without telling anyone?"

The thin face closed and the boy's eyes skittered away from hers once again. "I go for ride."

Nancy said nothing, sure that the boy would tell her more if she waited. He quickly proved her correct.

"I run away," Ngyun admitted at last. "I no go back."

"But you can't do that," Nancy protested. "Your aunt and uncle love you, they'd never let you leave them."

"They send me away. They think I steal. The sheriff tell them I bad. I not take jewelry, so I no can give back. They take Cochise away." Tears filled the sad, dark eyes. "He mine, I not steal him."

Understanding the boy's feelings, but sure that she couldn't let him go, Nancy took a deep breath and began to tell him what had happened to her the night before. She described how she'd followed the pinto horse into the wash and nearly died for it.

As she talked, Ngyun nodded. "Horse like one in canyon," he said when she finished. "Maybe he ride that horse?"

Nancy smiled at him. "That's what I think," she confirmed.

"What you do?" Ngyun asked. "How you find out?"

"Do they ever leave the canyon?" Nancy inquired instead of answering.

Ngyun thought for a moment, then nodded. "Sometimes. Why?"

"I want to search that cabin," Nancy answered. "If they are the ones causing all the trouble that has happened to you, there should be some clues down there. Something that will tell me why they are try-ing to frame you."

Ngyun grinned at her. "I make them chase me," he told her. "You go down cliff."

Nancy shook her head. "That's too dangerous. If they shot at you before, they might . . ." She was given no chance to finish, as the boy raced across to Cochise and jumped into the saddle. Ngyun waved to her, smiling as he rode away.

The young detective hesitated, afraid for the boy, yet longing for the chance to prove him innocent of the charges that the sheriff would be bringing against him. Finally, she sighed and made her way to the top of the rocky cliff. She stretched out on her stomach again so she could look down into the huge ravine.

It seemed only a few moments before Ngyun appeared in the mouth of the canyon. When no one noticed him, he began to shout at the two men. His words were jumbled, but she could make out "thief" and "gold."

The men hesitated only a few seconds before they dropped their picks and shovels and raced to the corral to get their horses. In no time, they had sad-dled up and ridden out of the corral.

Once they disappeared around the rocks at the

mouth of the canyon in pursuit of Ngyun, Nancy cautiously edged over the lip of the outcropping. Her toes sought and found a narrow ledge, and in a second she was climbing down toward the canyon floor.

Since she slipped and slid a good part of the way, the climb took only a few minutes. Once she reached the base of the wall, she could see that the men had, indeed, been digging into the rocky soil of the cliffs. Still, she didn't take time to study their prospecting, preferring to head immediately for the small cabin.

Once safely inside the squeaky door, she paused to look around and catch her breath. There was little to see. A table and two stools stood by the single window, and two unmade cots were pushed against the other walls. A single, rough shelf held meager supplies and utensils for cooking and eating. There was no sign of a stove, and provisions consisted mostly of canned goods and crackers.

Since there was not much to search, Nancy went immediately to the old, brass-bound trunk that stood beside the door. It creaked slightly as she opened it. Then she gasped. Beautiful pieces of jewelry were scattered on top of a jumble of clothing!

Silver and turquoise were spread out in lavish array. Semiprecious stones set in imaginatively worked, silver settings made two squash-blossom necklaces outstanding. The same delicate workmanship and design were repeated in a bracelet and in the setting around the single, large turquoise of a ring. Nancy nodded to herself, confident that she had found the Bascombs' stolen property.

Carefully, she shifted the jewelry to look under it, hoping for some clue to the identity of the thieves. However, when the faded denims and torn, red flannel shirt were moved, she found only a battered old book. "Big Jake Harris's journal," she murmured. "So they took that, too, and probably set the cottage on fire to get it."

Nancy sat back on her heels, frowning at the contents of the trunk. Should she leave everything here and go for the sheriff? Or should she take the shirt, the journal, and the jewelry with her? It was a hard decision.

It would be best if the sheriff saw the stolen items himself, she knew. But she was also afraid that Ngyun's appearance might have been enough to frighten the men into leaving with the treasure. She suspected that they would come back and take the things away while she was riding to the resort for help.

Suddenly, she heard sounds from outside—hoofbeats coming closer and closer!

Nancy scrambled to her feet and moved to the window, peering through the dirty glass. To her horror, she recognized the riders as the returning prospectors. They were already so close she could hear their voices clearly.

"Did you see where he went, Sam?" the blond man asked his smaller companion.

"Little brat ducked into those rocks and just disappeared," the darker man replied, riding into the corral. "What do you think we should do, Joe?"

The big man shrugged as he dismounted. "Maybe nobody will believe him," he suggested hopefully. "I heard that the sheriff was at the resort today, so the kid is in a lot of trouble over the jewelry we stole."

The men chuckled evilly as they closed the corral gate and stood in the shade of the cabin wall. "Mr. Henry isn't going to like it, if the kid talks to anybody about us," Sam observed.

Nancy gasped. Was the McGuires' friendly neighbor her unknown enemy?

"So what do you want me to do?" Joe demanded. "Do you want to ride to the ranch and tell him the kid was out here again?"

Sam shook his head. "He's coming out tonight, anyway. Said he wanted to look over what we've dug out so far. He doesn't think we're in the right place yet."

"He'll change his mind when he sees the nugget you found this afternoon," Joe said. "This has to be where the gold washed out of the mountains in the flood last spring, 'cause this is the end of the ravine. We've prospected every other inch of it on his ranch and on this one."

"Don't tell me," the little man said. "Let's just see what else we can uncover before dark."

"Whatever you say, Sam," Joe replied with a sigh, "but I'm getting mighty hungry."

The men moved away from the cabin, still talking in low voices, but Nancy could no longer make out the words. She watched them till they reached the cliff face and took up their picks and shovels, then she leaned against the wall and looked around.

There was no way out. The door and window were both on the side of the cabin, facing the spot where the men were working. Nancy nibbled at her lip. The land all the way around was totally open, so the men couldn't miss seeing her the moment she stepped through the rough, squeaky door. She was trapped, and it was only a matter of time before someone came inside and found her!

16

A Great Shock

Nancy looked around the small room once again, then crossed to the trunk and carefully returned it to its original condition. That done, she assessed the situation, seeking some solution. But none came.

The only hiding place appeared to be beneath one of the cots. The area was tiny, but the blankets, carelessly thrown off, hung to the floor and would give her some protection.

Having decided where she could hide, Nancy returned to the window to watch the men as they dug lazily in the crumbling cliff face. Gold! That had to be the answer.

The mention of Mr. Henry had been a terrible shock. He'd been so friendly to the McGuires, so helpful, according to Heather and Chuck. Yet she did remember that Heather had said he'd once offered to buy the ranch.

An hour dragged by, then another. The men worked without enthusiasm, taking frequent breaks in the shade of an old mesquite tree that grew beside a small spring. Nancy watched longingly as they dipped up the water. She was both hot and thirsty in the dusty cabin.

When the shadows moved across the floor of the canyon, the men stopped working, throwing down their picks and shovels and heading for the cabin. Terrified, Nancy slid into her small hiding place.

Heart pounding, she crouched in the dark space and waited as the two men argued about which cans to open for dinner and what they should tell Mr. Henry about Ngyun. Sam wanted to keep it a secret, while Joe muttered dark predictions of what their boss would do to them if he found out that they hadn't told him. She was glad when they went back outside to put the grill over their small campfire.

The smell of the heating food soon penetrated the cabin, and Nancy became aware of her own hunger. She couldn't stay hidden here forever, she realized. But what to do? She couldn't slip away, even after dark, for the men were cooking only a few feet from the door.

Uncomfortable in the stuffy darkness under the cot, Nancy shifted her weight and tried to stretch her cramped legs. But her riding boot caught in the blanket, which in turn caught around the leg of the unsteady cot. To her horror, the whole frame shifted, tipped a little, then rocked back against the wall with a loud bang.

At once, there were shouts from outside, and the next minute the men burst into the cabin.

Nancy did not dare breathe, but with one man holding the lantern and the other searching the room, they discovered her almost immediately.

"Look what we've got here!" Sam shouted as he pulled the girl from underneath the cot. "A spy!"

"Just what we need," Joe grumbled. "I wonder what—"

He was interrupted by another man who at that moment walked through the door. *Mr. Henry!*

"Well, if it isn't the nosy Miss Nancy Drew," the rancher said. "You certainly are a stubborn young woman. Anyone with normal good sense would have paid attention to the letter I sent." He smiled evilly. "Or to the scorpion I put in your suitcase."

"You know her, boss?" Sam asked, his dark eyes bright with curiosity.

"She's the one you shot the arrow at, you idiot,"

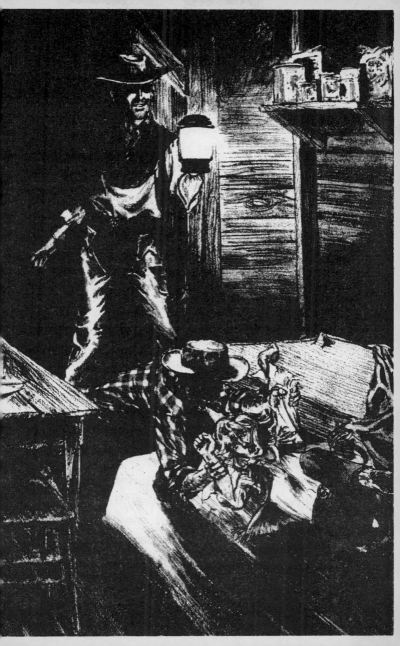

Mr. Henry snapped. "If your aim had been better, we wouldn't be having this problem."

"Ain't my fault she moved after I let go of the arrow!" Sam grumbled.

"How did you get out of the wash before the flood, Miss Drew?" Mr. Henry asked, ignoring his employee. "Sam said he had a tough time escaping the water with you so close behind him."

"I got out," Nancy said curtly. "And I didn't get hurt in the station wagon, either, when you forced us off the road the day we arrived."

Mr. Henry did not deny that he had caused the accident; he just glared at her. "Too bad!" he sneered.

"What do you want to do with her, boss?" Joe asked.

Mr. Henry sighed. "I suppose we might as well tie her up till I can think of a convincing accident for her. We certainly can't let her leave here since she obviously knows what is going on."

"What is going on, Mr. Henry?" Nancy asked, hoping to sound innocent.

"Get some rope, Joe," Mr. Henry ordered, then gripped Nancy's arm tightly.

Nancy drew in a deep breath, waiting till Joe was in the cabin and Sam had his back to her. It was a desperate move, she realized, but her choices were very limited. She lifted one foot and brought the heel of her boot down on Mr. Henry's instep with all her strength. He bellowed in pain and rage, but most important, he let go of her arm!

Nancy plunged wildly out of the flickering light of the campfire and into the deep shadows of the brush and trees that grew near the small spring. Once in their concealment, she paused, not sure what to do next. She'd escaped for the moment, but she had a terrible feeling that she was only delaying whatever Mr. Henry had planned. There was nowhere to run!

"Block the canyon entrance!" Mr. Henry was shouting. "Put more wood on the fire. Get torches. We can't let her escape us now!"

Nancy moved cautiously in the brush, grateful that the rain had kept it from becoming dry. Any loud crackling of twigs or branches would give her location away. As her eyes adjusted to the darkness, she saw the rocky hillside ahead and moved toward it, seeking a large rock or depression where she could hide while she tried to decide on her next move.

There was little choice, but the biggest of the rocky formations did offer a small, cup-shaped hole behind it. Nancy slipped into the hole and snuggled down against the still-warm earth as the cold of the desert night began to seep through her light shirt.

The crashing and shouting from the cabin area continued for quite some time as the men began to spread out to search. Then, suddenly, everything grew very, very quiet. Nancy, who'd been crouching low in fear, lifted her head, sensing at once that something had happened.

She heard the tattoo of approaching hoofbeats, and suddenly the air was full of shouts and shots. Nancy got to her feet, recognizing the voices that were calling her name.

"George, Bess, Heather, Chuck!" She ran through the brush and into the arms of her friends.

For several minutes, they all talked at once. Then, as the first relief died away, Nancy looked around. She saw that Ward, Chuck, and the sheriff were holding rifles on Mr. Henry and his two men.

"How . . . how did you get here?" Nancy asked.

"Ngyun came riding into the resort about an hour ago, shouting that you were in terrible danger," Heather replied. "We didn't know what to think, but he insisted that we call the sheriff. When he calmed down a little, he described Leaning Tree Ravine and Canyon to us, so we knew where to find you."

"Thank goodness he did," Nancy breathed, feeling a little weak with relief now that the danger was over.

The sheriff walked up and addressed Nancy. "Are you going to tell us what is going on here, Miss Drew? Mr. Henry is claiming that you sent for him. He says you had some complaint that his men were trespassing on the McGuire Ranch."

"This is McGuire land, isn't it?" Nancy asked, shocked by the man's quick lies.

Everyone nodded.

"Well," Nancy began, "his men have been doing more here than just trespassing."

It took nearly an hour of answering questions for the sheriff, helping him to search the cabin so he could examine the contents of the old trunk, and interrogating Mr. Henry before everything was completely explained. The rancher admitted to setting the fires and being responsible for the other incidents that were blamed on Ngyun. The boy was innocent of all the crimes of which he'd been accused.

Finally, Nancy asked, "Is it possible that there really is a valuable gold mine in this canyon, sheriff?"

"Probably not a mine," the sheriff replied. "You see, when we have bad floods like we did last spring, shelves of rock and shale break loose from the sides of the ravines or from cliffs like those over there." He indicated the end of the canyon where the men had been digging. "When that happens, small pockets or short veins of gold are sometimes uncovered. I suspect that's what has happened here."

"You mean we have gold on our land?" Heather asked.

"What do you say to that, Henry?" the sheriff asked.

Mr. Henry glared at them all, then shrugged. "We haven't found too much yet, but it has to be here in the canyon. I discovered a couple of nuggets late last fall when we were cleaning the debris out of our end of Leaning Tree Ravine. I figured it was coming from somewhere along the ravine itself, so I made you the offer on your land in case I didn't find it on my property."

"You would have bought the resort for the gold?" Heather sounded skeptical.

He shook his head. "If you'd taken my offer, the gold would have been pure profit. The land is worth that much, anyway."

"But we didn't take it," Chuck reminded him.

"And we didn't find any gold on our end of the ravine. We went over every inch. These two idiots were supposed to casually check your territory, but they let that sneaky kid catch them digging around in the ravine not far from here."

"So what?" Nancy asked.

"So they couldn't risk having him talk about what he'd seen." Mr. Henry's face was cold.

"So that's when you decided to see to it that Ngyun was sent away?" Ward looked as though he'd like to hit the handcuffed man.

"He never said a word to us about seeing the men," Heather murmured. "I wonder why."

"He just thought they were prospectors," Nancy answered. "He didn't even know this was your land. He's seen lots of people prospecting in the mountains."

"Well, we all know whose land it is, and now we know what has been going on," the sheriff said. "I suggest that we get our horses and head for the resort. It's a long ride over rough country and it's getting late. Where is your horse, Miss Drew?"

"Up there," Nancy said, pointing to the side of the canyon. "At least, I hope he still is."

"If you left the reins trailing, Pepper Pot is still there," Heather assured her. "He's very well trained."

"I'll take you up there, Nancy," George offered. "You can ride double with me. Let's go get him while they finish up everything down here."

Nancy nodded, suddenly glad to be getting away from the canyon and all the frightening things that had happened to her here. She was proud of having solved one of her mysteries and having cleared Ngyun's name, but her mind was already returning to the second mystery—that of the Kachina spirits that still haunted the resort!

17

Celebration

Once they reached the resort and the sheriff left with his prisoners, Maria served a huge meal, restoring Nancy's good spirits. She and Ngyun told and retold their stories of what had happened during the long afternoon and evening.

Nancy was just finishing a detailed description of how she'd managed to escape her captors when Heather spoke up, changing the subject. "I know this is a nice dinner and everything, but I think we should have a real celebration," she began.

"What do you mean?" Nancy asked.

"How about a party for all our friends and neighbors? I'm sure they'd love to meet Nancy and hear about what she has done. And it will give everyone a chance to make Ngyun feel welcome in the area after all the trouble he's had." She paused, then asked, "What do you think?"

"How about having it tomorrow night?" Chuck suggested. "It could be a welcome home for Grandfather, too."

"Is he coming back?" Heather asked. "Why didn't you tell me?"

"Actually, I've been too busy. In case you've forgotten, I was talking on the phone to him when Ngyun rode in, and after that . . ." He broke off with a grin.

"What kind of a party shall we have?" Maria asked.

"How about a barn dance?" Heather suggested.

"Don't you need a barn for that?" Bess asked. "I mean, your stable is very nice, but there isn't any room for dancing." She looked around. "That is what you do at a barn dance, isn't it?"

Heather laughed. "As a matter of fact, we do have a barn, a genuine, old relic from the days shortly after Jake Harris died."

"You do?" Nancy frowned. "I don't remember seeing it."

"You haven't," Chuck confirmed. "Or rather, you saw it, but you didn't know what it was."

"What are you two talking about?" George asked.

"How could we see it and not know what it was? A barn is a barn."

"True," Chuck conceded. "What I meant was—we drove by the barn on our way here, but you didn't know it was our barn. You see, after Jake's death, there were all kinds of rumors about this old house. People were always claiming to see lights in it at night, things like that. Anyway, the people who took over the ranch didn't want to live here, so they built a small house and a barn on what was then the trail to town. We passed it on our way here from the airport."

"And the house?" George said. "I don't remember seeing any house that close."

"The house burned down years ago," Heather answered. "We talked about tearing the barn down, but then we decided that our guests might enjoy an old-fashioned barn dance from time to time, so we fixed it up instead. Now what do you think of the idea, Nancy?"

"I think it sounds just fantastic," Nancy told her. "I can hardly wait."

Heather got up from the table. "You folks enjoy dessert," she said. "I'm going to start making some phone calls. We'll never be ready if I don't."

"And I'd better start planning the menu," Maria

decided. "We'll need lots of food and some punch, of course."

"What can we do?" Bess asked. "Can't we help?"

"You can be the cleaning and decorating committee," Chuck told them. "That way, Heather will be free to help Maria with the cooking." He paused, then added, "The barn is weather-tight, so it isn't real dirty, but it will need sweeping out and some kind of decorations."

"We'll do it," George agreed, "if we can borrow the jeep tomorrow. We'll have to go into town to get the decorations."

"It's yours," Chuck told them. "In fact, you could use the station wagon in the morning, if you like. I will have to have it in the afternoon, though, to pick up Grandfather."

"The jeep will be fine for us," Nancy told him, her eyes sparkling at the prospect of a party. "Besides, it may take us till afternoon to decide what we're going to use for decorations. We haven't even seen this barn yet, you know."

The rest of the evening passed quickly as plans for the party grew. Still, Nancy managed to slip away for a little while to follow Ngyun to the stable, where she found him leaning on the stall door, petting Cochise.

"He mine forever now," he said, looking up at her. "I thank you."

"And I thank you," Nancy replied. "If you hadn't come back here and sent help, I could never have escaped. You were very brave."

"I try keep men away," he went on. "They almost catch me. I hide. I sorry they go back."

"You did just fine," Nancy reassured him. "We're a great team."

Smiling at each other and laughing together, they gave Cochise and Pepper Pot each a final pat, then went back to the house.

Everyone was still working on plans for the party, which was to include a number of the children in the area and their parents, as well as young people of Chuck and Heather's age. By the time she said good night, Nancy had decided that it had been a truly satisfactory evening after all the bad hours she'd spent in the canyon.

The next day dawned clear and beautiful, but Nancy woke with a feeling that all was not well. As soon as she opened her bedroom door, her premonition was confirmed. George was standing in the hall looking very unhappy. Nancy quickly asked her what was wrong.

"It's back," George announced.

"What is back?" Nancy asked.

"The Kachina ghost. Bess and I saw it last night."

"You what?" Nancy frowned. "Where did you see it? Was it in the hall?"

George shook her head. "Outside. I thought I heard something, and when I went to the window, it was over on that little ridge. I thought maybe I was seeing things, but Bess woke up and she saw it, too."

"What was it doing?"

"Just watching the resort. At least, it didn't do anything else while we were looking at it."

Nancy sighed. "I wish I'd seen it."

"What would you have done?" George asked.

"I don't know," Nancy admitted. "Maybe asked it for a clue." She forced a laugh.

"It probably would have given you one, too," George told her, joining in her laughter.

"Well, I guess we'll have to wait to find out," Nancy said. "Now, how about some breakfast? I think we're going to have a very busy day, don't you?"

"The way Heather has been planning, I'd say so."

The barn proved to be a real challenge—one that they met with brooms, mops, and dust cloths. Once it was clean, there were decorations to be decided on. A trip into Apache Junction provided a wide selection of colorful Mexican hats and baskets, which they stuffed with bright paper flowers.

Ward and Chuck brought in a half-dozen bales of hay for makeshift benches, and a number of folding tables and chairs for the more conventional guests. Paper streamers and more flowers were draped from the rafters to finish the effect, and the barn was quite festive by the time Nancy and her friends were through. They were feeling quite pleased with themselves as they drove back to the resort to have dinner and change for the party, which was scheduled to begin at seven sharp.

Dinner was a very simple meal, and they ate by the pool so they wouldn't get in Maria's way as she finished fixing the food for Ward and Chuck to take to the barn. Mr. McGuire, a friendly, white-haired man with a white mustache, was now happily settled in a lounge chair, his wrist still in a cast and his knee resting comfortably on a padded cushion.

As soon as Nancy filled her plate, he signaled her to his side. "I want to hear all about your finding Big Jake's journal," he said. "Chuck barely mentioned it on the way home. He was too busy telling me about your adventures in the canyon at the end of Leaning Tree Ravine."

"That's a strange name for that ravine," Nancy observed. "I don't remember seeing a single tree, let alone one that was leaning."

"It was named for an old palo verde tree that died years ago, I think." Mr. McGuire laughed. "The story was that when the tree was blown over, the roots were full of gold."

"Gold?" Nancy raised an eyebrow.

He shook his head. "I don't believe it either. Most of the washes and ravines have names like that and stories to go with them. We may change that one to Golden Gulch, however, if there is a pocket of gold in the cliffs of the canyon."

"That would be quite appropriate," Nancy told him. "I hope it works out."

"Now, what about the Kachina you saw? Tell me all about it. What was it like?"

"Well, to begin with, it was the Cloud Kachina, or at least it looked like the Cloud Kachina painting." Nancy did her best to tell him everything that she'd seen and heard that night.

Once she'd completed her story, Mr. McGuire began describing his experience with the same spirit. When he finished, he asked, "Do you think that was the solution? Finding the journal, I mean. Have you routed our resident ghost?"

Nancy sighed and put down her fork. "I'm afraid not."

"What do you mean? Have you seen the thing again?"

Nancy shook her head. "I haven't, but George and Bess saw a Kachina on the ridge outside last night, and I've heard the chanting every night I've been here." The young sleuth sighed. "I don't know what it means, but I'm sure there is more to this mystery, and I'm still trying to solve it."

"Well, you just watch yourself," Mr. McGuire told her. "I don't want you to end up in the hospital the way I did. You have taken altogether too many chances already."

"I'll be careful," Nancy assured him. The conversation was ended by Heather's announcement that they had less than an hour to get ready for their guests.

The moment she entered her room, Nancy sensed a change. She looked around quickly, seeking a reason for the feeling. At first, everything seemed to be in order. Then she saw that the bedspread had been disturbed.

Remembering the incident with the scorpion, Nancy approached the bed cautiously, not sure what to expect. However, when she eased the spread back, no dangerous creature awaited her. Instead, she found a feather lying in the fold of the heavy material!

It was very old and slightly dusty, and when Nancy picked it up, she gasped. She recognized it as being from the headdress of the Kachina spirit she had followed in the hall!

18

Barn Dance

Nancy stood quite still, her heart pounding. Then she heard the soft sounds of chanting once again. She ran quickly to the window, then to the hall, but there was no sign of the Kachina spirit in either place.

Disappointed, Nancy sat down on the bed. She realized the feather was a message or perhaps a summons, but she had no idea what it meant!

Swallowing a sigh, she placed the feather carefully in the drawer of her bedside table and turned her attention to what she had come to her room to do. She had to get dressed—the celebration was about to begin!

Nancy donned the blue-and-white gingham peasant dress that she'd bought while they were in

Apache Junction shopping for decorations, and studied her reflection in the mirror. The square neckline with its feminine, white ruffles was very becoming, and the blue ribbon sash made her waist look tiny above the full, swinging skirt. White sandals and a white crocheted shawl completed the outfit, and she felt very festive.

Nancy had already decided not to mention the feather when she stepped out of her room. She smiled easily at Bess and George, who were waiting in the hall. Both girls were clad in dresses similar in style to Nancy's—George's in shades of gold and brown, Bess's in a rose that brought out the pink in her cheeks.

Bess twirled on her toes. "Don't you just *feel* like dancing in a dress like this?"

Nancy laughed. "You'd feel like dancing in jeans and cowboy boots," she teased.

"Well, of course I would," Bess admitted, "but this is better. I hope Chuck likes it."

Nancy laughed. "I know he will."

"Let's go," Heather called from the lobby. "I hope you don't mind walking. It's only a little more than half a mile, and both our vehicles are loaded with food."

"Lead the way," Nancy told her.

The path they followed was clear of rocks and led

up to a ridge, then wound gently down the other side to where the barn sat near the road. As they descended the hill, Nancy could see the jeep and the station wagon at the rear door of the barn, while several other cars were already parked in front of the well-lit, old building.

Lanterns glowed in all the windows and light spilled out the open doors. As the girls drew closer, they could hear the sounds of the band tuning up their fiddles and guitars.

Floyd, Tim, Diana, and the rest of their companions from the night of the barbecue were waiting near their cars. As soon as they had greeted the girls, they all went inside. Once they began dancing, they were joined by dozens of other couples.

It was a fine party, but different from any Nancy had ever attended. Whole families arrived, some bringing food which was delivered to what had once been the feed or tack room of the barn.

Babies were settled in baskets on the hay bales, while children Ngyun's age and younger ran in and out, laughing and playing. Everyone seemed to know and like everyone else, and they all greeted Mr. McGuire warmly and congratulated Nancy on solving the mystery that had surrounded Ngyun and the theft of the turquoise jewelry.

The music the band played was a mixture of country-western tunes, square dances, modern pop, and old favorites—something to please everyone. Nancy found herself with a different partner for every dance and had to plead exhaustion before she was allowed to stop.

Floyd escorted her to the punch bowl which rested on a table opposite the small bandstand, and poured a glass for each of them.

"How do you like our country dance, Nancy?" he asked.

"I love it," Nancy admitted enthusiastically, "but I don't know where some of the people get all their energy. That older couple out there hasn't missed a single dance—fast or slow."

Floyd laughed. "They're my grandparents, and you can bet they'll stay on the floor all night. They are members of a championship square dance club, so they're in terrific shape."

Bess and Chuck came over to join them. Bess accepted a glass of punch, then asked, "When do they serve all the goodies I saw Maria fixing?"

Chuck laughed. "Bess, your appetite is incredible!" Then he looked at his watch. "In about half an hour," he said. "We try to serve the food early enough so the children can eat before they wander out to the cars to sleep."

"Is that what happens?" Nancy asked. "I wondered, with so many children here."

"Everyone brings blankets, and when the younger ones get sleepy, their parents just settle them in their cars."

"Sounds simple enough," Bess observed.

Chuck nodded. "Well, a couple of times people have gotten home and discovered they have the wrong child, but since everyone knows everybody else, they just settle it with a phone call and trade back in the morning."

Nancy and Bess giggled, then Floyd took Nancy's empty punch glass and set it on the table before whirling her back out onto the dance floor. The time passed pleasantly, and when the feast was spread out, they were ready to do it justice. The hard exercise on the dance floor had whetted every appetite.

Later, however, when the music grew slower and the crowd had thinned a little, Nancy slipped outside alone for a breath of air. The night was clear, and though the moon was no longer full, it was still quite large enough to give plenty of light to the now familiar desert landscape.

She moved away from the barn into the quiet of the desert, hearing the distant howling of coyotes as they serenaded the moon in their own fashion. Just then, a movement on the ridge that hid the resort from her view caught her eye.

Nancy's heart pounded as she recognized her guide from the previous night, the Cloud Kachina! It moved with ghostly grace along the rough ground. The moonlight glinted on the white feathers that adorned its colorful face mask, giving it almost a halo effect.

Nancy gasped as it seemed to turn her way and gesture with one red, yellow, and white–painted arm. It wanted her to follow it!

Everything else forgotten, and totally without fear, Nancy turned her steps in that direction, cutting across the rougher ground to save time as she hurried after the apparition. As she neared the top of the ridge, the spirit vanished from her view, and for a moment she was afraid that she had misunderstood the signal and perhaps frightened it. However, when she reached the crest, she could see it ahead of her, drifting unhurriedly toward the resort.

Breathless with excitement, the young detective followed the ghostly spirit as it skirted the old, stone structure. It led her around the front, into the shadows on the side of the building opposite from where her room was located.

Few lights were burning in the windows on this

end of the building. However, the moonlight on the white feathers made the Kachina visible even as it ventured into the brush and trees that grew in thorny profusion near the wall.

Nancy stopped, unsure what to do. The Kachina halted, too, barely noticeable behind the mesquite and cactus that protected the wall of the building. Once again, the arm signaled for her to approach. Nancy obeyed slowly, feeling in her dress pocket for the matches she'd put there when she'd helped Maria light the candles on the serving table.

"Too bad you spirits don't supply flashlights," she told the apparition as she approached, making her way cautiously, not wanting to snag her new dress on any of the thorny plants.

The Kachina remained in place till Nancy was almost close enough to touch it. Suddenly, it was gone! Nancy hesitated, then carefully lit a match. The light helped only a little, but she did catch a glimpse of color low on the wall before the match sputtered out.

The next one lasted longer as she held it down near the ground so she could see what was painted on the wall. A fierce-looking Kachina stared back at her from the slits of its black mask, and Nancy shivered though the night was mild.

Several more matches showed no further clues.

There was only a single painting and it was too dark for her to study it. She finally left the shadows of the house.

She'd wanted a clue, and now the Kachina spirit had given her one! The only trouble was, she had no idea what it might mean. With a sigh, she started back toward the barn, aware that her friends might have missed her and that they would worry if they had.

Floyd was waiting for her when she reached the foot of the hill. "I've been watching for you," he told her. "Where were you?"

"Out to get some air," Nancy said, deciding not to mention the ghost just yet. "Did I miss anything?"

"Not much. The band took a break and Mr. McGuire gave a little speech, explaining to everyone what happened. He praised you for your excellent sleuthing, and Ngyun for his bravery. The boy really loved it; he's quite the star of the evening."

Nancy laughed. "He deserves it after all he's been through."

"Well, he does share the limelight with you, Nancy!"

Nancy blushed. "My job isn't done yet," she said. "I haven't solved the Kachina's secret yet!"

"You will," Floyd said with a chuckle. "And I bet it won't take long, either."

"I'm certainly going to try," Nancy replied, thinking of the painting her elusive guide had shown her tonight. Tomorrow, in daylight, perhaps she'd be able to make some sense out of the strange, little Kachina with its ferocious appearance!

19

A Ghost Beckons

After she got into bed that night, Nancy opened the drawer of the bedside table and took out the feather. She held it lightly, studying it, wondering what the morning would bring, then she laid it gently on the other pillow before she went to sleep.

Thanks to her impatience, she woke early in spite of the late night. When she was dressed, she armed herself with some stout clippers from the pool storage shed and made her way around to the far side of the old, stone building.

It took her several minutes to locate the small painting. Once she did, she spent nearly half an hour clearing away the worst of the growth in front of it. Even when she'd finished, she wasn't surprised that no one had found the painting before. It was in a hidden spot, shielded by the very unevenness of the wall itself. If it hadn't been for her guide, she would never have found it.

Suddenly, there was a sound behind her, and she whirled around, startled.

Ngyun had come up to her and pointed at the picture. "What that?" he asked.

"I found another Kachina painting," Nancy replied, then told the boy about her mysterious guide the night before.

"It not like others," Ngyun observed after he'd inspected the painting.

"I know," Nancy agreed. "Is your Aunt Maria awake yet?"

"She fixing breakfast."

"Would you mind asking her to come out here when she has a free minute? I'd like to know what this Kachina represents. Then maybe I can figure out why it is in such a hidden spot."

"I go ask," Ngyun agreed, and disappeared around the stone wall at a dead run.

Nancy busied herself clearing away more thorny limbs. She had a fair space opened up by the time Maria and Ngyun came to join her. She got to her feet and moved to one side so that the Indian woman could have a clear view of the small but surprisingly well-preserved picture.

Maria leaned down, then gasped and stepped back, almost involuntarily. "It's *Hilili!*" she whispered.

"*Hilili?* What's that?" Nancy asked. "Is it some special sort of Kachina?"

"It is a Witch Kachina brought to our tribe from the Zuni. You see the wildcat skin draped over its shoulders? It's a mark of fierceness. It is often a guard at our ceremonials."

"A guard?" Nancy frowned. "But why would it be painted here?"

"To guard the house?" Maria suggested.

"I don't think so. A guard would be near the door." Nancy studied the painting again, then asked, "Is it authentic? Jake didn't add or change anything, did he?"

Maria bent down and examined the picture carefully. "I've seen several, and this looks exactly like the old ones," she declared. She peered at the heavy growth of cactus and thorny bushes on each side. "How in the world did you find it?"

"The Cloud Kachina brought me here last night," Nancy answered. "It was trying to tell me something, and—" she added with a sparkle in her eyes, "I think I know what it was!"

Maria stared at her, realizing what Nancy meant. But her dark face showed no emotion. Instead, she firmly took Nancy's hand. "Before you go any further, I think you should come in and have some sausage and pancakes."

Nancy giggled. "I might as well."

"What you think?" Ngyun inquired curiously, tugging at her hand.

"You'll find out in a little while," Nancy told him.

When they joined Bess, George, Heather, and Chuck around the kitchen table, the others sensed immediately that Nancy was up to something.

"Are you going to tell us what is on your mind?" George asked. "You've been sitting there looking like a cat with canary feathers on her whiskers."

"Have you made a discovery?" Bess added curiously.

"As a matter of fact, I think I have." Nancy smiled at them. "As soon as you're all through with breakfast, I have something to show you."

With such a promise, plates were quickly emptied, and everyone followed Nancy out into the sun and around to the side of the house. She pointed out the small painting and explained how she'd been guided to it by the ghostly Kachina.

"I don't understand how you can follow those things," Heather said with a shiver. "I'd be scared to death to even see one up close."

"But it has been helping us!" Nancy reminded

her. "First, it showed me where to look for the journal, now this."

"What does it mean?" Chuck asked. "Have you figured that out?"

"Well, Maria gave me the best clue," Nancy answered. "She says this is *Hilili*, a guard Kachina."

"So?" George asked, when Nancy paused.

"So I think it was painted here because it's guarding something," Nancy replied.

"The treasure?" Bess gasped.

"Nancy, really?" Heather asked.

Nancy shrugged. "We won't know till we do some digging," she told them.

"I'll get the shovels," Chuck said. "You decide where to dig."

Nancy studied the area, trying to judge the age of the various plants. Then she noticed that Hilili was holding a single thin, green, yucca leaf whip in one hand and that it seemed to be set at an odd angle, unlike the several whips in its other hand. With her eyes, she traced the direction in which the painted leaf was pointing and marked the sandy soil with her toe.

"Is that where the treasure is buried?" Heather asked.

"I'm afraid we'll have to dig to find out," Nancy admitted.

"So let's get started," Chuck said, handing a shovel to Nancy. "You can take out the first shovelful."

"We're going to have to take turns," Nancy warned as she started digging. "It's hard to tell how deep we have to go. She hesitated, then added, "Provided there is something buried here. I can't guarantee that, you know."

"So dig," he teased. "We'll never find anything speculating."

Soon, the laughter died away and was replaced by serious work. The hole was growing, but the earth was so hard they had to fight for every foot. Chuck and Nancy had soon given their shovels to Bess and Heather, and they in turn yielded to George and Ngyun. Maria was kept busy bringing out cold drinks and other refreshments to keep the workers going.

As it neared noon, Nancy and Chuck once more took up the shovels and stepped down into the hole. Nancy worked on one end, her hands sore and perspiration forming on her face as the day grew warmer. However, as she forced the shovel in for the fourth time, there was a dull, clanging sound, and the shovel refused to move when she leaned her weight on it.

"Hey," Chuck shouted, "you've hit something!"

"I hope it isn't another rock," Nancy said.

"That didn't sound like a rock," Chuck told her. "Let me see if I can uncover it."

Excitement made the soil fly, and in a moment the top of an old, metal trunk was uncovered. Everyone was anxious to help, and in a short time, Chuck was able to free the small trunk from the clinging earth and lift it out of the hole.

For a moment, they just stared at it. Then Mr. McGuire, who'd been watching the entire proceedings from a lawn chair in the shade, called, "Break the lock on it, Chuck. Let's open it up!"

Chuck stepped forward and used a pick to hack away the old lock, but instead of opening the trunk himself, he turned to Nancy. "I think you should do it," he said. "You're the one who found it."

Everyone nodded agreement. Nancy took a deep breath and moved forward to touch the metal lid that was warming now from the sun after being so long in the cool depths of the earth. Her hand shook as she began lifting the rusty lid!

20

Hilili's Treasure

Once the lid was open, Nancy gasped in delight as
the sun touched the slightly faded, but incredibly
beautiful Kachina dolls within. Maria cried out and
came to kneel beside the trunk, tears running down
her brown cheeks.

"What is it?" Mr. McGuire shouted, struggling to
his feet and limping over to join them. "What is the
treasure?"

Nancy lifted the first of the Kachinas with rever-
ent gentleness, recognizing it at once as a replica of
her guide from the night before. Time had dimmed
and broken its feathers, and the paint on the colorful mask was faded, but that only made the little
carvings more precious.

"They aren't gone!" Maria whispered. "We always believed that they were taken away or destroyed when the chiefs fled to Mexico. We've mourned their loss all these years."

"There are some papers in the bottom of the trunk, Nancy," Chuck said, leaning over her shoulder. "See, under the Kachinas."

Nancy moved the dolls very carefully, slipping the dusty pages out. "From the journal," she said. "I recognize Jake Harris's handwriting, and remember, I told you some of the pages had been torn out."

"What does it say?" George asked. "What are the Kachinas doing here? Did he really take them from the Indians after all?"

"I think we should go inside with all this," Mr. McGuire said. "Nancy can read to us from the journal while the rest of us study the Kachinas."

After they were all settled in the living room, Nancy scanned the pages quickly, then began to read:

> *Deer Slayer and the other chiefs have come again and this time they left their Kachinas behind for me to guard. They say that Winslow has hired some bad men*

*to follow the members of the tribe and
they fear those men will steal the sacred
dolls for his collection.*

*There have been fires in the hills again.
I thought it might be Deer Slayer's people
camping nearby to protect my house, but
last night a fearsome torch was burning on
the ridge and the riders who set it were
white men. The door was not fastened
when I came home tonight, so I fear Winslow's men have been here searching for
the Kachina dolls.*

"Big Jake escaped their first visit," Bess murmured softly, "but obviously not their second one."

Nancy nodded, shifting to another page. "The
next couple of entries are about his being afraid to
go out and not knowing where to turn for help,"
Nancy told them, then went on reading.

*I fear the Kachinas will be stolen from
me if I don't hide them. I've chosen a safe
place to bury them and painted a guardian
Witch Kachina to mark the spot for Deer
Slayer if I'm not here to tell him myself.*

*Dawn is near and the fearsome torch
just beyond the door is burning out. To-*

morrow night they may burn even this house to the ground. I shall wait till daylight when they hide from my sight and I'll bury these few pages with the sacred dolls. When they come tonight, I'll have my rifle ready.

Nancy put down the stained pages. "That's all there is," she said. "He must have done what he said, buried the trunk, then barricaded himself in the house to wait."

Maria shook her head, turning her attention at last from the Kachinas, which she'd been examining very carefully. "Poor old man, he was so brave. The collector Winslow and his people must have come just as he expected, and he was so old and frail the strain killed him."

Mr. McGuire nodded. "You can bet that they were the ones that ransacked the house. And they were the ghosts that haunted it the next few years. They knew that he had the Kachinas and they were determined to find them."

"But they didn't," Heather reminded everyone with a grin. "That took someone as smart as Nancy."

"With a lot of help from the Kachinas," Nancy reminded them modestly, as she picked up the Cloud Kachina doll that had been her guide.

"So what happens to the treasure now, Mr. McGuire?" George asked. "I mean, it really is a treasure, isn't it?"

"For my people, the Kachina dolls are beyond price," Maria whispered.

"Indeed, they are extremely precious," McGuire agreed, "and they shall be returned to their rightful owners as soon as possible."

Maria turned to him, her dark eyes luminous. "You mean it?" she asked. "You know how valuable they are and they were found on your property. There are collectors who would pay any price you ask for them."

The old man smiled at her. "Your people trusted Big Jake to protect their most sacred treasure, and he managed to do so at the cost of his life. That doesn't give us any claim to them. Besides, wasn't your great-grandfather one of the chiefs who entrusted them to Jake?"

Maria nodded. "He died in exile in Mexico, driven there by those who claimed that he and the other chiefs had caused the death of Jake Harris."

"That terrible collector Winslow probably made up the story to cover his own guilt," Bess said.

Everyone nodded.

"What do you plan on doing with the Kachinas, Maria?" Nancy asked. "I mean, how will you go about returning them to your tribe?"

Maria leaned back, lost in thought for several minutes, then she smiled. "I think I would like to have Ngyun help me return them," she said. "He is a descendant of a chief, and it would truly make my brother's son a member of the tribe."

"Oh, how wonderful, Ngyun," Nancy breathed. "You'll be proud to do it, won't you?" She looked at the grinning boy.

Ngyun was too overcome to speak, but his happy face when he nodded was answer enough.

"Will you be here for the ceremonial?" Maria asked Nancy.

The girl sighed, then looked at the circle of her friends. "I'd love to," she replied, "but now that both mysteries here have been solved, I probably should be getting back to River Heights."

Little did she know that soon after her return home she would be confronted with a new mystery called *The Twin Dilemma*.

"How about lunch?" Bess suggested, changing the subject. "Finding treasures makes me hungry."

"That makes two of us." Chuck laughed and put an arm around the pretty girl. Chatting happily, the young detectives all headed for the kitchen, leaving Maria and the wide-eyed Ngyun alone with their precious Kachinas.

The Chalet School Series

by Elinor M. Brent-Dyer

Elinor M. Brent-Dyer has written many books about life at the famous Alpine school. Follow the thrilling adventures of Joey, Mary-Lou and all the others in this delightful school series.

Below is a list of Chalet School titles available in Armada. Have you read them all?

The School at the Chalet
Jo of the Chalet School
The Princess of the Chalet School
The Head Girl of the Chalet School
Rivals of the Chalet School
Eustacia Goes to the Chalet School
The Chalet School and Jo
The Chalet Girls in Camp
Exploits of the Chalet Girls
The Chalet School and the Lintons
A Rebel at the Chalet School
The New House at the Chalet School
Jo Returns to the Chalet School
The New Chalet School
The Chalet School in Exile
Three Go to the Chalet School
The Chalet School and the Island
Peggy of the Chalet School
Carola Storms the Chalet School

The Wrong Chalet School
Shocks for the Chalet School
The Chalet School and Barbara
Mary-Lou at the Chalet School
A Genius at the Chalet School
Chalet School Fete
A Problem for the Chalet School
The New Mistress at the Chalet School
Excitements at the Chalet School
The Coming of Age of the Chalet School
The Chalet School and Richenda
Trials for the Chalet School
Theodora and the Chalet School
Ruey Richardson at the Chalet School
A Leader in the Chalet School
The Chalet School Wins the Trick